DIVINICA

JP Roth · Dawn McTeigue

JP ROTH

DIVINICA

MYTHMARKED

CITY OWL
PRESS

DIVINICA
Mythmarked, Book 1
By: JP Roth

CITY OWL PRESS
www.cityowlpress.com

Cover Design by MiblArt. All stock photos licensed appropriately.

Edited by Lisa Green.

For information on subsidiary rights, please contact the publisher at info@cityowlpress.com.

Print Edition ISBN: 978-1-64898-527-0

Digital Edition ISBN: 978-1-64898-526-3

Printed in the United States of America

ALSO BY JP ROTH

ROTHIC REALMS

Ancient Dreams

REM 8

Southern Nightgown

Theory of Magic

I dedicate this book to my husband. Regardless of how my world has turned, you've always been the hero in my tales. I will love you in all my lives, so swear you'll find me in the next.

PART ONE

PROLOGUE

Just another wide-eyed girl

Divinica's Diary. Read or die.

Dear Divinica—that's your name by the way. None of this is going to make sense, but read it anyway. Chances are, you'll die if you don't.

It happens every thirteen days. One moment you begin to remember, understand, perhaps even feel. Then the red wave comes, and everything is gone. Past, present, and future, things you once loved, dissolve like smoke. There are blips of space where you wonder why anyone bothers surviving at all. Sometimes you think you're the only one in the world who experiences brief, unsatisfying flashes of what used to be. The only soul who has the barest conception of the events that transpired—the single bang that tore through the fabric configuring this universe and in one blow basically fucked up even the mere concept of what "once was."

Once you had a family, or at least that's what you assume, but every time the red wave comes, you can't remember their faces.

You're not sure where you are geographically, but that hardly seems to matter. You make your home with the rats and share the outdoors with the Tardigrades, or Rades, as you like to call them. Creatures that were once microscopic and always indestructible, now the size of a small SUV due to the obscene amounts of radiation left by the waves, which are systematically killing the rest of us. Those critters are some of the beings that survived the great destruction. The rest of the animals, trees, and most plants died when the moon slipped from its orbit by inches. Lunar fragments crashed into Earth changing the landscape and causing irreparable damage. Tsunamis struck. Fires raged and humans died. Billions of them. You don't have all the details, but whatever happened soundly shook the structure of the cosmos, and we who remain are lost in the aftermath.

You live in a small, stuffy room with a single window and cement walls painted a slightly nauseating shade of green. If you wake up in a blue room, leave it immediately. You always have nightmares in the blue rooms. You sleep a lot, and there are days when you can't remember your own name. You have thirteen tattoos running straight down the middle of your body. No, don't look right now. Just trust me.

Sometimes, between the red waves that take everything, you can almost imagine what used to be. Home, family, babies, purpose, love. Then the red waves come, and the feelings vanish like mist in a November wind. It appears the Earth has turned on itself, like the cosmos overlords—whoever they may be—allowed a total breakdown of natural law, and it all just burned to fucking ash. You don't know how long humanity has survived in this broken rhythm. Lately, you don't care.

Your life sucks. You look for food and struggle to survive the violent repercussions of the endless red waves. You stare out the window a lot. As far as you know, it's always the same broken landscape.. It snows a fuck ton—you've literally almost frozen to death twice.

Here are three things you have to know. One: Stay awake when the cold gets bad. Two: Hunt with a bow and not a gun. The third is a fundamental truth you can't let yourself forget. If this world was something once, that once is now gone. Cities are charred down to their bare bones, bodies rot everywhere, lying where they fell. Everything has been reduced to nothing. Only the highest mountains stand untouched, capped in snow, mysterious, rugged, old. They look safe. You think about running to them and finding a cave to wait out the rest of your days, but you don't because you hate the fucking cold.

You dream all the time, at least you think you're dreaming. Use the paint by the door to scribble your dreams on the walls before you forget. When you're feeling artsy, your tattoos glow, and sometimes you hear people whispering behind you. Don't freak out. They're nothing more than echoes in a howling wind that exists somewhere beyond the confines of your world.

Always when you search your mind for thoughts that might bring a modicum of clarity, you encounter only sticky darkness and miles of white emptiness. It is endlessly infuriating.

Of course, there was a time before this moment, but you can't remember it. For you, your life starts today. Lying on your lumpy bed in an institution that used to house the mad and is now a haunted graveyard void of memory, twisted enough to drive its only resident insane. You call this place Styx, but there's a broken-down plaque outside with a single word inscribed on it. Hadamar.

Okay. This is the worst part, are you ready? You lit a candle and walked through a *glowing archway. You watched the birth of Aphrodite, and it was horrifying, beautiful, and scary as fuck. You drew her face on your wall. It's fine, but you could've done better. It's possible this was a dream, probable even.*

You miss something every day. So badly that it's turned into a chronic, constant ache. You have no idea what it is. This pisses you off worse than the days when you don't remember your name.

You think you're going to die in this room. Some days, when the red waves come, you wish you would. Lastly, read through this book every time you wake up. Otherwise, don't think, don't plan. There is no escape. Just sleep.

CHAPTER ONE

The red wave

I think I've seen him before, with his dark eyes, wavy curls, dirty hands, and furtive smile. He's shuffling through my food cans, piling up the ones he likes, the little thief. I look at him for a moment longer than necessary. Something about his slender face and wind-chapped cheeks is familiar to me. Covered in the purple dust of our world, he's camouflaged so well I almost missed him. He looks up from sorting through a smaller stack of cans, glowering. I flinch from the window, press my back flat against the wall. Holding my breath, I wait for him to look away. I feel as if this is a game the two of us have played often, though no images or recollections come with the feeling. Eventually, he stops trying to see through my dusty window, and he returns to the larger stack of cans. Something is in his right hand. A ball of jumbled, multicolored wire with a pale green light blinking in the middle of the mess.

It reflects weirdly against the approaching red wave, like a dying android's malfunctioning heart. I suddenly remember what androids are. I start to run. My feet scrape over the uneven floorboards. The boards are rotten in some places and chipping badly. I close my eyes and breeze past the morbid paintings on the old walls. All of them depict humans screaming in agony, strapped to torture devices or wrapped up in straitjackets, limbs fixed to the wall with dirty metal chains. White faces, wide-open mouths, and eyes silently begging for release or death. To me, they are the faces of Styx, this crumbling asylum—the only home I know. I think at one time a human face contorted in that much agony wasn't normal. Things seem to be quite different now. My own face belongs up there with them. Everything in this world is misery and pain. If I were a braver girl, I would unalive myself and hope the next life offered me something more. I honestly don't know why I haven't done that very thing.

Maybe it's because I know I've forgotten something vital, and I refuse to shuffle off this mortal coil until I remember what the fuck it is.

I stumble to the wide double doors and slam my palm against the latch. It gives way, and the doors swing outward on their rusty hinges as I run outside.

"Hey!" I scream at the boy, who's in the process of kneeling. He doesn't turn around at the sound of my shriek, but his shoulders stiffen, and I watch him place his blinking device dead center in the tower of my cans. When it's done, he spins and backs away from his homemade bean bomb, tossing me an innocent shrug that fits well with his rapscallion smile, a smile that makes me feel like I've taken a kick to the gut. My heart stutters painfully. Looking in his big, brown eyes, I'm disturbed by the irrational impulse to wrap my arms around his slight body and never let him go.

"What the hell do you think you're doing?" I shout.

He laughs. The cynical, childish sound does more twisting things to my heart. "You're on my turf," he accuses me, tucking his hands—all covered in chunky silver rings—in the pockets of his dark pants and casually glancing over my shoulder at the approaching red, electric waves.

He looks like such an imp, I struggle not to scream at him, though I don't know why I would bother. "You the one who torched all my rice?"

The twin dimples in his smile deepen as he shrugs. "I sure as shit hope so."

I frown at him, then at the ticking bomb about to destroy what's left of my food. "Aren't you a little young for that kind of language."

"No one's young anymore," he says. I frown. *Real, depressing, hard facts.* The back of my neck prickles. Behind his head, the sky blackens. I feel like darkness in this place is its own dimension, stuffed with the screaming music of monsters. This boy seems to think so too. Trepidation hoods his next skyward scowl. "That red shit is close. I don't think you want to be chatting out here with me when it hits," he says, sounding as scared as I suddenly feel.

I sigh. "Why are you blowing up my food?"

"Cause you stole my home. I was here first, and you're annoying as hell. I hear you at night, screaming and tripping over your big feet." He sniffs loudly and swipes the back of his hand over his red-tipped runny nose. "Sometimes you scare the hell out of me, but I can't leave," he says and kicks a flat rock that flies for a second, then lands in the shadow of Styx.

"Why not?"

"I don't know, but I think I made a promise." His eyes crinkle at the corners, and for a second I think he's going to cry. He gives me a shy look through lashes as thick as mine, then he squares his shoulders and says, "Sometimes, just before the red wave hits, I see pictures..." He breaks off to kick another rock. This one releases a jet of steam when it momentarily parts with the ground. The steel toe of his left boot nudges another that rolls over under the persistence of his foot. The ground beneath hisses and churns like running lava, boiling up until it's a tiny hot spring of black fire, melting all the snow around it. It's freezing today but sweat carves a wet path along the center of my back, itching like a dozen biting fire ants. I take a step toward the boy, careful to avoid a patch of black thorns jutting from the ground, longer than my forearm and sharp as daggers.

"What do you see?" I ask slowly.

"I don't know, actually. I don't have a name for most things. There's a lot of bright stuff, sometimes the sky is light blue, or all cluttered by white, fluffy clouds that look like cotton balls." He scowls up at me, an invisible fish hook lifting his brow. "Why? What do you see?"

"Flowers," I say, not thinking. His eyes widen.

"Flowers," he says, a reverence in his whisper. "Yeah, flowers, yellow, red. I remember flowers," he says, seconds before his ears perk up and his shoulders hunch.

He's wearing a black jacket covered in smudged metal studs painted murky violet by the colors of our dark world. His wardrobe fits the moment, but I think it makes him look too strong for his age. I keep that thought until he glances into the turbulent distance and fear fills his eyes. He slinks down into the oversized garment, and just like that he's a frightened little boy who's strayed too far from home. I follow the path of his eyes and see moving shadows in the roving dust clouds. Two-legged figures too tall to be men, with long tails that whip and swirl the air.

Suddenly, the boy dives for his ball of wires and places his hand over the lime-colored flashing light. The child's chaotic actions distract me from looking for things that shouldn't exist. I watch as he pulls two wires from the center of the tangled mess. The light stops blinking. "There," he says and throws his broken bomb to the dirt. He tosses a glance over his skinny shoulder, and for a second we both stare at the approaching wave. "Hope those blasted things stop at some point."

I shake my head. "In this world, hope is a dangerous thing. Why did you destroy your bomb?"

He snorts. "Hope is a dangerous thing in all worlds. And no reason, really. I just don't like doing anything important when that red shit is on the horizon.

'Sides, I feel like I know you. It's weird. I think about blowing up your food and it gives me a pang." He touches a spot just below his heart. "Hurts right here."

"I feel like I know you too," I say, staring deep into his almond-brown eyes.

He scratches his head, flicks something behind his ear. "What's a memory?"

"I don't know," I say, but strangely, I believe I just might. The meaning of it is trapped somewhere in the fog that fills my mind. I search the endless expanse of white emptiness, then smile when I unexpectedly find the answer. "A memory is something once experienced. A repetitive vision of a moment lived and lost. It is an impression of the experience that will always remain," I say.

His face screws up, and he shakes his head. "Well, I don't know about all that bullshit—except I don't know who I am, but I'm sure I know you."

His words make more cold sweat break out on my brow. I lift a hand to wipe the clammy moisture away. My body starts to tremble. It feels as if a wild, taloned creature, like one of the radioactive rats that share my bedroom, is alive in my mind, desperately trying to claw its way free. As the red wave draws nearer, the creature inside me fights harder for release. The first hints of fear creep in, not fear for myself, but fear of what is about to be taken away from me once more.

I realize I've been silent for a few seconds too long, just staring hard and seeing nothing, because the boy is glaring at me, an unfathomable expression on his face.

"What?" I snap.

"A beach," he says, seemingly unbothered by my vitriolic tone. "We're standing on a beach making sandcastles, you throw sand in my eyes, and I kick you in the shin—go me. You're limping when we make marshmallows. You hug me even though I hurt you, you call me an annoying little shit and tell me no matter how wretched I am, you will always be my big sister." He meets my eyes. "Is that a memory?"

I can't speak, I can't breathe. I feel his voice inside my head. His every word is a picture, and they fall atop each other like so many discarded drawings. I see it all. His cheeks are chubby, rosy as a California dawn. Not pinched with hunger and neglect like they are right now. The sun in those pictures is bright and golden, not the color of blood and dust. It's a different world that he paints with his words, one of light and laughter. Not a red wave or a decaying dead body in sight, but a world as full as this one is empty.

"Well?" he presses, his eyes glinting. "Is it a memory?"

"I don't know," I say, but again, I just might. My brain is at war with itself, but the knowledge in my heart is steady and pure. It tells me this boy is somehow mine. All I have left in the world. The only thing I live for.

The red wave is close now. I see it building behind him, gathering height like an angry tsunami. The heat baking off of it is incredible. He turns to stare at it. We both do. For a few moments, there is no sound but the electric crackle and our linked, panting breaths. When he swivels on his left foot to stare at me, I see the fear in my soul mirrored in his eyes.

"It will crash over us soon. Take me away from you," he says, and I know then that he has said this exact same thing to me many times before. The look on his face, the tears gathering in his eyes tell me that he knows it too.

A sudden high, screeching sound makes him fling up his hands. It drives us both to our knees. His fingers clench as he covers his ears. He rocks back and forth, his parted lips emitting a thin stream of agonized wails as the earth shakes. I don't know what I'm doing, or why, but watching his pain is more hurt than I have ever known. I crawl to him, and wrap my arms around his slight, trembling body. Tears flood my eyes. The second I touch him, I know him— better than my own soul. "Daniel," I whisper.

He flinches, then stares up at me. His tears magnify his huge eyes. "Yes, that's my name. Daniel. I'm Daniel, and…and you're my sister." He hiccups and uses the back of his hand to swipe at his runny nose. "I remember…I—it was the day the first red wave came. The news said all the polar caps were officially melted. We came here together, you, me, Mom, and Dad. We were running, Dad was holding my arm." He points to a pile of crates leaning against the south walls of Styx. "I went that way, I thought you would come and find me," he says wrathfully. "I waited and waited, but you never came, you never came."

"I'm so sorry! I'm so sorry," I cry, rocking him.

"What happened? I've been so alone."

"Oh, Daniel, I don't know. I don't know!" My voice sounds like the cry of a dying thing, and = I'm holding him tight, but he doesn't seem to care. His tears are wet on my neck. I'm crying hard now, it's getting difficult to breathe. I lean back and hold him at arm's length so I can stare at his precious face.

"I'll forget you," he says and looks again at the approaching wave, sees the colors it paints on the rushing sky, all the varied shades of blood—the forerunners of our doom. I want to tell him that it is impossible, that I could never forget what I love so much. I stay silent because anything I say will be a lie. I pull him close, and he smells like sweat, dirt, and Daniel. I want to scream and run, stitch his skin to mine, never let him go. Instead, I cup his face in my hands. Kiss his flushed cheek. "Only my mind forgets," I tell him. "Only my weak, stupid, human mind. Not my heart, my heart never forgets you." I touch my heart. "Here I will remember you forever."

Daniel's face resembles a clenched fist, and he hiccups again. "When the red wave comes, if no one remembers me, do I even exist?"

"Of course you do, sweet boy, of course you do. Of course you do," I say, over and over, while I pull him close and rock us back and forth, back and forth. I feel like my insides are being drawn through the eye of a red-hot needle. I taste bitter tears in my mouth, and they fill my stomach with nauseating acid. I swallow the lot and squeeze him tighter.

"A memory isn't a thing you have, it's a thing you are," he says, and I nod. He's right, a memory is thousands of glass shards that construct your breakable shell. In moments, all those shattered splinters of me will be taken away, and the fear is that I will be reduced to nothing except vanishing smoke and ashes. I let go of him for a second, grab the first stick I find, and quickly write in the muddy snow. I dig the words deep as I can in the time that I have.

Daniel is my brother.

He takes the stick from me when I finish carving the last *r*.

Divinica is my sister, he writes and sits back on his heels. Together we stare at the words.

"I love you, Daniel."

He throws himself back into my arms and locks his fingers behind my neck. "It's coming," he says.

"I know," I tell him.

Daniel grabs, then shakes me for emphasis as he yells, "It's here! It's here!"

I know that too. I close my eyes and take a final breath before I can't breathe at all. I crush his head to my chest and use my back to shield him from the initial hit. I grit my teeth and brace for it. The electric wave slaps against my bowed spine with the force of a thunderclap. I arch in agony. Then, the shimmering waves cut through me, touching every nerve with liquid flame and soldering irons. I scream. I can't help it. I hear Daniel screaming too. I pull him closer. It feels like streams of sun-fire carve a blinding path through my flesh and bones, burn across my heart, singe my eyes, and fry my brain. Everything is red lightning, screams and pain.

Daniel fights wildly against the irrepressible agony. Through grinding teeth, I yell that I love him. That I won't leave him, that I swear to find a way to save him. All hideous lies, but I can't stop babbling, I want him to know—need him to understand how I'm feeling right at this moment.

"I love you too," he says, and his voice is a screaming, electronic sound. His head twists a little until his skin is taut and bulging. As I stare at his face, his skin starts to stretch, all seven layers vibrating madly, then tugging and jerking to opposing sides, until it looks like he is wearing a mask made up of flesh and fresh blood. Then, his eyes roll back in their sockets, and I see flashes of his skeleton as the waves hit us again and again.

We scream together.

The mystifying heat torches my hair, rends the sparking, tearing synapses in my ravaged mind. We break, we burn, we scream and scream. It goes on and on. I don't know when I let go of him, but I sob when I feel the loss of his body in my arms—cry like I'm being flayed alive. We writhe side by side, creating clouds of steam with our hot, thrashing limbs. In the distance I think I hear other screams. I yell as my body is flung to the side. Daniel's hand flails in front of my face. I grab it, grit my teeth, and tug him close, my arms shrieking with pain. I scream behind sealed lips as he curls against my chest, and locked in each other's arms we try to survive the unsurvivable.

Finally, it is done, our bodies fall still, our limbs quit their twitching, and we fall quiet. All is silent. For a time, we hover in that weightless place between life and death. My mind repeats his name like a mantra. Daniel, Daniel, Daniel, Daniel, *Daniel, Daniel, Daniel, Daniel.* I say his name until I forget it. I say his name until the red wave decimates every thought, every feeling I've ever. Nothing is everything. Nothing is all I know.

I open my eyes. The air is hotter than normal, and I don't know why. The sun is dark, and the black clouds are low. It's snowing, but sweat runs down my neck. Something murky and unnamed has burned the chill away. I have no recollection of what it could be. A warm body lies atop mine. I look down at the curly head tucked against my chest, at the ashen skin and closed eyes. I wrap my arms around the slight body, heave a tremulous sigh, then shove the body away from me in the same breath. The little boy hits the ground with a thud, sending up a huge cloud of white vapor that merges with the one already shrouding us. He opens his eyes and looks at me. The second our eyes meet we scramble to our knees, coughing, spitting dirt. He speaks first, rubbing purple dust and soggy gray snow from his eyes, then wiping it away from where it collects at the corners of his mouth.

"What the hell do you think you're doing?" he shouts.

I draw back, then hold up my hands in a defensive pose, beyond stunned. "You were lying on me." , He gives me a look full of wary hatred.

"Then why did you have your arms around me, huh? I think I'm a little young for you." He picks up a small rock resting beside his left foot and instantly hurls it at me. "Geet!" he spits. "This is my place, find your own!"

I hate the loathing in his eyes. It's breaking my heart, and I don't know why. "How did we even get here?" I ask, but he shakes his head until his hair falls into his eyes. He has no answer for me. I back farther away from him, scooting along on my hands and feet like some strange variant of confused spider. I use my boot to draw a line in the mud that separates us, with little more than a foot on each side. The meaning of it is deeper than the indent I made. I point toward his side. "Don't cross this line, and I won't kill you.". The words sting my mouth, as if saying them goes against everything I am.

The boy snorts and shoves a dark lock of hair out of his red-rimmed eyes. He looks down at the line I just drew and the words beside it. He scrunches his nose. "Who the fuck is Daniel?"

"No idea. Just don't cross this line."

"Maybe I will, maybe I won't," he says with bravado, but he looks as dazed as I feel. He inches back another two steps and laughs, it's shaky and joyless. I understand the tone. There can be no humor in this dark place. I turn away to walk back inside the safety of Styx. The boy picks up a can and throws it at me, and it hits my shoulder. I flinch but don't turn around.

"I hope I never see you again," he rails. "Never...never, never."

I rub my eyes, shocked to realize I'm crying. I look at the evidence of tears on my fingertips, which only makes them fall faster. My head aches, and my skin is burning as if every inch of me was branded, yet the anguish in my heart obliterates all else. Ten more steps, twenty, thirty-five. I walk back inside my abandoned fortress of horrors and ghosts. The heavy double doors slam behind me. Any thread of light from the outside world is instantly extinguished. Everything is darkness, pain, and fear.

CHAPTER TWO

Visions and star doors

I wake up with a shout. My mind is filled with ten thousand shades of disbelief. I've dreamed of the seafoam goddess again. I was her, my mind and soul trapped in the body of a creature born of earth and stars. Her life was mine. My heart was hers. We were one. I still hear a battle cry and the scream of a violated woman. I remember her and not myself. Aphrodite.

I feel insane.

Scrambling to my feet, I cast my narrow bed a filthy glare, then rub my smarting eyes. I try to swallow, but my mouth and throat feel stuffed with cotton balls. I stumble to my canteen of filtered water. When I kneel down, my stomach lurches. In the reflective surface of the canteen, I see the tattoo on my forehead. It glows electric-yellow. I jump, so stunned that I drop the canteen. It clatters over the uneven, tiled ground. I kick it away. Content to deal with the thirst for a bit—because kicking something felt so good—I hardly feel the sharp jolt of pain that lances through my big toe. I grab my box of storm matches. Their sulphur tips are lime-green and spark boisterously when I strike one on the ground.

I reach for the squat candle sitting beside them. My fingers shake when I strike the match a second time. Finally, the wick ignites with a few more insolent sparks. A bright, flashing one lands on the underside of my wrist. I hiss as I shake it away.

My breathing is unsteady, my heart is racing, but I sit still and watch the small flame catch, then glow. A high-pitched ringing sounds in my ears, so loud

I want to plug them to block it out. I don't, because I know it will be useless. My right arm starts to shake, then burn. I drop the match, and the flame dies against the tiles. I take off my jacket and slowly look at the stinging underside of my wrist.

As I stare, dumfounded, flaming writing carves into my skin, searing its way from the base of my hand to my elbow. The writing starts to smoke. I smell my own burning flesh. It makes me hungry and sick at the same time. I swallow hard and begin to read the words aloud.

"Misplaced powers scattered through time. I travel through firelight to make them mine."

The moment the final word falls from my lips, a gust of wind cuts through the room. It howls like a wild animal, so loudly it drowns out the ringing. I don't look away from the words sprawling up my arm. I am utterly immobilized as the letters begin to flow off my arm and swirl around me. I feel like I should stumble back, fall over, and scream or faint dead from lack of air and shock, but I don't do any of those things. I hardly move as my reality challenges the confines of pure fantasy. The letters reshape in front of my eyes mold themselves until they look like...*Hieroglyphs*. The word blasts through my mind, followed by more forgotten words—*desert, sand, pyramid*. I can almost feel the burning heat on my neck, taste the gritty dust on my tongue.

Spinning and twirling, the letters stack atop each other. They create an ornate archway, then shiver into stillness. Just then, I know I've seen this archway before.

"Nokomis," I whisper.

The room is so bright now. The letters have all become symbols, and I have to squint to see each shape individually. I stand up and take a step toward what is now an animate object. "I'm dreaming," I say. I even pinch myself, quite hard. It hurts but I don't wake up. I didn't think I would. Somehow, I know I'm meant to walk through the trellised arches to whatever lies beyond the brilliant portal which is currently changing the structure of my nauseating green walls. All at once, the tattoos running down the front of my body start to burn. I don't look, but I suspect they're glowing. They pulse with each racing beat of my heart. Thirteen tattooed symbols, thirteen beating drums that rush together and make a discordant, compelling sound. The candle flame brightens. Through the archway I see a million stars, colorful nebulae, and spinning galaxies.

"If I'm not dreaming, this is a really stupid choice," I say. No one contradicts me. A rat—one of the many that share Styx—chills at the foot of my bed, electric green eyes staring at me. He's deeply unconcerned with my drama, thus offers little advice. I pick up my cropped, black jacket off the floor and put it back on, take a breath that I don't release, and step through what I now call The Gate of Stars.

It's like stepping off a hundred-foot cliff. My stomach drops to my toes. I'm not sure if I scream, but I assume I wail, and then I'm falling. Stars shoot past my eyes. I see a pale moon smeared by a bloody shadow. Behind it the sky is drenched in colors I can't describe. I hear hundreds of tiny sounds and loud, thunderous roars. A bird is singing somewhere, and as I plummet, the bird's song grows louder than the rest. My bed, Styx, the four cramped walls of my bedroom, and that one filthy window all just fall away. Gone, like they never existed. I am gone too. My shell dissolved in the endless sponge of glittering space. My soul is free. Flying. Untethered. I continue to spiral, ever downward, shooting now like one of the stars, like a blazing comet. I feel a surge of power inside me, as if a liquid light has replaced all the blood in my veins. I can't think, I can't breathe. The sounds become unbearable, and the speed at which I fall threatens to tear the skin from my bones. Just when I think I'll die, just when I think my soul can't manage all the opposing ages stretching it apart, the stars disappear. I hear a wolf howl, and the bird sings again. I open my eyes and stare at the swirling sky, all ink and moonlight, supernovas and whirling black holes. My last sight for a long time is that sky and a pale, blood-soaked moon.

CHAPTER THREE

First sight

I open my eyes, I'm on the cold floor. My gasping breaths are loud as screams. My hair is twisted around me, thick strands fill my mouth, lie across my face, and clog my sight. I brush them away, coughing. Terrified, but also relieved to see the familiar lines of my room. The candle is lying on its side near my drawn-up knees. Hot wax spills all over the floor. It feels like a ton of bricks is lying on my chest. My first couple of breaths are a struggle. I groan and hold my head with both hands when I sit up. I don't bother reaching for my water, even though the thirst clawing at my throat feels like a living thing made of uncut gasoline and flame. I dive for my paints. I'm moving as fast as I can. I hit my knee hard against my bedpost, but I don't care and I don't stop moving. I must draw her before the images fade. Every second my mind feels more stuffed with fog, every breath I take, further dissolves the pictures still flashing in my mind. I kneel in front of the west wall.

Moon goddess. Nokomis.

The world outside is pitch black when I stop drawing. I twist at the waist, trying to loosen a few aching muscles, then groan when something in my lower back spasms. I could've kept trying to get her lips right, but my mind went blank some time ago, so I put the paints down. I've just been doodling in my notebook since. I stand up, stretch my arms above my head, then bend down to touch my toes. I'm starving. I don't know when I last ate. Hours, days? I feel weak, and if I get any weaker, I won't be able to hunt. My stomach stopped rumbling around the time the pictures in my mind faded, and I don't know if that's a good sign. I leaf through my black notebook and my mess of scribbles, looking for clues. My notebook is full of a thousand words I don't understand. Still, if I didn't have it, I think I may very well starve. On the third page, written in my bold script, it says:

> Daniel is your brother! Find him. Remember him! Your Tardigrade, or Rade—as you seem to prefer—lives in the back courtyard. His name is Boogles. You love him. He's saved your life at least a hundred times. Trust him. Your saddle is downstairs, two doors right, three doors left to another set of stairs. Don't fall again. One long hall. First door on the right, second shelf to the left. Your knife is there too.
>
> Ride east. Cloud raiders are north. You hate them! Villains. Stay away from the Burning tribe. Bald, sores, red capes, cannibals all. They've tried to eat you twice.
>
> Then there's Valance. Skylord and lost cowboy extraordinaire. It's complicated with him. You hate and love him. He drives you mad. The way he looks at you makes you melt. He's dangerous, but if you need help, you always run to him.
>
> Dayle and Rashid are your friends. Trust them.
>
> Radiation from the waves is killing everyone. Even Daniel. You seem to be immune— It might not be a good thing.
>
> Did you read what you wrote above? Daniel is your brother. Daniel. Small, brown-haired boy, you'll know him when you see him. Remember him!
>
> He's sick. Help him. Remember him. Help him.

There are a few jumbled lines that mean nothing to me. The scribbled words are splattered by what look like tearstains. I skip the page.

> Red waves come, and each time you forget everything. Don't try to fight it, it doesn't change anything.
>
> There is an old military silo beneath the earth in the back

courtyard. You find what you need there. You hunt and steal the rest. You found an old well pump behind the south graveyard. Stop forgetting how to use it.

I close the notebook. I don't know how to feel. I try not to feel anything. I open the book again and write:

You lit a candle and the tattoo on your arm started glowing. You read the words, and they made an archway. You walked through it and fell into a shit ton of stars. You're sixty percent sure this happened.

I shove the notebook under my pillow and lift my cloak from the end of my bed. The cloak is one of my favorite things in the entire world. I made it out of a survival blanket, according to my y notebook. It keeps the sun from scorching me during its hottest times, and the icy night wind from freezing my bones. I pull my long hair back and tie it in a knot, then lift the hood of my cloak to cover my overflowing mass of dark curls and give my room one long, last look before I leave it. My legs are shaking when I walk down the set of crumbling stairs that exit Styx. It's impossible to know if the shaking is just general fatigue or a byproduct of my recent free fall into insanity.

Boogles is lying just where my book said he would be. The size of my pet shocks me. He's resting on his side, looking like a two-ton ball of pure fat. He perks up when he sees me. His face scrunches even more until his nose looks like the indent made by a finger in a fluffy pillow. I scratch the top of his head and hand him a can of beans. He nudges my shoulder with one of his trunk-like paws, then eats the can and the beans. I place the saddle on his back while he eats. I made it out of some old Kevlar vests I found in the silo, the same material my jacket is made of. It stops knives and most bullets. My notebook says it's saved my life more than once.

"How you doing, boy? Let's find ourselves a bird and pick its bones dry. What do you say?" I attach the hanging straps of the saddle under his huge, swaying stomach. He snorts through his trumpet nose, then kneels on his front haunches so I can climb on his back. The night is drenched in silence, the eerie kind. I clench my teeth to keep them from chattering.

The air freezes the moisture in my nose, coats my tongue in icy shards. I pull my cloak tight, lifting the crinkly cloth so it covers everything except for my eyes. Night thickens as we ride. Cliffs in the distance create a gloomy, jagged pattern on the low-hanging sky. Their scope enhances my loneliness. I load my crossbow while we make our way. Under the murky, wavering moonlight, the earth looks bruised and wind-chapped.

A shape moves behind me. I twist and hold up my crossbow, then stare down the glistening edge of the bolt. Whatever it was vanishes behind a blackened tree stump and a pile of rubble filled with jagged metal pipes and bricks turning to purple dust. Boogles snorts and keeps running. I shift in the saddle, scanning the endless stretch of snow and the cliffs that jut from the ground like the broken bones of a dying earth. No birds, no light. Too much fog to see any stars. No hint in the landscape of what this world was like before the waves, not what it is now, the dying dregs of a once great humanity.

A few feet in front of us, I see something slither through the snow. I make a clicking sound with my tongue against the roof of my mouth, then grip the edges of the saddle as Boogles comes to a stop. He snorts and shakes his head as I dismount. My boots sink deep in the freezing earth, leaving prints I wish I could cover. It's so dark, I use my ears to find the creature. It's a snake. I hear the ice particles crunch under its slithering belly. My eyes widen, and I scan the darkness until I see a glimmer of moonlight on its striped black-and-bronze scales. When I think I'm close enough to take the perfect shot, I kneel and aim the arrow. I'm so involved in my kill, so wrapped up in my own hunger, that I don't hear the footsteps behind me. Someone throws a bag over my head.

I don't scream. I don't think. I fight. My foot lashes out. I strike something soft and hear a satisfying grunt. The bow is torn from my grip. Gloved hands wrestle with mine, trying to lock them behind my back. I twist my right arm free and claw the hand around my waist. My fingers grate uselessly against cold metal. An arm brace of some kind. A hand grabs my throat, trying to squeeze the life or, at the very least, the consciousness from me. I struggle for air but only manage to suck in a mouthful of cloth. It tastes like dirt and sweat. Another hard hand grabs my left thigh.

"Let me go!" I scream. "Fuck you! Let me go!" Something hard strikes the side of my head. The world sways. Harsh, raucous laughter makes me taste rage.

"Keep her Taga quiet. Kill the beast if you must, the skin of a Tardigrade is good trade," someone says.

"No!" I scream. Instantly, I stop struggling. "Don't hurt him. I won't fight anymore, just don't hurt him."

"Take the beast then," the hard voice says and nudges my waist with his elbow. "We'll bring them both as a gift for the Skylord."

Someone laughs. "If she starts kicking again, we can kill it then."

I stop listening after the first one said "Skylord." Valance. My notebook says I love and hate him, and I almost snarl. *Way to go, Divinica. Keeping it real and cryptic.* I take a deep breath. *Steady, steady, steady.* I repeat the word to myself as they tie my hands behind my back with metal twine and rope, then toss me face-first over Boogles's saddle. He snorts happily when he feels my weight but then grunts in anger. I assume someone has given him a hard tug with whatever they looped around his neck.

We start to move. I hear the heavy footsteps of other Tardigrades. It sounds like a large procession, with at least ten humans besides me. I count to a thousand six times and focus on my breathing. It's not his fault, really it isn't, but every step Boogles takes threatens to drive all available air from my lungs. My ribs are screaming when one of the men finally calls halt. I lift my head, blink rapidly, and try to see through the dirty cloth. I smell fire. Once my eyes adjust to a sharp infusion of light, I see it burning in hollow, metal drums. Orange flames that bleed thick, black smoke.

I try to keep my promise not to struggle when they pull me from Boogles's back. It's difficult, the need to fight seems as intrinsic as breathing.

It starts to snow then, light flakes that target my exposed skin and wet the cloth over my face. The melting liquid makes the smell worse. I think of wet dogs and moldy socks. I cough again. Breathing is a struggle. The air feels heavy here, dusty and thick.

Just when I fear I'm in real danger of suffocating, one of the men tears the bag off my head. I blink rapidly. I don't look directly at my attacker, not yet. I look over his shoulder. I see dilapidated concrete running off a huge, three-tiered structure that blocks most of the low wind and disturbs the slanting light running off the horizon. Broken bricks and glass clutter the ground. A twisted, deeply rusted staircase is perched haphazardly against a rubble slide. The staircase leads to a broken window, standing without walls. The remaining glass pane clings weakly to the plastic frame, both swaying in the low, freezing wind.

Someone comes up behind me and shoves me to my knees. Sharp rocks grind against my bones. It hurts, and I am proud of myself for not making a sound. One of the men kneels in front of me. I have a second to take in the foulness of his breath before he pulls off one of his leather gloves, grabs my chin, and turns my head from side to side, inspecting me while making appreciative sounds deep in his throat. Red, weeping sores split his nails. He strokes a finger down my face, leaving a gooey trail of pus on my cheek.

I spit in his eye. My actions are, devoid of rationality considering my current circumstance. It felt so good though, and I almost hock back another loogie to do it again.

But before I can, he cuffs me. Fire blooms in my jaw, and the hit knocks me over. My face smacks the ground, and rocks gouge the soft skin of my chin. I straighten and look him in the eyes, spitting blood and hoping he drops from the heat of my death stare. Without the canvas material muting my vision, I see my attacker clearly. The meager light touches his face and shows me a monster. More red and oozing pus-soaked sores cover his lips. The whites of his eyes are the color of urine. His skin is dark and pierced, and three deep scars warp the left side of his mouth. From what I can see of his companions, they are equally pierced, tattooed, and afflicted.

I notice a persistent feeling between my ribs, like I've swallowed lava, or maybe something blazing and dangerous, raging and mystical, that's hovering somewhere just out of my reach. I have a sense that if I could touch it and use it, I could split the very foundations of the earth. It's a weird sense, and I chalk it up to wishful thinking while the men form a semicircle of horror around me. I focus on my surroundings instead of them. The square concrete building with its front blown off casts weird shadows on the ground. Each level of the dilapidated structure is stuffed with small electric bulbs, shedding pale-white glows. There are long halls leading to nowhere in particular and deep windows with cracking glass. Barbwire drapes the three-tiered structure, running up the floors and climbing the walls, like some exotic, alien vine. A sort of throne made of twisted metal pipes sits on the highest platform, overlooking it all. The chair is empty, but I see black shadows moving along the back wall.

I want to ask where the fuck we are, but it hardly matters. If I've been here before, I can't remember. What's more, the way home is a mystery. I bite my lip to keep silent. Regardless of where I am, if I don't find a way to escape, I think I'm dead.

The man who struck me stands and rocks back on his thick heels. The movement makes the chains dangling from his black canvas jacket rattle and sing as they clash against each other. "You'll do," he says.

"For what?"

"Micha's fallen out of favor," says a thin man to my right tossing a weathered thumb in the direction of the hitter. The others laugh. The sound is dangerous.

"I'm sorry for Micha? What the fuck does that have to do with me?"

"You're a peace offering," says another. More laughter.

"The Skylord loves beauty, and you..." The man called Micha reaches out a grimy finger toward my cheek. "You're the prettiest thing I've seen."

I snap my teeth at him before he touches me. He backs away. "How the hell do you know?" I screech, but no one's listening. They speak among themselves for a moment. I see each of their names tattooed on the backs of their hands and understand why they've done it. Micha walks back to me and reaches for a lock of my hair. Even though I yank my head away, he manages to catch a few strands and rub them between his fingers. "I am no one's peace offering, and your *lord* can go and—"

Micha cuts me off. "Fine, maybe we kill and eat you, find a different offering. Maybe another woman who's not so angry."

"I dare you to cut these ropes and try," I say. Something in my eyes makes him take a step back. He looks like he wants to hit me again for a second, then laughs. The others join suit. I imagine myself jumping on Micha's broad back and snapping his neck between my knees like a dry twig. The laughter cuts off abruptly when we all hear footsteps riling up the snow. As one, we lift our eyes to the owner of those heavy steps. A few of the men bow low. Micha inclines his head, and I see his left hand inching toward the knife in his belt. I think about the knife I shoved in my boot and decide that the second they untie me I'm going for it. I fear this new evil will make the villainy of Micha seem like puppy love.

"Here we go again," drawls a smooth voice that makes the skin on the back of my neck prickle. I hear a sigh, deep and exhausted. "Well, Micha, what have you brought me today?"

"A gift, my lord," Micha says, tilting into a slight bow, then shuffling his body to the side. A dark shadow crosses mine. The tension in my body makes my limbs feel brittle. I lift my chin, and my gaze crashes into a pair of astonishing blue, deeply set eyes. Breathtaking eyes. I gasp as a spasm rocks me. *The fucking Skylord, I presume,* my mind snarls. I don't know him, but my body reacts like it does. My own lips throb when I look at his. I'm dizzy, confused, mentally and physically reeling, but I won't be the first to break the stare. Finally, he drops his eyes, and I take the opportunity to give him a once-over. He's wearing steel-toe boots, canvas pants, and a black T-shirt that looks three sizes too small. His hair is the color of sunlit gold. On him, it is a musical color. His face is so stunning, I am momentarily struck speechless. I must gasp again or make some sort of embarrassing squelching sound, because he smiles and hunkers down in front of me.

Inspecting his gift, no doubt. I feel my teeth worrying at my lower lip. He is the most startling thing I've ever seen, but I refuse to disgrace myself by gasping again, so I bite harder on my lip and choke back any more untoward noises.

"What happened to her cheek?" the Skylord says, his voice is strangely cool, yet I think of the eerie calm before a storm. The silence that comes before the wave hits with the fury of an exploding star.

"She spit at me," says Micha, by way of explanation.

Blue eyes clenches his fists, then he shakes his head, sighing again. "Micha, it is a daily struggle not to kill you. Tie up her Tardigrade and bring her to me. If you put one more mark on her, I will cut off both your hands and hang them on my wall," he says, then turns to stride away. His casual, dismissive movements put me in a killing rage.

"I'll fight you until I die," I say. It sounds like a promise.

His voice changes, becomes low, almost tender. "Oh, I know you will," he says. Then, "Better leave the ropes on this time."

CHAPTER FOUR

All the stabbings

My captors drag me down a long hall. It is dimly lit by soft blue lights swinging on white cords that are affixed to the concrete ceiling. More white wires run along the walls like vines, twisting, then conglomerating in ungainly clumps. People wrapped up in rags watch me through mistrustful eyes. They cluster in groups, arms around each other like I am the source of evil in the room. Paintings cover the walls, beautiful, colorful landscapes filled with light green trees and dark blue water. Suddenly, I remember the sight and smell of a beach so clearly that I can almost taste the salt in the air. White-capped waves crashing onto sandy shores. The rare gold light in a setting sun, the reflection of a moon on black waters.

The painting to my left shows a white ship sailing peacefully into the watery reflection of a melting, silver moon. I want to stay and look at them all. I want to recreate them. Especially the one on a grayish-white, deeply cratered plain full of shadows, traversed by men who look weightless in their strange white suits. The letters N-A-S-A boldly featured over their hearts. They look free, alive. I have no time to think about it, because hard hands push me farther down the hall. I walk so that I don't fall. I am tense, observant, as we move through a labyrinth of cramped hallways dotted by high, square-cut windows. The air is damp and stuffy, the lighting is different too. Broken bits of furniture litter the doorways and sloping staircases. Seems the old pieces were left where they fell. I have to step over a toppled chair, then stub my already damaged toe on a bedside table missing its back legs.

We make two more sharp turns and climb a long flight of spiral stairs with metal railings. Hands shove me again. I stumble into a wide, brightly lit, concrete room. The same room I saw from outside with the throne of twisted pipes. I realize we are on the top level of the structure. I blink my eyes and scan my surroundings. Dark, velvet curtains framed by tattered gold tassels are strung along the back walls. Huge, multicolored rugs, circular, pentagonal, and all the shapes in between, decorate the hard floor. Every inch of the walls that are not boasting velvet drapes is covered in wild paintings, a hundred or so, maybe more. *One hundred and three,* I think, and then I know I've been in this room before and have counted all the paintings. The smell is also familiar. Paint. Canvas. Storm. Rain. Home.

I see his shadow before I hear his voice. "Come in, Divinica, it's rude to lurk." I have to crane my neck to see his face. He looks so much larger inside the confines of walls and roofs. We both take a step back. He holds up his hands in a defensive pose. The shadows he stands in do little to mute the overwhelming brilliance of his eyes. "I would untie those," he says, pointing to my bound hands, "but it's been a long twenty-four hours, and if you stab me again, today might very well be the day I finally lose my temper." His chin tilts up in a brief nod directed at one of the cretins behind me. The man understands the silent command and starts to fumble with the ropes binding my wrists behind my back. The knots loosen for just a split second, but I go wild, kicking and thrashing. It takes three of them to hold me while another reties my hands, crossing them tightly over my lower stomach.

The blue-eyed cowboy watches it all impassively, as if the spectacle I'm making of myself is nothing new. Maybe it isn't. When my hands are fully secured, the men step back to a safer distance. The Skylord lifts his chin again, another barely perceptible move, and the men fall farther back. "Leave," he commands sharply, and they do.

I keep my defiant eyes on his face, free of boils or scars. He has a tattoo on his forearm, a bird in flight, taloned claws extended. Formidable, dynamic, dominant, intoxicating. "I stabbed you?" I ask. The notion seems absurd.

"Multiple times, actually. You've given me thirty-six scars in two years." His eyes scan me from boot to hood. It should be creepy, but it's not. Instead, it's a slow, mesmerizing perusal. I feel like he's looking for further injury. Assessing my overall damage score. I don't think he likes what he sees. I don't like it either. His look makes me feel hot and faint. Randomly, my palms start to sweat. *What in the actual hell is wrong with me? Maybe I'm getting sick.*

No, it's him, my mind says. His smell, his eyes, that face, which has turned me into a mass of pins, needles, and fluttering nerves. I hate it. I imagine kicking him where it hurts worst, then dancing on his writhing body. His keen eyes seem to read the thoughts straight out of my head, because the right corner of his mouth kicks up. He crosses his arms over his chest and motions with his chin to a red bean bag sitting amid a pile of overstuffed, colorful pillows. "Take a seat, if you will." He gives me a little bow. I don't understand the gesture. "That one there, it's your favorite."

I eye him warily and walk backward to the fluffy seat. I fall in the bag, and it puffs up around me, cradling my sore body. I close my eyes, groaning in absolute bliss before I realize what I am doing. My eyes snap back open.

He takes the seat across from me—a velvety, orange couch—draws up one knee and slings his arm over it, letting his large hand just dangle in the space between us. For a long time, we just stare at each other. It's not an overly comfortable silence, but not a violent one either. I feel like I know him, like I've met him before, maybe a hundred times. The feeling is just as unsettling as everything else.

It's so quiet I can hear the distant rumble of voices downstairs, the busy hum of the electric lights, and his slow, steady breathing.

"You look hungry," he finally says.

I roll my eyes at that. "Thanks for noticing. I was hunting before your men grabbed me," I say, then take a breath. "When was the last time I stabbed you?"

"They're not my men, and about twenty days ago." He pulls back his black cotton sleeve to show me a deep gash running high up the underside of his arm.

His words shock me more than the nasty-looking cut. "How do you know that? How do you know the days?"

"I know a lot of things."

"Like what?" I snap.

"Like your name, your favorite food, where you live. I even know how long you've been there. In fact, we've had a version of this conversation fifty-five times. The beginning is almost always the same, the ropes, the red bean bag." He pauses, then lifts the hand hanging in the space between us to point to my cheek. "Your face. One day, I really am going to cut off that son of a bitch's hands. I'll hang them on my wall right next to that Monet. I'm not sure which decoration will bring me more joy."

"Versions of this conversation?" I ask, ignoring the rest.

His smile makes his face startling again.

"There are a few differences here and there. Untying you really changes the script." He rolls his eyes. "Each time is its own adventure."

I shock myself by letting out a laugh that turns into a sharp snort. It's an alarming sound. I fall silent and puzzle over what the dust is wrong with me. I never smile. I certainly don't laugh. I briefly wonder if any of this is real. Maybe I am dreaming, maybe the red wave killed me. I kind of hope it did. I open my mouth to ask if I am awake, but he speaks first. Answering my unspoken question.

"Yes, Divinica, you're awake," he says. "And I'm with you. I don't think it's all real either. Sometimes I pinch myself but never wake up. I try to console myself with the knowledge that humans are the only animals who can't distinguish fantasy from reality, so in a way we kind of had it coming."

"Great. Brutal capture with a side of dry wit, how lucky am I? Did you come up with that?"

He shakes his head. "No, some dead guy did, but it's true. Everything is X-rated fantasy these days. It's the constant dark. It's the 'gets in your brain and stays with you' kind."

He's right, so I don't say anything more on the topic of reality.

"Will you please untie me? I promise not to stab you."

He laughs outright. "Do you realize I've fallen for that exact line thirty-six times? Goddamn. Must be your eyes," he says in that deep drawl of his that I think I could become addicted to. Still smiling, he leans back in his chair and folds his hands across his flat stomach.

"Have you ever untied me and I didn't try to stab you?"

"Nope, but I keep hope alive."

"How do you have your memories? Are you really a Skylord? Or a god? Or whatever?" I expect him to make another joke, but his lips tighten.

"I suppose that depends on how you look at it, and who's doing the looking," he tells me rather caustically. The moment he says the words, I am sure we have had this conversation before. Even the depth of his left dimple seems familiar.

"What's the longest amount of time you've kept me here?" I ask.

He sits up in his chair, curiosity replacing the challenge in his eyes. "You've never asked me that before."

"What do I normally ask you?"

"You ask me why Micha brought you to me."

That makes me pause. I gnaw at my lower lip, then realize he's staring at the tormented spot, so I bite my tongue instead. "I was going to ask that, but I thought the other question might have a better answer."

"It does. Once, you were my guest for eight days."

"Your guest?" I say and lift my bound hands.

"No, your hands weren't tied, it was one of the times you stabbed me."

"I don't feel like stabbing you right now."

"That's okay. The electric storm is eleven days away, so there is plenty of time to change your mind."

"Electric storm?"

"You call it the red wave."

As soon as he says those two words, I remember the pain. I shiver hard, and goosebumps break out all over my skin. Screaming, tearing, ringing in my ears that splits my skull. Breaking bones, twisting ligaments, bursting veins, burning skin. When I finally find some words, my voice is chicken scratch. "It takes everything away. Why does it take everything away? Do you know why?"

"No, I do not," he says.

"Does it take it away from you?"

"No, it does not."

His monosyllabic answers infuriate me. "Why?" I demand.

"Because I wasn't here when it happened."

"When what happened?" I nearly shriek. When the first wave hit and destroyed what was left of humanity that hadn't been killed by climate change, disease, and natural disaster. I wasn't here. I was in space with two other guys."

"Space?" I echo, sounding like an intoxicated parrot.

"Yep," he says. "I was on a three-man mission to Mars, refueling on the second International Space Station when the first wave hit. I didn't feel it, but I saw it. Surrounded our beautiful blue-green planet in a red-electric haze. Like a bloody disco ball. After a year without a single word from command, we packed up and headed home—to all this splendor," he says, motioning to the expanse of the concrete room and the strange throne of twisted pipes. "Found some folks held up in this abandoned parking structure. The moment they saw us, they fell to their knees. Pretty weird being bowed to for the first time, I gotta tell ya. A bunch of these guys watched me fall from the sky. When our pod broke atmosphere, we turned into what must've looked like a spinning fireball of death. Naturally, everyone thought we were gods. They drew pictures of the whole event on that big wall out back that they all write their names on."

"What happened to all the cities, the trees and plants? Why does the world look so different? Everything is so…ravaged."

He shrugs and stands up, then starts to pace. "Can't say for sure. Do you remember what it looked like before?"

I have to think about that for a second, then realize I don't. "Just flashes, pictures in my mind that disappear when I try to look at them. Why do you ask?"

"Sometimes you remember things, other times you don't. I'm always trying to see if there's a trigger," he says.

"You're a confusing guy. Did you know that?"

He nods once, as if absently registering my words. "Whatever that red shit is, it's radioactive and causes catastrophe. It's something that transfigured everything, then restructured it all. It has to do with time, or the lack of it, I guess." He stops pacing to give me an owl-eyed stare, crossing his arms over his chest. "It's gone beyond apocalyptic."

"So, what? We're all just trapped to live the same set of days, again and again?"

"Maybe. I think it depends on you."

"Me?" I almost choke on the word.

"Yes, you, Divinica, I think you are somehow at the epicenter of it all."

He's finally rendered me speechless, so I stare up at him in silence, struck again by how he dominates all the space around him, making me feel small. "How did I manage to stab you thirty-six times?"

He looks like he wants to say something for a moment, then he throws up his hands, as if dismissing my question. "I told you. I think it's your damn eyes. The last wave hit the day before yesterday, right?" he asks, staring off in the distance, clearly distracted.

"You're asking me? How the fuck should I know? It's all just one big blur. I know the words of things my mind doesn't think it's seen. There are times when I don't even know my own name."

"Yeah. That seems to be the nature of the beast. It only takes the soul, obliterates only what matters. Love, friendship, memories, family, life. Your name is Divinica, you're nineteen. You're an Aries, born on April 8th, if that matters to you."

Nineteen. Fuck! "And it doesn't affect you?" I'm almost yelling. "Not at all?"

"No. It's what makes me think you had to get hit by the initial blast. The guys I was with haven't lost anything either. They're like me. Sometimes I think we might have it worse. To remember what used to be and have no idea how to get it back?" He shakes his head. "It's a fucking horrifying nightmare is what it is." He starts pacing again. "People remember a few things as we get closer to D-day. Ten, maybe twenty seconds before it hits, they remember just about everything. You remember the most. You have a brother, by the way. His name is Daniel. You love him like crazy, really, it's almost holy. You're a good sister, the best. I never had any siblings, never saw what that kind of love looks like. Rashid, my first mate, is the closest thing I have to a brother, though recently—" He breaks off, leaving his thoughts unfinished. He clears his throat and tries again. "You're a legend around here. People draw pictures of you on their walls right beside their sketches of me. They call you 'the ghost of Styx.' Sometimes, I think it's a fitting moniker."

"Why?"

"Well, beside the fact that you and that old wreck you live in often disappear from the face of the earth, you seem immune to all the viruses killing the rest of the population, dwindling as it may be."

"Why?" I whisper again with feeling, like I am incapable of saying any other word.

"Darlin'," he says in that honey drawl that makes my skin tingle, "I ain't got no idea. Rashid thinks you're a witch. A year ago, he wanted to kill you and burn your bones. He said it would exonerate the world. Kill the witch, break the spell. He's changed his mind though, right when I thought what a grand idea it was. Traitor. Rashid may be blood, but lately we've been fighting over your fate like an old married couple."

"Fighting over my fate? How dare—" My angry words cut off as I realize what he just said. "You wanted to kill me?" I snap, drawing up my arms and flinching into myself, then hunching my shoulders, as if I could somehow protect my person if he decided to throw his bulk at me.

"I'm not gonna lie, I've thought about it," he says and smiles at me. His smile is cold, and so beautiful it stops the breath in my chest. "Especially the tenth time you stabbed me, right in the back after you kicked me in a place meant to be kissed."

I hiss at him.

His smile broadens. "I've considered all options. I'm desperate, we all are. Once, you considered it too, the day before the red wave struck, last August. You thought if I killed you, it would save your brother, and you begged me to do it. Even gave me the knife. I couldn't do it, but we have to do something. Humans are dying out. Our once glorious race is being systematically destroyed. Someone is doing this to us. There is an ancient legend of a Sumerian king who ruled in Mesopotamia. He took all the memories of his people using a device powered by the stars. He did this to save the planet they were killing. No memories, no desires, no gluttony, no greed. Humans have always felt so evolved, but what are we without our memories? We're stupid. We intentionally closed our eyes to all that had come before, so someone took away what was. That's my theory."

"Who? Who took it away? Who are they?" I ask.

He looks up and finds my eyes, his piercing gaze cutting right through me. "I think you'll figure that out before any of us. I feel it in my gut."

I throw up my hands. "Your gut? Oh, that's great. Are you going to keep me prisoner?" He starts pacing again.

"I haven't decided yet." He strolls away, leisurely walking to a long table at the far side of the room. I can't stop watching him. The world is brighter wherever he is, like his energy is at war with the ever encroaching dark and is constantly winning. He picks up something undecipherable from one of the plates strewn across the table and pops it in his mouth. While he chews, I watch the color of the humming electric lights wash over his face. White, pale green, and golden yellow. It makes him appear like one of his paintings. His beauty enrages me. Beauty doesn't belong in this world. It makes him alien.

He turns to look at me and with a single glance correctly reads my expression. His shoulders shake, and I think he's laughing. Again, I imagine kicking him in that place he mentioned while I struggle silently with my bonds, trying to twist my hands through the rough gaps in the wires and rope.

I hear him sigh as he takes another bite of whatever is in his hand. "I know, I know, don't say it. You hate my face. It makes me alien. Sometimes I feel like one too, trust me."

His last statement, spoken like a command, makes me smile. "Never," I vow.

He turns back to the food, frowning. "Would it be redundant for me to tell you I knew you were going to say that?"

His words give me chills. I wonder how much he does know.

"I'll tell you something new," he says. He lifts a hunk of curious meat and a bowl of something, then walks back to me. He stops a few feet in front of me, close, but not close enough to annoy. I stare up at him coldly. I can feel the mutiny of my glare as he looms over me. "You're gaining a resistance to the waves. Each time, you remember faster. The last three times you were captured, you fought harder. Every time I see you, there's more strength. You wear it like an aura. I want to know how."

"Like I told you before, I don't know what the fuck you're talking about," I say. My lie has a hollow echo in the room. In my mind, I see two faces, a woman made of seafoam, and another a moon goddess who runs with warriors and wolves. The pictures come in flashes. Then, a candle, a flickering flame, small black letters that morph into golden symbols. I see a high archway. Through it thrives a world of glittering stars.

"Fine, don't tell me," he says, sounding almost comically petulant. I get a whiff of whatever is in the bowl, and it smells sweet and spicy. My mouth instantly floods with water. We both hear the unholy rumbling of my stomach. I drop my eyes as my cheeks burn.

He watches me for a moment, then says, "Let's play a game, shall we? It's called twenty questions."

"I hate games," I say acerbically, trying to be cruel.

He winks at me. "I know."

"I don't want to ask you anything," I say, shaking my head so my hair curtains my blush. Internally, I suspect that he knows I'm lying again.

"Bummer for you. I have a million questions for you, and since, for the moment, however fleeting, you're at my mercy, I'm afraid your compliance is mandatory."

I don't say anything, because what is there to say? He's right, I'm trapped. But would I walk away from him right now if I could? That's the real question. I lift my eyes to look at him and see he's gazing directly at me. Roasting me from the inside out with the heat of his challenging stare. The air feels ridiculously hot, and I imagine that I must lower my eyes or be burned. I don't. "Fine, ask your damn questions."

For a moment he continues to stare, his piercing eyes peeling back layers of me. I feel raw, exposed, known. Sitting here with him, there's a strange sensation of safety. I hate it because it feels like a lie. I'm alone. Always alone. *Why don't I feel like it? Why do I feel found? Home?*

Finally, he takes a breath, then sighs. "Somehow, you're managing to break free. The wave just hit. It affects everyone differently, of course. Some weep, some wander around confused and lethargic, and others, like Micha and his crew, follow a set course, or a predetermined sequence of events, if you will. You might follow a path right after the wave hits, but for the most part you make your own rules and—"

I interrupt him with a screeching, indignant sound and sit up straighter. "Excuse me. I don't weep."

His dark blond eyebrows rise. Their pointed arches are dramatic. I notice a jagged, slanting scar cuts through the left one. A single slash of white. The flaw, like everything else, only adds to his pagan beauty. "See, how do you know that, Divinica? How do you know this early on? How do you know what you do and don't do?"

I don't know the answer to his question, so I don't bother to reply.

He sighs. "You're pale, Divinica. I want to give you this food, and you hate it when I offer to feed you, so," he pauses dramatically, "I'm going to untie you, but if you stab me, so help me god—"

"I swear I won't," I quickly say. I think we're both surprised that one didn't sound like a lie at all.

He goes down on one knee in front of me, then sets the food on the ground beside his foot and starts working on the knot in the wires and rope. Regardless of my promise, I fight the violent urge to use my knee on the underside of his chiseled jaw and make a break for freedom. In end it's easy to keep my word because his cool hands against my hot ones feel good, and so does the rope when it lets loose and ceases its mission of twisting my skin. I rub my wrists while he turns away to lift the food before handing it to me with a grin.

I take it. "Don't expect me to thank you. I'd be full and in my own room if your men hadn't jumped me."

He sits back on the overstuffed couch across from me. "Again, not my men, and, Divinica, I've learned it's best not to expect anything when it comes to you."

"Do you know where we are? In the world, I mean," I ask, taking a sip of the brown mush in the bowl. It tastes like dirt and pepper. The mystery meat is chewy, probably some sort of snake.

"That sounds like a question." His tone is leading, and he wriggles his brows. "Let the games begin?"

"Whatever. You seem to magically know my name. Before we play, tell me yours."

"It's Valance Lord."

"Your name is really Lord?" I ask skeptically.

"Yep, it sure is. The Lords are an old Kentucky family. Southern blood, hot tempers. To answer your first question, we're in Germany. For both of us…it's a long way from home."

"Do you know where I'm from?" I ask, hearing awe in my voice.

"You're American, you were born in California, as were your mother and father. It's my turn to ask a question now."

"Fine," I say.

"Fine," he echoes and smiles again. "Why is Styx only visible twice a day?"

"It is?"

"Yeah, like Briga-fucking-doon."

"Briga-what?" I'm shrieking again.

"Old story about a town that only appeared once every hundred years. Good movie," he says. Seeing my blank look, he shakes his head. "Never mind. What's in the lab underground?"

"I didn't know there was one." I sound defiant yet honest, but there's hesitation in my tone as a wild thing tugs at the fringes of my memory. Ruins and humming symbols. Needles, ink, and knives. Pain that's white and red, pain that shocks and tortures, pain that lingers.

Valance scowls at my answer. "Where did you get those tattoos?" he says, motioning to my body with his chin.

I almost throw my hands in the air, but they hold my food, so I settle for rolling my eyes. "I have no idea. Tell me, have you had much success with this line of questioning in the past?"

His eyes flash. "Is that one of your questions?"

"Fuck you," I say, my voice soft.

He's shaking his head again, the smile in his eyes now something else. "Oh, darlin', I don't think we should pull that thread."

"You're impossible, tell me about the red wave."

"No, ask better questions," he says.

I put my food down. If I eat another bite, I'll hurl. "Why are you asking about my tattoos?"

"You won't believe my explanations," Valance says.

"Why? Have you tried them on me before?"

"Yes."

Unblinking, I stare at his face. "Tell me."

"Star travel is one of the most common legends in all pantheons of ancient mythology. Typically tattoos, like the ones you have, were used to harness star energy, and in rare cases, open doors. Star-tech, to put it in sci-fi nerd terms."

"Sci-fi what?" I gasp.

Valance waves my outburst away. "These doors tear a shortcut through the space-time continuum. Wormhole, or black hole, but really just a door. Creating a traversable wormhole requires more energy than humans have ever been able to produce. We simply didn't have the tech. Millions of times more energy than a nuclear bomb. Still, many believe we had it at one point. Hell, I think there's even a portal somewhere in Michigan called the Michigan Triangle. There's the Bermuda Triangle, shit, Stonehenge, the damn pyramids for Christ's sake. I studied all this in senior year. I think it's what started my obsession with Mars.

"I know every symbol on your body, the ones I've seen, that is. I can tell you which goddess they belong to, and from which mythology. You always tell me you dream you're walking through a gate of stars. I think you use that gate to travel to the lives of the goddesses whose symbols you're wearing. You have Sumerian hieroglyphics all over the grounds surrounding Styx. The place is like a damn magical fortress."

I think then that my blank look must hold a lot of comic value. I blink. He's crazy, I'm crazy, we're all drowning in insanity, even the sun and moon have taken leave of their senses, locking those who remain in a reality that shouldn't even be imagined, much less lived. "Have you told me all this before?" I ask.

Valance draws in a deep breath and rubs his eyes. "Yes, so many times. I am locked in the weirdest Groundhog Day of all time. I'm getting less diplomatic with each explanation."

"Groundhog? You say strange things," I tell him.

Again, he waves my words away. "I used to spend hours trying to convince you. Once, I had Rashid and Dayle hold you while I ripped off your clothes so you could see the tattoos for yourself. You didn't like that, you stabbed me in the shoulder blade. Hurt like a bitch and took forever to heal."

"You're fucking crazy. You're talking about magic, aren't you?"

"Could be. What is magic except the ability to alter the confines of known reality?" He motions to where we sit, points to the broken world through the window. "I hate to be the one to tell you, but our reality has been fucking altered. Magic or advanced science, it's all one and the same. Something happened, call it whatever you want, but it turned us into a species inflicted with short-term amnesia—maybe we always have been."

He isn't making sense. Sweat is starting to dew my forehead. Suddenly, I want to see Boogles, I want to sleep in my bed. Out loud, I say, "I want you to let me go."

His shrug is nonchalant. His eyes on my face keep their intensity. "Fine, you'll be back, we'll talk, you'll remember, we'll get close to figuring it out, then the wave will hit. And this?" He motions to the space between us. "This will begin all over again."

I stand up and turn on my heels to make my way to the door. Behind me, I hear him stand. "I'll walk you out," he says. "It's incredibly boring when you get lost."

"Do what you want," I say, comforted by the weight of my knife tucked in my boot. His giant presence looming behind me makes my heart beat faster than it should, but I'm not afraid. Not really. It's something else. I pace my steps, but my feet are itching to run. I turn the short, sharp corner and nearly crash into a man walking briskly in our direction. He catches the top of my arms to steady me. I tense, ready to attack. He lets go quickly and steps back. He's smaller than Valance, with deep-brown hair and olive skin. He looks incredibly happy to see me, like he is holding himself captive, like it's taking everything in his power to keep from wrapping me in his arms.

"You're back!" he exclaims. "I'm Pollox Rashid, you call me Rashid. We're besties and have been since I gave up on trying to kill you. You look like shit, girlfriend," he says and reaches into the pocket of his cropped jean jacket. "Here's a power bar. It's not your favorite, but you keep it down. Eat it, you're pale. Wait!" He grabs my arm and in the same instant lets me go. "Leaving already?" He holds up a circular disc with bright green writing printed all over it. "I got a movie, it's a comedy. I know, I know we managed to do it. Finally got the fucking TV working. Wires really do bow to the power of my fingers. Come watch it with me," he finishes, and I feel like I've just been blasted by a speeding north wind.

"I...I..."

Rashid grabs my hand. "Just come, I'm going to make you laugh, then you can leave."

I say nothing. My book says to trust him, so I allow myself to be dragged back to the red bean bag. Rashid fusses with a slender, rectangular object while I peel the wrapper off my power bar. Valance sits as far away as possible, on the floor near the twisted throne. He opens a black box, and it glows blue in the muted light. My mind names the device: *computer*. Rashid follows the path of my eyes and nudges my shoulder. "He got all the computers working five waves ago. Smart fucker. He really can fix just about everything. Youngest person to ever venture into space. It's another one of the reasons the general populace thinks he's a god." Rashid sighs, "That, and he's a hot hunk of man." He flips his hand at me and purses his lips. "You think so too when you're not in such a foul mood."

"I think so right now," I mutter. Rashid giggles, then lays his head on my shoulder. We watch the movie, but I don't laugh once. Just stare at the flashing pictures so full of all the vibrant colors I've forgotten. At some point during the film, I realize my cheek rests on the top of Rashid's head. He smells like wind and strawberries. Valance remains sitting in the far corner of the room, near his throne. Now, he's rifling through random stacks of paper, seemingly absorbed in his task. Somehow, though, I still feel his eyes on me. A tall, dark guy—who looks like the physical embodiment of the strong, silent type—comes into the room and talks with Valance for a time. They speak in hushed tones. I strain to hear their words but manage to catch only snippets. Valance calls the man Dayle. Another name in my book, another person I'm supposed to trust but don't remember. *Ugh! I hate my life.*

When the movie is finally finished, my mind feels soggy and oversaturated. It's Rashid who walks me to my Rade. "What up, Boogles?" he says, reaching out to scratch between my pet's eyes. Boogles makes a trumpeting sound—angel song meets whoopee cushion—and nudges Rashid's hand as he's turning to face me. "Any more star door action?" he asks, and I almost tell him. "Well, remember what I said, don't fight the fall. Let the inertia take you."

"Take me where?" I whisper. Wind blows threads of my voice away.

"Wherever the dick it wants you to go. Valance is right, your symbols definitely have a lot to do with—" He motions to our surroundings. "All this."

I remember something then. A brief, sparking flash that lights up the dark behind my eyes. I remember seeing the reflection of my face on the smooth surface of my canteen and watching Aphrodite's symbol glowing on my forehead.

"Yeah, I see your mind moving. You're a smart girl. Just notice what symbol is interacting with the door. Valance can tell you which goddess each of them belongs to. If you find out where they are from, you might have some idea where you're going."

"You act like this is all so normal," I say.

His eyes pin me in place. "Listen to me, Divinica. Remember this. Make it a 'dear diary' moment if you have to. Shock and disbelief don't belong in this world. It's a sickness of the old world that makes you stupid and slow. Now, if your eyes see it and your body experiences it, I've learned it's best to just accept it." He kisses my cheek, the lightest brush of friendship. I don't like being touched, but I don't mind the kiss. I don't knock away his hands when he helps me saddle up. "Don't worry, it gets easier with time. I promise."

"Does it really?"

Rashid's smile stays pinned on his face, but something dark creeps into his eyes. "No. I don't think it will."

I turn to leave, pause, and glance over my shoulder at the concrete structure straddling the horizon like the old body of some crumbling, petrified dragon. Valance sits on his throne watching me. His face is in shadow, only his eyes catching the light. We share an electric look filled with the questions I could not answer, and the ones he did not ask. I feel his eyes on me long after I ride away.

The sun is low, melting into the break between earth and sky when I finally crawl under my emergency blanket—the one I didn't make into a cloak—close my eyes, and fall asleep without a second thought. My dreams come instantly and with incredible savagery. Volatile colors and screaming sounds, a living blackness that has breath and motion, a white emptiness that tastes like loneliness. I dream I'm in that lab underground. The one Valance talked about. The walls are narrow, the ceilings low, both covered in shiny, white tiles.

I'm freezing. My white jumper is unzipped. I open my eyes and stare into three circular, flat bulbs, all beaming a burning-white light. My eyes tear, but I don't close them. My hands and feet are strapped to a metal table that looks like a butcher's bench. Two needles are sticking out of my arm, and there's a tube shoved under the skin of my wrist that feeds a thick liquid into my veins. The liquid swings in an IV bag above my head, undaunted in its steady drip, drip, drip. I'm dizzy, achy, and when my tongue flicks out to lick my lips, I taste my salty, drying tears. A woman leans over me, her hair a waterfall of silver running across my stomach. She's pressing down on my forehead, digging deep with a flat needle covered in glowing symbols.

I gasp or make some gutted sound. She must hear it because her head snaps up. She has three of them—the middle head—watches me. Her eyes are shot through with black starlight, gleaming like an overturned jar of ink. The profile heads are ghostly, almost transparent, but threaded with color, like holographs from the old world. Each profile has white hair hanging in messy braids, straight, silky strands, and wild, looping curls.

"I don't expect you'll live," the middle head says. Her voice echoes with a hollow twang. "All the others have died screaming. Thirteen symbols, you are the thirteen-thousandth girl—I wonder—"

"Please," I whisper, but I don't know what I'm begging for.

"Not much longer." She keeps drawing on my skin. When she's working on the first symbol, my body starts to shake as pain seeps into my nerves by slow degrees, mirroring the steady drip, drip, drip of the IV bag swinging from its skinny metal arm. During the creation of the third tattoo, I'm panting, my palms slick and sweaty. On the fourth symbol, the needle feels like a firestick. A brand charring my skin, again and again. Tears blur my vision. I focus on the triangular device suspended over my head, a four-sided prism. The interior of the prism is swirling like a million constellations trapped in a glass jar. By the eighth symbol, I'm screaming. As she starts to carve the twelfth symbol, the edges of the prism pulse. She finishes with the thirteenth symbol, etching it just below my navel. I feel a jolt that threads through my new, aching tattoos, and I wake up sweating and screaming, scaring the rats calmly sleeping at the foot of my bed. They screech and run for cover, scurrying to the safety of their hidden corners where they can watch my endless drama through glowing, green orbs.

I blink and rub my eyes. My room is dark and silent, even the storm lamp has extinguished. I sit and swing my feet over the edge of my bed. The floor is ice cold, but I am too tired to go on the search for my shoes. I reach for the box of matches and light the storm lamp, pushing the match through the tiny opening in the lamp's glass shell. When the light in the room is enough to read by, I take my black book from under my pillow and start writing before I have fully collected my thoughts.

Skylord captured you, apparently for the fifty-fifth time—the worst! He thinks you have something to do with the red wave. You want to kick him in his special place, but he could be right. He says there is a lab under Styx, you dreamed about it tonight. It might be the power of suggestion, it might be something more. Valance is a wild card. You don't think Rashid will hurt you.

Next time you see Micha, it's important you punch him.

I thumb through my book and read some of my past notes until I find what I am looking for on the second page I ever wrote.

You dreamed about a torture device in the basement of Styx. There was blood on the floor, your blood.

I turn two more pages and read another paragraph. My writing is shaky here.

Tonight, you dreamed of a woman with three heads. She has a crown of stars on each head. Don't speak to the right head. She's a monster.

I close the book. If Valance is right about the tattoos and the star doors, I need to know. I pull back the sleeve of my jacket and look at the markings on my arm. They are black and calm, not glowing or crawling off into outer space. I reach for my matches again and light my candle before I think better of it. I feel the symbol in the center of my stomach start to pulse. I don't have to look to know it's shining that soft, golden light. I see it falling around me. The jagged tiles make the ring of light look like the broken halo of a fallen angel. I sigh, so deep it moves my whole body, then I read the words.

"Misplaced powers scattered through time. I travel through firelight to make them mine."

Just like before, the writing on my arm ripples and begins to shift, as if propelled by my expelled breath. The archway forms, and through it I see the Gate of Stars. I walk forward and step into oblivion. My mood is dark. The place I travel to is so much darker. Dying worlds and broken promises. A goddess enslaved by a husband who was also her brother. For a nebulous moment in time, I experience life through her eyes. I watch her lie, trick, and eventually poison to reclaim her light. The light she once sacrificed to save Ra's life. In Isis's body I use poison and force him to tell me his real name, then I twist the power of the name and use it against him. My spell immobilizes him. I watch dispassionately as the great ruler falls limply at my feet. I hold the vial of poison in my hand, then press it to his lips and see pure firelight seep from his mouth and eyes.

Something jerks at the base of my spine, and I drop the vial. It doesn't shatter but only rolls unevenly over the golden ground. The second jerk arches my back, making my hands fly out on either side of me, and I'm falling again. The final jerk tugs me into the endless swirl of dimensions through a white, glimmering spiral of planets and stars. I see a tree. Its bark is mother-of-pearl. A planet hangs from each of its branches, spinning and swinging like living, breathing ornaments. I have a moment to think how much I hate it that Valance is right before I am pulled straight into the land of unconsciousness.

CHAPTER FIVE

The irrepressible passage of time

I have tears in my eyes, they dry while I draw her. Isis.

I know Valance told me I'm from California, but I can't remember anything about it or about my childhood at all. I don't know what my favorite color or food is, but I do know what it felt like to be inside her body. Isis. Isis. Isis. Alien. Goddess supreme. The power, the cruelty, the lust, the brilliant understanding of what had come before, and a working knowledge of the drama that would follow the disintegration of my bones. A creature from another place with a mythological knowledge of the stars. She's difficult to draw. Her lines are too smooth and symmetrical. She's not human. She's something more. My hands are aching when I finally sit back on my heels to inspect the piece. I must have redrawn the left eye a dozen times. It's finally correct. I wait for her image in my mind to fade like all the rest, but it doesn't. It's strange living in these other worlds, times, and dimensions, strange the way they feel more real than my own.

Isis was so strong, connected to the universe in a way I'm sure almost no woman has been for thousands of years. She was a goddess of light and strength, and she knew it. Then there was Aphrodite, a juxtaposition of vapid and wise. Formidable as wind and earth. In my tiny room, their power stays, lingers. I lay down on my back, ignoring the hard, cold floor. I throw my hands out to either side of me, close my eyes, and then feel it, live in it. For a time, I am all of them in one. Formidable, eternal. Goddess divine.

I'm rudely reminded of my human status when I'm forced to get up and pee.

I flush the toilet with a bucket of water dragged from the boiling hot stream that winds like a snake around the back of Styx. I have a water pump but always forget to prime it. Not surprising, I forget a lot of things. While I'm getting the water, I see small footprints left in the mud by the water's edge. Valance, and my book, says I have a brother named Daniel. I wonder if he left them. They are like tiny marks of something once remembered, now about to be washed away. Trying to find his face in my mind is an impossible mission, but there's a burning thing alive in my heart that won't quit. I search for more signs of Daniel while I make my way quickly inside. Nothing. The mists lie low on the ground and swirl around my boots, little shards of ice, sharp as glass, lacing every breath I take. When I walk through the gate and shove open the old double doors of Styx, I'm shivering so bad it looks like I'm on the verge of a seizure. Back in my dark room, I pace and stare at the pictures I painted until my eyes fuzz and cross.

Frustrated, bored, miserable, and lonely, I make my bed and open a can of beans with the blade of my sharp little knife. I really can't believe the whole stabbing thing. Unless…Valance must let me get pretty close. He must trust me, at least a little. Which sucks, because now I feel horrible for betraying him, for being the cause of his pain, of any pain, any at all. The jagged edge of the can's metal lid slices my thumb. It cuts deep. The weird sensation makes me a little ill. My toes curl. I hiss and stare at the wound, watching the way the blood bubbles up out of the skin. I stare until the drops hit the ground, then I wipe my thumb on my knee-high socks. They must have been white once, but now they are dirty and maroon like everything else around me. I eat quietly, write in my book, and read the passages I wrote before, finding mentions of symbols carved into the grounds, the ones Valance talked about earlier, and more crap about that underground lab. My book is filled with all sorts of ramblings, most of which mean nothing to me, but that lab—it triggers visions of dreams, and I feel like I'm just stupid and bored enough to go looking for it. I stand up to do just that. Suddenly, strangely, I can't move. Not won't. *Can't*. I want to, but my limbs refuse, and my heart starts to pound and my breaths shorten. It takes me a few long seconds to realize that what I'm feeling is fear, and I decide that I hate it. Fear is a dark color, something damp and restless, each fitful molecule sharp as the point of a knife. It's a living thing that crawls down the back of my neck. My scalp prickles. The silence around me is eerie, deafening. I try to take a step. My leg shakes so bad, my foot taps against the floor. My hands are drenched in sweat, flexing, quivering. I can feel my knuckles clanging together. I shake my head to clear it. "Come on, Divinica!"

Dragging in a breath, I clench my fists, grit my teeth, and start toward the door again, my steps harsh with intent. My mind shouts out images of my dream, images that haven't quite left my head—an anomaly in itself. Three heads and jet-black eyes that never stop staring at me. I remember the brilliant needle covered in symbols, glowing the same exotic, golden color that shines from my tattoos. I think of the cold chills and hot pain. The quakes attacking my limbs intensify.

I make it out of my room and about ten feet down the hall. My limbs freeze again when I reach the landing of the seemingly endless staircase leading to the basement. The choppy, concrete-and-tile stairs descend sharply, disappearing way down into a swirling ebony. I rest a hand against the rusty metal stair rail. My breaths get tangled up in my chest. Black spots obscure my sight. I spin away, run back to my room, collapse at the foot of my bed, rest my elbows on my knees, and breathe rapidly into my cupped hands.

"The fuck is wrong with me?" I rasp. The room and rats have no answer. I stand up and leave another angry shout bouncing around the room in my wake as I storm off to find Boogles. As long as the basement isn't my destination, my legs seem to work just fine. Still, my skin is clammy when I wrap my cloak around my body, pulling it high to cover my face in case the winds rise.

I don't mark the passage of time as I ride. All I know is that the sun is dark and appears to be hanging perilously low. Everything is sharp angles and purple haze. Time must move, warp, shift, or perhaps rewind, because before I know it, I'm sitting in the freezing rain staring up at the three-tiered concrete structure with the twisted metal throne.

Valance is standing outside waiting for me, following a playbook written in a language I don't understand. I sigh. I thought my mind had redefined his face while I was sleeping and dimmed my scattered recollections, adding impossible beauty to the mundane. It infuriates me that it did not. He's wearing a tan, wide-brimmed hat that casts his face in deep shadow. His arms are crossed over his chest, his shirt has a trippy checkered pattern, and the sleeves are rolled to his elbows. The red in his shirt against the sky makes his skin look dipped in gold. His jeans are dark, and distractingly close-fitting.

"Good afternoon, Divinica." The rumble of his voice sets off tidal waves in my veins.

"Is it?" I ask peevishly.

Valance seems to appreciate my petulant mood. His smile is like the sun, and I look away to remain unburnt. "We have Pop-Tarts," he says.

I screw up my face while trying to put a picture to the word. My mind draws a foggy blank, but my senses apparently understand. I swallow back a gush of water that floods my mouth, and I dismount. "I tried to find the lab."

His brows arch. "Really, how did that go?"

"Great. I couldn't. I couldn't move, couldn't walk. It was the best. I think something pretty horrible happened to me down there."

Valance nods. "I'm sure it did."

"I had a dream."

"Did you now? Something to do with ancient Celtic symbols, pyramid devices, and witches with three heads?"

"Something like that," I say, still not taking a step toward him. I cast my eyes around. Anything to avoid looking directly at him. I'm afraid that every time our eyes meet, he captures a little more of me forever. It's an illogical thought. I blink hard, then try to focus on my surroundings. Hunched humans mill about, women with children clinging to their legs. Other children sit alone, staring into the distance or using sticks to draw in the icy mud. Men wash laundry in huge, steaming metal basins, then hang it up on tattered lines. The rest cluster in huddles, stewing more mystery meat over dumpster fires.

"Valance," I ask, my voice unintentionally soft. I feel him staring at my profile. "How many people live here?"

"Two hundred and four," he says. "We used to be two fourteen, but the Burning tribe ambushed us last week."

"You didn't see that coming, oh almighty one?" I ask. My voice is crueler than I intend.

Valance's mouth draws in a thin line, and it's a long time before he speaks. Finally, he rocks back on his heels, then smiles that cryptic smile of his. "Every god has their blind spots. What are you doing here, Divinica?" he asks pointedly, sounding years beyond tired.

"What do you think?" I snap, meeting his glare with one of my own. "I'm here, apparently, to ask you the same questions all over again." I roll my eyes. "But you already know that, right?"

Valance's smile broadens, igniting the swirling indigo in his eyes. Without deigning to give me another word, he turns and walks away. I grit my teeth and slowly follow.

Valance goes around to the back of the building. I continue to follow him in silence as we take a broken flight of stairs to a dilapidated landing braced by a high, white-washed wall, about fifteen feet long and eight feet high. Children kneel in front of the wall, dark cloths covering their heads, sticks of chalk and coal in their hands. A myriad of writing styles pepper the wall. Pictures, engravings, and names, so many names. As we walk past it, I turn to Valance and meet his eyes. At my look of askance, he says, "Our wall of memories, like your notebook, only cooler."

"All the names," I whisper. "There's so many—" My voice shakes, and I clear my throat before I ask, "Don't your people write those on their hands? I saw Micha and the others—" I shrug as my voice breaks off again.

"Hand-names tell a person who they are. Here, on this wall, we remember our dead," he says, and his words ache inside me. I was afraid he was going to say that. I swallow hard and don't ask any more questions.

The image of the memory wall stays with me as I eat two Pop-Tarts. Little girls and their hollow eyes, writing names of people they once loved, because if they don't, no one will remember. I try to put it out of my mind. It's just the way of the world, but sharp misery clings to my skin like oil. I wish I could stop caring. Caring brings more pain, and I have enough of my own. Tossing the last bite of Pop-Tart in my mouth, I chew, wanting water. I throw my gaze around the room to see where some might be hiding. Instead, my eyes touch on Valance, seated in his throne like the king of rubble and threadbare remains. There is a pageantry in his relaxed stance. Something in his pose that hints at regal. "Did you travel last night?" he asks bluntly, no preliminaries.

I try to guard my expression, but my lips tighten, and I suspect my eyes narrow. "Yes, it was horrible." *Why did you tell him that? And why, oh why, do you want to jump in his arms and cry until you sleep?* my heart demands. "My tattoos glow before I travel," I admit in a lower tone.

Valance nods absently and fiddles with the cuffs folded at his flexed elbows. "Your tattoos are an enigma to be sure. I know the symbols and their correlating goddesses, but I haven't been able to study all the nuances. I know she left codes in the lines. If I could enhance an image, I believe I could see the structure of the code, or at least an indication of it. I've looked at them, especially the one on your forehead. Sometimes I'm almost sure it moves. I'd like to look at the ink under a microscope."

"She who?"

Valance lifts his head. "Beg your pardon?"

"You said she. She left codes. Who is she?"

"The three-headed goddess. Hecate, I assume. That's what you've always called her anyway,"

"What do you need from me?'

Valance smiles darkly. "Oh Divinica, that's a loaded question."

I roll my eyes. "Only because it appears you have a filthy mind."

Valance's upper lip lifts on one side in a sharp, almost pointed arch, showing me his top row of straight, white teeth, then he growls—actually growls at me. A low rumble in his throat, it's a thirsty sound that makes me shiver. "You don't know the half of it."

"Awesome. I'll put that on the list of things I'm grateful for."

Valance stands, a slow, genuine smile transforming his face. He takes a step in my direction. His movements are almost hesitant, as if I might bolt or attack. "I want photos. Well, I really want you on my makeshift operating table downstairs under my microscope, but the last time I tried that you freaked." He takes another step. "I didn't know about the lab, back then..." he says. "If I had known, I never would have—"

His bronze skin goes a few shades lighter, and for a moment it looks like the memory of trying to strap me down is causing him physical pain. "That was not a good day," he mutters, taking another step. We are less than two feet apart now, but it feels closer. His stance is casual, but tension is in every muscled line of his huge shoulders. Our gazes collide and duel. I find myself wishing I could read his mind. There is so much emotion in his eyes that I can't decipher. Standing this close to him, I'm overwhelmed by a sense of belonging. As if right here beside him is the only place in the world I'm supposed to be. My breathing is erratic and loud in the sudden silence. We keep staring, falling deeper into each other. It's like he's willing me to remember something, to remember him. I try. I reach into the cacophony of my brain. The confusion up there is paramount, dense, and sticky. I feel like I might have more success trying to shove my fist through a boulder. Still, Valance is there, in the cold whiteness infesting my mind. His eyes, his smell, the electricity in his hands, but the recollections are foggy. Trying to touch them is like attempting to read the writing on a penny at the bottom of a foggy pond. Like trying to see the color and shape of a star through a storm cloud.

Finally, Valance drops his eyes, breaking our scalding contact. I blink. "How did we first meet?" I whisper, trying to end a silence beginning to feel lonely.

"The day my ship crashed," he says, turning away and walking back to his twisted throne. The seat is low, and the ground is raised where I stand. For once, he isn't towering over me, and I realize he sat on his throne not to dominate the room but to put us on eye level. "You were very alert, no sickness or boils, just clear, beautiful skin and wild eyes. I was fascinated. You just stood there, staring up at me, unafraid. I grabbed you and kissed your cheek. I don't know why. Maybe it was three years in a metal cage with two men, or it was that I was so happy to see someone who didn't look like they'd just been vomited up by an apocalypse. In hindsight, it wasn't one of my brightest ideas. You took that fucking knife out of your boot and buried it to the hilt in my thigh. First cut was definitely the deepest. Three nights later, Micha brought you to me. You come back nearly every day, Divinica. You remember more each day. We get so close to figuring it all out...so close."

"Why don't you come with me to Styx?" I blurt before I can think better of it. His eyes go wide. "I mean, I paint most of the symbols on the walls, and a few of the faces that I see when I travel—" My voice cracks when his body jerks. His eyes are suddenly alert. Flashing sapphire lights. "What? Have I asked you to come with me before?"

"Yes, but normally you ask me on day six."

"Have you ever been inside?"

"No," he grumbles, "the damn place hates me."

"Sometimes people make it inside. Dark shadows that walk through my halls, looking at my art. I hide behind the slats of the wooden walls in the corridors and watch them touch my things. I think that's why they call me the ghost of Styx. Or the dead artist, I've heard that one too."

Before I finish speaking, Valance bounds to his feet, rushes forward, and grabs both my hands. I flinch away, but he doesn't let go. "Divinica, do you realize what you just said?" he almost shouts. "How do you know that? How can you possibly remember that?"

I search my mind. *How did I know that?* "No idea," I breathe.

"Look at me," Valance demands. I do, and his eyes are heartbreakingly desperate. I can't be sure, but I think I see something else there, a brilliant emotion I've long forgotten. Hope. "Do you—" His voice breaks. He clears his throat and tries again. "Do you know me, Divinica?"

Yes! Yes! Yes! No! No! No! my mind screams. "I...no...I—" My words break. *Do I know him? Do I? Do I? If not, I fucking want to.* I won't try my audible words again. I can't find any that will make sense, but the answer is I do know him, every fiber of my being knows him, yet, at the same time...I don't.

We stand still for a vibrant second, my hand in his, just staring at each other. The air is filled with the sounds of his quick, rasping breaths and the smell of him. Winter, dust, and rain. Seconds tick like a countdown. To what I don't know, but I think I'm afraid of their destination. We stay, panting in the twilight. Our gazes so fused, I wonder wildly if my eyes will ever be capable of looking anywhere else.

Footsteps echo on the stairs. Valance starts and drops my hands as if my blood is lightning. We both step back. If moments had a sound, our moment breaking was a shattering crystal.

CHAPTER SIX

Flashing lights

People wrapped in rags and tattered scarves burst through the narrow doorway. They carry rough woven baskets—which seem to be filled with diverse types of trash—and rush to lay their gifts at his feet as he reseats himself on the throne. Valance thanks them sincerely, sounding like a benevolent god. A wicked twinkle flashes in his eye when he winks at me. I turn away to glare out the concrete, square-cut window. Broken buildings dot the horizon, remains of the distant city. They are no more than jagged black shapes against the ever-weird purple sky currently overrun by scurrying, silver storm clouds. Purple dust covers each rock and thorny shrub. It soaks its color into the melting snow. Our world, systematically incinerated by the red waves, bleeds violet and shadow.

My thoughts are disturbed by a sharp tugging on my belt. I spin around and look down at the little person making a bid for my attention. It's a girl, small, thin, and pale, stringy hair, and eyes all shot with blood. "Yes," I say, clearing my voice to take the sharpness from it.

"Are you a god too?" she asks in broken English, dragging out the last word. Making it sound like an off-key note in an old song. *Toooo.*

"No, I am not a god. I'm Divinica. I'm a human just like you."

The little girl shakes her head, strands of her hair lash her face. She shoves the hair aside, showing me the blue-black shadows under her eyes. The color of crushed violets. "No. Not like me. You look strong and super-fast. I'm neither of those things. Besides, the wall in my room says I'm dying. Radiation poisoning."

The girl relays this horrid information with no hint of inflection in her voice, as calm as if she were commenting on the miserable state of the weather.

"The wall in your room?" I ask, hunkering down to put us on eye level.

She nods again, giving me a strange look through her lashes. "We write our stories on the walls of the rooms we lock ourselves in before the wave hits. We write what we like, who we love." She scrunches her pert nose. "Don't you write on your walls?"

"I do actually."

A small flush infuses her cheeks, and her pale lips seem to consider smiling. "Good, you would be silly if you didn't. How would you know anything at all?"

"How indeed? Do you know your parents' names?"

"My wall says my parents are dead. They killed each other after the ninth wave. Obviously, they didn't write on their walls. It's a shame. If I remembered them, my brother says I would miss them."

"I think your brother is right," I tell her.

Her hands are shaking, and she laces them together. She draws her slight gray shawl tighter around her shoulders. I see her little body shiver. "I don't though, so I don't," she says and finally smiles, a ghost of a smile that dies before it's fully realized. Now her cheeks are the color of a pink rose. Suddenly, I picture a rose in my mind, brilliant and in full color. Blood-red petals folded over each other, green stems, and sharp, twisting thorns. I know if I closed my eyes right now, I could smell the sweet, husky fragrance.

"Why are you so strong?" she asks. "The only people I know who aren't sick are the gods."

"I don't know," I say honestly.

She thinks about that for a moment, then sighs. "Maybe you are a god, and you just don't know it," she says. She walks away to take her place in the crowd of people beside a tall, thin boy, with eyes identical to hers.

When it's the girl's turn for an audience, Valance lightly touches her forehead. A deep frown pulls the corners of his mouth. I watch him turn to shuffle through a wooden box until he recovers a blue syringe. The silver needle tells me what instrument it is right away. I shiver. I'm afraid of needles. Terribly afraid, if my suddenly wet palms and pounding heart are any indication. It would be freaking great if I could remember the reason why, but if I were a betting girl, my money would be on Hecate and the damn lab.

Valance squeezes the girl's hand, then switches to flawless German. I must know some of the language, because I understand a few of his words. "Hey, Tawna. Take a deep breath for me, yeah?" he asks with a kindness I would've sworn he wasn't capable of. Tawna obeys. She's calm. She obviously doesn't remember the cringy, piercing pop-pop a needle makes as it stabs its way through skin. I do. My hand squeezes a phantom ache in my chest as Valance pokes the needle into Tawna's arm. I flinch when he presses down with his thumb on the plunger and injects the blue liquid into her veins. Her little body shudders. Her brother stands beside her, looking vague, bored, dispassionate with the whole scene, unaffected by her pain. It's a monstrous travesty. They are blood. They are strangers. The girl sways on her feet for an unsteady moment. Her brother offers no help, so the girl wraps her arms around her stomach and deals with it herself. She leaves, others take her place, and Valance shoots more blue shit in their arms.

I sit in the far corner of the room, draw up my knees, and rest my chin on top of them. I watch each face, staring in every pair of eyes that passes through the throne room. Human faces stamped with sorrow and confusion. Empty bone bags, with vacant, disillusioned stares. My lids begin to droop, and for a space, time moves on without me.

When Valance and I are alone again, a low, silver light rides the horizon. I wonder if night is falling. He stands from his throne—now I almost understand the point of it—flexes his hands, then stretches them above his head. The crack of his knuckles is stark and jarring in the silence, and it makes me cringe. He stretches his arms higher, arching the crick in his neck. Light falling through the square windows at his back casts him in mercurial hues, crisscrossing his body in triangular shapes of varying shades. His black T-shirt rides up, showing me a thin line of bronze skin pulled taut over the chiseled shadows of his stomach muscles. His checkered shirt is casually flung over the throne's armrest, and the sleeves of his dark T-shirt are rolled to his elbows.

Sighing, he faces me. Dark smudges frame his slightly bloodshot eyes. He looks as exhausted as I feel, a bone-tired that no sleep can heal. I understand. Really, I do, because there's no *true* sleep in this world, just that nebulous intermediate between reality and dreams.

"Why are you helping them?" I whisper. My voice is scratchy from lack of use, and it sounds overly loud in the stillness.

"I'm no hero, if that's what you're asking. I hate seeing their pain. My ma always said I was a big softie hiding under a slab of granite."

"Your mom. Do you remember her? Oh, of course you do," I say, realizing how silly I sound. How easy it is to forget that he's not broken like me.

"Yes. I remember her. A verbose woman who thought far too much of me. She was the last person I saw before I left Earth. Three years later, when I finally made my way back home, I found her on the living room floor with a picture of me on the day I graduated the academy in one hand and a discharged gun in the other. From what I can surmise, she shot herself sometime between the third and fourth wave. She always lived with so much hope, for me, for humanity. I think losing her hope is what killed her. These people here, they have no hope either. They don't remember what was, so they have no idea what could be."

"Was Earth perfect before the wave?" I ask, staring up at him, unmoving.

"It had its moments," he says, then tucks his hand in his pocket and drags his lower lip between his teeth. The blue of his eyes is so crystal bright, it looks like bottled lightning. "But no, in many ways we were as broken as we are now. It was ten years ago that the danger posed by the climate crisis started taking us all out. Then, there were the magnetic storms that blew holes in our ozone caused by solar flares taller than Earth. The green started fading and just never came back." He takes a step toward me, then another, until his nearness seems to suck all the air out of the room. I, in turn, take a few retreating steps until I feel the wall at my back.

I drop my eyes to study a scuff on the right toe of my boot. "So…you want to save humanity, is that it? Bring back what was?"

"Yes, bring it all back, but better."

"And you need photos of me to do this?"

"I know how it sounds, but yes."

"Because I'm connected? Because star doors and portals are real, because my stint in some blood-smeared German lab isn't just a dream?"

"Yes," he says deeply.

"If that's not a pick-up line that gets results, I don't know what is," says Rashid, storming into the room and rushing to my side. He drags me away from Valance and hauls me into a backbreaking hug, then spins us both and holds out his hand to Valance. Valance gives the extended limb a long, questioning look. Rashid rolls his huge, dark eyes. "Give me the damn camera, I'll take the pictures—don't worry, darling," Rashid says to me. "Beautiful as you are, my fascinations are of a different variety."

Valance flinches, his teeth clenching until the hard line of his jaw resembles a sharpened blade. "No," he snaps.

Rashid whistles through his teeth, then lowers his hand. "Oooh, so fierce. Protective as a lion with his prey."

"I am no one's prey, and I'll take the damn pictures myself," I say. My words tumble out too fast, revealing their absurdity.

My blurted statement is met with a tense silence, then Valance casts his eyes toward the ceiling. "That's…an idea," he says, his voice oddly thick.

Rashid slings his arm around me, rests his weight on his right hip, and leans his head against my shoulder. "You've just written the script for the next two weeks of Valance's dreams," he says and laughs.

Valance throws Rashid a withering look. Rashid shrugs, feints to the right, then snatches the device out of Valance's hands. He turns and gives it to me, smiling. I feel the weight of it in my hands. I know what it is instantly. Camera. I've used one a couple times, I know this, but I can't remember even one of those times. I never had much use for actual cameras, because I always just used my phone. *My phone!* I think, missing the tiny thing with a weird pang. *But if I had it in my hand right now, who would I call?* I have no answer. Sadness settles on my shoulders like a storm cloud, and it feels terribly heavy. I step out from the shelter of Rashid's arm and stumble back, staring at the glass-and-metal contraption. "Have you made me do this before? I mean, do you have a file full of naked Divinica somewhere?"

Rashid laughs loudly. "Huh! Valance wishes. Don't worry. You're never so lucid this early in the game, by day ten…when we finally have all of you back… well…" His words drop off as he glances between Valance and me. "Valance never wants pictures after the fifth day."

"Just show her where she can take the damn pictures," Valance says. My stare moves to him, and I can't understand his undertone of frustrated rage. I feel Valance's eyes burning deep holes in my back as Rashid links his fingers through mine and leads me away. He takes me down a flight of stairs to a small room filled with more broken furniture and one flickering white bulb. When he leaves me alone, I understand the paradox of deafening silence.

I unzip my jumper and step out of it. Even though it's unnecessary, I hide my bare breasts behind my arm and try to set the camera on the old leg of a broken chair. It takes me a moment to balance it, to tilt the little glass eye in my direction and keep the damn thing from slipping clean off the chair. When it's done, I set the button on the back of the camera, and it starts counting down to ten. I don't know how I'm remembering to do any of this, but I don't have time to care. I rush to stand in place, squeeze my eyes shut, and clasp my hands over my breasts so hard it hurts. I stand like this for five full seconds, each feeling like a thousand years, and wait for the mechanisms to click and flash.

What the fuck am I doing, naked in room I don't know, with people I can't remember? Something small inside my mind struggles with that thought while the camera snaps another picture. I put my clothes back on after I've taken three photos. The flash was blinding. My vision is still spotted and hazy when I find Rashid waiting for me in the hall. "I can't fucking believe you just did that, girl," he says, waving a hand past my face and snapping his fingers. "Two fucking years I've needed these. Do you know how much this is going to help? Valance wasn't a believer until about five months ago." His voice drops low. "After he saw the tattoos glow with his own eyes, you know—" He stares at the zipper running down the front of my romper. "The hidden ones."

"He did?" I whisper.

"Um-hum, you showed him."

I gasp. "I never."

"You did, girl, not that I judge. That boy could talk anything out of its pants." He sighs. "I've always had a thing for charming Southern boys, more's the pity."

"Have you ever…" I clear my throat. "Have you ever had a Southern boy?"

"No…though I probably should at some point, and you're deflecting. You know, I'm proud of you, Divinica. You're breaking out of it somehow, all on your own, resisting or gaining immunity to the electric waves. I don't know how you're doing it, but you really are. You almost remember me, don't you?"

"Almost," I say. Just then, as sudden as a thunderclap in a summer storm, a face flashes in my mind. Dark eyes, dark curls, adorable smile. A jolt goes through me. Something like a memory. Pictures that will not fade. *Golden sun, surf. White-capped waves and laughter. So much laughter. Dad says sunny days are beach days.* Then I think of Daniel. His face takes up all the empty spaces in my mind. My heart twists, my vision blackens. It feels like the ground is splitting under my feet. Like the world stops spinning, then starts up again with too much speed. Memories come, brilliant and startling, as the camera flashes. I gasp and grab my chest, stumbling. I crash against the wall, my jacket droops down my shoulder, and I feel the rough bricks skin my upper arm.

Rashid spins around, takes in the look on my face, and kindly says, "Remembered Daniel there, did ya? I know that look. I've seen it a dozen times. I call it the 'brother pang'." I hear pity in his voice.

"I…I…" My stutters are uneven, and my breaths hitch. Rashid's face is a blur. My eyes are seeing something else. A world the color of blood in which I'm screaming, running toward Daniel, wrapping my arms around his little body, crying, praying for death as the wave washes over us, teaches us about pain. *"I love you. Only my mind forgets, never my heart. Love you. Love you. Love you." "What's a memory?" "Daniel is my brother." "Divinica is my sister." "I hope I never see you again, never!"* The last words he said to me hit me like a slap. I feel the color drain from my face, my heart is in my toes, my stomach an endless pit of ravenous, clawed things, and unshed tears start burning holes in my eyes.

"You're okay, he's okay. This is crazy! You usually only remember him on the last day," Rashid says, his hand patting my shoulder in a consolatory fashion while his eyes study me with shock and deep curiosity. "How are you doing this, girl?"

"Who the hell cares? What can you tell me about Daniel?" I almost screech. I hate how suddenly he's the most important thing in a world, where moments ago he scarcely existed. I find it all horrible and deeply unfair. I want to stomp my feet and shout my righteous rage, but Rashid holds out his hand to me. I take it, hesitating just slightly. Rashid kisses my cheek, then pulls me down the hall, back to the throne room and to Valance, who is sitting cross-legged on the floor, surrounded by piles of books and loose papers, highlighted blue by the glow falling from his flat, yet slightly curved computer screen.

I give Valance the camera, and his hand has a slight tremble when he reaches out to take it. His eyes are at once shadowed and fever-bright.

"I'm going to find Daniel," I state baldly, blinking at the stupid moisture in my eyes.

Valance glances up from his computer. His eyes fix on my face, and the hardness in them softens just a bit. "Divinica, come here."

I don't move, not because I don't want to, but because it feels like my feet are nailed to the ground and my body is pressed down by the weight of my heart. I shake my head. Valance stands and moves toward me slowly, as if knowing I startle easily. I can't breathe, not one tiny bit when he reaches out and takes my hand. His skin is warm, hot even. I jump but don't pull away. "Come," he says again. When I still don't respond, he shakes his head and drags me forward. Now I pull away, wrenching my hand loose from that devastating touch. I'm trembling, hot, and annoyed. He gives me a patronizing glare.

"What?" I snap. "Everyone here is always dragging me everywhere. I can move on my own."

Valance chuckles. "Can you? Show me. Come sit, Divinica." He stares up at me, a sideways tilt to his head. "I can't believe you already remember Daniel. Can you see his face in your mind?"

"Yes," I breathe.

"Do you remember the last thing he said to you?" he asks.

"Yes," I say again, louder this time.

Valance nods once, then strides across the room and snatches a chunky, checked cushion from the lumpy, orange couch. He tosses it on the ground and tells me to sit again. I obey with a scowl. He kneels, reaching past me for a stack of papers. As he does, his arm brushes my waist, and his bare skin glides over the cloth covering mine. I feel the contact like a bolt of electricity. We both jump. He quickly hides the movement with a cough. I hold my breath as he pretends nothing happened and continues to stare at his computer screen. He clicks some keys and squares full of moving pictures open after a split-second delay. I intuitively know what I'm looking at. The feed of a hidden camera placed somewhere in Styx. I would recognize those walls anywhere. The windows show me images of a little boy sleeping on a dirty mattress, curled up on his right side, his hands folded, cradled under his round cheek. My breath rushes out in a gush of trembling sounds. I place my right hand, fingers splayed, against the shining computer screen. "Daniel." My voice shakes. *Daniel, Daniel, Daniel, Daniel.*

"There's no point rushing to him. He has no idea who you are, and he's a fierce little warrior. I let you go to him about a year ago on day six, and he tried to shoot you. Consequently, you cried for three days. It was—" Valance shudders —"It was something I wouldn't want to live through twice. We installed these cameras after that. Now, I'm always watching him. I promised you a year ago I would never let anything happen to him. For the rest of us, we only see the damn place when the sun rises and sets, and sometimes not even then. When it is visible it seems to breathe, phases in and out, sometimes the picture is grainy or frozen altogether."

"Who installed the cameras? You said you've never been inside."

"I haven't. Stupid place won't let me. I only got them properly working about two weeks ago. You installed them with Daniel half a year ago. It was your idea to put them up in the first place. The camera feed stays live even when Styx is invisible."

I shake my head. This whole conversation feels disconnected and dreamlike. "That sounds crazy."

"Doesn't it though? It gets one thinking, especially one like myself. I studied pyramids, star doors and ley lines my whole life. We found pyramids on Mars in 2020. That was it for me. The subject of star travel, mergers, and points of invisibility around the planet enthralled me."

"Enthralled. I love that word," I say, realizing I do.

He smiles, and it's unusually authentic, making him appear human, vulnerable. "I know, you love all my big words, so I try to use them as often as possible. You must have loved reading in your other life."

"I did," I say without thinking. "You think Styx is magical, like it's one of these points of invisibility around the Earth?"

Valance reaches out before I can blink and tucks a lock of hair behind my ear. His knuckle brushes my cheek. I don't know when Rashid left the room, but I realize with a start that Valance and I are alone. Behind his head I can see the full moon through the window. It seems pale and tired, worn down by the misery of its sister, Earth. Slender, silver-tipped clouds scuttle across the sky, casting long, traveling shadows on the ground.

"Science or magic, call it what you want. That place has been badly tampered with. It's…alive," Valance says.

I glance up. His eyes are such an alarming shade of blue, like he managed to capture a slice of sky from the old world and wear it forever. His lips are so full. I think about kissing him, pressing my trembling lips to his perfect ones just to see what the hell it feels like. I suspect—though I can't be sure—that I've done it before. He leans toward me, only an inch, and just like before, all the air in the room is suddenly gone. My murky world is abruptly teeming with sound and light. Time freezes, I freeze, I feel like the entire world is simultaneously gasping and holding its breath.

"Well…" Valance jerks back, effectively snapping the moment like a piece of old plastic. He returns his attention to the blue screen. So do I, but I'm half staring at his profile, and the shimmering reflection of the screen in his eyes. "I watch Daniel all the time, he sleeps a lot, rarely eats, likes to trash your food. He's a good kid."

"He's the best," I say, feeling more tears torture my eyes. Valance places his hand on my cheek and turns my head toward his.

"I can't believe you remember him." He shakes his head, then rests the tip of his index finger against the point of my nose. "You know what? You're the only thing that surprises me anymore." I open my mouth to say something, but he cuts me off. "I have your photos here," he says, turning back to the computer. He clicks a few keys, and my half naked body fills the screen. "I downloaded them. You're right. I can't see much."

I scoff as my cheeks go up in flame. "You can see every single one, except the one below my panty line, and I wasn't going to take those off for you. Not even to save the world."

He smiles. "Flattering, Divinica, always so flattering. These," he points to the three tattooed symbols running in a straight line between my breasts. "These all belong to the goddesses painted on your walls, the ones you talk about in your notebook. This one here, Kali, she's the East Asian goddess of wisdom and war. It's strange that she would be placed so near Athena, Greek goddess of the same. The two are almost mirrors of each other." Using his left forefinger, he touches Kali's symbol on the screen. "Have you traveled to her yet?"

"No, and I don't want to, there's enough war in this world, I don't need to go looking for it in another. Besides," I rub my hands over my face, "what's the freaking point of it all? I hate these other worlds. They are so bloody, the stories are so strange and sad."

"Oh, there's a point." he says thoughtfully, eyes still on the screen.

"Yeah, what's that? Torture Divinica? Maybe I deserve it, maybe I killed kittens in another life or something."

"No, Divinica, it's no punishment. You're special, plain and simple. Maybe one of a kind. Somehow these tattoos are taking you back to specific moments in time, letting you be a part of some incredible events. You were pretty out of it for the first year, and I thought you were a madwoman, so I didn't put much stock in what you said."

"A madwoman, what a common label for an intelligent girl," I say snidely.

Valance winks at me. "Yes. After nearly thirteen months of unquenchable idiocy, I realized the error of my ways and started listening to you. You told me the first time you star-traveled. You thought it was a dream. I did too, actually. But time passed and your stories barely changed. You've described hidden technologies, and artifacts that could fracture time, end wars, cause invisibility. Shit, even immortality. It's all fucking crazy and firms up a theory I've had since I was a kid."

"What theory?"

"That so much of Earth's future has always been locked in the past."

"I have no idea what that means," I say.

Valance smiles and touches my cheek again. I think there's a purpose to these touches now, as if he is intentionally trying to remind me who he is. And it's working. Every second I feel I know him more. "It means there might be something in the past that can help us change this future. That's why I think you're the key, or at least a huge part of it." His hands fall from my face, and he turns away from me. "I keep telling you to bring stuff back with you. Have you done it yet?"

I narrow my eyes. "No."

"Why not?" he demands.

"First, because I don't remember you telling me to do anything. Second, because I don't have to do what you tell me. And third, because my only thought beyond personal survival is getting the hell out of there." I close my eyes and exhale through my nose before I add obstinately, "I don't think I want to do this anymore. I get lost in their minds. Their thoughts, feelings, and emotions erase me. Sometimes I'm afraid I'll get so lost it will be impossible to find myself again. They're each incredibly powerful, like individual forces of nature."

"And you're not?" he asks, lifting his eyes again to mine.

"No, I believe I am, but it's different. Also, I get why I'm fucking sad, for the most part anyway. But their misery is a mystery to me. When I'm in their bodies, their thoughts are everything. My own go quiet. They subsume me."

"Bring something back, Divinica," Valance almost commands. "I don't care what it is, just grab the first thing you see that looks significant, then get the fuck out of there."

"Why? For what?"

"The item you retrieve will be proof positive if nothing else."

"Proof of what?" I ask.

"Star doors, time travel, wormholes, ancient tech instead of spells, all of it."

"Do you think Styx has one of these star doors?" I ask. I want to sound doubtful, but my voice comes off husky and convinced.

"Yes and no. I think the star door is you, and I tend to believe those symbols on your body are some kind of advanced technology rather than your garden-variety hocus pocus. Tech is just a small word for it. In my mind, it's something far more profound. Perhaps a supreme plan for humanity that went awry." He takes my hand, and my fingers tremble. I don't move, and I scarcely breathe as his finger follows a line cutting a groove through the center of my palm. "I've seen strange things in the stars, including crafts that moved faster than I could blink. I was never proud enough to believe the human race is the only intelligent life in the solar system. Actually, I know it's the exact opposite." He drops my hand, and I notice a chill in the air as he continues speaking, his voice low and totally bewitching. "There have been many cultures, not all of them human, hiding in plain sight on Earth for thousands, probably millions of years. Cultures with sciences so advanced, our minds could scarcely comprehend them. I've seen things in the past two years that taught me everything I thought I knew is unequivocally incorrect, like the Reptilians, for instance. An advanced civilization existing under our feet for a millennium. What's occurring on Earth right now is no magic or happenstance. The waves are timed to a mathematical perfection."

Most of his words fly over my head, but I love watching the way his lips move when he speaks, and his hands as they run through his hair. I realize—to my dismay—that I'm *enthralled* by him. I don't think I know much about men, but I do know he's that bad type of trouble. My mind throws up a caution sign, but the warning is lost on my racing heart. All I want is to be closer, closer, so much closer. Under his skin, tasting his breath, feeling his strong hands make me gasp his name.

"I'm going home now," I say, unable to meet his eyes. I need to get away from him, hide in my dark, terrible room and write my thoughts in my notebook before I do something stupid, like throw myself at him.

"No, not yet. Cloud raiders always attack tonight. In fact, the first bullet will strike the side of this building in exactly nine minutes. If I let you go, you often end up getting assaulted." My hand edges toward the knife in my boot. "Don't you dare touch that thing," Valance snaps. "Fuck me, I can't even see a knife any more without shuddering and thinking of you. Rashid's right. I am PTSD boy." His eyes rove back to the screen, he flips through my other two pictures. I see a tick in his jaw. His lips are twitching, like he wants to say something. I hope that he will, but there is only silence, and that strange, unexplainable, crackling electricity between us. I feel it so strongly. I wonder if he does. *Does he? God, I hope he does. How could he not when it's all there is?*

CHAPTER SEVEN

Violence is a disease

Nine minutes later—I check the digital watch on Valance's wrist—a bullet strikes the building.

"Fuck," he mutters beneath his breath. His arm wraps my shoulders, and he drags me to his chest. His hands are as hard as iron. I don't resist as more bullets hit the outside wall in rapid succession.

I press my hands against his chest. My palms tingle, and I hear his breath catch. "Let me up, I can fight," I demand.

"You always do. I've learned there isn't a thing I can do to stop you. Leave that fucking knife of yours sheathed." He reaches to his lower back and withdraws a gun. "You know how to shoot a gun. I taught you two years ago. Just point this end at the target and pull this trigger. The rest will come naturally." He places the piece on my outstretched palm. I make a face, and he winks at me. "Trust me."

"I suppose I must," I say, taking the gun and assessing the weight of it in my hand.

Valance glances at me curiously through thick fans of black lashes that would make Aphrodite weep with envy. "Don't shoot yourself in the foot," he says.

"You always say that, and I never do," I snap, not thinking about my words at all.

"Fuck, Divinica!" He drags a hand through his wild hair, messing it adorably.

"You shouldn't know that." Another round of bullets splatters the left wall. He shouts over the noise. "Stay here, please!"

"Do I ever?"

Valance gives me a foreboding look, then dashes across the room staying low, moving from side to side, clearly traveling a memorized route. He flinches to the left, and a second later two bullets fly through the window and smack the wall, passing directly through the space where his nose was moments ago. Valance barks out a series of sentences that sound like commands. I can't make any sense of the words. I can barely hear them over the crackle and pop of gunfire. Unconsciously, my eyes flick back to Daniel's face on the screen. The feeling in my chest is becoming downright unbearable. Something dark shoves and shoves at my mind, pressure pulsing, pounding, watering my eyes. *Daniel, Daniel, Daniel, my Daniel.* Sleeping on his back now, his hands flung out to either side, he's perfection. His eyes move rapidly beneath his closed lids. I wonder what goes bump in the night for him. Does he dream? Are the dreams about the underground lab, our parents, or maybe me? I can't help wondering if I dream of him. Is he scared? Does he ever miss me as badly as I suddenly miss him? I want to kiss his precious cheeks, to break into that tiny room of his and pull him into the biggest bear hug ever. I want it so bad my arms ache. I stare at him until the image goes all fuzzy, then fuzzier still, until it's replaced by the strange picture forming in my head. A memory of a slight woman with hair like mine, packing duffel bags in the trunk of a silver car. I blink my eyes, but the images stay. A hard man, with black hair and wire-rimmed glasses, helps her lift a huge container of water.

"Don't you touch my chips," a younger Daniel yells.

The woman laughs, her lips are painted bright red, her teeth are stark white. I know her well. She's my mom, and the man running his hand through her long hair is my dad. Daniel, annoying little shit, is my brother. This is my family. The images make me feel so alone. Where are my parents? What happened to them? What the fuck happened to all of us? My mind cringes away from the answer to those questions the same way my body cowered from the mental images of the underground lab.

"Divinica!" Valance shouts. I spin toward him, and from the frustrated grimace he wears, I know he's been shouting my name for a while.

"What?"

"I have to go help Dayle. There are casualties in the east wing. I need to make sure everything is—" That hand rakes through his hair again. "Just stay by the door. Count to one hundred and twenty-five, then turn left, take a small step, and shoot." He holds up his hand when I start to speak. "Don't argue with me this one time—I'm literally begging you. Just shoot, aim low."

"Fine," I sigh.

"Fine," he says and leaves the room, still crouched at the waist, a gun in both hands.

With deep reluctance, I do as I was so vehemently instructed and walk to the door, staying low, my ears perked to every sound. Memories or not, one does not survive the apocalypse without being overly attuned to their surroundings. Everything takes you by surprise. Most things are trying to kill you. Eyes and ears are the best weapons. The second you forget those three golden rules, you're dead. Slowly, I start to count.

Shouting replaces gunfire. I hear Valance loudest of all, his booming voice is at the heart of it. *Fifteen, sixteen, seventeen, eighteen.* Scrunched up in the darkness, I close my eyes as cool night air blows through the windows, though it doesn't have much effect on the cold sweat running down my neck. Pins and needles attack my feet, sending weird, lancing pains up my tense calves. *Fifty-three, fifty-four, fifty-five.* I feel hideously helpless. My heart is pounding, my foggy mind confused. *Have I really lived through this more than once? Multiple times? One hundred and twenty-two, one hundred and twenty-three, one hundred and twenty-four.* A drop of sweat trickles down my temple. I hold my breath. *One hundred and twenty-five.* I take two steps to the left, drop the gun barrel a smidge, then fire.

The sound is deafening. Miraculously, I'm prepared for it and don't jump at all. The smoking chamber smells familiar, like death and protection. I close my eyes and breathe deep, almost counting down to the shout I somehow know is coming. "Argh! My knee! You shot me, stupid bitch!"

My eyes open slowly, and I glance down at the body of a man writhing on the ground. He's bald, black tattoos interspersed with open, bloody sores covering the top of his head, piercings stringing his ears in sharp, silver spikes. He's clutching his knee as dark blood spurts between his fingers. I start laughing, I know it's terrible, but I do. Maybe I'm in shock, maybe I'm broken, my soul darkened and trashed beyond repair. I stagger back, clapping a hand over my mouth to gatekeep my insanity.

I realize that Valance and his overconfident, regal attitude is possibly a product of his inability to miss his guess. I can hardly believe he knew each moment of the future down to the very second, yet the proof is here, mewling on the ground.

I hear footsteps pounding up the stairs. I know they belong to him. Valance bursts into the room. His eyes find me first. He looks me up and down. After a heartbeat, his shoulders sag in a sigh.

"Think of the devil," I whisper.

"And he appears," finishes Valance, and he winks at me again. "You always say that. Are you good?"

"Yes. What happened down there?"

"They attacked, like they always do, because they're hungry and confused. I feed them, give them medicine to combat the radiation, and they leave. Four days after the next wave hits, they'll attack again." He pauses to scratch at the back of his neck. "Their camp is an old train station at Bahnhof, near the city center. From there you can clearly see this place on the days when the fog lifts, right on the horizon line. It sucks. I would pack this all up and move if I could." He rubs the heels of his hands into his eyes. "Shit, I want to get the hell out of here."

"You don't want to lose anyone along the way, do you?" I ask, impossibly hearing everything he didn't say.

Valance nods, his movements are a little sluggish. "You're remembering the oddest things. I'm not going to even question it anymore." He stashes his pistol between his belt and lower back. "You've never been like this," he says.

I sigh. From the corner of my eyes, I can see the blood seeping through the tense fingers of the man I just shot. It spurts with every failing beat of his heart. "So I've been told, repeatedly."

Valance laughs. He looks troubled, amused, and desperate all at once. "You've always been a shocking individual, Divinica, I don't know why I'm surprised." His hand flashes out, and he swipes a lock of hair off my forehead. I freeze when the tips of his fingers brush my jaw. Fire blooms on my skin. Shivers race down my neck, and I can hear my breath accelerate. Can he? He stares at the tattoo on my forehead. I stare at his eyes. "Are we…have you and I…did we…you know?" I blurt but don't finish any of my sentences, just letting them hang awkwardly in the air.

"No, we've never…" His eyes drop to my lips. "No."

I want to ask him more. Ask him why not, when it seems to be all I want. Why, when he looks at me the way I know no one has ever looked at me before, like he wants, needs, craves me. If I could, I think I would stand here and stare at him forever, but the man on the floor whimpers like a wounded beast demanding my attention. "Are you going to help him?" I ask, hardly interested in the man's fate. Should I care more? Perhaps. But I'm glad I don't. Caring is as dangerous as closeness. This world takes everything away.

Valance looks undecided. "I've taken a shit ton of bullets out of this man. Cloud raiders started attacking about nine months ago, yet he always follows the same damn path." Valance hunkers down beside the man, who is now emitting a steady stream of weak groans. "It really seems to make the stupid stupider," Valance says, casually inspecting the man's knee. He presses a finger to a spot just above the knee. The guy screams like a Rade with his paw in a trap. "Thank fuck! Nice shot. Bullet went through and through. Just nicked some upper thigh meat," Valance says acidly. He sounds disgusted. Standing, he nudges the man's shoulder with his foot. "What a tosser." He kicks him again. Harder. "Get up and get out of here, dude. It will take time to catch up with your tribe. You should probably know they didn't think twice about leaving you behind. You might want to find a new crew to roll with." He shrugs. "Just saying."

Crying snotty tears, the man drags himself to his one good knee. Blood rushes down his leg. I don't think it's funny anymore. I turn away from the damage I caused and feel the chilly wind wash over my heated face while I listen to the scuffling sounds the man makes as he lumbers from the room. I feel sick. Valance comes up behind me, grabs the tops of my arms, and turns me to face him. For a brief moment, the expression on his face is unguarded, and I see the aftershocks of real terror.

"What?" I ask in a whisper. "I'm fine."

Valance sighs. "And thank fuck for that, but events change sometimes. I never know if—I'm never a hundred percent sure you're going to be alright."

My teeth lock. "I can take care of myself."

His sudden smile melts me. "Better than anyone I know."

"What happens if I don't shoot him?" I ask, wanting to break the spell our silences weave.

"You would be on the floor beneath him, fighting for your life. The first time he attacked you, I broke his nose and jaw but spared the bastard's life. I've regretted it ever since. Mercy is an old car with the propensity to backfire."

I press a hand to my gut and break away from his devastating eyes to stare out at the dark night. I watch the low, thick clouds rush across the barren earth and drape themselves like blankets over the snow-drenched mountains. "I'm a killer when I inhabit the bodies of these goddesses. If that's what I'm actually doing." My statements sounds so insane it was a struggle to make the words leave my mouth.

"Makes sense," Valance says, his voice deeper than normal. I feel him take a step closer. The heat baking off him makes my palms sweat. "This world has always been drenched in blood. Power is best gained at the tip of a sword, and all that."

"I feel like I'm cursed. Do you think curses exist?" I ask, turning as if pulled toward him by an invisible, irresistible force.

"Everything exists, and if you're cursed, so am I."

"Why?" I whisper. "How?"

Valance closes his eyes and takes a deep breath, his chest brushing against mine. The tips of my breast tingle, making me jump. "This is my curse," he says in a coarse, grating tone. I either stumble or step back, I don't know which. He catches me, his huge hands wrapping around my waist to hold me steady. He dips his head so that his lips nearly brush my cheek and my world spins, stumbles, breaks. "You are my curse, Divinica." A sudden buzzing in my ears makes his voice sound far away. A memory of him is struggling to break through. Valance and me, standing in these same shadows, his hands gripping my waist, his lips on my skin.

I breathe raggedly, unable to break the peculiar spell. I feel so comfortable in his arms, like it might be the one spot in the world where I am truly safe. Safe in this place full of shadowed moonlight and the merging colors of our souls.

His head dips lower. I think he'll kiss me—I want him to. He smells so good, like whisky, rain, and him. I think about pressing my lips to the tan line of skin showing just above his collar, and my whole body starts to ache. I lean in close, closer...the moments stretch, tremble. Each breath Valance takes is deeper, huskier than the last. The air in my lungs is useless vapor, and I grapple with my equilibrium. I close my eyes and tilt my face toward his lips. I suddenly want to kiss him more than I want my memory. Crave it more than I desire sanity. Valance stiffens and clears his throat, his hands drop, and he steps back. "Good night, Divinica," he rasps. Disappointment floods through me as the shivering spell is broken. I leave him quickly before it can reform.

CHAPTER EIGHT

Artifacts

I haven't seen Valance in a while. I sit here in my bed freezing instead. I'm cold as fuck, but too afraid to light a fire. I'm terrified of the flame and where it will take me. Valance said I would return to him, and even though it's the hardest thing I've ever done, I haven't. If I've broken his timeline of set events, so be it. I want to make things different. I want to understand what drives us to sleep, to wake, to take our next breath in a world where death is everywhere. It follows us like a pack of wolves waiting to strike at the weakest members of what remains of our race. I see it always, tripping over bones of babies and mothers with their arms outstretched. So many bodies lay strewn across this broken world, silently wanting to return to dust. Will I return to it soon? Will I lay my bones with the beasts and the birds and let what memories I have left flow away? Who will fire the final shot? How far will I fall? What pleasure will there be in the release from this prison of body and mind?

So many answerless questions make my head ache. I rub my eyes, but that action extends the pain to my retinas. If Valance is right about everything, have I had these thoughts before? Will I ever know? I need to know.

Chills are making my teeth clack, and my limbs are trembling like a bunch of independent dancers, but I get up, toss off my emergency blanket, and turn on my generator. Tiny, confusing metal box in the corner of my room. Last time I woke up—whenever that was—I randomly knew what it was. I strike a match and light the storm lamp. A soft glow spreads about me as I pore through my black notebook, trying to find a similar vein of thought in my previous ramblings. When I find it, my body gets cold, then hot all over. A wash of fiery chills makes my fingertips numb. I freeze, falter when I realize the question is not if, but how. How many times have I thought these thoughts, found this same passage, and felt the fiery chills? I read the words, once, twice, and on the third round I wonder if I'm going to fucking cry. I wonder if I even can.

Today my eyes die. Today I forgot myself. Today I am as I once was, unformed, new, broken. Someday my ashes will return to the ground and free me of this. But today is not that day. Today I am living, and I am shattered.

I assume I knew the wave was coming when I wrote that, but the sentiment rings true today. Today I am living, and I am shattered. I lie down and close my eyes. It's snowing again, and my notebook says to stay awake when it's this cold, but I just can't. I suppose I must sleep because my dreams are full of him. The fucking Skylord.

I sleep. I wake up. I open more cans and eat more mush. I think about Daniel. I want to go to the south hall and knock on his door, but don't. Instead, I listen to the small sounds he makes and occasionally watch him from my window, ducking and weaving like an acrobat when he looks in my direction. I write in my notebook, but with little to say, my words are shy and turn to doodles, horned bugs with three eyes and wingless butterflies. Through it all, Valance remains forefront in my mind, inhabiting my thoughts and ceaselessly haunting my dreams. I think about him telling me to use the star door to bring something back, and I wonder if I even can. It *would* be proof positive if nothing else. Something for me to touch and know in my dark moments that I'm not insane. It takes a long time to work up the courage and reach for the candle under my bed.

After a great deal of fevered deliberation, I light the damn candle and watch the letters on my arm start to glow and then transform. The fall through the gate of stars is brief, the landing stunningly painful. I can't think properly when I'm in these other worlds, lost in alternate, hostile timelines. In Aphrodite's body, I am young and full of fresh life. It's hard to organize the cacophony of nonsense in my head. I take the first shiny object I can find—a singing shell that has a soft-blue glow and never shuts up. The music is melancholy, and I wish I had stolen something that wasn't so annoying—then I get the hell out of ancient

Greece. Still gasping, drowning, flailing, I light the candle and do it all over again. The fall, the blood moon, the tree strung with glimmering planets, and the drop into another time. Another body.

In Isis's world I am terrified, my once glorious race is dead, the planet of my birth destroyed. My brother wants to create a new world where the Anunnaki reign supreme. He wants to enslave every living thing to his toxic power. Even me.

Four times I travel back to the places I previously visited. I walk in the worlds of goddesses long dead. I collect the items that glow, and each artifact I steal deepens my confusion. After Aphrodite's shell, the second item I bring back is a peach from the tree that grew out of Magu's dead body. An ancient East Asian goddess who sacrificed her life to save another. I don't eat the peach, even though I'm starving. I barely want to touch it. The peach glows bright as a new bulb. The damn thing looks radioactive. Running through the free lands of Nokomis's world, a huge bird that looks like a cross between a giant woodpecker and a flaming phoenix latches its claws onto my back and falls through stars with me. In Isis's world, I take the light of Aether, which I steal directly from Ra's lungs after he drinks poison from my own hand. I escape his incestuous touch the first moment I can and gag for hours after I get home.

In the undefined hours that precede my return, I write in my book and paint to pass the time. I paint a picture of the peach I stole, then sit the luminous item beneath my messy painting. It's a stolen memory in a world devoid of them. I don't know what any of it means, and it pisses me off. I do the same for all the other artifacts I collected. I draw a picture of their likeness and place the item beneath it. Most of them I set on old upside-down cans. I can't do anything about the bird though. He makes his home in the rafters of Styx and screams every time I light the candle.

I don't know how many hours or days these weird trips take me. I have no concept of time at all. I'm exhausted when I finish the last painting and set the light of Aether beneath it, the light I stole from Ra. I stomp around my room for a while. There's a fire blooming in the distance, sending reels of black smoke into the roiling sky. I watch it for a time. Making up stories in my head about who or what is behind the explosion. I'm stalling, I know it. Even though I can't remember all the times I've traveled to them, the worlds of Aphrodite, Isis, Magu, and Nokomis feel familiar to me. Kali's world is unknown. The longer I stall, the hotter my Kali symbol glows. Every time I try to think about something else, the damn tattoo pulses relentlessly, a painful reminder.

Is this really what happens at the end of everything? Have I found the fifth dimension through the cracked barriers of the fourth? I put my hands to my head and squeeze my skull, trying to shut out the questions that have no answers. "Argh!" My wail bounces around the room, taunting me with its notes of frustration and hopeless rage. I drop my hands and look down at the writing on my arm. "Aw, fuck it!" I moan. I know what I have to do.

CHAPTER NINE

Don't you fucking dare

I'm lying on a riverbank. The moon is full and high, bathing my limbs in liquid silver. It's a beautiful moon—an alien moon. Nothing like the one in my world. I try to sit up, but my body shakes and refuses. My nerves are screaming, and my skin feels stretched and torn. My ears are bleeding. I can feel the hot liquid dripping into the hair at the back of my neck. Two more tiny rivers of blood stream from my nose, and a trickle seeps from the corner of my mouth. I swallow a gulp of blood and wonder why my body doesn't shudder at the awful metal taste. It's like my mind is crumbling. I don't know how I'm breathing when my brain is telling my body it's fractured. I instinctually know I'm no longer under the cloud of my civilization, that the parameters of my personal reality have been expanded. I am somewhere in a time that's not mine.

The air is fresh, new, and clean. Each breath intoxicates, strengthens, revives. No polluted or radiated air.

I try to sit up again. My head spins. Then, a shadow moves over my body. Hard hands touch my skin. I realize with horror that I'm naked. The shadow leans down to kiss me. *Are you fucking kidding?* my mind screams. I try to kick him away, but my legs don't belong to me. These are not Divinica's legs. They're slimmer, longer. Stupid legs that don't care about my internal panic. They wrap around the shadow's waist.

No! No! No! No! No! the voice in my head wails. *This is my body! It's mine!* But it isn't. It's hers, and the way I need this shadow man is a tangible thing. Every cell of this body I inhabit loves him. Has loved him for what feels like forever.

I look at him, at myself. The writing on my arm is still flaming, the symbols reforming themselves into that collection of toxic words.

Travel through time my ass. Wrenched through earth and space, split apart by the sky is more like it.

My skin is darker, beautiful and rich as this land itself. I glance around us trying to figure out where I am. All I see are dead bodies and blood. There's blood on my hands, on his hands, blood on our lips and skin. The world is bleeding.

I try to fight again. Swing my fist and kick my legs, but I'm a prisoner inside this body and the violent action happens only in my mind. In reality, I press closer to him. In this place with a thousand bodies, we are the only ones breathing. His kiss, my moan, his hand between my legs, my teeth biting into the taut skin of his powerful shoulder. This body I wear does belong to me, but it also belongs to him. He is my lover, and this is our place. He looks like an ancient legend. His hair is shaved to the skin, but a long blue braid runs down the center of his bald head and follows the path of his spine. It's a war braid, and it's long because he has never been defeated in battle. This knowledge belongs to the body I inhabit, and it matters to her. This man is her warrior, her god. I run my hands over his face. I know him, but that knowledge doesn't come with pictures, just a feeling so deep it stuns me.

Why is this happening to me? Words I want to scream out loud. I want to lift my head and holler rage at the sky. I don't say a word. I only gasp. My lips belong to him. I almost glance over my shoulder to look for the damn star door, but the man takes my face between his huge, bloody hands and kisses me savagely until the entire world dwindles down to a single, myopic focus: His lips and what they're doing to me. Just like that, I'm her again, I've been with him before, and I know what to do. I arch into his bloody hands, my body begging. Wanting.

He's not gentle, but neither am I. I've killed today, I've tasted blood, and my throat is still sore from my battle screams. I feel no guilt. My soul isn't in torment—quite the opposite, it's vivid and alive. I turn my head to the side, he kisses my neck, and I see our reflections in the stream. I watch how he moves and notice the way individual strands of his hair that have escaped his long braid blow in the wind. He's tall like Valance, smells the same too. I run my fingertips along the base of his spine and feel a set of sharp spikes like dragon fangs dug into his skin. He's a beast and I'm his woman, lost in another dimension of time.

Ecstasy is my breath, blood, and bones. We move like thunder over water, like jagged lightning crashing into the sands of a blood-red desert. I'm screaming, begging, scratching, demanding more. I tilt my head back and see his eyes. Blue eyes. Valance's eyes. With or without my memories, in any world, any time, any dimension, I would know those eyes better than my own.

My mind is so open, so full of science and astrology. I understand mathematics and know the foundation of sacred geometry. Vaults of information lost to time are stored in my head. Equations modern scientists would kill to read. I know that our world histories are wrong, and legends are true. I understand time and its constructs. I know it's a spherical, invisible cage, and I have the key to open the door. I know that bodies are merely fancy dolls, mortal vehicles for our immortal souls. I know that each soul has lived an infinite amount of lives. He and I are twin flames, luminous galaxies, each caught in the other's orbit, forever destined to collide in any century, in all lifetimes.

He keeps moving, it's a torment and the best thing I can remember feeling. For a time, heaven and hell coexist right beside each other.

When it's done, when the crescendo inside me feels like it has shattered the surrounding mountains, I lie on my back and stare at the sky. It seems fuller somehow. All that endless midnight blue, broken only by tufts of fluffy white nonsense and piercing starlight.

I stand up, feeling sore in all the right places, and make my way to the stream. I don't care about the blood and broken bodies rippling on the glassy surface or floating face-down. Death is just another version of life. I wade into the water. It rushes around me, covering me like a warm blanket. I duck my head beneath the surface, wash the blood and the smell of what we did from my skin. I feel the earth around me. If land can have emotions, this land has rage. It's in everything, even the water. I taste it as the cool water fills my mouth and washes my eyes. It's a world that eats the weak, then spits them out and uses their shattered bones to clean the flesh from its teeth.

When I come up for air, I wipe the water off my face, but it's too late, it's in my skin, my blood. I am this land, and this land is me. I am the goddess of death in my time. I am a warrior, and I am queen. On the walk back to shore I remember my name. A powerful, immortal name, one that will be spoken until time runs into itself. In this time, my name is Kali.

The man with Valance's eyes sits up and watches me. "Peace tonight," he says, "let me have you once more under the stars."

"It doesn't matter how many times you have me. I'm going to kill you at dawn." I shudder when the vow leaves my lips, but I don't take it back because it's true. Tomorrow, I will kill him. His continued life means the death of my gods, the death of the world and the people I'm sworn to protect.

He only laughs. "Ah, you cannot spill my blood, and well you know it. I am a hydra. Every drop that falls to the ground spawns more demons to menace your Earth."

"I know who you are and what you can do. I won't spill a drop. Raktabija, I have loved you since we were children, since the sun was young in the sky and Saturn had no rings, but I will not let another of your kind walk this Earth. Your time has passed. The powers that be are quiet, the old gods are sleeping. Soon you will sleep with them. This night is your last."

"If you truly loved me, Kali, then you could not kill me."

"Little you know. Your soul is trapped, Raktabija and I will set it free, to wander untarnished until you find me in another life, as you have done in so many lifetimes past."

He stares at me unafraid. I see nothing of the demon that I know lurks inside of him, the same demon who destroyed one of my villages last night. He killed with his bare hands, ate the hearts of the strong, drank the life force of the young. The monster is dormant—now there is only the man I love and have loved, it seems, forever.

He stands and walks to me. "You're the only one I fear, Kali. If death is on my horizon, I pray it is delivered by your hands. You are and have always been the love of my life. Even the demon loves you. Wants you."

He reaches for me, and I go to him. I love him, and always will, but this land is my heart, these people my blood. "Tragedy is contagious in this place—you make it so." I press my hand to his heart. "If I was a human girl, I would run away with you, even knowing that you would eventually devour me."

"But you are a goddess of this land who demands I pay homage with my death," he says and dips his head. I want to kiss him so badly, my palms are sweating, my clenched fists a sign of battle or restraint. "I want you, Kali. If you kill me, we will never touch, never love again." His voice is so deep and alluring, it almost sways me. I stare at him with my heart in my eyes.

"That is my curse. Ecstasy and pain are mine to feel. It's the nature of this game, and the exquisite beauty of all emotion is the prize in the center of the trap. We souls want to be human so we can feel it all, then when we feel it, we scream that it's too much. We die, we forget, we come back and do it all over again. One day, my sisters and I will create a being strong enough to harness the power you squander. Wild enough to merge the monster and the angel. In this story, you and I are both villains, but I fight for this Earth, and you destroy it."

Pain and rage twist his lips. "Kali! I fight through the darkness! I strangle the monster, just for these moments with you. If you were dead, I swear to you, good would never brighten my thoughts again. I would crave only the release evil brings."

"And that's why you have to die."

"But not tonight."

"No, not tonight," I say, and pull him back down to the grass, still mussed by the imprints of our bodies. His mouth travels down my stomach. "Kali, if you kill the monster tomorrow, know that the man will love you past his dying breath. I will find you. I will always find you. In any life, in any time," he whispers. His tongue is wicked fire, and it makes me scream. Our previous incarnations merge with our sweaty bodies, Parvati and the great god Shiva. I still remember his brilliance before the fall. If anything, in this life we are better together. I make myself remember every detail of him. Under the brilliant cover of a star-soaked sky, I see the reflection of my face in his smoldering gaze, and I'm wearing Divinica's piercing, emerald eyes. Strange, but I think of her now as a distant creature, something not yet created, and I wonder, if Divinica had not used the stargate, would Kali still have chosen her? Or did Divinica merely plant her face in Kali's mind when she unwittingly inhabited a goddess's body?

Sunrise brings no answers to my questions. Rage and denial it has in spades. I must have slept for a while. When I open my eyes, I see the man I love is gone, the demon sits in his place not ten feet from where I lay. His skin blue as a robin's egg, he holds a scythe in each of his six hands, and his tongue is bright red, hanging out of his mouth like a felled flag. His eyes are the blackest of tar, and in them I see no traces of my man.

I tune out his taunting laugh, close my eyes, find my center, align my chakras, and realize my place in the connected web of universe and mind, then I reach for the goddess within. It only takes seconds to find her. I calm my racing heart, mentally take a back seat, and let my own demon grab the metamorphic wheel.

When I open my eyes, the blue of my skin is brighter than his, and I have eight swords in eight hands. My tongue is thick, red, and heavy in my mouth. It craves the taste of his blood. I raise my swords. Some small, nearly forgotten voice screams in my mind, *Get out! Get out, get out, out of this body, out of this time!*

This vision is not like the others—there is no eject button, no retreat. I want his blood. I will not leave this place until I have drunk the last drop. I charge at him, snarling my battle cry. He lifts one of his right hands, and our swords clash and spark. The land under my bare feet gives me power. I feel the vibrations of the earth thrumming in my blood, hear the melodic wail of the wind. Kali is screaming, Divinica is screaming, Raktabija is screaming. I wonder if this is all there is for me now, battle, screams, and death.

I fight like I was born to do it. My blades sing as they shred through the dusky, morning air. I jump and spin like I have springs for feet. He can't touch me, and he slashes and shouts rage-filled curses when he misses me by inches. My movements play out a deadly choreography. I feel fire in my eyes, taste blood as the tips of my fangs scratch my tongue. Familiar anguish wells up inside of me. I hate killing, and killing him will be the worst. Because as much as I love this land, I do love him and have loved him in so many lives. Memories of past times rush through my screaming brain, so awful I can barely stand it, so incredibly enthusiastic I can't stop it. I see us practicing swordplay as children, the way he would lean in and steal a kiss each time he bested me. The first time the win was mine, he wrapped his hands around my waist, lifted me above his head, and spun us both in a wide circle, over and over, until I was dizzy from it. I see the laughter in his eyes and remember the way they burned when he first told me I was the one he was in love with, would always be in love with.

I should've killed the monster years ago, but I just couldn't. Even wearing the face of the demon, even knowing a single drop of his blood would spawn more villains for me to destroy, even knowing that my hesitation smeared the blood of every innocent killed by him on my own hands, I just couldn't. I told him that he wasn't the love of my life. I lied. At this moment, my heart wants to let the land burn, let its people die, hell I want to set the blaze myself if it will save Raktabija's life. These thoughts take mere seconds to flash through my mind—mainly while I'm spinning in midair and dogging a well-aimed blade poised to strike my heart. As I land, two of my swords connect with one of his on a downward tilt. The fury of my strike knocks the blade from his hand. His eyes flick to the felled sword, and I see my chance. I plant an elbow in his throat with all my strength. I hear something crack. He drops another sword, the empty hand grabbing his throat as he claws at the spot I hit, choking wetly. I hit him again but pull my punch, careful not to make him bleed.

He goes to his knees in front of me, two of his arms still swinging their swords. I draw back my foot and kick him in the chest. He wheezes and drops his head, and then his eyes flick up and catch mine. I gasp, stumble back, and I think I scream. He's wearing Valance's fathomless blue eyes again. The blue tint fades from the skin on his face, and the lips transform. A moment more and the change is complete. The blue body belongs to the demon, but the face is the one I love.

"Kali," he says in a voice I have no idea how I'm going to live without. "You can't kill me. This will never be finished. I'll come back."

I raise all my swords. The curved blades create a frame around my face and wild black hair. I know in my eyes he looks for the girl but sees only the goddess. "Don't come back like this," I tell him. "I'll only kill you again."

He smiles a crooked smile that does unspeakable things to my much-abused heart. The sudden silence is a scream in my ears. He just watches me like I am the sole source of life and breath. I can't kill him. Not when he looks at me through Valance's eyes, not when he smiles Valance's smile. My arms start to lower. I stumble back and see the blue beginning to fade from my skin. The girl in me is seeping through, and there is no way she can do what must be done. How can she? When even I, an immortal goddess, choked at the finish line. All I want to do is wrap my arms around him and beg him to run away with me, to another place, another solar system where no actions, whether good or bad, are worthy of death. One of Raktabija's arms points the blade it's holding at the wrist of another arm. The small action snaps me from my melancholy introspection. He's going to cut himself, release more monsters for me to fight. It's an old trick. One he's used on me before.

I don't want to fight any more, I just want it to be over. I dive at him. One of his fists hits me in the jaw, but it's weak. I'm so much stronger, I overpower him in seconds and sink my teeth deep into his throat. Then I drink and drink and drink and drink.

The taste is divine. The blood of the monster feeds the darkness in me. My eyes roll back in bliss as his life force rushes down my throat. Like a mad, starving vampire, I suck out all the blood. I drink every drop until the demon with the azure skin is gone, and his skin is once again as it was, deep, russet gold that has always reminded me of sunrise.

It's fast and brutal. The blood makes me drunk and dizzy, makes me moan and whimper. I hate it and I love it. I want to run from this place fast as my legs can carry me. At the same time, I want to stay exactly where I am. Here with my lips locked to his throat, wishing the drink would never end. I feel it the second he dies. The moment I taste his death, Divinica is not distant—she is me, and she is disgusted. I crumple to the ground, full and sick. The goddess who possessed me departs as quickly as she appeared, the blue fading from my skin. I have two arms again, and I wrap them around my waist and roll onto my side. I lie still, shocked, gutted, and heartbroken.

CHAPTER TEN

That's literally disgusting

My palms are sweating puddles. I unclench my fists, then press my trembling hands to my chest. The air I gasp is crisp. The ground under my trembling body is hard, and sharp rocks dig into my side. I don't care. I hardly feel them. Crepe jasmine surrounds my body like a fragrant shroud, or a gravesite made by angels. I lay still as a tombstone. In the wind I hear a series of harsh, guttural groans, thick sobs, and wheezing moans. It takes a few breaths for me to realize the sounds are coming from me. Then, I'm screaming, crawling to his bloodless body, and wailing like a maniac. I close the blue, dead eyes. All their fire is gone.

Now, they stare into the great nothing where I have banished his soul. I press my cheek to his and half fall, half lie down on my right side. I gasp and rock, back and forth, watching my tears fall to the earth for which I had killed the love of my life to protect. "I want to go home," I moan. My words surprise me. Apparently, the horror of Divinica's world is better than this. Everything about Divinica's world is full of danger, the dark and brutal variety, but I never once drank all the blood from my dead lover's body—at least...not that I can remember.

"Don't vomit," a sobbing Kali says.

"I want to go home," Divinica nearly wails. I hold his body until it begins to feel cool against my sweaty breasts. I want to push him off me, shove the death away, but I only hug him tighter. Horror is too insipid a word for what I'm feeling. Searing, tearing agony, pain so sharp it erases thought. All this grief, terror, and misery, for what? I have to tell myself there is a purpose. Something grand and eternal, because if this is all random pointlessness, I fear I will find a way to set the earth ablaze so I can laugh while I watch it burn.

The truth? I'm in way over my head here. If I keep traveling like this, living these other lives, constantly feeling all these torrid emotions, there is a distinct possibility I'll lose my mind, and perhaps I already have. Here I am, lost in some ancient jungle, a goddess, a villain, a murderer. Maybe this is what madness feels like. *Breathe,* I tell myself, trying to feel my own mind, understand where I begin and Kali ends. I try to find myself, but I see only her. Only blood. *Just breathe, in the nose, out the mouth. One gasp at a time, allow your heart to beat, just breathe.* I can't obey the directions of my mind, even though they are spoken in Valance's deep voice. Seems he's always commanding and overbearing, even in my subconscious.

Mere moments before I start to abandon hope, something crackles and sparks about three feet away from me. My whole body jumps like it was electrocuted, but I don't make a sound as the star door begins to form right in front of my eyes. It's a white rip in the air and sky. Piercing, burning, white light chars all the ridges of the tear. Fire gnaws at the molecules, and the break in the fabric of time expands. Soon, I see the glowing tree, leafless branches strung with planets. The space behind the tree holds more stars and galaxies than I have brain cells to count.

I stand up and climb out of Kali's body. I am made of smoke and starlight. The colors of my soul are violet and maroon. I'm a spirit now. A time remnant. A ghost. I feel a split second of remorse for Durga, the girl, just barely a woman but already a murderer a thousand times over. She is possessed like me, and it sucks to leave her like this, knees curled in the fetal position, arms wrapping the body of her dead lover. I look at her for one long moment, but she doesn't see me, only her falling tears. I glance over my shoulder, feel my eyes widen as they lock on the ever-expanding star door. Through it, I can see the tall smokestacks and cracked windows of the old asylum I call home. Suddenly, nothing else exists. A collage of faces flash through my mind. Daniel, Valance, Rashid, Dayle...even Boogles lives there with the others, trumpeting through his adorable snout.

Then, our eyes meet, and the girl on the ground has once again become the goddess. Kali stares back at me through her own terrifying eyes, her irises drowning in the blood she drank. The blood I drank. Kali knows me. She sees me. Really sees me, right down to my marrow. I think of Valance then, remember him telling me to travel here, to Kali. My mind replays my pert response. *No, and I don't want to, there is enough war in this world, I don't need to go looking for it in another.* I had been right, no part of me wanted to travel here, yet strangely, now that I am here, my feet on this ancient ground, a part of me has no desire to return home.

Kali sits up just as I'm on the verge of saying something dumb, like, *Please let me stay* or *Is there any way I can jump back inside your body?* Her hands touch her face, her hair, and she clutches at her knives, then hands me one of the blades. "Take it," she almost shouts. "Take it, Divinica, quickly before our time runs its course."

Instinctively, I recoil at the casual use of my name and violently flinch away from the proffered blade, as if she were handing me a hissing viper. *No freaking way.* Her eyes narrow and look dark and ravenous. "Take it," she demands, in the voice of a thousand goddesses. It sounds to me like a million crashing waves or the scream of colliding galaxies.

"Aw, fuck! Fuck, fuck, fuck! Fuck this! Fuck me!" I want to sound angry, but my voice shakes. I keep looking from the star door to her desperate face. I think of Valance telling me to grab the first shiny thing I see and get the fuck out of there. I wince and run to her, trying to keep myself from frantically glancing over my shoulder at my expanding escape route. I lean down and grab the scimitar she's offering. My fingers slowly wrap around the handle. Our eyes lock and hold. "I don't want this," I say. "Whatever you and your tormented goddess friends have planned for me, I don't want it."

"You chose this a long time ago. You are merely living your decided fate."

"I don't believe that!" I shout. She doesn't say anything, and she doesn't need to. The look in her eyes says more than I want to hear.

Kali shakes her head. "We are one, you are the soul who cast the spell, you can't escape this." There's a fierce note of regret in her voice that makes me all the more enraged, because despite everything in me rebelling against it, I believe her.

I turn around, run, and jump through the star door, holding the scimitar close to my chest. I can smell the blood still coating my tongue, sweet and metallic. I start to fall and close my eyes. I can barely think and hardly breathe as I tumble through the cosmos. The fall is brief, the landing hard and painful. I hit the floor of my bedroom with a powerful thud that echoes. I cry out as something in my back twists, and a muscle pulls sharply in my right calf. I roll onto my back and pound the floor with my fists in a useless display of anger. "Gods!" I half roar, half moan. I roll across the floor toward my bed, trying to get as far away from the candle and its damn smoking wick as I can. Fuck that thing. Halfway to the safety of my bed, my stomach lurches sickeningly. Cold fear seizes my body as a small part of me realizes what that means. There are moments in time—or whatever poses for time in my reality—when the stillness is strangely mimicked by every object in sight. Like all things are trapped in a place where time has folded in on itself. As if the world and all it holds ceases to vibrate for a single breath.

My stomach rumbles a series of loud, gurgling pops. I can taste something hot and sweet trying to climb up my throat. There is no help for it. I drag myself to my knees, pinch my nose, and lock my hand over my mouth, but nothing is going to stop it. Cringing, shaking, I suck in a breath of ice-cold air and vomit what can only be described as a pool of blood. I heave and heave again, as I purge every morsel of food from my body. The adrenaline from my fall through the stars begins to fade under the bracing chill of current reality. I yell and scream, even as my back arches and my body shakes. Blood pours from my mouth like a waterfall. The second it hits the ground, the blood starts to hiss and smoke. Black clouds stuffed with a noxious odor mushroom around me. The smell of the air—dead bodies, rotting food, mists—makes me gag again.

The rats watching me through their glowing, green eyes rush for cover as the size of the fog increases. The sizzling cloud of smoke grows denser, then begins to take shape. I remember Raktabija and his hydra analogy, the way Kali had sworn she would drink every drop of his blood, and she had. I was the idiot who brought a stomach full of demon blood back to my home, then vomited it up. *Good job, Divinica,* my mind sneers. I see six blue arms slowly emerge from the black cloud, then the thick, red tongue hanging just below a pair of glossy-black eyes that are the very definition of hellfire.

Oh, fuck. Fuck, fuck, fuck, fuckity fuck! I raise Kali's sword, still clutched in my right hand. The demon I just stupidly vomited up casts a single glance at the sword, then backhands me across the face. I was not expecting the attack, and the shock makes me slow, leaving me momentarily defenseless. I go flying. Literally soar across the room. The sound of my body hitting the wall rings in my ears. Something twists in my left arm as I slide down the ugly green paint and thump against the uneven ground, yet I somehow manage to keep the sword's handle clutched between my trembling fingers. Agony shoots through my ribs when I move. I get back to my knees and almost scream at the bone-grinding pain, when my wounded arm jerks and twists.

The bright-blue creature advances on me. With the wall pressed against my back I have nowhere to go. I desperately cast my eyes around my confined surroundings. My vision blurs, and I realize my flight and subsequent landing took the wind from me. I wheeze while trying to get my bearings. I see the window and discard it as a viable escape route instantly. It's freaking locked anyway, who knows why or when I did that. I grit my teeth, and my eyes swing to the partially open door, then flick back to the creature's face. It takes everything in me not to flinch and scream. Towering at least ten feet, he's a mythological nightmare. His dangling tongue is terrifying, and his teeth look like hunting knives.

He makes a grab for me. I don't stop to think as I lunge forward instead of dodging his hand as he must have anticipated, because the creature roars as he grabs a handful of air when I duck beneath three of his arms and make a mad run for the door. I use every ounce of energy I have, and then some, to go faster, faster, faster, zipping through the room like a charged current.

I almost shout when the door handle is finally in reach. The corner of the door whacks me in the center of my forehead when I fling it open, but I hardly feel it and don't even use the tenth of a second it would take for me to glance over my shoulder. I burst into the hall, lower my head, and run for my life. Terrified, confused, and pissed don't even begin to cover it. I make two sharp turns, nearly crashing into an old, overturned bookshelf, then take the stairs to the basement three at a time. I don't think I've ever moved so quickly in my life, yet I can feel the creature lumbering behind me, barely a breath away.

I throw open the heavy metal door, dash in the lab, slam the door, and drop the dead bolt. I do a quick scan of the room. Fuck if I know what I'm looking for, but according to my black book, I've found strange knives in here. Once, I think there was a flare gun. But now, there's nothing, just an old metal table— which, according to my book, and my dreams, I may have been tied to at some point—a shit ton of broken glass, and a plethora of twisting symbols.

I run to the far side of the pentagonal room where, I remember, a back door lurks. I see it often in my nightmares. Somehow I know it leads to the courtyard, and to Boogles. Suddenly, I want the comfort that seeing my cuddly monster will bring me. I run for the trap door, because the creature has reached the metal door I bolted shut and is trying to kick it in. I think the lock can only take a few more hits, and I'm right. Three more to be exact, because on the third kick the door flies off its hinges. Spinning out of control, it soars straight at me. I barely have time to dodge the projectile. It hits the wall with a deafening crash, inches above my head.

I look up and freeze. The creature looms over me, so close I can hear each of his breaths. Wet, heaving, repetitive sounds. He sniffs, spits, then reaches for me. I lift my sword and stand and without hesitating, I take a swing—not aiming, just hoping. My blade strikes the elbow of his extended arm. I hear a wet crunch —bone shattering under the touch of steel. I grit my teeth and shove through the sudden pressure of skin, tendon, and tissue. His arm hits the ground at my feet, the hand still clutching his sword. The creature lets out a roar of agony. A geyser of hot crimson splashes my face, soaks my hair and chest and momentarily blinds me. His remaining arms flail in all directions.

I look at the flowing blood in horror, wondering if I have inadvertently unleashed a horde of monsters who will surely kill me. My thoughts are abruptly truncated when one of his hands strikes my jaw, another lands a solid punch to my gut. I grunt as the hit knocks me off my feet, and I fly backward for the second time in as many minutes and land hard in a pile of glass. A jagged piece cuts straight through my romper and stabs me in my right thigh. Blood gushes, dark crimson, the color of my day. I try to stand, but I slip on all the blood and fall again. More glass cuts my palms and shreds the skin of my fingers.

The monster reaches out and grabs a handful of my jacket. He hauls me close, then shouts something in a language I no longer understand. "I don't know what you're saying!" I yell. My voice sounds mad, not scared, which makes me smile and gives him pause. He says something again, then shakes me so hard that I rattle like a broken doll. My eyes roll back in my head. but when he is done, I shrug and smile some more. This time, my expression enrages him. He lifts my limp body above his head, shakes me, then tosses me again. My body arches when it hits the table in the center of the room. My hip bone strikes the cold metal, and the impact clicks my teeth, jarring my arm unbearably. I swallow a shriek. I'll die before I give him the satisfaction of my pain.

I roll over, groaning, and tumble off the table. When I hit the ground, I land on something that shatters and cuts my stomach, slicing—sharp as the broken glass—straight through my Kevlar jacket like it was my own skin. It feels like glass, looks like glass, but as I sit up and touch the crystal material, it turns to dust and blows away in a sudden, invisible wind. The device that the crystal shell was sheltering lays on the ground near my hand and is pyramidal in shape. Sizzling, violet-colored electricity cocoons it. I start to back away from the thing when the earth shakes so violently it knocks me off my knees. I hear a large crack, like the shattering of a megalithic stone, and the quake ends as suddenly and inexplicably as it began.

I have no time to go into hysterics over this fresh anomaly. Raktabija grabs a handful of my hair and hauls me to my feet. He throws me again. This time, I curse dramatically as I hit the ground face-first. My bottom lip splits, making my mouth fills with blood. I spit it out. I don't stand, because what's the point? I've lost Kali's sword sometime in the last few minutes while I was busy getting my shit rocked. I remain where I am, hurt and defenseless.

Fog obscures my vision as Raktabija lumbers to where I've fallen and lifts me again, by the throat this time. Blood drips down my forehead, but I blink it from my eyes and kick him in the junk before he can throw me again. I'm guessing the chances of me saving my own life will dramatically decrease if I pass out. I kick him again, just because I can. He yelps, and all his hands save the one holding my throat rush to cradle his injured parts. I claw at the hand cutting off my air and feel my face turning red. I know my eyes are bulging out of my skull. He squeezes even tighter, and my world begins to blacken at the edges. I scratch, kick, and wail, but Raktabija and his iron grip are unmoved. Of his own volition, he suddenly lets me go. I fall six feet to the ground and land directly on my ass. Agony rockets up my spine. I ignore it, because from my miserable vantage, I can see my fallen sword. Without bothering to look up at Raktabija , I dive for the blade.

The creature screams another set of unintelligible words. I wish I could make sense of what he's saying. Maybe I could find a way to convince him that killing me isn't the best plan. I reach out my hand until my fingers brush the hilt of the sword. The moment I have the cold hilt in a firm grip, my random wish is answered. When the creature screams again, I understand every word. I freeze in the act of standing and stare at him through the curtain of hair falling over my face. Witnessing his babble turn to sense right before my eyes somehow scares me more than anything yet.

"Doomed bitch!" he yells. "Vile offspring of earth magic. By what dark power do you summon me?"

"What?" I scream, with a bravado I am far from feeling. "Summon you? You're just the product of a good hurl after a bad hangover."

He lifts a thick, black brow, crooks a finger, and beckons me close, ignoring my wit, which stings—I thought it was a good one. His tongue lolls limply from his mouth, and his eyes swirl in their ink-black sockets. "You need not follow the edicts of your creator. Choice is your only way of escape. Come, darling, we shall go to the afterlife together."

"Wow," I say. Finally standing, I hold the sword across my chest like a shield. "Hard pass, and there's a lot to unpack in the sentence. First, I don't know who you think I am, but I'm no one's damn darling, certainly not yours, and second—"

"They have used you," he says ominously, cutting off my angry tirade. "They have trapped you as they themselves are trapped. Humanity deserves no more chances. You should not exist. You must not exist. Humanity is a plague we have nearly exterminated. I will not be the one who allows you to live and undo all we have done."

"Oh my god! Make sense, asshole! I am no one!" I scream. I grip my sword tighter as he stares at me through those terrifying, flaming eyes, which look like burning tar. I want to fight, but I'm so tired. I want to curl up and sleep in my bed. I want to clean whatever is left of this creature's blood off my floor. I want to feed Boogles, because he's probably starving, and more than anything I want to see Valance. I'm consumed with this insane, desperate desire to be wrapped in his big, strong arms, as if, for some crazy reason, they could make everything better.

The creature stares intently at my face as neither of us say anything for a time, both deciding on the best way to kill the other. I believe he sees the fight going out of me and thinks I'll be a quick kill. Silently, I pray he's dead wrong. I tuck my chin to my chest and charge at him, hoping I can prove him wrong. But I never make contact. Something strikes me from danger's path. I fly to the far wall, hit it hard, slide down slowly, and stay unmoving in the pool of my aching, rubbery limbs. A roar rips through the room, like the howl of a ravenous beast who's finally managed to catch his prey. The snarling continues, each growl louder than the last, until I think it's coming from the floors and walls.

There's a *hiss*, then a drawn-out *sizzle-pop*. Black smoke instantly fills the room, thick as pudding. It burns my throat until I feel like I'm being strangled. Tears start to pour from my eyes, and I squeeze them shut, holding the sword close to my chest. The naked blade feels cool against my burning tattoos. I drop to my stomach, trying to get beneath the toxic smoke, then crawl like a legless butterfly with a broken wing. My arm flops uselessly, and my left knee refuses to bend, but I scoot on my stomach to where I think the door might be. I can't be sure though. I'm busy being blinded by the black smoke and fervently wishing for my imminent death.

"Divinica! Divinica?!"

I stop crawling, instantly recognizing that deep, husky voice. Much like his eyes, I think I would recognize Valance's voice anywhere, in any dimension, any life.

"What!?" I shout.

"Stay low!" he demands, his voice hoarse, probably from all his growling.

Behind my closed lids, my eyes roll. "What the hell do you think I'm doing?"

"I don't know, I can't see you," he responds reasonably.

"Ugh! You're so annoying! Did you see what the hell I'm fighting?"

"Yes."

"Do you think we can kill it?"

"I don't think I should spill its blood—"

"Not sure that's working anymore. The whole demon, hydra thing. I cut off his arm, and I'm covered in his blood but—"

"No more demons," Valance says, finishing my sentence. I hate and adore how he does that. *Has this all happened before?* My mind trips. If so, I'm mildly ashamed of myself for being so stupid. More than once.

"Divinica, get up and get the fuck out of here!" Valance says.

"Don't tell me what to do!" I shout. Then, in a smaller voice, "I'm trying, I don't know where to go, I can't see anything. What the hell is all this smoke? It's horrible." I shake my head, trying to clear it. I'm starting to feel a bit frantic, and I sound like I'm about to cry. I feel like it too. I crawl a foot farther, then something brushes my hand. I flinch back and scream.

"Divinica, it's me," Valance says, and my whole soul seems to relax. His hand brushes my cheek, his fingers threading my tangled hair. The second his skin makes contact with mine, there's a vivid spark between us, and from the way he flinches, I'm positive we both feel it.

"Divinica, are you alright?"

Relief rushes through me, a deep, calm, sensational feeling that leaves goosebumps on my skin. I want to curl up in his arms and kiss his lips. I bite out my reply. "Do I look alright?"

"I don't know, I can't see anything. Smoke in the eyes, remember?" he says softly, and I can hear the smile in his voice. "Are you hurt? Can you move?"

"Kinda, to both questions." I say, gasping as I drag myself forward another foot. Toward him. "It's more function over form right now, but I think I can make it."

Something light and fiery brushes my forehead. His lips? *God, I hope it was his lips. Ugh! What is wrong with me?*

"Good." His hot breath tickles the shell of my ear, and the shivers that race down my spine are almost painful. "Rashid is on the stairs," he says, then he's gone. I call his name, but he doesn't hear me, as he's off, ferociously growling again. I hear a wet thud punctuated by the demon's rage-filled wails. Cursing under my breath, I half crawl, half squirm toward the door and toward the safety of the stairs beyond.

After a few agonizing moments, I reach the bottom step, drag myself up, and sit down. I push strands of hair from my face and wipe the tears and blood from my eyes. A hand pats my shoulder. Blinking, I glance up and see Rashid's smiling face through a hazy blur. He's sitting cross-legged on the second to the last stair, smoking something that smells like burning grass and sunshine. Then I wonder how I know the smell of sunshine when I have no accessible memory of such a wondrous thing. Rashid tucks my hair behind my ear, and his beautiful smile dies when he gets a good look at my face.

"What the shit, girl? Are you good? You're wearing a blood mask. It's giving angry vampire. I mean…it's a look but—"

"It's not my blood," I gasp, still struggling to catch my breath. "Well, not all of it."

"Oh, that's comforting. Valance is going to get one good look at you and go supernova, can't wait," he gushes.

"Valance," I whisper, quickly glancing past the busted doorframe, trying desperately to see through the thick, midnight smoke. I take another breath, and it ignites a horrible tickle in my throat that makes me cough until my eyes are streaming all over again. "Why are we just sitting here? We have to help him," I say, when I finally can.

Rashid giggles. "Help who now? I hope you're talking about that giant blue monster, because your cowboy is fine."

I almost hit him. "Why are you laughing? This isn't fucking funny!"

"Ha! Maybe not for you."

This time I do hit him. "This is horrible, and it's all my fault."

"Respectfully disagree. Best drastic timeline change yet. I, for one, am loving this, and trust me, Val is having the time of his life."

"That creature will kill him. He's literally a demon from the past," I insist, trying to stand up. I sway on my feet for a second before Rashid takes my hand and pulls me back down beside him.

"I suppose there's always the chance of brutal death, but that's what makes it so exciting," he says.

I notice that Rashid's eyes are bright and full of smiles. Today his hair is a deep pink, and his lashes are long and curled. He looks like a mythical creature, something I would find in one of my other worlds. "You're pretty," I say without thinking.

"Thanks, girl, I would say ditto, but you literally look the worst."

I nod. "Yep, feel like it too," I say not offended. The words hardly register as they leave my mouth. My eyes and mind are focused on the battle in the lab. I squint, trying to see through the smoke.

Rashid waves a hand in front of his face, then rubs his red, watering eyes. "Pepper bomb," he says. "It will clear soon, but it's too bad." He elbows me lightly in the ribs. "We're missing a hell of a fight." Rashid takes a long drag and blows out a ringed cloud of smoke. He leans back and rests his elbow on the next stair, then shakes his head. "Shit, I love watching that boy fight."

"We have to help," I say again, tugging on his arm. Rashid ignores me completely, even as a deafening crash punctuates my plea. I flinch, and my stomach turns over as I desperately try to find Valance through the haze. Rashid blows out more smoky rings, and I almost howl at his nonchalance. Just as I'm about to dash into what I am sure will be only disaster, the smoke begins to clear, not a lot, but enough so that I finally see Valance. He's locked with the demon in what looks to be an ancient death dance. I barely notice Rashid's whooping cheer because I'm transfixed by what I see. Terrified, fascinated, and, as always, completely enthralled.

Valance fights like he was born to kill. There's a beautiful synchronization in his moves and godlike qualities to his stance. He's in his zone, a place I know well. Absent of thought and full of action—I go there when I paint. In the same fluid move, Valance jumps, spins, and then kicks the demon in the face. Blood bursts from the demon's nose as the heel of Valance's booted foot breaks it. The creature screams through bloodied lips. Two of his arms, scimitars in hands, strike out. Valance is light-years too fast. He jumps from the path of the blows onto the metal table, then slides the length of the shiny surface on his knees like some iconic rock star. I remember those few fair folk. Their bright faces, true talent, fake smiles, they died with everyone else.

Black jeans stretch over the muscles in his legs, fitting him like a second skin, the black T-shirt showing every perfect line beneath it in harsh relief. He's intoxication personified. I watch as Valance reaches for a metal bar above his head, grabs it with both hands on the first try, and swings it directly over the creature's head. The creature spins about looking confused, and it's almost comical to watch pure befuddlement transform his ferocious face.

Still holding tight to the bar, Valance drives his knees into the base of the monster's skull, who stumbles forward, nearly tripping on his giant blue feet. Valance grabs onto another metal bar running parallel across the ceiling. The muscles in his back and arms bulge under the strain of his weight as he swings across the room, flips twice in the air, then lands directly in front of the howling monster.

The muted light from the single bulb weakly flickering at the top of the stairs tangles in Valance's hair and turns each individual strand to a million shades of painted gold. As the light pours down his profile, each flash of the bulb alters the color of his skin.

Fuck me, he's hot, my mind practically wails, while my teeth sink into my lower lip. I realize— when the rest of the smoke finally dissolves—that I was so captivated by the man at first sight, I didn't see what he was holding in his hand. I give it a good look now and shudder. Valance grips the blue arm I chopped off, the fisted hand still clutching the wickedly curved scimitar. "He's resourceful, I'll give him that," I say and clearly hear the awe in my voice. From the corner of my eye, I can see that Rashid is looking at me with pointed interest. I'm staring, and I know it. My cheeks start to heat up under Rashid's perusal, but I don't look away from Valance, I can't. "Where did he learn to fight?"

"*Puh-leeze,* that boy's been punching and getting punched since he was on his mama's knees. His dad was a shit drunk, but he was the senator of Kentucky and wealthy and powerful to boot, so no one lifted a finger to stop the bastard. He used to kick the stuffing out of Val and his ma when he was in a bad way. Fucked 'em up good for years, all the way until Valance got big enough to fight back. That guy can take a punch like no other."

"That's horrible," I whisper.

Rashid shrugs. "That's life, babe. We got in our first real fight when we were twelve, at a rave no less."

"Why?"

"Some kid called me a homo. Valance knocked out his front teeth. It became pretty commonplace after that. He hates to see a big guy picking on a little guy. Shit, I had to bail that boy out of the box like ten times before the military got him." He throws me a wink. "I didn't mind doing it. I liked the flex. I used to be crazy rich. Huh? I guess in a way I still am. LOL."

"Laugh out loud," I say, finally spinning to face him, forgetting Valance for a second as I feel my face light up.

A huge grin transforms Rashid's handsome lips, touching all the flecks of gold in his mahogany eyes. He reaches out to tuck a few strands of hair behind my ear and trace a finger through the blood coating my cheek. "You remembered," he says softly.

I nod. Silent. Awed.

"About fifteen days ago, I told you what it meant, for like the hundredth time," he says.

I cut him off. "I said I won't forget again," I blurt, shocked, almost remembering the exact moment when I spoke those words.

"I guess you didn't. Good for you, doll."

I smile. "I guess I didn't. What do you know? Good news can arrive even on those days when you're covered in demon blood."

Rashid laughs, but the sharp clash of swords cuts off his mirth and makes us both spin our heads. It takes me a second to realize Valance was the one who launched the attack. The creature is clearly on the defensive. The severed blue arm is now lying near Valance's feet, and Valance is holding the sharply curved sword in his left hand. Thrust, parry, charge, retreat, Valance moves like a warrior in a dream. The creature battles to defend himself from the assault with his five remaining hands, but it's easy to see that Rashid was right. I never had any reason to worry. Even four feet shorter and outarmed, literally, Valance has the advantage.

He's too fast and fights like a berserker, his lithe movements little more than a captivating blur. He spins, flips, strikes, and I am spellbound. My jaw drops, and I can't find the strength or desire to pick it back up.

Rashid makes a series of strange, chirping sounds. I cast him a look, brow raised. "What?"

Rashid's teeth are a sharp slash of white as his smile turns knowing. "Girl, please, could you want him more?" he asks and starts to laugh. I kick him, but that only makes him laugh harder.

You could try to be a little less obvious about it, my snarky mind informs me, but my eyes inevitably go back to Valance. I feel the binding touch of that ever-present pull between us, magnetic, eternal, unbreakable. I find it strange that a phantom, and most likely imagined, connection with a man I barely know somehow feels like the realest thing in my life.

"It's okay to want him, he's your boo," says Rashid, nudging my shoulder and blowing more smoke in my face.

"I don't even know what that means," I say, blushing again. I don't bother to duck my head to shake my hair and hide my bright-red cheeks, because Valance has the creature up against the wall, a blade to his throat. I see real fear in the monster's black eyes.

"He's yours, and you're his. You can't fight it, Divinica," Rashid says, patting me on the back. "You've both valiantly tried for more than two years. But it's impossible. I'll tell you something, I've seen that man with all his women, and never once did he look at one of them the way he looks at you. He would kill for you, die for you. I mean, you know, he would totally go all Romeo and Juliet for you at the drop of a hat. No matter the state of our world, that's a beautiful thing. Wish someone would want me like that, but all the good ones are dead."

"Women, how many women?" I ask, then instantly wish I hadn't.

"Since he was thirteen, girls have been chasing that boy like he has rosé in his back pocket," Rashid says, then winks. "You've chased him too, once or twice."

"Have not," I snap, my blush so hot I think my face might implode.

"Fight's over," Rashid says, using his chin to point to where my eyes are glued.

Valance increases the pressure of his hold. The knife draws a drop of blood from the thick, blue neck. The demon roars something in a language I no longer understand, but all the bravado is gone from his voice. There's murder in Valance's eyes, and the baring of his teeth is his only response. I don't breathe, I don't think any of us do.

CHAPTER ELEVEN

Hush

It's morbid, but I like how terrified the creature looks, as if he's considering his own mortality for the first time. In retrospect, I don't think he likes the color of his life-thread. At least, not in my present time. He opens his mouth to say something else, but Valance has no time for last words. He flexes his arm, then slices off the creature's head with a single, terrifying stroke.

Geysers of boiling, blue-black blood drench the air for the third time today. I make a sound like shattering glass, my voice echoing loudly through the close stairway and adjoining lab. Rashid stands in the rush. Valance drops the sword like it's a burning brand, and I can see that his hands are shaking. Blood flows down the decapitated body and sizzles when it splashes the wall and cracked tile floor. Not one of us dares to breathe as we wait in silence for the worst to happen. It seems like forever, but it can't be more than a few moments before the dangerous blood blackens and turns to dust.

Valance's shoulders slump on a long exhale. He puts a hand to the back of his neck and twists his head, then drops his hand to his side. Our eyes meet across the pile of demon ash. His wild, slightly unfocused gaze roves desperately over my face. The way he looks at me is pain and pleasure rolled into one, the feeling both jarring and sharp. Memory and need, confusion and white silence. Another snarl starts to build in his throat when he notices the blood all over me. Before I can blink, he's kneeling in front of me, pushing my messy, blood-smeared hair from my face and cupping my flushed cheeks in his hands, still soaked in the creature's black, drying blood.

I don't say anything, I can't with my words are all tangled with the breath caught in my throat. I simply stare at his perfect, sweaty face, hopelessly lost in the moment and stunned by the naked emotion in his eyes. His touch makes this old world, and everything in it, just...hush. There's peace in this silence, and I want to stay in it, with him, forever.

"So much blood. I hate not knowing if any of it is yours. Is any of it yours?" Valance asks. His hands brush my face and neck and skate down my arms. A low hiss escapes his lips as he touches a sore spot just above my right eye, and I flinch.

"You mean there's actually something the great Skylord doesn't know?"

Valance doesn't take the humor bait. His eyes are dead serious when he says, "Yes, and I fucking hate it. You changed the timeline and made me feel mortal." He glances over his shoulder at the still twitching, decapitated creature. "Sometimes these friendly creatures come back with you. This isn't the first we've killed." He looks at the blood dust and shrugs. "Their powers rarely seem to work in this time, but I haven't quite been able to figure out why."

"Shocking," I state, deadpan.

Rashid gives a crack of laughter, quickly covering it with an awkward cough. "Sorry," he says, sounding anything but. I can hardly give any credence to his sarcastic jibe. Valance's eyes are devouring me, and I stifle the urge to touch his jaw, his hair, to lean forward just an inch and kiss him. An awkward silence between the three of us ensues. I want to look away from Valance's face, but I can't. He holds me tethered like gravity. My palms are sweating, and I wipe them on my romper. Valance moves a little closer.

Rashid fake-clears his throat. "Well," he says as he dusts off his hands and stands. "I'm totally sure I have somewhere to be. Suppose I'll figure out where it is as I'm on my way there."

Neither Valance nor I say a word. His thumb is gently touching the cut on my lower lip, and a sudden, rampant case of goosebumps is making me dizzy. "Have I ever changed the timeline before?" I ask when the sounds of Rashid's footsteps fade away.

"Small things, yes, but nothing like this. This was too much. Four days! Fuck, Divinica, I haven't seen you in almost four days. I've been going out of my damn mind."

"I'm sorry. I was upset after we last talked." I shrug. "I hate thinking I'm not in control of my own life. I wanted to change it, wanted to prove that I could. I think I slept. I don't even remember traveling to Kali. Though—" I pause to bite one of my bloody fingernails. I shudder when I realize what I'm doing and drop my hand.

Valance raises a brow. "Though…"

"Well, I guess I do have a slight memory of reading the words on my arm and thinking, fuck it, I know what I have to do, but that's your fault more than anything. You told me to go, and now I wish I hadn't listened." The swinging bulb above his head casts his face in varied slashes of flickering light, highlighting a touch of golden stubble on his jaw and black bags under his eyes.

Valance's eyes dart to the bloody scimitar. "Now I really can't tell myself this is some wild hallucination."

"I've brought lots of things back."

"Oh yeah, like what?"

"In my room, I can show you," I say, watching the light in his eyes flare. I clear my throat awkwardly. "Shit's getting wild," I whisper.

"Yeah. It is. I mean, a lot of weird crap has gone down in the past two years. Once, I even had to fight off a bunch of Reptilians that came to kill you, but this —" Valance drags a hand through his hair. "Div, I really don't know how you did it. Sheer stubbornness would be my guess. I've tried to change the timeline before, so many times, but events always circle back. Seems like you had to be the one to break the cycle."

His finger traces an invisible, electric line down my jaw. I'm shocked that I can form coherent words. "It does?"

"Just swear you'll never do it again. I really did think I was going insane. I know you barely know who I am, but I know you, Divinica, and I know what will happen to me if I lose you."

My mouth goes dry as Valance's words sink into my skin. I can hardly find it in myself to blink. I don't know why, it's just…I feel like missing even a single moment of him is somehow criminal. Like, maybe it's something I once promised myself I would never do. *I'll never look away, never, never!* I remember dimly saying those very words while I held his face between my hands. I know the memory is wrong, because in it, Valance's eyes are soft, adorning, peaceful, the violent opposite of their current state. Now, they're the swirling pallet of exhaustion, rage, want, and desolation. He looks gutted. Actually, to my current recall, he always looks fucking gutted.

"How did you get in here?" I ask when the thick silence gets uncomfortable. "I thought you said this place was—"

"Invisible? Yeah, it was. Not sure what happened. Something must have broken, maybe the device holding the cloaking shield in place."

"Cloaking shield?" I ask dumbly, remembering the strange thing I landed on that shattered like glass but moved like watery air.

"Rashid's name for whatever tech protects these grounds," Valance explains, moving to sit beside me on the top step. He lifts the hem of his shirt, showing me a generous portion of bronze skin and a set of flawless abdominal muscles. I swallow hard, gulping down a mouthful of liquid fire, and quickly glance away. Blasted man makes my mouth water. He uses the hem of his shirt to wipe at the blood coating my cheeks. There's so much blood, in various stages of turning to dust. Like everything else in this world, the blood will eventually blow away. His actions are unnecessary enough to have alternative intent, but I don't move. Why would I? I'd rather be nowhere else in the world. Touched by no one else. Ever. My mind quickly trips to my time in the lands of Kali. I remember the way her lover touched me, and I swallow another ball of fire. This one cuts me on the way down.

"I saw you in the cameras, the second you dashed into the hall with that blue piece of shit chasing you," Valance says, pointing to the headless body and effectively snapping my attention back to him. "My fucking heart stopped."

I hear nothing beyond the word *cameras*. "Cameras?" I ask, my voice shrill. "You have cameras in my—"

"No, not in your room, of course not. If I had, I would've been here a whole hell of a lot sooner." Valance wipes his free hand over his face and shakes his head. "Lot of fucking good that would have done. This house and you in it might as well be made of smoke. We finally did get here, then nothing. Over the last two years, I've tried to time the sequence of the Styx vanishings, but they follow no mathematical pattern. They're so sporadic, in fact, it hints at intelligent construction." He pulls a device out of his pocket, lit up with the same luminous blue light as his computer. *It's a phone*, I think, and then I know I've stared at one a million times. I remember that there was a time when I thought I couldn't live without one. He clicks the silky screen, taps on it a few times, until I see my hallway reflected in the sparkly glass. It's a strange angle, making me think of the way a bird might view the world.

"I heard you scream," Valance says, his fist tightening on the phone until his knuckles go white. "Then I had to watch you run for your life, afraid I wouldn't get here in time. I watched you fight him, saw him throw you across the room, and I couldn't—" His voice, tight and strained snaps on the last word. He clicks the phone again, and the picture on the screen changes. Now I see the inside of the trashed lab, I see us, too, so close our heads are nearly touching. He clears his throat. "I couldn't get to you. Not gonna lie, I just lived through the worst thirty minutes of my life."

"Then how—"

"There was an earthquake. 4.0 at least. Knocked Rashid and I off our feet. Split the earth and caused an avalanche. When it was done, this place was ten feet in front of me, larger than life and untouched by the general mayhem. While Rashid was picking your locks, I almost tore through the front door with my bare hands." I see his broken nails, the red, swelling marks on his knuckles, and I know he's not lying.

"I'm sorry," I say again because I can't think of anything else to say. My thoughts are as scrambled as a dust cloud in a thunderstorm. We are face to face now, and each breath he takes becomes mine. He runs his big hands over my shoulders and down my arms.

"You've nothing to be sorry for, Divinica, this is on me." Valance's eyes drop to my lips, then to the hollow in my throat. His gaze moves downward and stops abruptly on my shoulder. He makes a low, broken sound. "What?" I whisper, suddenly feeling dizzy, as a dull, throbbing pain starts to trace from just behind my left ear, continuing clear down to the tip of my spine.

"Your right shoulder is dislocated," Valance says, sounding horrified. His eyes are flat and hard, holding mine captive.

"Crap," I say, my whisper breathy, and I clear my throat. "Is that bad?"

"No, Divinica, it's the best," he tells me, that one mocking brow raised high enough to tempt cirrus clouds. His voice is so completely deadpan that I burst out laughing. Which hurts, badly. I bite my bottom lip to keep in the giggles. It doesn't work.

Valance leans back a bit, his shoulders rigid, his mouth set in a fierce line. I watch his gaze go to my lips while my giggles twine around us, tinkling like a tumbling bell. "Smile while you can, this is gonna fucking hurt."

His cool, collected voice dims my shock and brightens the pain. I lean my head against the dirty green wall at my back. "It already fucking hurts," I groan through my teeth.

Valance doesn't say anything, but his expression darkens by degrees. He leans over me, and I can feel the heat radiating off him as he places one hand gently on my shoulder and another on the right side of my collarbone. I open my eyes and stare up at his face looming less than an inch from mine. He's sweaty, but I don't care. I want to peel the clingy black T-shirt from his chest, rip it off and watch his body glisten in the flickering light. I want to paint him, just as he is now, sweaty, rumpled, dangerous, and captivating. I want it so bad my fingers itch. *What the actual hell is wrong with me? Hormones much?*

"Bite down on my shoulder," he grates out, speaking through his teeth. "Scream if you want to."

I sigh. "You don't know me at all if you think I'll do either of those things." I take a deep, shaky breath, close my eyes, and lock my teeth. "Just do it, and be quick, will you?"

Valance nods and sets about it. He doesn't hesitate. His hands tighten on my body, and the one pressing into my lower spine causes my back to dramatically arch. The action drags the tips of my breasts across his chest. A sound escapes my lips, squelched and desperate.

"Dear god," Valance bites out, I feel him shudder. His heartbeat accelerates against my nipples, and they tighten in a rush. Valance goes completely still for a second, then groans and closes his eyes. He lifts my left arm, and I hear his teeth lock with a click before he shoves down hard. His strength is incredible. My shoulder pops back into its socket with a sickening, audible snap. I scream, I can't help it. The pain is monstrous, white-hot everywhere, possessing everything. It's too much. I'm too weak to be brave. Midnight threads of unconsciousness suck the blinding, spinning light from my vision. I slump against him.

Valance's hand cups the back of my head, and his fingers run through my tangled hair. Unconsciously, I lean into his touch, and it feels like heaven. I want to push him away, and be strong, be as fearless as this world requires me to be, but I don't. I can't. I'm lost in the pain and sensation of him. After an interminable space of time, the agony starts to fade, until I feel nothing at all. Everything is black and silent.

CHAPTER TWELVE

So, leave then

"Divinica, Divinica, fuck, baby, open your eyes." I hear Valance's voice coming down what feels like a long, black, foggy tunnel. I want to do what he asks, but my eyelids seem to be made from the heaviest metal on earth, and I find I can't comply. "Please," he begs. His lips brush my cheek, light as a feather in the wind, and his kiss lingers at the corner of my mouth. "Come on, baby, just look at me, yeah?"

I feel a breeze against my face, then hear two sets of approaching footsteps. "What's wrong with her?" an airy voice asks. Rashid, I think. Then a deeper tenor voice, clearly Dayle, asks, "Is she okay?"

I try to sigh, but I get no air. Crap. Everything is so hazy. I'm trapped in a distorted dream of pain, of warm hands and Valance's soul-binding lips kissing every inch of my face. *How did I get here? Where is here?*

"No, she's not fucking okay, she's exhausted. This shit's killing her," Valance says through his teeth. He seems incandescent with rage, but when he lifts me in his arms, his touch is almost achingly gentle. He holds me close to his chest as he ascends the rickety stairs, carrying me like I weigh nothing and cradling me against him, close, so close. But not close enough. I want to burrow myself under his skin. Valance seems to feel the same. His arms are iron bands beneath my hips and around my waist. My cheek is pressed against his shoulder, and I feel the muscles flex as he moves. Slowly, his hand travels up and down my back. I know he intended to soothe me, but as his fingers brush the curve of my waist, I think it becomes something more.

For the few minutes it takes him to reach my room, I feel like the most precious thing in the world. I blink when he lays me on my narrow bed, then the mattress dips as he sits beside me. I blink again and find the line of Valance's profile in the dark. The meager light streaming through my window highlights each one of Valance's dramatic features in crimson and silver. The distant, glowing moon commands the color palette of this night, and the lines and shapes in my room appear otherworldly, glowing like the alien objects I brought back from all those other timelines.

"Thank you," I whisper, touching the forearm Valance is resting on his knee. I hear him catch his breath as his head snaps in my direction. Relief and something else, something more, floods his eyes. It's the same thing I feel when I look at him, an emotion too powerful to quantify.

"Divinica, thank fuck." Slowly, he lowers his forehead until it rests against mine. "I've aged ten years in the last hour."

My hand moves to his cheek, and I feel a hard shudder race through his body. "Sorry."

"No, I'm sorry," Valance whispers. "This is my fault. I'm the one who told you to walk through your glowing archway two years ago. I acted like I was humoring a crazy person, but I think...even then, even though I didn't want to believe it, I think I knew you were somehow the key to ending all this madness. The cure if you will. I should've left you alone. Turned around the second I saw you and walked the fuck away. I couldn't. I knew I would hurt you...I knew I would hurt us both, but I just...I couldn't."

"Hurt me?" I try to clear my throat. "You have an annoying habit of saving me."

"I'm using you, and it's killing you."

"Using me how?" I ask, unconsciously stroking the light stubble on his cheek, wholeheartedly hating the pain in his eyes.

Valance places his hand atop mine, and the look we share has a depth I know I could lose myself in. "This is all so fucked up."

"Then explain it to me...though I'm sure you already have," I say on second thought.

"So many times," he says, then winks at me. "You're a little forgetful, you might want to work on that." Even in the middle of all this, he makes me smile. I feel my face light up and see some of the tension around his shoulders release.

I hold his gaze with feeling. "We're trying to save the world, right?"

"Yeah, I guess we are."

"Then go ahead and use me," I say, dropping my head and my hand, then closing my tired eyes.

"Dangerous words, baby," Valance says. My eyes snap open. I see his smile, bold and hot. My eyes adjust to the muted light, focusing on his gold hair, drying around his face in long, angelic curls. The few slow streams of irrepressible moonlight paint a glow around his head and touch the hot, blue light in his eyes where my reflection dances.

It is on the tip of my tongue to object to his casual endearment drop, but instead I ask, "Why? Why are they dangerous words? I mean them. I think I would let you do anything to me. I know you, Valance, I don't know how, but I swear I do."

"You know almost every part of me," he says, and the honesty in his eyes is pure.

"Whatever we're doing, it's killing you too, isn't it?"

"Yes." He flexes his fingers and sinks them deep into my hair. "These hands have had to let you go so many times. Each time you forget me, it destroys a piece of me. I wonder how many more pieces I have left to break."

"I'm sorry," I say again, and mean it. But I'm sorry for him, because in this hallowed moment I feel his pain as if it were mine. "Kali told me I chose this fate years ago. I don't know why I would choose something so horrible. It's enraging. The forgetfulness is like spiders crawling in my brain. Hazy pictures burn like acid, they never really stop. I hate traveling to these other worlds, all fucked up on so many levels. Living inside another person's body, I'm forced to experience their life, their battles, their lovers—" My voice drops. "Their deaths."

Valance exhales a giant breath. His whole body goes strangely still. His hard fingers stiffen in my hair, then he withdraws them slowly. I see his face and watch my words explode through his brain. "What did you just say?" he asks, his voice low and as cold as I have ever heard it.

"What? That I experience their deaths?"

"No, not their deaths…" he snarls.

Crap, way to go, Divinica, my mind wails. My hands start to shake, and I shove them flat beneath my hips and sink my teeth into my lower lip. "Yes…well Kali, she had…I mean when I fell into Kali's body, she was with…" My stuttering words die a sad, squelched death, and I shrug. "It's her life, her body, not mine."

"She was with what?" Valance bites out, his carefully spaced words adding menace.

"Don't make me say it again," I beg.

Valance fixes me with a deadly glare, and now my heart is beating so fast I'm sure he can hear it. "No, Divinica, I think you're gonna have to."

I sit up, ignoring the lightning strike of pain that numbs my arm. "Kali had a lover. She was with him...like that...then she killed him. It was all rather morbidly poetic. Gruesome and romantic. She—I drank his blood. He was the one you killed. Again."

Valance shoots to his feet and starts up a wild pacing around my small room. His size and crackling aura dwarf the four peeling walls. I can feel rage radiating off him in waves. I hear that low rumble deep in his chest, but now it's more wounded animal than frenzied predator. He stops on the far side of the room, makes another jagged sound, then punches the wall, putting his fist straight through the old boards. "Fuck!" he shouts, so loud I jump.

"I didn't really have a choice, did I?" I shout back. "You were the one who told me to go to her," I finish, throwing my words at him like poison darts. I feel guilty and insulted at the same time. I hate it. "I'm trapped in someone else's body, in case you forgot. Stuck in their system like a damn virus."

Valance doesn't say anything, and I'm dying, aging, fading. My throat is a desert filled with burning sand. His face is now white, the single spill of moonlight pouring through my window enhances his pallor. He links his fingers behind his neck and drops his head. I wrap my arms around my chest in a form of self-protection, suddenly noticing how freezing it is in this horrid room. My heart feels like it's clawing its way up my throat, and now I'm shaking so bad that my teeth have begun to chatter. The silence between us thickens. Then, he drops his hands and looks up, his face a cold mask of blank rage.

"Damn it, Valance! Why are you looking at me like that? I didn't have a choice."

"Maybe you did, maybe you didn't," he says cruelly.

I can see in his eyes that hurting me is his intent, and he strikes true. My blood runs cold. "What the hell does that mean?" I shriek. My jaw is starting to ache. Horribly, I know I'm seconds from bursting into tears. I think I've always been like this. A girl with her anger valve directly linked to her tear lever. Valance stares at the giant hole he made in the wall for so long I think he's not going to answer. Then, he narrows his eyes at me, and my heart stops altogether. "What did you let him do to you, Divinica?"

My voice is a scratchy whisper. "Nothing! How could I let anyone do anything? I wasn't in my own body."

"Did you like it?" he asks, his tone low, deadly.

"Oh my god, how can you even ask me that? I don't like any of this. I have no control over the body I'm in. Pain, death, rage, love, I feel it all! It's monstrous, but you told me to go there, and I did."

Valance drags his hands through his hair, a wild look about him, as if now the wounded animal has become insane. "I've gotta get the fuck out of here, right now, before I say something I'll regret."

"Don't you mean something we'll both regret?"

"No, Divinica. You won't remember." The ice infusing his tone is a slap in the face.

Still, I want to beg him to stay, using any words I have to convince him not to leave me when I'm already so alone. I don't say anything though. Sitting here protesting my innocence just makes me seem guilty, begging...seems too needy and risky. So, we stare at each other until the silence starts to scream. "Go then," I finally say. I want to sleep. I want to forget. I don't wait to see what he'll do. I lie back down and roll onto my side, facing away from him. I hear the sound of his footfalls moving across the room. After the door clicks shut, I close my eyes.

CHAPTER THIRTEEN

Death by cold fire

I don't drift off to sleep, not right away. Sleep runs from me as if it were prey, laughing, taunting me from all its hiding places just beneath the fringes of my consciousness. I chase its blessed oblivion down the long, painted corridors of my mind. For an indeterminable amount of time, I drift through the soft-cotton space of the in-between, lost in the limbo that braces both wakefulness and dreams. There is peace in my solitude, knowledge in the endless unknown. Dreams eventually come, wild and colorful. I watch them play out through a golden frame of flames. The monsters who have haunted all my lives visit me in this one. I run but my legs refuse to move. I scream out worlds of silence.

When I finally wake, the light in the room is violet and hanging low. In my sleepy state, I think it makes a haunting sound as it travels through my room, leaving long shadows that waver. I sit up and rub the heels of my hands into my eyes. I'm more exhausted than ever, but I can't keep lying here. I'll truly go mad. As I stand up, my wobbly legs protest at my weight, but they eventually hold me.

Standing in my freezing shower, I lean and rest my forehead on the old yellow wall, cracking with mold, time, and age. I'm glad I primed the pump, though I have no memory of doing it. While the freezing water runs down my body, I listen and respond to the voices in my head as they argue the merits, validity, and reasons for Valance's heartbreaking departure from my room. It makes me miserable all over again when I think about the look in his eyes. I smack my palm against the shower wall, then flinch at the pain.

How can he hate what was done in another time, another body? He is not mine, and I am not his. Or am I? Is this thing I feel for him real, but only forgotten?

Guilty. That is the consensus reached at the conclusion of my shower rant. I decide Valance is at fault for being unfair regardless of what we might be to each other. How could I change the actions of a goddess, in a place and time I have no control over? Would I have tried harder if Kali's lover hadn't been wearing Valance's face? The question hardly bears consideration. The answer is, of course, a resounding yes. I would've fought like a fiend. I would've done my best to take control of Kali's limbs and cut the man's throat before he could touch me. However, I saw his eyes, bright blue and alluring, and I could only submit.

I should probably let Valance know about his doppelganger. Maybe the knowledge will help ease the blow I delivered with a slip of the tongue. At the same time, it might privately assuage my own guilt for lying down with a man who was not my golden Skylord. I almost smack the wall again before I shut off the shower. The loneliness that always plagues me is somehow worse today. It aches. I tell myself I'm crazy, because the truth is, I'm forever alone, living out a broken time that seems to loop in on itself for infinity. I owe no one anything, besides Daniel—who wants nothing to do with me. So why do I somehow feel like I unwittingly betrayed the love of my life?

I open a can of sliced peaches, bobbing in some chemical, sugary goodness. I eat them while I get dressed, lace up my knee-high boots, zip up my tight romper, then brush and braid my hair. Nothing goes right during my morning ablutions. I poke myself in the eye when I lift the hood of my cloak into place, after nearly tripping over the damn candle still laying in the middle of the floor. I level a nasty look at the candle, then kick it hard. It flies under my bed. Good riddance. I hope it stays there and dies. I shiver, then wipe my hand over the back of my neck. First cold, then sweaty, my body seems at war with itself. My heartbeat is an erratic gallop that speeds incessantly the closer I get to walking out my front door.

When I saddle Boogles, I'm armed to the teeth and angry. I can't be sure, but I don't think I'm an angry person. The rage feels strange, the way it's all hot and wrapped up in my chest, as if the barbed metal wire that drapes Valance's concrete castle is twisting all around my heart.

The world I ride through fits my mood. Above my head, the roving sky looks ruptured, done in by humanity, even before the world fell to pieces. Heavy clouds riding low on the horizon obscure what remains of the dying sun. Purple snow covers everything. I think that soon this world will be washed away, all manufactured things eventually devoured by the hungry, radiated earth.

In the books I found in the old silo, and the subsequent notes I scratch in my notebook, I read about nuclear war. Scanned through numerous accounts of what it did to these skies, and creatures like my Boogles. My notes also say it was the humans who made our oceans boil by something called global warming. A phenomenon ignored by those in power who lived and ruled pre-red waves.

As I continue to ride, I stare at the icy edges of my world and find myself wondering, as I often do, what our Earth used to be. Was it green and lush like Kali's world, or wild and full of ancient spirits like the free lands of Nokomis? Was it soaked in blood, misogyny, and fire like the kingdoms of Isis? Or was it all those things? Beautiful, magical, dense, and dangerous. I hope it was all those things, life and death and the miracle that might be found in between. I wonder if the people of such a mysterious place had lived each day to its max, felt nothing but grateful for what they had? Or did the Yin too far outweigh the Yang? If all things exist as inseparable, contradictory opposites, as Magu's culture believed, was pain all we ever knew?

"Doesn't fucking matter now," I say aloud. Boogles snorts at the sudden sound of my voice, raspy and unused. I scratch the top of his head, and he trumpets contentedly, then continues plodding along. A wake of gentle ripples shake the earth with each of Boogles's heavy footfalls. Spiked and poisonous shrub creatures mark our passage through yellow eyes, curious but unafraid. They are the true masters of this terrain. I am the intruder. I can't feel anger at that. From what I read, it was the stupidity of my race that lost us our place on the food chain.

I pass remnants of family here, a loner there, disintegrating bones and crumbling stones set as grave markers of death, all sanded down by the steady destruction of time. The sun is fully set behind the arching mountains dominating the distance. Sleeping giants that guard the spaces between air and earth. My eyes are drooping by the time I see the single window standing proudly in its broken frame. I feel a strange affinity with the old thing. Alone as I, hard braced against the wind and elements set to destroy. I keep my eyes on the window even after Boogles stomps past it. I finally turn and see him. *Him, him, him, him, him.* My mind whispers the word, makes an endearment out of it.

Valance sits on his twisted throne, watching me. I shift and sit up straighter in the saddle, then reach for the knife I stashed in my right boot. Valance looks to be in a fighting mood, and I mean to be prepared. Head held high, I ride on, pretending to be unaffected by the way he burns me. I pass a group of people sitting and warming their hands around a dumpster fire. Clustered like drowning ants. They wear an assorted collection of threadbare rags, old sweaters, gloves, woolen hats, and jackets of all colors and sizes. The purple, icy mud slathering the ground buries them all in its clustered folds, like they're already among the dead, relics of what once was, gargoyles waiting for the sun to rise so they can take their final breath.

A young boy with bright mahogany eyes toddles around, yelling happily and brandishing a stick for a sword. He's adorable. He paints pictures in my mind of another little boy who sat beside me on my mother's knee—Daniel. My brother. My heart twists like it always seems to when I think of his name. I remember my mom used to bounce him on her hip as he screamed, and she used to sing to hush him. It was the only upside to the howling that went on all night. My mom had a beautiful voice. I remember. For a second, I can almost hear it. I swallow hard and turn away from the child. I wonder if his parents will remember him when the next red wave strikes. No, they won't, I decide. Soon, the thirteen-day wave reset will break over us, and this little boy in front of me will be lost and alone like the rest of us.

The downward spiral of my morose thought ends as that invisible pull between us drags my eyes back to Valance. I lower my head and watch him through the cover of my lashes. He's standing now, arms folded, the lines of his face set in a harsh, unreadable mask. I feel the heat of his stare like fingertips on my skin as I dismount and scratch Boogles on his trumpet snout. I kiss my pet on his goofy nose. "Wait here for me, okay? I'm gonna see about finding you some food. Be a good boy, will you?"

Boogles snorts at me. His smiling, squinty eyes say he's always been a good boy. He nudges me in the chest, and I chin-bump his forehead, then stride from Valance's line of sight, past more clusters of people with blank or terrified faces, and march straight up the stairs, in the direction of the fight I mean to pick. I nearly crash into Dayle at the top of the stairs. I remember his name right away. He's twice my height and three times my size. Overall, unforgettable. Looking up at him from my vantage gives me a bit of a shock. I trip, and he catches me by the shoulders a second before I tumble head-over-heels backward down the stairs to my doom.

"Déjà fucking vu," Dayle says and sets me on my feet, then quickly drops his hands and steps back to a polite distance.

"Sorry," I mutter, looking at the ground.

"That's alright, girl, running into you is always the best part of my day," Dayle says. His voice is excessively deep. *If mountains could speak*, I think, then know I've thought that thought before.

"Go on up. He won't admit it on pain of death, but that boy's trippin' hard. He needs to see you. Careful though, he's in a rare mood."

"So am I," I say, then smile, nod, and walk past him, too tired for any more pleasantries. Besides, I need to conserve my energy for all the screaming I'm about to do. Dayle seems to anticipate my hasty retreat. He smiles as he turns to let me past, humming a slightly familiar tune when he walks away.

CHAPTER FOURTEEN

Portals, stone circles, black holes, or star doors, all just shadows of the same

Valance is watching me when I walk in the room. He's standing in front of his strange throne, backlit by the silver moon. As I step fully into his lair, his sharp eyes go to my boot and the knife sheathed there. He nods his head as if confirming a private theory. Slowly, his eyes travel back to my face, then wander to my lips. He swallows hard. I see his throat move, and then he takes a deep breath, the exhalation of it ruffling the golden curls hanging over his brow. "What can I do for you, and your knife, Divinica?" he asks, his tone polite as if we were strangers.

The tone makes the madness build in my bones. "That's a stupid question," I snap, hating his calmness when I'm seething inside. Hating how badly I want him and hating that I don't know why. I instantly lose whatever cool I gained on the ride over here, and my heart starts its erratic, racing beats all over again. Every pump of blood feels like a punch in the chest. "There's a crap ton you can do for me. You can tell me why you left, why you blame me for something I can't control, why you're looking at me like I've betrayed you when the truth is I don't even know you!"

When I stop shouting, the room falls silent again. Valance doesn't speak to my outburst. Instead, he turns away to face the open night and rests his white-knuckled fists on his narrow hips. His pose is that of a king surveying his kingdom and not liking what he sees. I came for a fight, but Valance's pensive mood is catching. The night is quiet, involved in that sacred kind of hush that whispers and echoes. I walk farther into the long, cluttered room, so full of items and pictures from the old world. Libraries and lovers, screaming children in parks and parties with colorful balloons. Things I can hardly imagine, things I'll never see again.

Piles of papers and shiny images lay strewn around the base of the throne. I try to see what's written on them, to soundlessly move even closer without drawing his attention back to me. I can't make out the words, but I understand the symbols, or some at least—pyramids, the eye of Horus, galaxy spirals depicted on stones or clay tablets. I see them in my dreams. Use them on my travels. There are other images, things I don't understand. Machines, or ships perhaps. Near my feet are shiny pictures—like the photographs I took of my tattoos—of empty corn fields covered by huge symbols that flatten the tall green-and-gold stalks.

"Crop circles," Valance says, turning and following the path of my eyes. "Dayle thinks if I stare at them long enough, some pattern, other than the known, will emerge."

"Has it?" I ask, stepping closer to the scattered images, and to him.

He cocks his head but doesn't look away from the pictures. "There's geometric symmetry, and a number of astrological correlations, but no, I honestly don't see shit. Far as I can tell they have similarities, but follow no order, like diametric clues placed to hinder, not solve." Valance hunkers down and rests his arms on his knees. I kneel beside him and reach for another image that catches my eye. I lift it and hold it up to the dim light.

"What's this?" I ask, hearing awe in my voice. The image triggers a deep feeling, if not a memory.

"Castlerigg," he says. I must make a face at him, because he smiles and explains, "A stone circle."

"What's a stone circle?" I whisper. I reach for another photo.

"No one knows. Variations of these circles exist all over the world, yet they've always been a mystery."

"I see," I say, though I don't. I lift the new photo I'm holding and turn it toward the light as I did the other. "And this one?"

"That's Stonehenge, the king of all stone circles, or the queen, if you prefer. Supposedly built about five thousand years ago in the Neolithic age, though initial construction started much earlier than that. The thirty standing stones are made of local sandstone, but these here..." He motions with his thumb to a set of smaller interior stones with a slight blue sheen. "These are called bluestone, or crystal agate, brought all the way from the Preseli hills, more than a hundred miles away. It was once believed to be the ancient stone of dreaming, with a strong connection to the electrical impulses or energies produced by the human body."

"It looks like some type of machine. I think...I think I've dreamed of this place, or traveled to it, I'm not sure, but I have a memory of a stone circle just like this one, only...less ruined," I say.

"Makes sense, time has a way of fucking things up. This circle in particular has always been associated with the disruption of time. If you were to stand in the circle's center on the equinox of the winter solstice, when the sun rises just to the left of the heel stone..." He points to an outlying stone standing north of the monument. "There may occur a form of transference—"

"I know," I say, cutting him off. "The rays of sunlight are channeled into the center, here. When time is exact, that sunbeam fractures and warps between these stones here. Then it shoots a beam of light straight up, bright enough to pierce through even the blackest storm cloud." My breath comes out in a rush when I finish talking. The memory I just had makes me dizzy. I clearly recall the way the sun beam seemed to glance off earth and sky. I wait for Valance to say something, maybe give me a metaphorical pat on the back for the superpower I just flexed, being able to remember something so incredible, and something that happened in another time no less. He doesn't though. Instead, he stays quiet long enough to make me swivel toward him and raise a questioning brow, mildly stung despite myself. Maybe he doesn't believe me.

His eyes widen briefly, then his face turns stoic. "What? Oh sorry, did you want a congratulations?"

"Uh, yeah."

"My bad, you've remembered that before. A few times. You were the one who made me think there might be more to these structures in the first place. After I got to know you, I was forced to admit to myself that you were most likely telling the truth. You weren't some spy or alien or sleeper agent with a plan. You were a girl who lost her brother and her parents and managed to survive something unspeakably horrific in the military lab of a dead German scientist. It took me longer than I'd care to admit, but I finally realized it's not in you to tell a lie. Eventually, I started listening to you, really listening. I would've worked it all out faster, but it sounded so fucking crazy. Goddesses from other times genetically alter a human girl to save the world from a device they created to destroy it. Even for someone who's walked on Mars, the whole thing just sounded—" He breaks off to run a hand through his hair. "In the end it was you. I believe in you. You convinced me of it all, and you didn't even mean to."

I drop my eyes back to the pictures. He doesn't look away from me. I put up with his stare for as long as I can. "What?

"What?" he echoes.

"I believe what you're saying, but I don't remember telling you any of that. The memories I do have are more confusing than helpful. What do you want from me?"

"Want from you? Fucking hell, Divinica. I don't want anything from you, not a damn thing," he says, shaking his head.

I look at him, lifting a single brow. "Nothing, really? Come on, your side-eye is raising the hairs on my neck."

Valance smiles that crooked, sexy smile I'm coming to adore. "You're incredible," he simply says. My cheeks go up in flames.

I drop my head, let the curtain of my falling hair hide me. "How so?"

"You're so strong. You're breaking out of it on your own. It's incredible and crazy, like watching someone escape Alcatraz in real time."

I scrunch my nose. "What's an Alcatraz?"

"A bird, and a prison."

"You think we're in a prison?"

"No, I don't think. I know."

"So, when you say I'm the key, you mean like an actual key. You think my tattoos are some sort of coded prison break?"

"I think you are rare and powerful."

"That's not an answer," I whisper, too captivated to break his direct stare.

The moment is so awkward, the silence momentarily so grim, a falling pin would be deafening. I watch his features harden by degrees before he says, "That's all I have, but it doesn't matter now. I'm going to put a stop to it. No more star doors, no more time jumping. I'm content to stay forever imprisoned, if it means dead lovers from past lives keep their fucking hands off you."

"The man was you," I blurt, hurt making a trembling mess of my voice.

Valance closes his eyes and drops his head. I think he's trying to catch his breath. "What are you talking about?"

I toss a hand lamely through the air between us. "The man Kali was with, he was different, but he was you. Your eyes, your mouth." My words break off, and I shrug, unable to finish whatever the crap I'm trying to say.

Valance lifts his head and glares into my eyes again. He stays silent for a long time, staring at me with what looks to be a combination of desire and dread. I can hear the low drone of murmuring voices coming from below, and the wail of the wind roving across the night, but between us is nothing save the sounds of our ragged breath.

"I don't care," he finally says. "I don't fucking care. I want it to be me." He places a big hand on his chest, touching his heart. "This guy, who loves plaid shirts, advanced geometry, and Mario Kart. I want to be the last man who touched you. My kiss the one you still taste on your lips." He moves closer to me, until our knees are touching, and his expression turns hungry, ravenous even.

My internal monologue is loud and argumentative. *Run, run, run, run, run, stay, stay, stay, stay, stay forever, let him kiss you, goddamn it, coward, kiss him first!*

We don't speak. We kneel together in the blue pool of spilling night, light peacefully streaming from the surrounding windows. The moment holds an intimacy for which I am unprepared. It's too hard to keep my expression neutral when I'm barraged by so many feelings. I try to break the spell and stand, but his hands flash out and grab my arms, fully preventing my retreat.

"No. Don't go." His whisper is broken, hoarse and pleading. His chest rises and falls, and my heartbeat is the sound of my imminent demise. "Divinica, Divinica, I know I must seem irrational, crazy, jealous even, but the truth is I am yours, and you are mine whether you remember it or not. The thought of another man touching you, kissing you when it's all I want to do—it tears my heart in half."

"It wasn't me!" I cry.

His face hardens, and he shakes me a little. "That doesn't matter. Can you even imagine what it feels like to be forgotten by the person you care about most in the world? No? Shocker! Well, I'll tell you. It's hell! Now, until the next wave comes and wipes your memory, it's him you remember, that nameless, faceless bastard. His kiss, his touch. I would kill for that. To be remembered by you. Fuck me! It's the only thing I want. I'm so desperate for some semblance of recognition, even a brief flash that tells me you know how much we feel, need, want. You're the only one. I'm in love with you, and damn girl, I know you're in love with me. We belong together, but every thirteen days—" He shudders. "God, this is the worst kind of torture."

I gasp and strain away, not because I don't want him, but because I'm terrified by how badly I do. I bring my hands to his chest, meaning to shove myself free of his hold, but my fingers disobey my mind's commands, and instead, they clutch handfuls of his black shirt and tug him closer, closer. Close enough to keep. *I'll never let him go, never, never, never, never, never, never,* I think as our hearts beat in perfect syncopation. He's looking at me like I'm the sum of all desires. I understand, because even though I don't know him, I know he's mine. I imagine that butterflies with wings drenched in so many extinct colors are battering at the frozen confines of my heart, the flap and flip of their wings heating all the places I've gone cold.

Valance's pupils are so dilated that the black has nearly eaten all the electric blue. My eyes drop to his lips. This time, I know he's going to kiss me, and I know I won't stop him. No freaking way. *Never, never, never, not until the stars fall from the sky, and the oceans turn to ash. Never. Not in this life or any that follows.*

The seconds tick. My heart is slamming against my chest so hard I'm afraid if he doesn't kiss me soon, that desperate beat will probably break a rib. I open my mouth to say something, maybe beg him to just fucking do it, and put us both out of our damn misery, but his hands fold over mine, and he presses them tighter to his chest.

"Look at me, Divinica, I mean it," he says when I don't comply. "I want you to see me when this happens." My head snaps up as his hands fall to my lower back, and he tugs me closer, only stopping when my body is flush against his. The nightlight makes him otherworldly. I can almost see our auras clash and intertwine. Mine is the purple hue of our world, his is dark and golden, together they make an unimaginable, powerful color. The color of life, passion, and desire. *He really is the most obscenely beautiful man I've ever seen,* I think, and I'm haunted by the horror of all I've forgotten.

Downstairs, the murmur has turned into an all-out commotion. There are a series of loud crashes and a few baritone shouts. I can hear the smack of the long curtains against the frames of the choppy brick windows, hear the wind washing the icy ground outside. Those things fade when Valance takes my chin between his thumb and forefinger. Then, his lips brush against mine, and all my next thoughts belong to him.

His lips are firm and dry, the touch of them light enough to be a figment of my outrageous imagination. Still, I'm lost. He doesn't deepen the kiss like I expect, but drops featherlight kisses over my mouth, and I realize he's giving me a chance to pull away. That simple act of care ignites a madness in me. My heart careens out of control, my head spins as my hands sink into his thick hair, and I breathe him in and kiss him back ferociously, nearly savage in my desperation.

Valance is ready for me. His arms tighten around me, and he crushes me against his chest. The strength in his hand as it runs down my back makes me feel all at once powerful, weak, and restless. He licks at my lips, then thrusts his tongue into my mouth and strokes it against mine until I think I'll scream. He steals my breath, and I let him. I beg him with my hands and arching body to do more. In Kali's world, with her lover—though he wore Valance's eyes—there was trepidation and fear. Here, there is only hunger and fire.

He tilts my head back over his arm, and the kiss turns indecent. He devours me and I let him, the nails I score down his back asking for more...they ask for all of it. For a time, this deadly, aching sensuality is our breath and blood, and I know he is as lost as I am. I want him, want him like I've never wanted anything.

He is my reality, my sanity, necessary to me as air and thought. Just as I'm ready to rip off my clothes and let him do whatever the hell he wants, Valance breaks the kiss. We stare at each other, shaking and winded. Distantly, I realize I'm nearly on his lap, and my hands are up under his shirt, pressed flat against his hard stomach. He makes me want things I can't name or describe. I want to ask him why he stopped. Instead, I stupidly say, "Why did you do that?"

"Why did you let me?" he shoots back, voice strained and low.

Why the hell do you think? I want you. Sometimes I think you really are a god, my mind screams, but my mouth says, "Don't deflect, I asked you first." I can't even recognize my own husky voice.

Valance tightens his grip on my waist. Shadows play over his face, and he looks like a predator, a rock dragon on verge of a death strike. "I kissed you because kissing you is all I ever fucking think about." The pad of his thumb brushes the curve of my lower lip before he kisses the spot he touched. "I kissed you because I want it to be my lips you think of, not some nameless lover, and I want my touch—" He breaks off and clears his throat. I drop my gaze to the scattered pictures, but he takes my face between his hands and lifts it so that our eyes meet. "I mean it, Divinica, I want to be the man in your dreams, the breath in your lungs. I want to touch your soul the way you've left handprints on mine."

I am silent. Struck dumb by the depth of sincerity in his declaration, and it makes my eyes water and my nose burn. "You...you are, you have..." I stammer. Valance's fingers dig deeper, stroking lines of shivers down my back, and any resistance that remains in me crumbles fast. I run my hand over the front of his body, stopping at the big, silver buckle on his jeans. His breath hisses between his teeth. My hand drops lower.

Valance catches my hand and brings it to his lips, nipping at my fingers before dragging my hand back down his torso. "You're playing with fire," he groans, then kisses me like he can't help it, and it starts all over again. The tandem pounding hearts, the wanting, the burning, the ragged, merging breaths that sound like muffled screams. Not breaking our kiss, Valance sits back on his heels, and I scramble all the way onto his lap, too crazed for finesse. He doesn't seem to notice or care when my front tooth knocks his lower lip or when I knee him in the thigh. His hands drop to my hips, he lifts me high, and I wrap my legs around his waist.

Valance grinds against me in an upward thrust. My head falls back as my bones turn to liquid lightning. His teeth graze my neck, biting down on my shoulder. "God, Divinica, I fucking want you," he rasps, taking my lower lip between his busy teeth. "Five more seconds of this, and I'm going to carry you to my bed and keep you there until the next wave hits." There's a blatant threat in his tone, but I can't think of anything I want more.

"You sure we've never…? In your bed…we've never? Are you sure?"

"Yes, I'm fucking sure. I've wanted to, god I've wanted to. I've imagined you there so many damn times."

"Why? If you want me, and it's been two years, then why?"

"You're never this lucid so early on. Last time we almost—" He breaks off and bites lightly on the shell of my ear. "Not gonna lie, these two years with you have been the longest and most frustrating years of my life."

"Do it now," I say.

Valance goes still. "Divinica." His voice is a gravel and velvet warning I don't want to hear.

"I mean it. Take me to your bed."

"Why? So I can have you for a night. Maybe two? Only to have you forget me all over again, hold you as you scream through the red wave, watch the desire in your eyes turn to distrust and hate, then go home, alone, to the smell of you on my sheets, the taste of you in my mouth redefining the parameters of desire?" His voice is wretched, and he shakes his head. "No. I can't. I'll go insane. If what I am missing is imagined rather than known, I won't kill someone when it gets taken away."

His reason is sound, but the rejection stings more than I care to admit. I drop my eyes and climb awkwardly off his lap. I see his fists clench, and I hope it's done to keep his hands from dragging me back and taking me up on my offer. His jaw is locked so hard I can hear his molars grinding together. I almost go back to him, force him to do what we both want so desperately, but I stand up and turn away, wondering if he can sense my inner battle as easily as I can read his.

"You take all the life from the air when you leave," he says, but he makes no move to stop me. My stomach is a tight ball constructed of a thousand knots. When I walk away from him and descend the stairs, my eyes prickle. I may take the life, but I think somehow, somewhere, I left my heart with him.

CHAPTER FIFTEEN

Fuck my fucking life

Leaving Valance tonight is the hardest thing I can remember doing. I'm silent as I saddle Boogles and ride home. The smoky, silver moon is high, and the world beyond Valance's camp is silent. Even the creatures seem to have taken refuge from the night's living dark. The stars, too, hide their shining faces, adamantly refusing to light my way home.

When I reach the crumbling asylum, I hobble Boogles in the back near the silo. I find two cans of mushroom soup in my rapidly diminishing stash, give one to Boogles and kiss his nose, then drink mine straight from the can as I walk inside and kick off my boots. I turn on the tap in the bathroom to wash the clingy purple muck from my face and hands, but the faucet spits and gurgles. I curse like a bandit when I realize I forgot to prime the pump after my shower. Misery makes me groan and bury my face in my hands. Fuck my life. I'm pissed and doomed to fall asleep smelling like him.

Does he regret letting me go as much as I loathed leaving?

Still cursing my head off, I stomp to my bed, flick back my wrinkled emergency blanket, and see my notebook lying in the center of my mattress beside my crude charcoal pencil. I snatch up both items. The familiar weight brings a sense of unstable calm. I hold them both to my chest, close my eyes, and take a second to breathe. I have so much to write, I'm not sure where to start. I place the items carefully on my pillow, then leave my room in search of the jerry can my notebook says I fill with water in preparation for moments like this. Back in my room, I unzip my jumper, unclasp my bra, and strip down, panties and all. When my clothes are washed and hanging at the foot of my bed, and I am securely wrapped in the emergency blanket, I open my notebook, lift my pen, and start to write.

You kissed him today—the fucking Skylord, or he kissed you. Does it really matter? You loved every second of it, it really was like kissing a god. You've hurt him by repeatedly losing your memories. You hate this and wish you could change it. You can't. Regardless, you're an idiot for forgetting him.

His touch is pure, unadulterated magic. Your life overall sucks the big one, but that kiss didn't. Your world is now spinning out of control, and Valance is the vortex responsible for its destruction. Ecstasy is too tame a word for how he makes you feel. He wants you too, but he's afraid, and it's your fault. Like I said, you're an idiot for forgetting him. Take some time today and feel like one.

You're going to see him again soon. I know it's nearly impossible, but do try not to act like you're not flying apart inside when his hand accidentally brushes yours, or he gives you a side look through those devastating eyes of his. Also, side note, this world sucks! You suck! Gah!

I snap the book closed and shove it under my pillow, then lie on my back and slam my fists into my uneven mattress. "Damn it!" I groan, rolling onto my side and punching my pillow with feeling. Goddamn it!

I don't know how long my body sleeps while my mind battles dreams, but I wake to the sound of a woman screaming, and for once it's not me. My eyes fly open, and I bolt upright. I drag my hands through my hair, suddenly remembering that I'm stark naked. The scream sounds off again, closer this time. I hear pure terror in every screeching note.

I dive for my clothes and throw them on as I dash for the door. I don't bother grabbing my bow, it's too slow at a time like this. I reach for my ax leaning near the door, my fingers wrapping around the handle before I scramble out of my room and run barefoot down the hall. I'm frightened and mildly enraged. Being woken by such a traumatizing scream has a marked effect on my mood. I dash hell for metal out the double doors guarding the front entrance of Styx. The moment my bare feet hit the dirt, I stop dead. Then, I sway a little, trying to hold back my own choked scream.

A woman and a young snot-nosed girl stand about twenty feet from the first of the crumbling statues lining my old driveway. Both seem to be in great distress, but it's the creatures surrounding them that grab my attention. There isn't much about them in my notebook, and looking at them, I can't help but wonder why the fuck not. In a world of unfathomable things, they are still fantastical.

My mind tells me it's impossible, but my eyes see giant lizards with forked tongues, each standing at least eight feet tall. Scaled skin and bright yellow eyes that fold in the middle. They stand upright like humans, but their arms, torsos, legs, and tails are Reptilian. They wear thick chains around their necks, carrying the insignia of a fire-breathing dragon surrounded by twelve stars. There are two of these creatures and three men, who I easily identify as members of the Burning tribe. According to my writings, they've tried to eat me twice. The men are staring luridly at the terrified woman and child, flashing broad smiles that show me the thick, black goo oozing between their sharpened, broken teeth. Red marks and open wounds cover their bald heads. One of the men has a weeping, red sore in place of his right eye.

Man or Reptilian, they all carry weapons forged in hammered steel—sharp, jagged edges designed for death alone.

"Hey!" I shout as I start to run again. My still sleepy, falsetto voice doesn't sufficiently draw their attention, so I swing my ax and whoop like a madwoman. The men cast brief, uninterested glances at me. The Reptilians hardly spare me a glare, their collective focus on the young girl with hair like a bright spill of sunlit copper. Two of the men grab the woman's arms and start playing tug-of-war with her shaking limbs. The Reptilians watch in silence, the gleam in their yellow eyes feral and deadly. When I'm less than ten feet away, I see Daniel out of the corner of my eye. The kid is wearing a rather cynical smile on his pale lips.

"Hey, you, stupid girl," Daniel calls. It's a deep credit to my insecurities that I instantly know he's referring to me. I wheel toward him.

"Daniel, get the fuck out of here!" My voice is hoarse and screeching.

"If I do, you'll be dead as well as stupid," he says, almost conversationally. I realize he's holding a hunk of metal in his hand just as he lifts it, then tosses it to me. I catch the makeshift club midair and turn back to face the men, my ax in one hand, Daniel's weapon in the other, and hope for the best.

"Thank you," I say, not looking at him, "Now will you please get out of here? There's a bunch of goddamn lizards. Lizards for fuck's sake!"

Daniel snorts rebelliously. "I know. Their faces are all over my walls, so I must've seen them before, kinda weird, kinda not. And no, I don't think I will get out of here. I—watch out!" he screams. Without hesitation, I take to the air, my body whirling so fast that the turbulent sky spins over my head, then I throw my ax at the lizard guy who's coming for me fast, claws extended, with what I assume is every intention of ripping my head off. The ax cartwheels through the air and strikes true, embedding itself dead center in the thing's chest and drops like lead, clawing at the ax's handle, gasping, gurgling. Now I have everyone's attention, and no weapon except for what Daniel gave me.

Great, Divinica, here goes nothing. I hoist the club, preparing to take them head-on. Two of the men rush at me. I wait until the last second, then let out another war cry and blindly swing again. The metal bar makes jarring contact with a bald, inked skull, instantly splitting the pale skin and releasing a geyser of blood that spatters my face. I strike again. The man drops to his knees as both his blistered hands go up to cradle his head. Heavy footfalls behind make me turn. Too slow. Something hard strikes my left temple. I stumble. My foot clips a devious rock that robs me of balance. Unconsciously, I throw out my free hand to break my fall. It's a bad move, the impact is terrible, and I hiss as something in my wrist twists. Alas, there is no time to cry over spilt Divinica. I roll onto my back in time to see the man with a canker sore for an eye diving at me, his filthy fingers racing for my throat. I spit dirt, lift both my feet, and kick him in the gut with all my strength.

The man staggers back. I jump up, waving my hands in search of my lost equilibrium. This time I take a second to get my bearings before aiming my club straight at his pockmarked face. The hit is direct and sends a numbing jolt up my arm. Vibrations ripple through the metal rod, making my fingers twitch like twigs in a radiated storm. It's a struggle not to drop the damn thing. The man sways precariously as a weird groan escapes his newly split lip. I land another spinning kick to his gut that knocks him on his ass. My arm is still numb, and my fingers are shaking hard, but I have murder on the mind and advance on him anyway. Seconds before I strike him again, I hear the young girl's muffled scream. The one remaining man and his lizard friend ignore the battle, apparently expecting their companions to make short work of me.

They have the struggling child on the ground. As the lizard pins the girl's hands to the dirt, the man wrestles with her kicking legs. Her skirt is rucked up around her chubby knees, and the sight makes me sick. I run for my ax, still embedded in the twitching reptile's chest. When I wrench it free, another spurt of blood splashes my face. "Still alive, pity," I cruelly say, but I'm feeling neither friendly nor forgiving. I'm confused, horrified, and scared. I use the back of my hand to wipe away the blood trickling down my cheek, slightly green and smelling like an open, well-used sewer. "Gross, gross, gross," I say, wanting to scrub it all off, but time, as usual, is not on my side.

Ax in one hand, club in the other, I dive for the man just as his disgusting hands go to the buckle of his equally disgusting pants. I feel rage contort my face as I swing with all my strength and stick the blade of my ax in the back of his skull, just above his neck. The woman screams as I twist the ax free, the blade dripping blood. I bring it up for another throw, hissing like the enraged animal I am. My breathing is shallow, and my ears are ringing, but I'm ready to see every last one of these monsters to the afterlife, regardless of their species.

Strangely, as I watch blood spill from the dying man's neck, the fear fades away. Power surges through me, and I can feel my tattoos glowing. They sting too, like a thousand hornets are attacking the middle of my body. Black dots obscure my vision, and I feel my body teeter to the right. I shake my head to clear it, but the darkness balloons, enveloping and smothering me. I see a dead leaf blowing through the air and watch it land on the feet of a statue, then flutter down the rocky base of its vaulted pedestal. The world sways and I plummet to my knees. I drop my weapons and grab my head with both hands as brilliant pictures barrage me from all sides, battering my mind. My grip on reality loosens. Through a busy haze, I see the remaining Reptilian advance on my unmoving body. I do nothing. I have lost control of my limbs, and my mind has taken flight.

Agonizing pain blazes through my brain, like an unseen force is cutting at the chunky scars of forgetfulness in my mind. Something strikes my face, more pain blossoms, and then I'm falling through an endless tunnel of discarded time and memory. The fall seems brief, and I blink my eyes until they tear up. When I can see my surroundings once again, I instantly notice that my world is completely different, changed, wrong. The men, the little girl, and her useless, frightened mother are gone. A man and woman stand in their place beside a shiny silver car. I recognize them at once. They are my mother and father, standing close, smiling. I'm there too, and Daniel. All of us. The sun above our heads is bright, hallowing my parents in brilliant happiness. Distantly, I'm aware of something hard striking me on the jaw, but the pain hardly fazes me, as if it's taking place in another, darker world where my mind is no longer a resident. The world where I currently exist is full of golden light and peaceful as a dreamless sleep.

Daniel gets out of the car, shades his eyes, and looks up at Styx, our new home for the next few months. "Wow, yuck," he says, "didn't know we were time traveling. This place looks like something on TikTok. It's a goddamn spook house."

"Language," Mom says, raising a brow and looking at her man. "You know how your father is when he gets a bee in his bonnet. It was Germany or nothing…don't blame me, I wanted to go to Paris."

"It's not a bee," Dad says, smiling at her. "This place will be the site of the first wave. I know it's coming soon. I'm not even sure I can stop it…if just one of my calculations is incorrect—"

Mom shrugs, with a "see, I told you so" expression on her face.

Dad steps closer to her. He combs his fingers through her ponytail and tilts her head back so that she's staring up at him, big hearts in her eyes. "I'll take you to Paris, my love, I promise," he says, then kisses her. Mom's whole frame seems to weaken as their lips meet, and she sways a little before pressing her body flush against his.

Daniel and I make a face at each other. "Ew," Daniel says. "Get a room."

I start to laugh at the expression on my brother's face, but the laugh dies a squelched death in my throat as the earth starts to shake violently. Little pebbles rattle under the soles of my brand new boots, knee-length faux-leather beauties that my mom gave me for my seventeenth birthday.

I see Mom's fingernails curl into Dad's chest. "What's happening?" she asks as the quake intensifies. Her voice sounds calm, but I'm not fooled. I can see her eyes. Dad takes his phone from his back pocket and taps on the screen. His face goes white as clotted cream. "Shit! Fuck!" he nearly screams, shocking me. I can't remember ever hearing Dad curse. "We've got to get inside, now!"

"Aw," Daniel whines. "But I wanna—"

"Now!" Dad shouts, fear twisting his voice to a nearly inhuman sound. Before Daniel can respond, a thousand explosions go off overhead all at once. I look up in time to see the sky I've known and loved my whole life inexplicably changing in front of my eyes. Black soaks through the blue, then all I see is red. Flashing, burning, an angry wall of crackling, electric light, wider than the Earth itself and tall enough to touch the farthest star. My dad's hands flash out, and he takes Daniel's arm and grabs Mom around the waist.

"Run, Divinica!" he shouts. I obey even though I know it's already far too late. My eyes crash into Dad's. We both know. I can't be sure, but in that moment, I think I see farewell in his eyes. We are running, still staring at each other, when the wave hits us in the back with what feels like the force of an atomic blast. Mom screams the scream of the damned. Daniel grabs the hand Dad has locked around his waist and hangs onto it as the wave punches the breath from his lungs. Heat surges through me. A million blistering flames chew at my nerve endings. My head cranes sharply to the right, my body spasms, and I scream as I feel myself fall. The pain of my face hitting the dirt counts for nothing. My skin is moving, melting, something pops in my ears, then I feel a hot liquid running down my neck. The pain goes on and on, rending the soul from flesh as it breaks and electrocutes my mind.

I'm dying, I think seconds before my mind is wiped blank as a new phone. The programs are there, but the files are empty. It seems like forever before the last burning pulses shred through us. I hear Daniel and my parents moaning, coughing, gasping. Confusion blackens my mind, daggers of agony split my head in two. Outwardly I'm scrambling to my knees, but inside I'm lost, screaming soundlessly in a world of white silence. Daniel looks around wildly, then jumps to his feet. His eyes are dazed, blank and bloodshot. "Run. I'll find you. Wait for me," I say, then wonder why I bothered to say anything at all. My voice sounds garbled, wavy, and distorted.

He gives me a single, chilling glare, then spins on his heels and runs flat out for the huge, gothic interior of Styx. He heads for the south wing, where I know he's been ever since. I don't know why I call out to him—I don't know him at all. I don't know myself. Everything is a thousand shades of nothing, and coherent thought is violated and torn. I fall more than sit before I crab-crawl backward. I have no direction in mind, I just want to get away from the site of so much pain. My progress is abruptly halted when my head and back slam into the base of a tall statue.

Mom makes a small sound as she stands, then runs her hands down the front of her body as if she's searching for injuries. Her nose and ears are still bleeding. I feel no pity for her, no connection at all. She's a stranger. Dad stands, then grabs her arm and spins her to face him.

"Let go of me! Let go! You bastard, let go," she shrieks. Dad's eyes blink erratically. He opens his mouth to say something, but no words come—like me, he has none. Mom slaps his cheek. The sound is like a thunderclap in the quiet. The confusion on my father's face instantly morphs into rage. He shakes her violently, making her head snap back on her slender shoulders. Mom screams, she struggles hard, raking her nails across his face. Dad's strong, and he doesn't flinch as she tears his skin. She kicks and bites. Dad lifts his hand and strikes her across the face. Mom crumples. She hits the ground hard, smacking her left temple on a sharp rock. She doesn't move again. A pool of crimson expands around her head, like spilt ink in the gray storm light. Dad stares at her for only a second before his soulless eyes lift and lock on me. He starts toward me menacingly.

I try to stand, meaning to run, but my trembling legs refuse to hold me. I crash back to my knees, flinching as the rocks cut through my jeans. Dad reaches for me. A shot cracks the air. I jump and scream but don't look away from Dad's face as a black dot seems to magically appear between his hazel eyes. For a split second, a flash of recognition sparks in his gaze, then he falls, faster than my mother. Like her, when he takes a breath, it's his last.

I shudder and spin around to find the source of a shot. A woman dressed in a glimmering, gossamer gown stands beside a statue that bears her likeness. She has luminous, violet eyes and three heads. At the moment, her three heads don't strike me as particularly odd. Everything around me is known, yet unfamiliar. I exist in a world stuffed with confusing items I recognize but have no name for.

"Come inside, Divinica," the middle head says, her voice sounding like a song.

"That's your name, you stupid girl," the right head snaps in response to my blank, dazed stare.

"Hey, stupid girl. Wake up! Hey—"

The distant shout makes me blink. The world tilts, spins, settles. The sky above me returns to the miserable edition of its former self. I blink again to see an older version of Daniel and know I'm back.

"Shit! Finally!" Daniel shouts, relief flooding his eyes.

He's on the ground a couple feet away from me. A stream of blood flows from a cut on his forehead, and his lower lip is split in two places. Terror stabs my chest. "Daniel, I'm sorry, are you alright?"

"Do I look alright?" he hollers.

I try to reach out for him, only to realize my arms are pinned to the ground. I look up. The one lizard I left alive is on me, its leering glare blocking out the dying sun. A horrifying scaled face hovers inches from mine.

Its claws coast down my body, looking for more weapons, I assume. I stare at the sky, trying to find the smashed pieces of my strength and put them back together. The feel of the creature's hot, scaly hands touching me is ghastly. When it comes, seconds later, the smile that lifts my lips feels icy. The creature leans in to take a long sniff of my hair—gross times ten, but bearable because the action brings their head close enough for what I want. I jerk my body upward, then slam my forehead into the bridge of their nose with what feels like tremendous force. The bone breaks with a satisfying snap. Blood spews, coating my vision in thick, dripping green. The reptile screams. An almost comical expression of shock paints its flat, cratered face. Its yellow eyes snap and shift in their sockets.

"Surprise, asshole, thought I was dead, didn't you?" I jeer.

"I did," Daniel says. There's no time to trow back a snappy retort to my brother's dry wit, because my arms are finally free. I draw back a fist and let it fly. The hit is bolstered by every ounce of my confusion, sorrow, and rage. It howls when I knock out one of its teeth. It would be a lie to say my own strength doesn't shock the hell out of me, but I don't have much time to dwell on it. I hit the creature again and again and again. Finally, it falls, groaning pathetically. I'm gearing up for a killing blow, right to its solar plexus, but suddenly Daniel appears at the thing's back, holding his metal club above his head. I cringe as he brings it down on the reptile's skull with all his little boy strength, hollering out his own—rather chilling—war cry.

A moan escapes the thing's scabbed lips, which blends nicely with the fading echo of Daniel's shout. Daniel draws back his arm and hits again. Then again And again.

"They're already dead," I say, sitting up and dusting my hands.

"Never hurts to be sure," Daniel pants, glaring down at his bloody handiwork for a second before he strides over to kick the man with the broken nose in the gut. "Who the fuck are these guys?" Daniel asks. I almost say "Language," just like my mom did in my memory.

"The lizards? I don't know. The others, I think they're part of the Burning tribe, cannibals."

Daniel snorts. "Ugh. That's so real. I mean…I kinda feel them though. I've certainly been hungry enough. They killed the woman by the way. I checked, she's not breathing."

My teeth start to chatter, and I hug myself, only now realizing how badly I'm shaking. "What about the little girl?" I ask, glancing around.

"She's right over there," Daniel says, motioning with his chin to a nebulous spot behind him. Daniel glares at the bodies of the moaning and the dead. "Nice folks, great world, so happy to be a part of it," he says, each word dripping with disdain. He lifts an imaginary glass to the sky. "Here's to the hope of dying young." His voice is so cold, I have to bite my tongue to keep from snapping at him. How can I say anything? Who knows what he's had to do just to survive?

Suddenly, my head spins, and my hands hit the dirt in front of me. I stay like that for a while, just wheezing, trying to catch my breath. The feeling that memory has thrust upon me is toxic. Watching my parents die, then seeing her, that three-headed creature. That was really the kicker. The straw that broke the metaphorical camel's back. Fucking Hecate, seeing her literally holding the smoking gun that killed my dad shook me to my core. I bring my hands to the back of my neck and twist my head from side to side. That fucking flashback gave me whiplash. While I struggle to regain at least a modicum of control, a part of me wonders if I will complete whatever world-changing mission

Valance has planned for me in one piece. The possibility is highly unlikely, considering my current state. I lick my lips, and they feel like sandpaper. My mouth is unbearably dry, and I'm the idiot who didn't prime the pump. Chances are the water in my room tastes like crap.

"Hey, you gonna sit there all day covered in bad guy blood?" Daniel asks calmly as he wipes his club on some dead man's pants.

"I want to."

"Don't think we live in a place where want has anything to do with it. I want to play video games, remember those?"

"I do, actually, though I'm surprised you do."

Daniel shrugs. "Memories and words come and go. I try not to think much about them." He sighs. "Well, get up then. I should warn you though, I feel like shit, and I'm still standing, so if you fall, I will laugh."

His mockery snaps me out of my session of self-despair. I roll my eyes at him and stand in one smooth move.

Daniel lifts a brow as he takes in my accomplishment. "You're really proud of yourself for pulling that off, aren't you?"

"Yes, actually. You have no idea how difficult that was. My legs feel like jelly."

"Well, to be fair, I have no idea who jelly is."

"It's not a person, it's something you eat."

"Maybe something *you* eat. Me? He stabs a thumb into his chest. "I try to stay away from eating people—best I can anyway."

I cross my arms and seal my lips before this tit for tat digresses, or before I tell him he's rubber and he assures me that he is in fact glue. "You're incorrigible," I finally say.

Daniel's brilliant smile is blinding. "Thanks, I like to think so," he says, then offers me his arm, surprising us both. "It's not gonna bite. Take it before you fall, I'll help you inside."

A bolt of feeling lurches through me, my eyes start to sting, and I blink rapidly to make it stop. It's a battle to fight the swirling emotions begging me to wrap my arms around him and give him the hug of his life. I take his arm in silence, worried to meet his eyes for fear there are tears in mine. He's grown so much in the last—what? Two years...has it really been so long? *Two years that I don't remember, strange that I still feel their loss,* I think. But I must've said something out loud, because Daniel gives me a weird look as we ascend the cracked tile stairs that lead to Styx. At the top of the stairs, I stop. "Give me a sec," I say and look over my shoulder. The child is still kneeling beside the dead woman with a lost expression of abject confusion painting her teary face.

"What?" Daniel grumbles, as he comes to an abrupt halt beside me.

"We have to help her."

Daniel's response is to throw up a brow. "Why? She's no good to anyone. Just stood there and wailed when those men attacked. Useless. This place will swallow her whole, sooner if we do nothing, a little later if we try to help. If you ask me, she's nothing more than death walking."

I let go of his arm, mildly shocked despite it all. "Geez, Daniel, that's dark."

"It's the truth. Doesn't mean I like it, it's just how it is."

I shake my head. "I would say don't let troubles take your humanity, but I have my doubts that you were born with much to begin with."

Daniel shrugs. "Good. That's probably why I'm still alive."

I lean back a little, to get a decent look at his face, and realize he's nothing like the kind, annoying little boy from my shining memory. He's hard now, no more teasing smiles. Unflinching. My gaze goes back to the girl. I won't say it out loud, but he's probably right, about everything. "We have to do something anyway," I sigh. Instantly, my mind goes to Valance. In that moment, his face is all I can see. My mind trips back to my previous encounter with him. Of all the memories I had to lose, the memory of being rejected by that man is the one I get to keep, at least until the next wave comes to take it away. *Fucking classic.*

I round on Daniel. "Stay here. Watch her, and don't move until I get back."

Daniel folds a set of rebellious arms across his chest, then throws me a look of defiance so fierce it's almost funny. "You can't just bark out a bunch of orders and expect I'll—"

"Please," I say softly, looking into his big, brown eyes, their shape so identical to mine.

Daniel throws up his hands. "Fine," he says, trying to sound pained, but his shoulders seem suddenly lighter, and I can sense the slightest crack in his bravado.

"Whatever. Fake pout all you want, you didn't want to leave her either," I say as I walk away, intentionally moving too quickly to hear his muttered response.

I walk into Styx and march down the drafty hall, hoping I'm doing the right thing and not setting myself up for more of that burning, maddening, intoxicating pain just being near Valance invokes. I spin around a few times before I spot a tiny, black ball in the upper corner near the staircase, which leads down to the lab. I stare into the coin-sized glass eye, finally recognizing the device for what it is. There's a small, red light blinking at the base, and I look directly at it. "If you can hear me, oh mighty Skylord, please come to Styx, there's someone here who needs you," I say, feeling ridiculous. Honestly, the man is insufferable even when he's not around. It really is like I'm praying to some invisible god—damn him.

The light blinks green, then flickers three times. I know it's a sign from my god. He heard my prayer and help is on the way. A warm sense of peace I don't want to feel courses through me. If I come to truly depend on him, what will I do when I'm alone once again? Regardless of what I want, as I walk back to Daniel, the peace remains. Then, since the moment I woke in a panic, I finally take my first deep breath.

CHAPTER SIXTEEN

I believe that when you die, memories are the only currency that becomes priceless

I'm sitting on the front steps beside Daniel, and the girl he decided to call Hope. Neither of us had any words of comfort for her, so we opted to sit in stony silence listening to her cry through a river of snotty tears. Daniel's nose bled like a faucet earlier, and now his head rests on my shoulder. It feels so wonderful that in this moment I might be able to vaguely comprehend the concept of heaven, of beauty, peace, and a single moment without fear. He did it a few minutes ago, unconsciously I think, because I felt him flinch when his cheek touched my skin. Neither of us commented on the awkward moment, but neither did we pull away.

Just sitting with him like this, at the end of the world, is perfect. In the silence we can both pretend that none of the awful things—some of which I'm only now remembering—ever transpired at all. I want so badly to blurt out that he's my brother, tell him I know what happened to Mom and Dad, confess I remember watching them die, and could probably find their bodies under the statue of the three-headed woman, now that I know what I'm looking for, or that I'm looking for anything at all. I gnaw my lips to keep the words in and wonder silently how the hell we both survived. I think about it long and hard until I see the dust cloud approaching from the east, signaling the return of my sky god.

All three of us stair-top critters stand to meet him. Daniel watches Valance—sitting tall in the saddle of his own Rade—barrel down on us with his usual glare of disdain, and Hope's sobbing increases in volume. Me? I'm breathless as hell.

Valance is shirtless beneath his NASA bomber jacket. I understand that compilation of letters now.

Valance quickly closes the distance between us. I love the way his thick hair slaps his jaw with each bounce and heave of the Rade's pendulous belly. His Rade wears armor like I've never seen. Strangely, the metal is molded to him, almost as if it's part of the creature's thick skin. As they get closer, I notice the stubble on Valance's jaw looks much thicker than when we kissed. *How long was I sleeping?* Valance vaults from his saddle, completes a near superhero landing, and runs to crush me in his arms.

I allow the hug for several beats, then step back to keep looking at him. He's as savage as this land. His eyes are twin lights, their visible heat contrasting sharply with the cool pallor of his face. He flexes, then fists his hands before running them through his wind-tousled hair.

"What the fuck happened?" he finally blurts. "You're covered in blood and looked half-crazed on the cam." He rubs his chest. "I know I'm fairly young, but I swear my heart can't take this shit."

"I'm fine," I say. "I heard a woman screaming, she woke me up...I was sleeping...I think I...I tried to help. Daniel and I, we had them. Truly, but then —" My voice breaks. I bite my lower lip to keep from screaming as my parents' bloody bodies flash once again before my eyes. I tell myself, *Be strong, Divinica, don't show fear, be strong.* "Shut the fuck up, I'm doing my best," I mutter beneath my breath.

"Beg your pardon?" Valance asks, that tell-tale brow raised.

I shake my head, gnawing at my lip until I taste blood.

Valance steps closer. "Then what, Divinica?" Another step, then another, ever closer, like he's being compelled.

Still, I give him no reply. I want to spend at least five minutes in this man's company without sounding like a crazy girl who belongs in this asylum I call home. I decide to go with a simpler truth. "The things that I just fought. I don't...I don't know what they were."

"We call them the Reptilians," he says simply, then holds up his hands. "I know, it's a bit on the nose."

"Have I ever fought them before?"

"I don't think so, at least not since I've known you. They didn't used to come out this way. They stay mainly on the fringes of big cities, picking off the weak. The lonely. Trimming down the herd. They're getting braver though, branching out of their sewers and caves more often. Dead humans mean more Earth for them. I think they might be trying to speed up the destruction, but I don't know how. Rashid thinks we should let them have it, the Earth, that is."

I look at the desolate wasteland around us, the sprawled bodies of the creatures I killed pouring more blood into an earth already drenched in it. "Where did they come from?"

"Fuck if I know facts, but were I to make an intelligent guess, I'd say they've always been here. Biding their time, waiting until humans obliterate themselves. Sightings and drawings of Reptilians spiral all the way back to Egyptian times, older even. Some say they were the first sentient beings to ever live. They trended hard at the turn of the twentieth century, when people and drones started snapping photos of them. The United States government threw around words like 'hoax' and 'conspiracy theory,' but cameras rarely lie. A week after I first met you, Dayle and I went to Munich for supplies and ran into a group of them. They fight like born villains, and those tails can take you the fuck out. I couldn't believe what I was seeing for the first few minutes, which made me take a couple of unnecessary hits to the face. I couldn't fight back. I could hardly think. My mind just short-circuited. Some are more human in aspect. I know one, a princess, or so she claims, in the right light and she could almost be—" Valance tilts his head as his eyes narrow thoughtfully. "This shit is wild no doubt," Valance says. "Then again, you ride a two-ton Teletubby that used to be microscopic. Giant lizards are scary, but not enough to paint that expression on your face."

I tense, still not ready to talk about my dead parents. "What expression?"

"Never mind," he rasps, then reaches for me. I try to push him away. If he touches me again, I'll remember what happened between us and I'll break, pass out, or burst into tears. Actually, the thought of doing all three is captivating.

Valance bats my protesting hands aside, locks his arm behind my knees, and before I can blink, lifts me in his arms. Gods above, I want to struggle, but it feels so good just being held by him.

"You look terrible," he tells me.

I gasp my outrage. "You look terrible—" I mutter, lying.

"Oh, good one," Daniel says.

"I hate seeing you covered in blood," he says. Valance takes the first few steps two at a time, then pauses to call over his shoulder. "Daniel, get the girl and find her something to eat, yeah? She looks like a starving kitten."

"Sure does," Daniel sighs, but surprisingly obeys.

"I don't need you to carry me," I say, sounding like a stubborn child yet praying to all that's holy that he doesn't put me down.

"Who says I'm doing this for you?" Valance asks, the sexy, rough tone of his voice making his words feel like a caress. My mouth goes dry, and my palms start to sweat—a weird combo. He strides down the narrow hall, kicks open the door to my room, then walks in like he owns it. He sets me down on my bed, and before I come to grips with his electrifying, life-altering touch, he lets go to pierce me with that intense stare of his. "Don't move," he breathes, then stands up and walks a few feet to my bathroom, only to reemerge seconds later. "You forgot to prime the pump," he says, a smile in his eyes and no hint of a question in his tone.

"Yes, I judged myself for it earlier, don't make me do it again." I kick off my boots and lie down on a heavy sigh. "There's a jug of water by the window," I tell him.

Valance looks at my pathetic jug, and the smile in his eyes starts to flirt with his lips. "Bet my life it tastes like shit. Poor babe, you must want a bath."

"More than anything in this wretched world," I assure him.

I close my eyes when I hear his low chuckle. He's gone for a moment, and I listen to his footsteps cross the room, pause, then make their way back to me.

"Sit up, love," he says. I open my eyes and see him kneeling beside the bed. I do as he says, swinging my legs over my lumpy mattress and letting them drop. His hands go to my knees, and my gasp sounds like breaking glass.

"Be calm, I'm not going to hurt you." He pulls my knees apart and moves between them. My world stops spinning.

I catch his gaze. "I'm not afraid of you, Valance," I whisper. My breath rustles the hair at his temple. His jaw locks with a click, and it feels like the very air between us starts to boil. We stare at each other for long seconds, our mouths close enough for kissing. But before anything happens, he breaks the connection, his eyes dropping to the floor. He reaches into his back pocket and pulls out a bright-red bandana.

"You really are just a cowboy in the wrong country, aren't you," I say. His head snaps up.

"What?" I blurt.

"Nothing, it's just that you always say that to me minutes before you remember me, remember everything."

"Do I?"

Valance nods slowly, his smoldering gaze all tangled up with mine. We aren't breathing at all steadily. "Yes, call me sentimental, but those words to me are the most magical part of this otherwise fucked-up déjà vu we've been forced to relive, time and time again."

Maybe it's his voice, perhaps it's his eyes, but I want to touch him, I have to. I reach out and brush my fingertips down the hard slash of his jaw. Valance closes his eyes. His parted lips are only inches from mine. Fuck me, he's beautiful, golden, spellbinding. "I thought you just shaved," I whisper, stroking his cheek up to the high arch of his brow.

"Three days ago," he says, moving away from my thirsty touch. He reaches for the water and pours a wasteful amount onto the bandana.

"Three days? What are you talking about?"

"You have a tendency to sleep, Divinica."

"Don't most humans?"

"Not like you. There've been times when I was afraid you would never wake up."

"Are you serious?"

"Yes, at least ninety percent of the time," Valance says, smiling. I smack his arm. He shrugs. "My theory is it's the goddesses in you. They were a famously exhausted bunch. Had a penchant for sleeping through millennia now and then." Valance starts to gently wipe at the blood on my face while I try to process his words.

"What do you mean, the goddesses in me? Like *in me* in me?"

"I think a part of them exists in you, yes. Over the last two years, I've seen you do some pretty crazy things."

"Things? Like what?"

"Well, you're ridiculously strong. Do you think I haven't tried to put a stop to all the stabbings? First few attacks took me by surprise. I was expecting all the others, and it hurts to admit you kicked my ass with ease. Shit, girl, when you get in those moods you could take me down in a fair fight with one hand tied behind your back, especially in the last six months. You read hieroglyphics like an expert—" Valance's words drop off as he pauses in the act of wiping a drying clump of blood from the curve of my neck. He sets the bandana on his thigh so he can press the pad of his thumb to my lower lip, the pressure feeling like a kiss. "There have been times, moments when you touch me, want me—" His voice drops off, he swallows hard, then continues, "I'm not too proud to say I've never once been able to resist the intoxicating spell of you. Somehow in this madness we created something sacred. Together we are chaos, and it's perfect."

"You let me go the other night," I mutter.

"No, I held on too long. I haven't been able to think about anything but you since the second you rode away. I've wanted you so bad these past few days, it's been damn near torture."

"Three days," I whisper, finally putting the pieces together. The second I understand, fear turns my blood to liquid ice. "The wave—"

Valance nods. "Soon," he tells me, and I watch the emotion in his eyes change from one of desire to being haunted.

"How long?"

"An hour, to be precise," he says, and the words sound like a death sentence. Valance leans down to pick up the bandana and starts to wipe at the blood on my forehead again. I knock his hand away.

"An hour! Why didn't you lead with that?" I can't help the unreasonable anger that surges through me, anger at everything, anger I choose to direct at him. "You shouldn't have come. What if the wave makes me mental and I try to stab you again? Ugh! No, no, *noooo*!" I wail.

Valance grabs my waving hands and pulls them to his chest. "I'll take my chances."

"I'll forget you, and Daniel, Rashid, Dayle, Mom, and Dad, the life we had." I jump to my feet and start to pace, too agitated to stay still. I chart the circumference of my small room in a few jerky seconds.

Valance slowly stands, then puts the bandana back in his pocket. "Divinica—"

"No! I don't want this!" I shriek. "Don't look at me like that, I know I sound like an angry child, but I don't care." I'm gasping so hard, my breaths are a series of distorted, wheezing coughs. The room starts to spin in the same second those horrible black spots cloud my vision, like a bad rash. I can't breathe, can't calm down. Soon more of that mental silence will come for me, those miles of empty white space that smother my soul in endless nothingness. That knowledge scares me more than fire, more than the star door and all the monsters that lurk beyond.

"I remember the last wave, you weren't here, I was alone and then...Daniel. You left me."

Valance's arms come around me, and I feel his lips brush the underside of my jaw. "It was a mistake. One I won't make again. I'm sorry, I'm so sorry, baby."

I wipe my face. "Why? Why did you leave?" Even as I'm saying the words, I know I shouldn't ask, shouldn't feel that he and I were meant to be together beyond death. But I do. I really do.

"We got close last time, so close. I tried to stay away, I thought maybe if mine wasn't the last face you saw, then—"

"What? I wouldn't come and find you?" I ask, pulling back against the hold of his arms to see his face.

"It was a fucking stupid theory. The private hell I designed for myself was all for nothing."

"Because it didn't work?"

"No, it didn't."

"Shocker!" Maybe it's the pain, or maybe it's him, but I'm suddenly angry as hell. I shove myself away from him. He lets me go but stays close as I march across my room and out the door.

"Where the devil do you think you're going, Divinica? You need to lie the fuck down."

"Is that what I need? Fuck you, Valance! What I need is for you to stop telling me what to do. What I need are some goddamn answers." I take the stairs leading down to the lab three at a time. When I stop and spin around, Valance is nearly on top of me, his big body blocking out the meager light flowing from the shifty staircase bulb. He's panting, we both are.

"I'm sorry," he says before I can spit out all the hateful words on my tongue.

I swallow hard but don't relent. "You're a coward."

He flinches, and anger finally washes over his face, bringing a slash of red to his cheekbones. "Divinica, last time if I had stayed with you for five more minutes, I would have ripped off your clothes with my teeth and fucked you until you forgot me," he growls.

I know his words are meant to hurt or warn, but my knees go weak, and I grab onto the metal table in the center of the room for support as he keeps talking, getting closer as his voice rises.

"I want you more than anything in the world, and have, I might add, for quite some time, but I can't act on it, not with the way things are. It's loss that's always taught me the worth of things. I've lost you a shit ton of times, Divinica, and I've come to learn that you're priceless. Along with your memories, the wave removes your freedom of choice. You don't know me. Not really. Thirteen days isn't enough time to make an informed decision, and that's all we ever have, darling."

I swallow at his words.

"I could be any random guy spitting pretty lines to get you in my bed. You would never know, not until it's too late. For you it's only been thirteen days, regardless that it's actually been two years, and you usually don't give me a chance until the eighth or ninth day. Then you start to remember, and at some point, invariably, we have this conversation. I'm no saint. One day I'll give in, and then you'll hate me." His eyes shine with a moisture that looks suspiciously like tears. "Up until the other night, I thought I couldn't live with myself if I did that to you. You are young, innocent, and a guy like me shouldn't be your first. But right now, all my good intentions are going to hell. I've wanted you so badly for so long, it's become an obsession. You're in all my thoughts, the unreachable quest in my every dream, but you're a virgin with a serious case of amnesia, and only a villain would take advantage of that."

"Well, you and you alone have the power to remedy at least one of those misfortunes," I say tartly. He opens his mouth to reply, but I hold up my hand. "You know, I wasn't going to tell you, because it sucks, and I'm not sure how to properly explain it, but I was forced to relive my parents' death today, and I'm fairly sure it wasn't for the first time. I don't know who I used to be before this world went to shit, but I deserve a good memory, at least one, and I want it with you."

"That's just the point. It's not a memory you can keep," he snarls.

I want to tell him I won't make the offer again, but it's probably a lie, so I keep the words behind my tightly pressed lips. I turn away from him and run my fingers over the still shiny surface of the cold, metal table that dominates the old lab. "I remember this table," I say absently. "You kissed me here once, maybe twice. Hecate brought me here after she shot my dad. First, I was confused, then scared. I kept asking what was happening, Hecate told me to lie on this table. The right head had only creepy smiles for me when I obeyed. I don't know why I obeyed. I was shaking, I wanted to run. I couldn't. The left head kept staring. Her eyes were huge, black pools, mesmerizing but so terrible. My stomach felt like it was falling in slow motion, all the way down to my numb toes."

"Yes, like spacewalking without a cable."

I glance up at him for a second before my eyes are dragged back to the table. "If you say so. Hecate undressed me, and I just stared stupidly up at that light and waited for it to be over. Then, she told me something like, I would probably die because all the others had. I didn't know what she meant. I still don't. She set thirteen glowing triangles around my body. Electricity started surging between the triangles. I didn't make a single sound of protest as she rolled me onto my side and stuck a ten-inch needle into the base of my spine. The pain was sharp and shocking. I screamed and tried to roll off the table. I couldn't move. I was frozen from the neck down. That's when I started to scream in earnest. The right head's smile turned savage.

"Hecate lifted another, thicker iron needle. I remember the tiny symbols carved into its surface. They glowed like distant stars. She picked up a small hammer from her metal tray of terrifying implements, dipped the needle into a pot of black ink, then used the hammer to drive the tip of the needle into my skin. The pain started slowly, like holding your hand over a candle flame, but the more she tapped the ink into my skin the more the pain grew until that's all there was. I was weak. It only took a few hours for me to beg her to stop. Beg her to kill me. Anything was better than the lancing, electric agony that came with each one of her steady taps." I open my eyes and look at Valance. "The right head never stopped smiling. It took hours, days, maybe, to create my tattoos."

"Yes, you've told me before. Interesting how I hate it a little more each time.

From all your recollections I've heard over the years, I think I've been able to piece together what happened. I'll tell you everything, or as much as I can, if you really want to know."

"Of course I want to know!" I shout.

"Fine. The short of it is, some chit with three heads used the implements and artifacts in an old Nazi army base to genetically alter you enough to traverse time. Your father was a scientist, quite well known. I looked him up a few days after I met you, and I studied all his work. He said the pollution and its effect on Earth's temperature would eventually trigger what he called 'the savior device,' a global reset, if you will. He thought he'd pinpointed its detonation location with a map he created using stones circles and the stars. Many of his theories were widely discredited by mainstream scientists, but social media believed him. He had millions of views on all his videos. He tried to warn everyone, but people are always blind to what they don't want to see. The negative press didn't seem to dissuade him. He came all the way from California to Germany, and he brought you. You were the one Hecate wanted. I think it's possible she gave him all the information to substantiate his theories in the first place. He was a genius, but it was you, Divinica Starr, who she was truly after. That's the simplified version. Rashid has a far more complicated explanation."

"She killed my dad, and she almost killed me." I remember the way that smoking black hole opened right between Dad's eyes, and my endless hours of torment at her hands.

"You weren't the first girl Hecate tried to make alterations on. From what you've told me, thousands have died over the centuries when their bodies rejected the forced change. By some magic, you managed to survive."

His words strike a series of chords in my brain, and my ears start ringing an offbeat, high-pitched sound. Suddenly, I'm seeing Valance, really seeing him for the first time since Micha dragged me from Boogles to lay me at the Skylord's feet. He's right. My father was all those things and more. "I gave you my father's full name, I showed you my passport. It's in my purse, under my bed. I have a purse, and a phone, oh my god!" I close my eyes and shake my head. I remember everything. My name is Divinica Starr, I was born in California, Alyssa and Frank Starr were my mother and father. We came here for spring break to chase another one of Dad's theories. Holy crap. I can't believe he was actually right! The savior device was real. I feel as if I'm having an out-of-body experience as it rushes back, all of it, stupid little memories, foolish human things that come attached with so much emotion it almost drives me to my knees. I sway.

Valance catches my elbows and holds me steady while a host of other memories lay siege to my mind. I remember how heavy my backpack was through middle school and recall skateboarding at the pier on sizzling summer days, cramming for my tests all through junior year, and kissing a senior boy I liked on the front porch of our beach house, then getting caught by my mother and having to listen to her tirade on safe sex for hours. I remember every iota of Mom's face, each detail clearer than the last. Each beautiful thing that made her comes rushing back, and the pain of her loss is sudden and deep. I can almost smell her vanilla perfume in the air. More details resurface, until it seems my whole life is flashing in an organized, coherent sequence through my mind.

I know exactly who I am, or who I was anyway. I also know it's all about to be taken away. Again. Valance must see the shattered look in my eyes, because his jaw locks and his hands reach for me. Just before he touches me, his fingers clench into fists that fall back to his sides. "Divinica," he breathes, and that's all it takes, just my name spoken in his husky, Southern tones I now remember so well.

"I know you," I say, clearly able to visualize the moment I saw him step out of that smoking ship. It's because of him I've chosen not to take my own life, like so many others—even his own mother—have done. He's the sole reason I'm breathing. The deep shock of the moment makes my voice shake as I whisper the three words again. *"I know you."*

Valance blinks twice, then his eyes harden into chips of flint. I can literally see him withdrawing from me. "Wave's almost here then," he says.

Knowing all that has passed between us, I understand his reticence and fear, really. I get why he wants to stay away from me, but it still makes me livid. "Did you hear me? I remember you, Valance, remember us." I reach for him, but he steps back, putting distance between us. I close it with a single step. "The day we first met, I followed the Storm tribe to the base of the Alps. I watched you fall from the sky. You stepped out of your ship and looked right at me."

"You were the first thing I saw," he says, so quiet I almost don't hear him.

"God! Oh my god, Daniel!" My hands fly up like I can find him in the thin air.

He captures both my hands. I can feel us both shaking. "No, it's okay. He's okay. Rashid and Dayle have him. He's safe as he can be."

The moment I touch him, so much comes back all at once, it's crazy. Every moment with him, every fight, every tear, every touch. How could I have ever forgotten someone like him? Like forgetting the air in your lungs or the sound of your own heartbeat. "Valance! I've missed you so much."

"I've missed you too, baby," the admission sounding like it was dragged from the depths of a broken heart. He drops my hands, but they rush to touch his face. I don't let him pull away. I kiss his cheeks, his eyes, the corner of his mouth. "I remember the first time you kissed me. It was the night before I turned eighteen. We were sitting on your throne, I curled in your lap, and you said kissing me was a crime."

"You told me, there are no more crimes left at the end of the world."

"It was a good kiss."

"Best of my life, well, up until that point."

I can't stop staring at his face. Every detail of him. so vivid in my mind, from first sight to this moment. He's always been there for Daniel and me over the long years, like a guardian angel or a benevolent god. "You're wrong. It isn't the same thirteen days. They change in all the ways that matter. I've gotten to know you over the years. You're smart, strong, you care when you don't have to, help when you shouldn't. You fight like a born warrior and kiss like a god. You've taken care of me and my brother like we were your own. I remember you, Valance, you're the love of my life."

Valance runs a hand through his hair, his eyes spark, and I can almost see the exact moment his control snaps. "Oh, fuck me," he groans, then squeezes my hand and pulls me close until my body crashes against his chest. He cups my head in his hand before his mouth meets mine. My lips part because they must. He tilts his head, and his tongue licks between my lips. I love the taste of him, the way it's always felt like I've known him for a thousand years. I see him and understand the man behind all that brawn, the astronaut who walked unscathed out of the smoking ship that brought him from another world back into mine.

I practically climb his body, needing to get closer. My legs wrap his waist, and I lock my ankles. His chest is bare, rising and falling hard with each of his labored breaths. I'm surrounded by the smell and feel of him, and I'm so fucking lost. My world narrows to that single point of focus. Him, always him.

I run my hands over his chest, feel his muscles clench and flex, then sink my fingers into his hair. Valance breaks the kiss and leans back to look in my eyes. I love the way our hearts pound in rhythm when we're like this. It's as if we've somehow locked onto the pulse of the Earth, as if in these rare moments, the world is only ours. His fingers find the pull of my zipper and slowly lower it. Our proximity drags the tips of my breasts across his chest. They ache, I ache. I am cinder and flesh, melting ice and scalding lava. "Don't you dare stop this time."

Valance's gaze locks on the shaky rise and fall of my breasts. "I won't, not this time. I don't think I can. Let me take you to your bed, at least there—"

"No! Fuck that. I won't give you a chance to change your mind."

"Divinica, I haven't lived a single moment of wanting anyone but you. Like I said, I'm no saint. Far from it. What I need with you is wicked."

I'm the one who kisses him this time, grabbing handfuls of his hair and tugging his head back down to mine. His lips are ambrosia, and I'm dizzy and drunk on the taste of him. Valance rocks his hips, and I can feel every hard inch of him pressing against me. He moves again. The friction of our bodies makes me shake. As his fingers skate across the underside of my breast, my world is a kaleidoscope of glittering prisms. His name leaves my mouth on a sigh. "Please," I beg, not caring that I think begging is for losers. I find the zipper on my romper and slowly tug it down past my navel.

"Fine, have it your way," he says, lifting me, then setting me on the cold table. "I'm not strong enough to walk away from this again. Fucking ironic."

"What is?" I ask.

"I wait two years trying to find the perfect time and place, only to finally take you covered in blood on this table of horrors."

"I don't care," I say, then scoot back to make room for him. He climbs up beside me and leans down to kiss me. Our lips never meet. The earth starts to shake, hard enough to make the whole lab rattle like an old bell. The quake ends as suddenly as it began, but we both know what it means. The timer has officially started on the reset clock. Our eyes meet and hold, the air between our lips is full of all the words we can't say. I study the shape of his mouth, the strong dips and plains of his face. Memorizing all the things I love before they are so cruelly wrenched away. The reality of what's coming permeates the air with black veins of poisonous doom, and I choke on it. We're going to lose each other again, it's only a matter of time.

CHAPTER SEVENTEEN

Twenty minutes to go

Valance sits back on his heels. I rest my chin on my elbows and stare up at him. Moments and tremble, and for a time, the look in his eyes is the primary substance of my world. His gaze finally breaks from mine and moves down my body. I scramble up trying to cover my rather large breasts with one hand, kind of failing.

"Well, if that wasn't the mother of all mood killers," I say, my voice as shaky as the recent quake.

Valance makes a squelched, coughing sound, then starts to laugh. I do too. I think in moments like this it's laugh or cry. We're both so scared and tired, even though neither of us will admit it. We're still burning from what we almost did on this table, panting, wanting. All these things, combined with the spiking adrenaline, make us laugh until we're both gasping and wiping tears from our eyes. We try to breathe through the emotional spasm, but every time we look at each other it starts all over again.

"You know, for two souls suffering cosmic loss on the reg, you're both *really* holding it together," I hear Rashid say. I glance across the room to find him standing at the base of the stairs, hands shoved in the pockets of his tight jeans, looking as sassy as his voice.

Maybe it's the joking twist to his lips, but I can't help it. I laugh so hard I wheeze. Rashid walks over to us, thumbs hooked through his belt buckles. "I'm taking Daniel and the girl back to camp before the wave hits. You guys good?"

"No. We're not, but I remember you, Rashid. I missed you," I say, still catching my breath.

"Sheeit, girl, I would lean in for a hug, but you're topless, and I think it would be the best way to get a punch in the face. We're leaving now, you can ride back with Valance."

My brow goes up. I look at Valance, but he's studying the table. "Are you taking me with you?"

"I want to try something else. Maybe if I'm the first thing you see, maybe if I tell you everything the second the red wave passes, maybe that'll change things."

"Alright, I'm down. You gonna tie me up or take away my knife?"

Valance lifts his head, eyes flaring. "Maybe both."

"Well, you two can argue out the kinky particulars. I gotta go. The wave is almost here." Rashid tips his cap to me, then turns to Valance. "Protect our girl."

"With my life," Valance says, and nothing has ever sounded more like a vow.

I blow Rashid a kiss, then listen to the airy *click-clack* of his footsteps recede. Valance and I spend the next few moments in charged silence. "You always look at me like that," I say when I notice him staring.

"Like what?"

"Like I'm the only food for miles."

Valance shrugs. "I've never loved anything in my life the way I love you." He puts a finger to my lips when I open them to say something. "I want to see you summon the star door," he says, shocking me.

"You do? Why?"

"Why not? It's unbelievable, magical, and an intrinsic piece of who you are. Would you mind?"

"No, I don't think so. Do we have time?"

"We have a little over twenty minutes to go. Why? How much time do you need?"

"Couldn't tell you. Time's broken for me, remember?"

"Always, baby. It's my curse." He tugs on a lock of my hair, then tucks it behind my ear before he leans close to press his lips to the tattoo burning in the center of my forehead. His lips feel like home. I close my eyes on a sigh.

"Alright, if that's what you want," I say.

"Sweet!" He kisses me again, then jumps off the table, lithe as a lynx. Smiling, he scoops his jacket off the floor and shrugs it on. He's all lean hardness and bunching muscle. It's difficult to decide where to look. My eyes run the length of his chiseled stomach. When my gaze reaches the waistband of his dark jeans, I notice the top three buttons are undone. My mouth goes instantly dry, and I lick my lips. I'm forced to drop my eyes before I reach for him again. I resist my hormones because he's right. As earth-shattering as I assume sleeping with him would be, the afterward—living a half-life, tormented by the permeating white silence so void of him—would really suck. Now that his hands and lips aren't bewitching my body and mind, it's possible for me to think with a modicum of rationality, and the truth is, I want him for more than twenty minutes.

Valance buckles his pants with quick fingers and winks when he catches me looking. I drop my eyes, blushing. He clears his throat. "Divinica, your hand isn't big enough to cover those gorgeous breasts of yours, not by half. You'd best put them away, darling, before I realize there's always another time to watch you tumble through a shit ton of stars."

"You read my notebook," I accuse.

"Not all of it. Your notebook was just lying open on your bed the night I carried you back to your room, begging to be read."

"The night you stormed out," I say, then remember the reason for his departure. Now that I know all that we are to each other, the idea of letting another man touch me, in any world, any time, makes me miserable. A new hatred at my situation twists my gut. I jump off the table before I say something stupid, and my hand slips.

I hear Valance groan. The sound is heartfelt. He reaches me in two long strides. I catch and hold my breath when he touches me. Gently, he helps stuff my stubborn breasts into the tight romper.

"Thank fuck this material stretches," he says, his voice rough as tires over gravel. When the zipper is just beneath the curve of my cleavage, Valance pauses. My breath deserts me like an unfaithful lover as he lifts a finger and traces an invisible line between my breasts. "You're like a siren, Divinica." His whisper is low, sensual, drugging. "Sometimes I don't think you're real. Maybe the wave did affect me, it's just that the walls of my prison are a little different. Perhaps you're the most gorgeous chains ever made, and the most dangerous. I would die a million times just to kiss you. Stay trapped for eternity if it meant I could touch you."

I can't speak. I want to remember him, imprint every single iota of him onto my traitorous mind, so that even when I forget, I'll always know him. He cups the back of my neck at the same time I go up on my tiptoes. Our lips meet with a bang. With a clash. With a clap of stormy thunder. With a catastrophic boom that ruptures the soul of my personal universe. His kiss is rough and intimate. I think this is our tenth kiss. Ten kisses with a man like this in two years, it just doesn't seem fair. I lean into him, wrap my arms around his neck, and wish for the moment to never end.

CHAPTER EIGHTEEN

A touch to die for

The earth shakes again, this quake more dramatic than the last. I lean back when it's over and look at him. "Valance—" My lips are dry, my fingertips like chips of ice. I can't finish whatever I was going to say. All I can think is, *It's coming, it's coming, it's coming, it's coming, it's fucking coming.* I part my lips to say something, anything, but the only sounds that emerge are strangled noises of pure pain.

I'll forget him again in moments, something powerful and unseen will reach into my mind and rip out this guy I adore. Soon, I'll blink the purple dust from my eyes, stare up at his perfect face, and wonder if he's a villain or a god. I know now why there isn't more written about him in my notebook. It's not that I don't have a thousand descriptive words storming my mind, my heart, begging to pour out of my fingers…it's just that by the time I remember, it's already too late. Too late to write, too late to think, too late to do anything but scream silently, fade slowly, hemorrhage eternally until I am ashes in a tornado, scattered, hopeless, lost.

There's nothing I can do. It's always too late. Everything I am, everything I know and love, will be ripped away again, and I will be a void of loneliness, waiting for and wanting what I don't know, trying to breathe, hoping to die.

Valance doesn't say anything, no admonition to be brave, no words of comfort, no false hopes or empty promises. We both know what we know. It's coming. Nothing is going to be okay. The truth is so huge and loud, there is no place for kind lies. Panic is seizing my lungs, and I want to fall to my knees and cry until my tears flood the Earth.

Last time the wave came I was with Daniel, and I told him I would never forget, but I did. The red waves made a liar out of me. The time before that I was in Valance's arms, crying buckets at the injustice of it all, cursing the gods of the past, damning the goddesses—using every foul word in my vocabulary to strike at whatever power ruthlessly locked me to this wretched fate. The time before that, Valance and I were on our knees just outside of Styx, between the statues of the goddesses with stone skin and vacant eyes. We were kissing when the sky blackened, then burned, burned, and burned until it turned my soul to cinders and my love to ash.

All the memories of all the waves are my noisy companions: Valance, Daniel, Valance, Daniel, Valance, Valance, Valance. My heart is breaking, tearing along old scars. "I can't, Valance, I can't. I can't go through it again. I'm not strong enough. I look for you in the pain, hold onto your name through the dark, say it repeatedly, only to lose you in the endless miles of white silence. In the silence I miss something, so badly it tears me apart. Not knowing it's you...not knowing what the hell it is makes the agony so much wo...wo...worse." I realize I'm sobbing tears of fear, regret, and a sadness so deep it slices through all that I am and leaves me in bloody pieces. The pain is an acid needle stabbing some vital artery.

Valance makes a deep sound in his chest. He sits on the edge of the table, places his hand on my waist, and drags me toward him. I flow over his legs like water, wrap my arms around his neck, and hold him. *Hold him, hold him, hold him.*

I bury my tear-smeared face in the curve of his hot neck, then count the seconds as he rocks me. He's holding so tight it's almost painful, but I don't care. I'll take any pain if it means I can keep him. I can't let go. I won't. *Not yet. Not yet, not yet, not yet, please, not yet.*

Valance touches my skin and wipes my tears as I stare into his eyes. I see what he feels, and feel more than I thought possible. Every emotion, every fear. Anger, helplessness, heartbreak, and worst of all, resignation. That last one kills me. It tells me there is no one coming to save us. No government agents or police with flashing lights and big guns. Those things are gone. Everything is gone. "Divinica, I swear I'll never stop trying to break the savior device. Never. The hope of you is why I'm alive. You're my light. When you forget me, it's always night. Full dark, no stars."

"I'm scared," I tell him and wonder why some words in the English language are so diluted and pale. Words like *love, pain, fear*. How can such small, nondescript words possibly describe such indescribable emotions? Feelings larger than the endless mass of space all shoved into four little letters—it's stupid and it sucks.

Valance looks down at me, eyes soft as I've ever seen them. He smiles a sad little smile. "I know, babe, so am I," he says, then his mouth is on mine, his lips firm and wet with tears. His and mine. He licks my lower lip and pulls it between his teeth with little bites that make me see stars. "I'd follow you into the darkness if I could. Take the pain a thousand times. Die for you in dreams, find you in the white silence. You are my forever, always."

His eyes are almost fluorescent in the darkness. "I'll lose you," I say. "No one should have to wait two years for anyone, you'll find someone else, you'll—"

"Never!" he rasps. "If winning our freedom from this hell takes forever, then that's how long I'll wait for you." His lips touch my ear and the taut line of my throat, brushing feather kisses over my collarbone. Two years of screams, two years of kisses, two long years of whispered words he knows I'll only forget. I stare at him. Memorize him. The muscular slope of his big shoulders, the way they hunch as he leans into me. My eyes rove over the hard slant of his jaw, the curve of his lips, the dramatic slant of his expressive eyes.

I hold him tight and scream into his shoulder as the earth quakes again. The harsh tremors come with the promise of approaching carnage, chaos, obliteration.

There are so few of us left, just a couple minutes and so many more are about to die. "We who are about to die—salute you," I say.

Valance flinches and places a finger over my lips. "Not you, Divinica, never you. Stab me as many times as you want. I'll never let you go."

"We're almost out of time," I whisper, nearly in tears over all the things I don't have time to say.

"Crazy, isn't it?" he asks almost absently.

"What?"

"Even though the whole world's gone to shit, time is still the most priceless thing in creation. Apart from you, of course. My beautiful time-walker. Because of you, of who you are, eventually it's all going to be okay. I know it. You are the wild card that will save us all."

I smile and touch his cheek. "You're fucking optimistic, I hate that about you."

"I know," he says cheerfully.

"You say stuff like that just to get a rise out of me."

"Well, that and you're also mighty pretty when you get angry."

My cheeks flush. "Oh my god, Valance, seriously?"

"See, there it is. Breathtaking."

I smack his arm, hurting my hand. I curse first at the pain, then at him when he doesn't even flinch. Valance lifts me into his arms and laughs all the way back to my room, even when he puts me down and I kick him in the shin.

CHAPTER NINETEEN

Yours, mine, ours

A gust of wind rushes through my bedroom, rustling and waving the hair falling in Valance's eyes. Under the muted light of the dying sun, he looks like an innocent boy, untouched by the sting of my dramatic storyline.

"Sometimes, oh all-knowing one, I forget how young you were when this started," I say as he sets me on my feet. I don't step back but just stand in front of him and stare up at the face I love. I touch his cheek, brush the hair from his eyes. "Perfect skin, muscles for miles, and the ability to predict the future, you really are the full package, aren't you?"

Valance smiles, all teeth, and heartbreaking dimples. "I'm smart as fuck too, graduated summa cum laude when I was fifteen. CNN called me a prodigy."

He's told me this before, perhaps a dozen times, but I don't let on. For once, it's nice to know what *he's* going to say. The earth shakes again, rattling all the artifacts in the room and opening Aphrodite's shell. It starts singing, and I have the unreasonable urge to smash it. I don't react this time. No screaming or tears. They are useless, and I'm honestly tired of snotting on Valance's neck. "How much longer?" I ask as the trembling of the earth subsides.

Valance glances down at his watch, his frown banishing his beautiful dimples. "Five minutes," he says, his face a mask of heartache. My fingertips go completely numb, and I can't feel my legs. Slowly, I disentangle our fingers—which seem to have linked sometime during the quake—and move away from him, walk over to my bed, then lie down on my dirty floor. I ignore the comical look of askance he levels at me and roll onto my stomach.

I can almost hear his brow lift. "Divinica? Dare I ask?"

I grunt as my chin bumps the floor. "You said you wanted to watch me use the star door, but I kicked my candle under here in a fit of righteous rage, and I need it," I say, reaching for the candle and stretching my arm until it feels like the joint in my elbow wants to pop.

"Can I help?" he asks. I can clearly hear him trying not to laugh.

"No, I've got it." I'm straining, and I definitely don't "got it," but now, for some idiotic reason, my body decides it must prove what my mouth so stupidly declared. My mom used to say, "Nothing in the world is as stubborn as an Aries." I hear her voice clearly in my mind, see the way she used to shake her head while looking at me like I was a burden the gods had chosen her to bear. Thinking of her makes me want to cry. So does the fact that I still can't reach the damn candle. It's there, in that moment, lying face-down under my bed, home of dust bunnies and rat poop, my arm stretched to the max and my tired muscles screaming, when I truly feel like throwing in the metaphorical towel. That or strangling myself with it.

Above me, I suddenly feel the bed shift. I shriek a little as the candle vanishes. "Uh? Divinica?"

I flinch, jerking my neck, then whack the back of my head against the uneven baseboard. "Ouch! Fuck! What?"

Valance doesn't say anything, so I scoot out from under my bed and roll over. Valance is sitting cross-legged in front of the damn candle, looking for all the world like a Buddhist monk at his prayers, Zen as fuck.

"What—" I sit and throw up my hands.

"It was looking like a bit of a struggle, so I just reached behind the bed and grabbed it for you."

"Don't expect a thanks. You robbed me of a possible, much-needed win," I say peevishly, pulling a wad of some unknown substance from my tangled hair. "You look so perfect sitting there. I wish I had something to throw at you."

"Maybe look under the bed again," he says, laughter lighting up his eyes. "I'll wait. I'll literally never get tired of staring at your ass."

I gasp and reach out blindly, grab the first thing I touch, and hurl it at him. His hand flashes out, catching the item midair, and too late I realize I just tossed him my notebook.

Valance opens it and makes a face. His brows climb slowly, until they pause imperiously in perfect twin arches. "Excuse me? I am not the vortex responsible for your destruction," he states categorically.

Snarling, I swipe my arm through the air, reaching for the notebook, but he makes a *tsk* sound and lifts his hand above his head, holding it well out of my reach. I stand, meaning to dive at him, but he moves fast and links his arm around my waist, then pulls me down on top of him. He shifts my body, and before I can take a breath, he's flat on his back and I'm sitting astride his waist, my unbound hair spilling like polished mahogany over his naked chest. My body rises and falls with each of his heavy breaths. In his eyes is an emotion so tangible I can almost hold it in my hands. He smiles, a slow, lazy smile, as if the two of us were still children of the old world, with silly, digital lives and nothing but time.

"You're so beautiful." He runs his fingers through my hair and traces an invisible line down my thigh. "Cast in the light of your artifacts, you look like a dream, a goddess," he says, and my annoyance is gone, my heart galloping all over again, racing, flying. Our energy kisses and crackles. I see his aura clearly now, golden as a desert at dawn.

He lifts his torso, holds himself up with one hand, and grabs the back of my neck with the other. He draws me down and our lips collide. This kiss is fireworks on the Fourth of July. Dynamite popping off in the center of a live volcano. A burning asteroid at the point of impact. I'm flying and my wings are on fire. I kiss him back with everything I am, dig my fingers into his shoulders, and tug and twist his locks of hair. Then, he's kissing me harder, molding me to him like he can somehow pull me under his skin and keep me forever. It's an earth-shattering kiss, and I think he must know it will be one of our last for a while. His mouth breaks away from mine, and he whispers my name against my throat. Beyond my window, I can hear the sky hissing and humming as thunder rolls over the Alps.

"This is the cruelest torture," Valance says against my parted lips, and he's right. I am pain and fear, I am a child of regret, a daughter of damage, the fading ghost of a borrowed soul.

"Valance, oh my god, Valance, Valance, Valance." His name, it's all I can say.

"I know. I know, baby, fuck! I know!" he grates through clenched teeth. I rest my forehead on his shoulder and let more tears wash my cheeks. He strokes my hair and drags his fingers down my trembling silhouette, sending shivers through my bones. Desire and dread.

"Please keep taking care of Daniel, I know I have no right to ask, but—"

"Divinica, I'll protect him with my last breath. The two of you are my family. My whole life."

"Don't let me stab you again," I sob, wiping hard at my drenched face. "Don't untie me, no matter what I say. I think I'm stronger since I brought back Kali's sword."

Valance smiles at me. "The heart falters at the thought, but it's easier said

than done. I feel like a felon when I see those rope burns around your wrists."
He brings my right hand to his lips, and his kiss leaves an invisible, glowing
tattoo in the center of my palm. "Must you fight so hard?"

I swallow. "I think so."

"Huh, figures. Probably one of the reasons why I love you," he says. I grab
those words and slather them all over my mind, begging it not to forget. When
he leans down again, I lift my face to meet his kiss. The man outside of time
who walked on other worlds. My cowboy-god.

This kiss is soft, achingly gentle. *He's saying goodbye.* I wish I had died a
thousand deaths in Kali's world before ever reaching this moment. Outside,
people are starting to scream as the wave overtakes them, and the tremors
wracking my body become an all-out quake. The kiss turns primal. It's the kiss
at the end of every good high school drama, the one that can make even a frozen
heart believe in love. But the truth is that the money shot is over, the set is
closed, the movie is finished, all the actors have gone home, and no one lives
happily ever after.

Valance kisses the tears from my eyes before his lips work their way down
my jaw, and he sucks at a spot on my neck hard enough to leave a mark. He's
oxygen. I breathe him in, but it's not enough. We melt into each other, but still,
it's never enough.

The earth shakes again, harder this time. Valance sighs and lifts me off his
lap. I settle on my knees beside him and notice how the sparse air in the room
goes suddenly arctic absent his touch. He reaches past me for my little box of
storm matches, then strikes one on the ground. Orange light seeps into the
approaching red glow that injects all the shadows in my room with the ruby
color of blood. Valance lights the candle, then takes my arm. The words are
already beginning to glow. As we both stare, they flake off the underside of my
wrist like pieces of dry skin and flutter around us. Radiant, moving.

I see pure wonder light up Valance's eyes as the magic happens. He looks like
a kid at Christmas, and I realize that despite his omniscience, he hasn't seen it
all. Not like I have. Dear god, not like I have.

The gate of stars constructs itself before our wide eyes with seamless
invincibility. Galaxies, star clusters, massive planets, and colorful supernovas
writhe beyond the forming gate. I hold my breath as the burning on my arm
subsides and the last of the letters re-form, then settle into place.

"Unbelievable," Valance whispers.

"It is, isn't it."

Valance meets my eyes. "No, I mean the portal is whatever. It's cool and all,
but you, Divinica, you are unbelievable." He takes my hand. "Come back here.

We only have about a minute left. I have to touch you." He pulls me close. "God, I want to keep you here, trapped with me in this moment forever."

"That's all I want," I say. I can see the wave through the smoky glass of my window, electric pulses changing the air and sky. The residents of my world are screaming, screaming, screaming, and soon I will scream with them.

I shove against Valance's chest, suddenly horrified he's about to witness all the ways the wave will break and change me. "Leave. Please. I don't want you to see this."

Valance grunts, then his arms tighten around me. My head is still resting on his shoulder even though I meant to push him away. I twist my neck to stare up at his face. Tears magnify his eyes when he leans down to kiss my cheek. "Not likely, Divinica. I love you. I hope somewhere, somehow, you remember that."

Tears slide past my closed lids and run unchecked down my cheeks.

The wave crashes over us, into us, damning us. Agony arches my back, twists my neck, and drops my jaw. I feel Valance's lips on mine, taste his breath as he whispers my name. I hold onto those things for merely a second before they're cruelly snatched away. Red floods my vision like the sky is raining blood. My mouth opens wider, but no sound emerges, except the charged hum and crackle of the wave that seems to infest every living thing. Even my rats are twitching and bleeding from their bright green eyes. Somewhere, lost in a distance of growls and dying wails, I hear Valance shouting my name as my body spasms violently. He yells, trying in vain to hold me together while the wave slices me apart. My ears pop with a bang. Hot blood runs down my neck, seeps from my tear-soaked eyes. Everything is a million shards of torment. I wonder if I really did die some undetermined length of time ago. Perhaps I went to hell and this is my suffering, a burning that will last for all eternity.

Valance takes my hands between his, squeezes tight to keep me from tearing out my hair, scratching off my skin, and clawing through tendon and bone just to get to the fire raging inside.

"I'm sorry, baby. Don't hate me for this. Your Freya tattoo is glowing," I hear him say. I feel his hands skim my waist, then cup my hips. "I'm sending you to her. If I have to listen to any more of your screams, I fear I'll kill us both."

Before I can yell in protest, he lifts me high and throws me through the gate of stars. Our hands hold on until the last possible second, our interlocked fingers sliding slowly against each other, reluctant to be parted. I see Valance's face through a dying haze. His tear-soaked eyes lock with mine, and he blows me a kiss as I start to fall, and fall, and fall forever.

CHAPTER TWENTY

The undisputed benefits of human sacrifice

The landing is stunning, and strangely brief for a fall that seemed to take a million eternities. I hit the ground face-first, graceful as a kicked stone, arms and legs spread like the Vitruvian man. My nose is squished, while my front teeth bite down into a patch of soggy earth. Dirt, grass, and a few slimy little bugs fill my mouth. It tastes like life and sunshine.

It takes an eon to sit up. My head is spinning, and I'm dragging for air when I finally accomplish the Herculean task. I shove long skeins of blonde hair from my watering eyes, then shake it over my shoulder. The locks fall down my back to the ground and beyond. The golden color of my hair scares me.

For a moment I think Valance threw me to Aphrodite's time, and I instantly loathe the thought of going through her world all over again. I take another deep breath and quickly reject Aphrodite's world as an option. The earth my knees are planted on is older than it was on the day of Aphrodite's birth, by centuries, maybe by millennia. *I'm a captain sailing uncharted waters, I'm lost at sea and lost in time*, I think, before my inner voice falls silent.

A sharp breeze rips around me, snapping my mind from the prismatic tunnel of confusion where it always lives after I take this kind of fall. I stand and look around me. The darkening day is overrun by gothic shadows that move like smoky nocturnal creatures. Light drips from the giant red sun, which seems to be hanging rather precariously, full as a soap bubble just before it pops.

No engine sounds break the music of this sunset. No electric lights from speeding cars cast their traveling glows. The air is crisp and smog-free like it always is when I fall into these other times. I look down at my feet, wiggle my toes, and smile. I'm wearing a pair of sandals that fit me like a dream. Around my toes are slender rows of tiny, flat buttons inlaid with veins of mother-of-pearl. Rose-gold laces twine to my knees, both tied off in a double knot that ends at the start of my slender thighs. Feels weird to apply the word *slender* to my thighs, but there it is. I'm in another body, that of a svelte warrior with flowers in her hair.

My dress is long and virginal white. It's made of a curious sheer material that feels like a strange combination of gossamer and silver nitrate. It glows and sways as I move my legs, almost like the cloth itself has breath and soul. My bodice is an armored vest, the material mercury and starlight. A twisted strand of river pearls wraps my waist, and the thick necklace hanging between my breasts is strung with sharp, white bones.

I can smell the flowers braided into the crown on my head. Its branches are silver and gold, and they move in time with me and the wind. I notice the color of each petal scattered through my wild hair. Fuchsia, topaz, lavender, white jasmine, and blood-red rose. I lift my eyes and take it all in. The sunset sky is a vase of swirling colors, studding with ink blots tar. The rising moon is huge and glittering like a disco ball. I spin in a full circle, arms out and hands open wide, feeling beautiful, young, and strong as the stone circle I'm standing in. I recognize it instantly from Valance's photos and my own pulsing memories. Stonehenge, untarnished, unbroken, and fully activated on this solstice, this midsummer's eve.

I notice I'm surrounded by only women, twelve in total. Staring and standing still like the statues in the driveway of Styx. They are different ages, colors, and races, gowned in various adaptations of my own white dress. I recognize the women. Nokomis, Magu, Kali, Isis…all of them stare at me, a plethora of emotions flashing through their luminous eyes. One of them even reaches out her hand to make sure I don't stumble and fall on my face again. *Do they know about the body switch?* my inquisitive mind wants to know. *If they did, would they care?*

In the distance, I hear the beat of drums, and the long shadows moving over the ground seem to bop to their pounding rhythm, to the eternal rhythm of the Earth's star glowing in the multicolored sky. *It's almost time,* I think, but time for what, I don't know. Two goddesses step toward me. One has a collection of hissing snakes for hair, and I know who she is by that feature alone. Medusa, the cursed. I wonder if she is considered a goddess by this circle because humans still say her name, paint her image and tell her story, thousands of years later. I open my mouth to speak, but Medusa holds up her hand.

"I represent revenge, moon creatures, and damned things," she says.

"I'm sure you do," I say. My voice stuns me. It's low and husky as a lounge singer, sensual as a candle beside a bottle of ruby-red wine.

The goddess beside Medusa moves. My mind intuitively knows her name and lore. Oshun. Her skin and eyes are bright, yet moody as starlit ink. She steps close and says, "I represent the damned. Souls who die and cannot be reborn are mine."

Another with a golden bow and arrow who I identify as Artemis, Greek goddess of the hunt, says, "I represent thriving life, innocence, and animals that cannot speak for themselves, creatures of sunlit meadows, jungles, and mountain tops."

I don't say anything inane this time. They are speaking to me, but I suspect they need no answer, rather their words are part of the spell this body I inhabit is preparing to cast. I can feel the incantation's magic building in my hands, surging through my core. My heart beats a staccato rhythm, and I feel my pulse throbbing in my throat and taste the energy in my mouth.

Now the sun hangs lower, drooping, falling, swooping, melting into place so it can pour over the distant, unseen horizon. I lift my hands, stare at my pale, slender fingers. I see then that I'm wearing about thirty rings, all heavy with glittering stones pressed deep in an alloy I can't immediately identify. A fusion of onyx and gold decorated with tiny, silver leaves and twisted forest vines covered in sparkling thorns.

I drop my hands and watch the sun settle at the pinnacle of the heel stone. Golden light spears through Stonehenge, hitting the thirty surrounding blue stones. The light charges each stone until it glitters, and white lightning crackles over the ground, hovering just above the thick green grass. In my mind and heart, Divinica fades as I drink in the power. It lifts my hair off my shoulders and uses my rings as energetic conductors as sparks fly from the tips of my fingers. I spin around and the next goddess I see makes my breath catch with a shriek.

Inside my mind, Divinica gasps, curses, screaming in silence, because she is not me, only a distant voice in my head. A voice becoming easier to ignore, second by charged second. The goddess is centuries, maybe millennia younger, but I know all three of her heads intimately. I feel no fear of her as Divinica did in her world. As I watch, Hecate lifts all six of her eyes to the glowing heel stone and smiles an old, dangerous smile.

She raises her hands to the sun. "We gather here on this solstice eve because I have foreseen the destruction of our Earth. We twelve sisters in power made a blood vow to protect our Gaia. Tonight, we gather to write the name of our incantation, *Kyma,* in the earth and stars."

"This is not the way, Hecate," says another, booming voice. The goddess approaching wears a gilded suit of silver armor. The breastplate fits her like a second skin, and the leather strap of the shield she carries looks molded to her arm. In her right hand she holds a sword. The blade is bathed in undying Olympian flames. I recognize their color, feel the strength in their heat. Her hair is a mass of chestnut curls that run over her shoulders like silk to brush her thighs, and her bright, amber eyes are the stuff of legends.

"Athena," I breathe.

Athena inclines her head. "Freya, I beg you, do not cast this spell. Thousands of innocents will die."

"There is no choice," says another, older goddess. Older than sun and time, wiser than stars and oceans. Ixchel, Mayan goddess of healing, birth, and moonlight. She is far older than I—I who watched the first dawn. I bow my head to her, but she has no time for my worship. "I will not sit and watch humanity obliterate this Earth I love," she says, motioning to the sky and the ground we stand on. "Gaia is all that is vibrance and life, she is too beautiful and rare to deserve so horrible a fate. As goddesses of this realm, it is our job to protect her. This spell will kill, but it will also save."

"I, too, do not wish to see innocents suffer, but I cannot bear to watch the destruction of Gaia. Though we cast it now, our hex will only be triggered by her imminent death," Magu says. As she moves, leaves flutter from her fingertips and a tree grows where she stands. "We must protect our Earth. We will take their memories, erase their histories, thus abolishing their darkest impulses. While humanity is in this state, Gaia will, for a time at least know peace for a time."

"What if we regret our destruction? Once it is done, can it be undone?" Athena asks.

"Perhaps," Hecate says, "though you will not exist enough to see it. These bodies that host your souls are advanced, created of more than tissue, bone, and skin. To humans you are immortal, but compared to me, you are not eternal. Eventually, the long sleep will call all of you. I alone will remain awake, as is my curse. Once started, this spell can only be broken by the force of our collective powers. If each of you chose to recant before you slumber, my sole power will not be enough to break our enchantment."

"No," Athena declares vehemently. "I will have no part of this."

"Perhaps humanity will surprise us, and this hex will never be," Isis says.

Artemis laughs. "Doubtful. They will never change because they refuse to embrace the laws of nature."

"There is one thing that can be done," Hecate says. "One small chance. A single probable future."

"And what is that?" Athena asks.

"There is a future where I use the star technology that formed me to create another," Hecate says. "I must search through time to find the human girl capable of holding a piece of each of our powers. It will be grueling, and many will die in the attempt."

"All will die. There's no human strong enough," Athena says.

Hecate shakes her heads. "You're wrong. I know she exists, I have seen her. She lives in the shadows of a million possible choices. Emerald eyes, skin like Egyptian gold. She is strong, brave, and capable. If she survives being mythmarked, there will be a chance. A chance of safety for humanity, a chance at rebirth for Gaia."

"I say let them be the masters of their own annihilation," Aphrodite declares. "We immortals will wait and see what comes next. Like any good woman, Gaia is a survivor. She will endure humanity."

"No," Athena says, and I am not sure what she is rejecting. Maybe all of it.

Aphrodite purses her full lips, then reaches both of her lily-white hands to the clasp of her necklace. A single, soft click and the necklace falls into her waiting palms. "Once I place a piece of myself in this, the first shell ever formed, how will this paragon of yours—who is more than two epochs from being born —get her human hands on it?"

"I will give her my ability to timewalk through flame, if she is smart and careful…" Hecate shrugs. "It should be enough."

"What this girl can heal, she can also destroy. If she turns on us, can we fight such a creature?" asks Ixchel, her fingers lazily stroking the head of the six-foot jaguar lounging at her side.

"No," Hecate says simply, "she will be beyond any of us. However, if she fulfills her purpose, she will be dead, and we will be safe."

More golden light spears through the tangle of vines draping the heel stone like a themed tablecloth. The sun drops lower, lower, lower still. "It's time," I say again. Now I know what it's time for. It's time for spells, hope, and death. "Are we all in agreement?" I ask, looking at Athena and Medusa in turn.

"Only if Hecate swears to find and mark this paragon, regardless of the cost," Athena says.

Hecate nods. "I swear it."

I take the wreath crown off my head with a sigh. My movements are slow and ritualistic as I walk to the outer ring of the circle and place my elaborate forest crown atop one of the shimmering blue stones. My crown settles, hanging a little askew. I think it's pretty, touched by the dripping glow of sun and moon. The wreath belonged to my mother, Freya's mother, rather—and her mother before her.

My people have many artifacts and talismans, but this one is special to me. I hope it will be special to her, whoever she may be. That thought makes me realize how far removed I am from Divinica now. Freya is strong, she is the sponge and I'm the water. She's sucked me all up, and there's nothing left for me to do but dry up and disappear. I step back from the iridescent stone and watch the other goddesses place their artifacts, each on their own chosen stone. When it's done, they step back as I did. Silently, we face each other, forming a full circle.

Hecate's primary head meets my eyes, and her left head gives me a nearly imperceptible nod. Immediately, to my surprise—not for the first time today—I start singing, or chanting, I can't be sure. My voice is stunning. Beautiful as birdsong at dawn, high, melodic, perfect. The goddesses move closer, and the circle tightens. My song increases in cadence as I feel the last rays of the sun on my face. I can literally see the musical notes flowing from my lips. Golden symbols glowing violet at the edges. Notes that dance and move through our circle, touching each goddess in turn. They twist and wind through the blue stones, soaking into the various artifacts.

My voice rises higher. The ground begins to shake, the colors of the music notes intensify, darkness seeping into the violet. Hecate takes my left hand. Oshun my right. The rest link their fingers in a similar fashion, and their voices join my song. Power surges, trembles, thrives. Light pierces the heel stone.

I sense movement beyond the circle. I don't turn my head, and the slight distraction has no effect on my song—because I know the cause. A spell, large as the one we mean to cast, always requires blood. The women of New Saresbyri are bringing me the human sacrifice chosen by my raven. I don't know who was picked by my gods, and I don't care. I close my eyes. I will look at their face once, when my blade opens their throat, then I will look no more. Whispers come at me from all sides but no sound of a struggle, which means my victim is placid, and I'm glad. I hate killing an unwilling, innocent human. They always beg to live a few more days of their short lives. It's horrible, like stepping on a butterfly.

I hear a thud as the martyr drops to their knees in front of me. I open my eyes. The sky is now painted in shades of indigo and scarlet. The distant mountains have stabbed the belly of the sunken sun, rivers of scarlet bleeding into the darkening twilight. I take a single step toward the man. My muscles tremble as my foot falls, and my power is everywhere. It touches everyone and everything, vibrates the air and the earth, and speeds the rush of blood through my veins.

"Freya," the man before me calls my name, and I pause. I know that voice. Like Raktabija's bright blue eyes, I would know it anywhere, in any world.

"No," I say instantly. "No. Not him. Anyone but him."

"Ah, Freya. Your raven landed on my shoulder. You can do nothing. It's a simple fate, unchangeable. Today is my day to die."

"The fates can't have you, Prince Steiner, you're mine!" I cry.

The Celtic prince nods, his gorgeous, golden hair blowing in the evening wind. "I am yours, Freya. It's to you, and you alone, I offer my life."

Freya doesn't move. She's thinking about his offer, actually considering killing the man she loves, but I'm screaming and thrashing inside. It's Valance. Not just his eyes. The face, hair, lips, and scarred bare chest all belong to the man I love. The idiot who threw me into this time because it was breaking him to hear me scream. Threw me here to this beautiful, terrible, terrifying, powerful place where a damn spell is about to be cast that will ruin my life and sanity in the future. He smiles up at me, and my heart stops. I fall to my knees in front of him, then throw my arms around his neck. His hands are tied behind his back, so he can't hold me. Instead, he rests his forehead against mine, then kisses my brow.

Him, him, him, him, him, him, dear fucking god, not him. I won't kill him. I won't!

I struggle to find my voice, my mind, and try to feel my discombobulated body. In utter desperation, I attempt to take control of Freya's limbs, try to use her lips to scream a thousand denials, but it's useless. She's too old, too strong, and her decision has been made. Even though I try to fight the action, I unsheathe the dagger hanging from the chain of pearls around my waist. The blade is wicked sharp and gleaming. It's going to happen. I know it. I can't stop it. I'm going to kill him again, and then I will go insane. I wish the red wave had fucking killed me. I wish he had let it.

CHAPTER TWENTY-ONE

You die, I die

The overall feeling is one of unknowing sentience and hopelessness. I don't need to be an ancient star witch to know the future. The spell to save Gaia obviously worked, or I wouldn't be here, trapped in the strange body of this beautiful enchantress, which means this prince wearing Valance's face dies. Hopelessness exists because I know there's nothing, nothing at all, that I can do except stand here and watch it happen. I can fight, I can rage, but if he managed to survive this, my soul would be home safe, and my body wouldn't be locked and listless in some starry vortex.

I fight Freya's strength anyway. Relentless, desperate, fierce. I think it's sheer determination more than anything else that lets me say a single word. "No!" A one-syllable denial. As luck would have it, it's the only word I need. "No, no, no, no, no, no," I chant, as if it can change events locked in time, when I know it can't.

One of the goddesses, a young girl who has until now clung to the fringes of our circle, turns to glare at me. She has snapping crimson eyes that make me think of radiated wolves prowling on a moonless night. I can almost hear their ominous howl as I stare back. A cowl of white silk drapes her yards of jet-black hair, the garment giving the impression of a living shroud. "You can't stop this," she says sweetly in a distinctly childish tone.

Tell me something I don't know, I almost snap, my thoughts vitriolic.

"It has been seen by the one who is three. This thread is formed and cannot be unmade," the young goddess says.

I shake my head in stubborn denial. The dagger falls from my numb fingers. It stabs hilt-first into the earth between me and the doomed prince of Gaul. He smiles at me. His teeth are shockingly white, and there's a scar that pulls just above his right eye, which somehow adds to the savage perfection of his bare chest, calloused hands, and big arms made for killing—or at times, made for holding me. I remember what Freya had with him in this life, and I know what he and I have in mine is more.

"Pick it up, Freya. I'd rather die by your hand than any other," he says.

"I won't, damn you!" I manage to gasp as Freya reaches for the knife. Strangely, my voice doesn't sound like Freya this time. It seems I've managed to find my own. I part my lips to say something else, but it's a struggle, like trying to run in quicksand. Outwardly, I'm as silent as a daisy. Inside, I'm a fucking madwoman, battling Freya with every ounce of my somewhat pitiful strength.

"I must save the Earth. I must take your life," Freya tells the prince, as if it's some kind of excuse. I can barely make Freya's fingers twitch, and she is seconds from the knife's hilt. I delve deeper, seeking the power within me instead of relying on hers—the power that hides in my soul like my own dark passenger, a gift these conniving goddesses planned for me on this cursed solstice night.

It's there, just a whisper, a sigh, as intangible as a prayer. I touch it, feel it. The power expands, rises, consumes. Gradually, using only my mind, I begin to lift Freya's body off the ground. I sense her eyes rolling back in her head, and finally, I can see clearly. I reach out to the lightning striking the ground, gather it, and cradle it in my palms. Then, I twist it, using it to soar higher, shine brighter, and for that fleeting moment, suspended in this way, I understand what it means to be star-born.

My head flies back as I call more of her lightning. It shoots from the sky, splitting the twilight with a thunderous boom that echoes through the mountains, beneath the oceans, and across the earth.

"Find another damn sacrifice," I snarl. This time my low, echoing voice sounds like I've swallowed a demon.

"There is no other. He is destiny's choice, and even I cannot deny her," says the beautiful young fate. As she speaks, her face morphs to the wrinkled, gray visage of her sister, and her single, eyeless, bleeding socket watches me balefully.

"The old ones, the star gods, want him," Hecate says.

I bare my teeth. She starts to say something I already know I don't want to hear, so I reach for a sharp thread of lightning, call it to me, pluck it from the sky, and hurl it at her. The bolt strikes Hecate square in the chest, and she goes flying. Her limp body lands a few feet from Aphrodite, who giggles shrilly and claps her hands.

I have no time for that particular goddess's antics. My eyes swoop back to the prince, who's watching me with a strange expression carving lines into his handsome face. I decide the emotion is confusion. I guess I'm breaking character, and I don't care. Strange, but in this moment, staring at him, knowing I'm probably about to see him bleed out, I find myself agreeing with Aphrodite. Let the fucking world burn, the only thing that matters to me is him.

I land lightly on my feet as Hecate sits up. She shakes her heads, then all of them glare at me with knowing smiles. I think she might see me—Divinica, not Freya. Her bottomless eyes scan me with a curiosity that has a hint of academic interest. It doesn't matter. She doesn't matter. None of them do.

Again, I fall to my knees and reach for the ropes binding the prince's hands, feeling possessed by a sense of déjà vu. As I touch them, the harsh hemp fibers submit to the energy flowing from my fingers and disintegrate like steam in a monsoon. The second he's free, he takes my face between his hands, the way he always does in my world, and when he looks deep in my eyes we could be back at Styx, sitting on my bed and talking about better days. I swallow hard. I know he's living in the last seconds of his life. I think he knows it too.

"There's something so different about you," he whispers, and now it's Freya who screams in my mind. I ignore her and hold on to my twisting, thirsty inner power.

My teeth clench as he kisses me. "I won't let you die," I tell him.

"All men must die. I've spent my life fighting for my people. Let me fight to help you save this world."

"No! You will live. You will succeed your father to the throne and be the king we've always dreamed of. The star gods gave you to me. They cannot have you back."

"Did they?" he asks, his eyes searching my face. "You are not Freya. She does not love me like this. Who are you?"

"I'm Divinica, and I'm going to save you," I promise.

His smile is of the heartbreaking variety when he runs his fingers through my hair and leans in to kiss me. A fraction of a second before our mouths meet, his body stiffens in my arms, then he slumps against me. Something crackles between us. I smell the sweet, sickening scent of burning flesh and glance down at our bodies, horror struck. Blood everywhere. It soaks through the fibers of my white dress, and I feel it, hot and sticky, running down my bare stomach. I cry out and catch him as he falls.

I lay him on the grass and look up. All three of Hecate's heads are smiling, and her hands are smoking. Murdering bitch. I want to rip out her throat. *Later*, I tell myself, and all my attention goes back to him. "A sword!" I scream, searching the surrounding ground for the dagger I dropped. I find it in Hecate's grip, as she smiles down at the blade.

"Hecate, please," I beg, "he must die with a weapon in hand, or he will not reach the gates of Valhalla. Someone! Please, please, please, dear gods above and below…please."

Hecate shakes her head. "That is not the way of this spell. He is not dying a warrior's death. Blood demands blood," she says, and none of the others disagree. I scream as more blood flows from his chest like water from a pressurized hose, soaking the earth of Stonehenge. The ground trembles, groans, and drinks up the offering. The surrounding light expands and brightens until it's blinding.

"No…no. Just stop, whoever you are," rasps the prince. "I have no wish to enter Valhalla." He coughs harshly, and blood splashes my face, but I don't wipe it away. "I want to stay a ghost of this Earth…I want to stay near you."

"Why?" I ask in a teary whisper. "You don't know me."

"I think I've always known you," he says. Blood drips from the corner of his mouth. I wipe it with my thumb, and he turns his head, dragging his lips over my wrists.

"Me, not her," I demand.

He nods once. It's not enough. I want his vow. I want him to search for me, not her. Freya's gods brought him here to die, and her lightning delivered the final blow. She is still his murderer even though she did not do the killing. She had her chance, her day in the sun with this god of a human, and she squandered it with bloody death. Now I am in her body, and the chance is mine.

The prince presses another hot kiss in the center of my palm, then shoves my hand into the pool of his ever-expanding blood. "Say the words, witch. Make it so," he demands.

"I vow it! From here to time's inglorious end, I command you to find me, in all lives, past, present, and future, even if it is only an echo of me living in another body," I add, covering all my bases. I lean down and press my lips against his, tasting his dying breaths. "I, Divinica, command it. This is my will, so mote it be."

He closes his eyes. "It's enough. I feel it. I will find you, even if it's only an echo."

I start to cry as his body begins to shake. The spell Freya cast is now out of control. Lightning thrashes the earth, and a brilliant pillar of it spears the darkening sky. It tears through the stones and pumps from the chest of each goddess. They're still holding hands, beatific smiles on their faces, and in a moment of blind rage, I want to kill them all, even those who opposed my creation and subsequent destruction. I close my eyes, cursing them and listening to his last, shredding breaths. When I open them, the stone circle seems to be spinning at a million miles an hour, so fast that if I turn my head and squint my eyes, it could be standing still. The artifacts are glowing, rising off their blue stones. They hang perfectly suspended, despite the howling gale, and I mark each of them for future reference, particularly noting the ones I don't have yet. Then, I rest my cheek against his sweat-soaked brow and damn every god who ever drew breath as the prince of Gaul dies in my arms. Heart all burned away, soul set to wander, I hold him until his chest and face turn to ash and bones. Freya is finally silent, and the tears that fall are mine. Divinica's tears. Divinica's loss.

When I see my portal tear open the electric fabric of these skies, I don't hesitate. I dive for Freya's crown of golden thorns and twisted vines, shove it down on my head, then run and leap through the portal, leaving Freya's body and the rest of them behind.

PART TWO

CHAPTER TWENTY-TWO

From the perspective of the cursed

VALANCE

I hated letting her go, but I had to. There was no way I could watch her go through that agony one more time. No fucking way. I would prefer to have each one of my fingers pounded to putty by a sledgehammer. I know she hates this time travel shit. I also know that my motivation for throwing her through the star door is based on self-preservation, but I do it anyway. Her fingers slide through mine, holding on until the last possible second, but it's not long enough. I think briefly about jumping in after her, but I hesitate. If I'm swallowed by some roving black hole, what good will I be to anyone? Best to keep my feet on solid, albeit currently shaking, ground.

Divinica's body hovers just out of my reach, weightless, as if she is a mermaid from a damn fairy tale floating on a sea of stars. Fucking poetic, I know, even for me, diehard lover of Keats, Jane Austen, and Shakespeare, but it's true. Divinica is my definition of fantasy.

I start to pace and run my fingers through my hair until my scalp aches. I think about punching her wall again, but shove my hands in my pockets instead and just stare at her. *Fucking longest wait of my life,* I think, even though I know it can't be more than a few minutes, because the red wave has barely passed us by when her body starts to twitch. Then, Divinica jerks like she's being electrocuted. I run toward her but hardly get a chance to blink my tired eyes before her body shoots directly at me with the velocity and pinpoint trajectory of a launched rocket. I catch her, turn, and let my backside take the brunt of what can only be described as a crash landing.

Divinica's instantly conscious, panting, shoving herself away from me, and scrambling to her knees. She looks up at me through her fan of intoxicating lashes, and to say my breath deserts me is an understatement. She's wearing a crown that makes her look like some lost, woodland princess, and just like that, I'm back in my fairy tale again. Her eyes are wild and dazed, and when she licks her lips, it takes everything in me not to yank her back in my arms and kiss her until she forgets whatever horror I sent her to live through. Was it better than surviving another round in the ring with the red wave? I fucking hope so.

"You're alive," she rasps. I can tell it's a struggle for her to speak.

"Yes, for now," I say, wondering why I added the doom and gloom. Like she needs any more of that. Not to boast, but in the past, I'd always had a way with women. It's my face. Girls get one look at it, and from that moment on, I can do no wrong. After a certain amount of hot side glances, a guy gets the confidence to be charming, but all my charm abandons me when it comes to Divinica. One glance from her enchanting eyes ties my tongue and turns all my fingers to thumbs. Been that way since the fateful second Rashid, Dayle, and I kicked our way free of the burning *Gravity*—the ship that brought us home—and I clapped eyes on her. God, she was a sight, a brilliant light in the middle of a shadowy world. Riding that giant Tardigrade of hers, she looked like a goddess from another time. It was months later when I realized that's what she actually was.

My mom used to prattle endlessly about fate, destiny, and the like. I thought it was all a steaming load until I saw Divinica. She's hot as hell, sure, but that wasn't what got me. It was the instant pull I felt between us. Like every single thing in my life was all connected, as if each choice made up the twists and turns on the road map that brought me straight to her. My feet moved as fast as my brain and heart did. I went to her, space suit still smoking, helmet tucked under my arm, and a bloody gash over my right eye, and expected her to love me on sight, as so many others had. Boy, was I disappointed when she whipped out her knife and stuck it in my thigh.

I grew on her though—a little. The first time she forgot me, it stung. The next time it hurt, and then it really hurt. Now, two years later it's living agony. But one I must survive. I exist for the moments when she looks at me and whispers my name, tells me that I really am just a lost cowboy.

I watch her now. I know my eyes are hungry, but I can't look away. My Divinica. Terrible and beautiful as the dawn. She stands, then runs on unsteady feet to her cans of paint and the bunch of brushes sitting in a clear solution that smells like turpentine and old coffee. Chosen items in hand, she glances around, trying to find a blank spot on the wall, I assume. The only place is the wall behind her headboard. She jumps onto the lumpy mattress, dips a brush in a tin of forest green, shoves hair from her eyes, and starts to paint.

"Have to draw her before she fades, should draw all of them so I know. Circle of goddesses, more like circle of evil bitches," Divinica mumbles, almost under her breath. I get a little closer, moving slowly so as not to startle her. I sit beside her on the bed. She doesn't look at me as the mattress shifts, doesn't remove her focus from the wall and the face quickly taking shape under her skillful hands.

Divinica's a beautiful artist. If things had gone differently, I think she could have made a career out of it. Had her pieces shown in galleries across the world, ten-million-plus followers and all that noise. She has an eye for color, and the proportions of her features are always flawlessly executed. It is fascinating to watch her work. I've seen the finished product but have never been around for its creation. I note the adorable way she scrunches her brow and purses her lips until they look like the bud of a blood-red rose. I fist my hands to keep from reaching for her. The girl gives me wild thoughts and makes me rock hard just by breathing.

"What's the circle of goddesses?" I ask, careful to keep my voice pitched low.

"Fucking bitches who did this to me. Protectors of Earth, my ass! Idiots didn't know what the hell they were doing. How's this bullshit better?" she shouts. "How?! God damn it, we're all fucking dying anyway, and Earth is beyond broken."

I sit up straighter. "What did they do to you?" I'm so calm, it's weird, because I want to rage and fire questions at her, but I can't. I never know when the radiated aftershocks of the red wave will take effect and wipe her mind clean of everything. Even me.

"Do to me?! What didn't they do! They ruined my life, all our lives. They took pieces of their hateful selves and stuck them into their stupid artifacts and...stuck them inside of...of me!" She turns at the waist to face me, then motions to the black ink running down the front of her body. "In these fucking tattoos!" she spits, and it's a struggle to keep myself from grinning. I love her dirty mouth. I don't even think she can blame it on this lovely apocalypse—it's just her. Goes with the whole artist vibe and pouty lips.

"Hecate's the worst. She was the one who marked me with their symbols and somehow gave me her power to time travel. Through fire, she said. What the crap does that even mean? These tattoos hold a piece of each goddess's soul. Hecate said many would die, and right now I wish I had."

Her words break my heart. "Don't say things like that, Divinica."

"Why the hell not? I think these symbols are going to kill me either way, it's just a matter of time. At least I know what they want me to do. Whether I'm going to do it or not is another matter."

"What do they want you to do?"

"They want me to collect all the artifacts, and once I have them, I'm supposed to use the star power embedded in my tattoos combined with earth energy to break their spell, a spell that should never have been cast in the first place."

"Do you know how to do that?"

"No. Of course I don't. I don't need to know. Freya knows, Freya will help me. Maybe some of the others…the others…others…" Her voice drifts off like the ending of a sad song.

I scoot closer to her as she shakes her head and flexes her drawing hand. The face on the wall is nearly finished. She has drawn a woman with bright, blonde hair. The painting is wearing the same intricate crown Divinica has on her head right now. I stare at it and at her. We're silent for a couple of breaths. Her eyes don't leave mine. She hardly even blinks. Then, she sighs dejectedly, and her drawing hand drops to her side.

"I have to paint her before she fades, have to draw…draw her…have to—" Her voice drifts away, her body goes limp, and the brush falls from her hand. I catch it before it leaves a smear of paint on her pillow. The crown tumbles off her head as her shoulders slump. I wrap my arms around her even though I know I probably shouldn't. She turns her body to face me. I take one good look at her eyes and choke back a cry of actual pain. I see zero recognition in their haunting depths. The green has gone all black and glassy. Fear washes over her face, sucking all the color from her complexion. My heart sinks to my gut and dies there. Slowly, I let her go and hold my hands up, dread making me shake.

"It's me, Divinica, it's Valance. You know, the guy who stalks your shadow and almost took your virginity on a metal table like an hour ago."

Divinica makes a small, strangled sound and backs up against her headboard, looking at me like I'm the resident monster from her worst nightmare. "No, fuck, baby, don't look at me like that. God damn it, Divinica!" I drag my hand through my hair, ripping out a few strands.

"What's happening?" she gasps, still shuffling back. "Who are you? What do you want?"

You! Fuck me, I want you! "I'm Valance, you're Divinica. You know me! I swear I won't hurt you," I say, but I don't think she hears me. Her fingers flinch.

"Wait, baby! No!" I shout, as she reaches for that blasted knife in her boot. How she always remembers the knife's exact location is fucking beyond me. I jump to my feet and suck in my stomach to the max. I'm a split second too slow.

The wicked tip of her blade cuts a long, diagonal slash across my chest. I hiss between clenched teeth. It stings like hell.

"Fuck!" I roar, and she starts so hard I can hear her teeth click. She gulps at the air like a beached fish, blinking rapidly, as if she just encountered a bright light. I charge at her, angry at the blank look, at the waves, at this girl I fell in love with at the end of the world.

Divinica swings her knife again, and the way she moves makes me think of enraged nymphs and Valkyrie battle cries. This time it's a swing and a miss, yet the knife's sharp edge cuts dangerously close to my jugular. I bring the side of my hand crashing against her wrist, and I don't pull my punch. I've spent two years learning how to disarm Divinica, and anything less than my full strength just won't cut it. She shrieks like a singed cat as the knife falls from her limp hand and clatters to the ground. She gives it a single longing look, then raises her fists and squares her shoulders, ready to take me head-on.

Once, when I was a child, my father and I were standing at the top of the spiral stairwell of the old Lord Plantation where I unfortunately spent my formative years. We were fighting. I wanted to watch *Star Wars*, he wanted to drink. I called him a dick, and he kicked me down the stairs. I was eight years old, and my young body was woefully ill-equipped to deal with a tumble of such magnitude. I lay for a long time at the bottom of those stairs, searching for air in a world full of it and finding none. Standing here, looking into Divinica's vacant eyes, I feel the same as I did on that horrible day, like I'm trying to breathe in a world full of air that has turned to sand. She's my air, and I'm losing her. Again. I thought that surviving on the surface of Mars for two years was a struggle. What an idiot I was, what did I know about struggles or survival?

I give it one last-ditch attempt. Why not? Might be interesting to see how much more damage my heart can take. "Divinica, please. You know me, look in my eyes. See me!"

"Get out!" she says coldly. "This place is mine. I don't know you at all. Leave." Her hands drop to her sides as she trembles all over. The ache in my arms is still there. They move of their own accord, as I reach for her before I realize what I'm doing. She flinches farther away, and I lower my arms with a sigh. I think then that all the philosophers were wrong. Dreams aren't what keep us alive, it's hope. Today, as I turn to leave her for what feels like the millionth time, my hope is gone.

I stomp from her room without a backward glance or another word. A last look would be too painful, and there's nothing left to say. She's afraid of me, and with good reason. I'm a stranger to her, again. I curse and kick my way out of Styx, stopping only to prime her pump. If I can't hold her when she wakes, at least I can give her a proper shower. Boogles watches me through slitted eyes as I check the saddle on my own Rade, Borax. But like Divinica, he doesn't know me at all.

"It's okay, boy. Don't worry. You're chill, it's all chill," I croon. His shifting, fearful stance is acid poured onto the open wound that is my heart. I want to curl up between the two Rades, close my exhausted eyes, and wait out the days. Watch the stars rise and set, wait for her to remember me. But I don't give in to the urge. I mount up. Borax snorts and tosses his head but obeys the silent command of my heels. I made Divinica a promise. For the next few days, Daniel is my responsibility. I told her I would guard him with my life, and I'm not about to get all mopey and break my word.

I'm operating on autopilot, and the ride home takes a while. There's no hurry, I know everyone is probably sleeping, as they tend to do after the wave. It's the pain—it's grueling and breaks them each time. I wonder, as I always do, how much more Daniel can survive before the radiation takes him. His body has already built an immunity to the Blue. I wonder how many more kids will die before this is all over. I used to think the worst thing humanity faced was the threat we posed to each other. Greed, guns, atomic war. I was wrong. It was the threat we posed to the Earth, and the rage we stirred in the goddesses who protected it. The savior device. What a stupid name. It saves nothing. Soon it will destroy us all, obliterate any chance we had to evolve as a species. Did the circle of goddesses know that?

In cultures across the globe there exists the story of a great flood that took place thousands of years ago. A savior device from another era, if you will. The gods wanted to destroy the Earth with a flood, to effectively press the reset button on people who had become too evil. Still, the gods wanted to give humanity a chance. The Bible's god looked for a worthy man and settled on Noah—in my opinion, a dubious choice at best. The story has some striking similarities to my current predicament, except in my tale, she's a girl and she's more than worthy. She's as precious and rare as a breeze in outer space, but is Divinica our slender chance at salvation or the catalyst of our final doom? As I ride, I decide it doesn't matter. If she elects to build an ark and fill it with a shit ton of radiated creatures, or go on a murdering rampage, I'd be with her either way.

Darkness holds the earth like a leather-gloved fist when I reach base-camp end, or BCE as Dayle likes to call it. He's waiting for me outside, arms folded, looking like a benched NBA player. Rashid paces in front of him, his nervous hands making a ruin of his pretty pink hair. How one even gets their hair dyed in this world is beyond me, but he manages. Rashid practically does a pirouette when he sees me, then he starts running, stopping only when his arms are locked around me in his dainty version of a bear hug. He squeezes me tight, right before he leans back and lightly smacks my face. The hit is nothing, but I'm so tired, I stumble a step backward.

"You scared me!" Rashid barks, but he draws his brows together and frowns when he gets a good look at my face. "Shit! Who died and made you king of despair? Seriously, bro, you look like you just killed your best friend."

I shake my head at him. "You know, Divinica's right, you really are a whole thing. The true travesty of the apocalypse is that you lost the opportunity to have your own reality show."

Rashid sighs wistfully. "I know. Sometimes I dream about spending hours in hair and makeup and wake up smiling."

I have no comment, so I turn to Dayle.

"You good?" Dayle asks, his voice low.

"No," I say honestly.

Dayle nods like he didn't expect any other answer, then reaches for Borax's reins. Borax snorts but allows himself to be led away with minimal fuss. "Meet you in the throne room," Dayle throws over his shoulder. "We need to talk."

"Alright," I say, wondering how much longer I'm going to be able to hold my eyes open.

Rashid links his arm through mine. I hate looking weak but let myself lean on him. I need support. "I won't ask if you're okay, 'cause my mama didn't raise stupid," he says, casting a glare at Dayle's retreating back. "But what about our girl? How is she?"

"She—" Words die. What should I tell him? What is there to say? I settle on, "She's breathing, though I'm not sure she's so happy about that fact right now. The way she looked at me when she forgot me—" I shake my head and try to rub away the physical ache in my heart. "The feeling it left me with will linger." I hold my thumb and forefinger to my eyes as a sense of unreality strikes me. It's starting all over again. Micha, the slap, the threats, the questions with looping, crazy answers. The disbelief, the way her body flinches when I get too close. "Fuuuuuck!" I groan. "I love her so fucking much! I don't think I can go through this again."

Rashid glances up at me. His face is full of sympathy, but I've known him too long to be fooled. "What?" he snaps.

"What?" I demand.

"Poor boy," Rashid says, using his exhale as an exclamation. "Why are you always so needy? The stud who managed to find a perfect girl at the end of the world is suddenly scared of the fight it takes to keep her."

"Asshole. If I wasn't so dead on my feet right now, I might hit you for that," I grumble.

Rashid tosses his luxurious hair. "Truth hurts."

"I'm not too scared to keep her, I'm just plain scared," I bark. "Oh, I saw her open the star portal, that shit's real by the way."

"Well, we always knew that, didn't we?"

"Knowing and seeing are two vastly different things, trust me. She said some crazy shit when she got back. Said her tattoos were star technology made specifically to interact with earth power."

"Alien?"

"Who the fuck cares? The point is, they did this to her, and she's pissed, or will be again when she remembers. From what I understand, the artifacts each hold a piece of a goddess. There are thirteen tattoos, so I'm guessing there's thirteen artifacts—"

"Wow! Did your three master's degrees from Yale help you figure that out?" asks Rashid, serving me buckets of raw attitude.

"It did, actually."

"It's pretty crazy," says Rashid. Shoving past me, he starts to climb the stairs leading to what the people have affectionately dubbed the throne room.

"Oh yeah? What about this particularly strikes you as crazy?" I realize I'm slurring. My mama used to say, "Boy could sleep on his feet." Turns out she was right.

"Well, we crash-landed on a big Earth after falling out of a bigger sky," Rashid says.

I start to yawn. "Your point?"

"Just seems strange to nearly land on top of the only girl who can save the world."

"Sounds like a coincidence," says Dayle from behind me, making me jump.

"Sure does, and I don't believe in those," Rashid says.

"It's not a fucking coincidence, or chance. It's fate. I think we would have fallen wherever she was. Sometimes I dream of her and I in another life. I tell her that I'll always find her, no matter how many lives I live. I press her hand into my blood and tell her to make it so. I've had the same dream for two years. She makes the vow, then I die. I didn't used to think it meant anything, but now—"

"That's dark, man, and beautiful. Way to go deep. I'm getting all choked up," Dayle rumbles.

I sigh and shake my head. "Fuck you, dude."

At the top of the stairs, Rashid flicks the switch he installed two years ago and floods the room with a soft, electric light. I blink, and my eyes water. The light illuminates all the things I've collected, once priceless works of art and culture, now forgotten relics of a lost age. I remember when we first found this place like it was yesterday. Almost five hundred people crowded together with their dead, existing in stench and misery because they forgot there was another way to live. They had a leader of sorts, the same guy who built my throne—for what reason, I can't fathom. I had to kill him in single combat.

It was fierce and bloody. It was also my first murder, and there've been far too many since. Rashid and Dayle carried on like cheerleaders during the fight. I hated it, or rather, I wanted to hate it, but some part of me—some dark, hidden piece—loved every second of it. I wanted to kill something after all the dead babies I had to bury earlier that day.

They chanted and called me Skylord. But that day, after I watched their leader machine-gun five kids to silence their crying before I could shout or stop it and I was forced to snap his neck with my bare hands, I felt like the lord of death. Felt like it ever since. I've lost two hundred and twelve people in two years, and only twenty-three have been born. I understand the numbers. Many have died during the waves. They smash their heads into walls or take drills and knives to their temples, anything to stop the pain. Who would want to bring life into such a horrible place? Randomly, I think of a little girl with Divinica's bright green eyes and my hair. The image of the imaginary child is so beautiful, it makes me want to punch a wall again. Instead, I shrug out of my jacket and pitch it across the room.

Dayle turns to face me. I'm a tall guy, a little over six foot three, but he towers about a foot higher. A lot of people told him he was too big and Black to be an astronaut. Dayle didn't care. He finished his training at Johnson, top of his class, and got himself not two, but three doctorates: engineering, biology, and environmental science. He was with me on my first flight, and I hope he's right beside me on my last, but sometimes I wish I was big enough to take him on. He's been hinting at a throw down for years, but I haven't gone for it, because I hate getting flattened by a best friend. You never hear the end of it. "You got a plan?" he asks.

"As if anyone could have a plan in a situation like this." I shrug. "Divinica will sleep for about a day, so I'll probably do the same. I don't even remember being this tired during hell week."

Dayle flashes me a crooked smile. "That sounds like a plan."

It takes physical effort not to flip him two birds.

"Seriously, though, it's the sadness, it exhausts you. When I lost my mom, I slept for two weeks straight," Dayle says, striding across the room to the jug of purified well water chilling in our makeshift cooler—an industrial garbage bag full of melting ice. He drinks down a giant swallow, then brings the jug to me. I thank him and drink the rest.

"Way to offer me some," Rashid whines.

"I han spit it bac ou if you lic," I say over the last mouthful.

Rashid makes a dramatic face. "Tempting, but I'd rather have a beer. I think I'll plan another trip to Munich, see if I can get more. Dachau's been dry for two weeks."

"Try Feldmoching, I hear there's two supermarkets we haven't hit yet," Dayle says.

"No, the Burning tribe have that town on lock—"

I cut him off. "No one's going anywhere. Rashid, how soon can we have the *Gravity* flight ready?"

Rashid gives me a patronizing look. "Well, considering it crashed, burned, and hasn't moved in two years, I'm gonna say a while."

"I need it operational in the next four days, or we're going to need to find another machine capable of getting us to England."

"Whoa, did I space out? We're going to England?" Dayle asks.

"Yes, I'm taking Divinica. One way or another, I'm ending this. My sanity depends on it. I can't stay stuck in this loop forever. I'm tired of the days of hate, I'm tired of digging graves for babies. If this whole thing is a spell, then spells can be broken. I would say you both don't have to come, but I can't pilot the *Gravity* alone."

Rashid clicks his tongue. "Boy, I followed you to Mars. England ain't no thang."

Dayle throws his bulk on the yellow couch, which squeals but holds him. "You know I can't stay behind. I get FOMO," he says, lifting Dan Brown's *The Da Vinci Code* and flipping to a page with a folded corner.

"It's true, I've seen it. Not pretty and…kinda sad," Rashid says, clacking his painted nails against his teeth.

"We're probably all going to die," I say cheerfully, looking through our first-aid kit for some rubbing alcohol to pour over the throbbing gash on my chest.

"*Valar morghulis.* All men must die," Rashid says.

"Don't quote *Clash of Kings* when I'm this tired, but thanks. I don't know what I'd do without you guys," I say over a yawn that won't quit.

Rashid winks at me. "You'd probably frown a lot more."

"I'm going to bed. We'll start on repairs in the morning," I say, yawning again, this one damn near breaking my jaw.

"Aw, stay. Dayle and I are going to watch a trashy romance and pick apart the main characters."

Dayle quirks his lip. "We are?"

"Immediately no, just no. I want to sleep," I say and start to turn away.

"You don't want sleep, you want dreams."

Rashid's words stop me in my tracks. He's right, that's all I want. "In my dreams, she always remembers me," I say. Silence follows me to the small room partially hidden by the giant throne. I fall face-first on my bed. Sleep finds me quick as a hired killer. I wish it hadn't, because my dreams are silent. I look for her, but Divinica is nowhere to be found. Maybe my subconscious knows that this time I've utterly lost her.

CHAPTER TWENTY-THREE

For all the stars that ever shine, one is yours and one is mine

DIVINICA

When I open my eyes for the first time after whatever happened happened—I am dazed, dizzy, and disoriented, like I drank too much of something that temporarily took my sanity. Thick, white mists stuff my head and create shadows that tantalize my tired eyes. My fingertips run down the center of my body and brush the mark just below my navel. It aches, and there's a pulsing glow emanating from it. I'm not sure if the glow and the pain are real or imagined, but it sucks just the same.

I remember the room I'm in. It's my room. Four green walls, rusted metal bars strung across an open window that shows me nothing I want to see. A storm of emotions rips through me. Rage at the white silence and twisting gut pain from a loss so deep, I know it scarred my soul. Disillusionment at the confusion that ensues when I try to recall…something…anything. I stand up and walk to the crude window. I can see the sky through the slender bars. The clouds look like giant bruises, black and sonic-green at the edges. The moment the dusky light touches my tattoos, all of them start to glow. Beautiful, like fireflies at twilight. It hurts too. Sharp pin pricks of fire that piss me off.

I turn and face my empty room with a sigh. A candle lies in the middle of the floor, tipped onto its side, a pool of melted wax its fixed companion. I think about kicking it and wonder if I've thought about kicking it before.

I hurt everywhere, as if the entire surface of my skin was branded. I sit back down on my bed. I braid my hair. I wash my clothes. I wash myself. I walk around the room naked and freezing while my clothes dry. I paint and scream at the walls. I stare into nothing forever. I touch the crown sitting on my pillow like it's always been there. It's glowing, like the other items in my room. A peach, a teardrop of light, a shell, a sword, and a big red bird that squeaks when I look at him.

Freya, that's the name in my mind. Her name, I assume. The goddess—the previous owner of this forest crown. I drew her on my wall, I almost remember doing it. I gaze at her for a long time. As I stare, I hear the crackle of lightning, and I see the bright blue eyes of man, feel his blood run down my stomach, hear the rumble of thunder, and watch him take his last breath. More pictures come. Dreams? Memories? I don't know. The sense of being horribly alone, of missing some vital part of myself, torments and consumes me. I lie down. I close my eyes. Toss and turn. The day darkens. The fog in my brain spreads to my eyes. And time—if that's even a thing anymore—passes on without me.

I'm something more than tired when I wipe my hand over my face and kneel on the small rug spread out in front of my bed. I see a black book on the ground and reach for it without thinking. The second my hand contacts the cold leather binding, I know it's mine. I pick it up, and it falls open to the fourth page. I start to read, happy that, apparently, I know how.

Twelve goddesses. Twelve artifacts. Thirteen tattoos. They did this to you, stupid mythical beings.
In these other realms, Valance always dies.

Valance. The name makes something sharp and poignant twist my gut. I breathe through it, then thumb back to the first page and keep reading.

The savior device Dad always told you about is real.

"What the fuck is a savior device?" I ask the room, and the bird squawks again. If he's saying anything of importance, I'm unfortunately unable to decipher it. I sigh and continue to read.

You lit a candle and the tattoo on your arm started glowing. You read the words, and they made an archway. You walked through it and fell into a shit ton of stars. You're sixty percent sure this happened.

I pause over that last line, then lift my pencil and write:

You're now ninety percent sure this happened. Maybe ninety-five. You've been collecting artifacts and bringing them back as proof. Go around your room and touch them, maybe they will help you remember. Right now, you have six in total: a peach, a damn singing shell, a bird, a vase of light, a sword, and now a crown. By the time you re-read this, you might have more.

I keep turning pages, and on almost every page in my boldest script, there's something along the lines of:

Remember Daniel, he's your brother.

I turn to a page in a back and continue reading.

Here are three things you have to know. One: Stay awake when the cold gets bad. Two: Hunt with a bow and not a gun. The third is a fundamental truth you can't let yourself forget. If this world was something once, that once is now gone. Cities are charred down to their bare bones, bodies rot everywhere, lying where they fell. Everything has been reduced to nothing.

I roll my eyes, wondering what the hell is wrong with my writing skills, a few helpful tidbits of information mixed in with all that confusion would have been preferable. With no explanation in sight, I shove the notebook under my pillow and lift my cloak from the end of my bed. I pull my hair back and tie it in a knot, then give my room a last look before I leave it.

Outside, Boogles is resting. Eyes closed, big body crouched in a tense, terrified pose. His back knees are almost touching, and his butt looks like it's trying to tuck itself between his legs. My book says he's a bit of a coward. I sing something pretty as I walk to him, a string of perfectly crafted lyrics. A gift from my subconscious. The music playing through my mind is a thousand threads of light that cut like daggers through the white fog. Boogles seems to calm as I enchant him with my song. I scratch the top of his head, then place the saddle on his wide back.

"How you doing, boy? Let's find ourselves a snake and put it in a stew. What do you say?" I ask, attaching the hanging straps of the saddle under his huge, swaying stomach. He snorts through his trumpet nose, then kneels down so I can climb on his back. A fine mist begins to fall, dampening my skin. Drops cold as melted ice. In the distance, black storm clouds pour like boiling water over the jagged, ice-capped mountains. I shiver hard. Almost instantly my tattoos start to glow. It hurts, like a million tiny needles stabbing my freezing skin. The glow brightens until it makes a halo around Boogles and me. Warmth flows from the marks into my veins and through my body. The shivers stop, but the glow remains.

Night thickens as we ride. Staring at the roiling sky, I find myself thinking of a wave, glowing, electric, red, and hot as a dwarf star. For a second, I almost feel myself screaming as the strong arms of a man throw me through a door to the outer confines of space and beyond the reach of time. Suddenly, his voice is a shout in my head. *"I'm Valance, you're Divinica. You know me! I swear I won't hurt you. Wait, baby! NO!"*

I resist the urge to scream as my mind circles back to what passes for my present when I see something slither a few feet in front of us. I make a clicking sound with my tongue against the roof of my mouth, then grip the edges of the saddle as Boogles comes to a stop. He snorts and shakes his head when I dismount. My boots sink deep into the gray slush covering the ground as the rain turns the powdered snow to mud. My feet leave prints I wish I could cover. I'm staring down at my boots, hoping the rain will wash the traces of me away, when a memory surges. I remember the first time I put these boots on. The zipper got stuck, and the buckles going down the sides of them were difficult to fasten. I remember spinning in a brightly lit kitchen. The hem of my white sundress tickled my knees. A little boy with dark, curling hair told me I looked like a slut-bag.

My lips part over a harsh exhale. The memory makes me want to cry. I shove it away and focus on the task at hand. It's so dark I use my ears to find the creature. It's a snake. I see a glimmer of moonlight on its bronze scales, hear a rattle in its tail, and follow it. When I think I'm close enough to make the shot, I kneel down and take my aim. I'm so involved in my kill, so wrapped up in my own hunger and random, shattering memories, that I don't hear the footsteps. I scream when someone comes up behind me, tossing some kind of sack over my head.

Rational thought abandons me. My foot lashes out. I strike something hard and hear a crack, then a man's low whine. "Bitch broke my fucking nose."

Good, I think, as hands wrestle with mine, trying to lock them behind my back. It takes at least three of them to subdue me, but in the end I'm conquered. Their hands are all over me like chicken pox. My body knows what those are even if my mind doesn't. Suddenly, I'm itchy everywhere.

I think then that the last time a man's hands were on my body, I was panting, begging, arching for more. I don't want my attacker's dirty paws to take away the memory of that other touch. I start to struggle in earnest, a little crazed, but a lot mad.

"Let me go!" I scream. "Fuck you! Let me go!" Something hard strikes the side of my head. The world sways. I stumble, almost falling to my knees. I hear harsh male laughter and see red, only red. Red, so much red. Always red.

No, it's coming, coming to take everything, coming to take him, coming on a whirlwind to smother me, a monster wearing a flowing cape of white silence, I think, then know the thoughts are too late. It already came. It already took. I'm broken again. Spliced. Split into so many parts, I fear I'll never find myself.

"Keep her Tardigrade quiet. Kill the beast if you have to," someone says.

"No!" I scream. Instantly, I stop my struggles. "Don't hurt him. I won't fight anymore."

"Fine. We'll bring them both as a gift for the Skylord."

"If she starts kicking again, we can kill it," says another voice, lower, more hoarse.

I stopped listening after the first one said "Skylord." *Valance.* My heart kicks hard. *I'm Valance, you're Divinica. You know me! I swear I won't hurt you.* The voice, his voice, subsumes my mind. Its accomplice is memories of firm lips kissing me into oblivion. Strong limbs tangled with mine. Hard hands shaping my breasts, fingers spearing through my hair, a hot ache between my thighs.

"Do it now!"

"Divinica..."

"I mean it. Take me to your bed."

"Why? So, I can have you for a night. Maybe two? Only to have you forget me all over again?"

Words, so many words run through my mind. They ring my ears and have a shattering effect on my heart. More memories come. I know that's what they are. Because in my mind, Valance and I are in my room. My gross green walls are his backdrop. He's holding up his hands, shouting and begging. *"No, fuck, baby, don't look at me like that. Goddamn it!"*

"What's happening? Who are you? What do you want?"

"It's me, Divinica, it's Valance. You know, the guy who stalks your shadow and almost took your virginity on a metal table like an hour ago?"

My whole body shakes as those last words shout through my mind. I take a deep breath. *Steady, be steady, just a little while longer, steady, steady, steady.* I repeat the word to myself ad nauseam as they tie my hands behind my back, then toss me face-first over Boogles's saddle.

I count to a thousand six times over and focus on breathing. In and out, one second at a time, because I don't think I can manage more than that. My ribs are screaming when one of the men shouts for the others to stop. I lift my head, blink rapidly, and try to see through the dirty cloth. I find that I can, a little, and through it I see dark, roving shadows, dilapidated ruins, and people, so many people.

I try to keep my promise not to struggle when they pull me from Boogles's back—it's difficult, the need to fight seems intrinsic for me as breathing.

One of the men tears the bag off my head, another shoves me to my knees. I look directly up at my attackers. When one of the men grabs me, and the open sores on his fingers smear puss on my chin, I literally can't take it—I spit in his eye.

CHAPTER TWENTY-FOUR

What does it profit a man, if he should save the whole world, but lose his soul?

VALANCE

I've been working on the *Gravity* for eighteen hours straight when I see her. I have a wrench balanced between my teeth and grease in my eyes, but my heart kicks me in the ribs so hard I almost fall over. She's on her knees where she doesn't belong. Micha grabs her face, and the second the man's filthy fingers touch her skin, I vow that this time I really am going to kill him. Divinica spits directly in his eye, brave boss that she is. I know what's coming. I don't think. I can only react. I grab the first thing I see, a curved scythe Dayle's been using for fuck knows what, and hurl it at Micha as he raises his hand to strike the girl I love.

The blade hits, nearly severing Micha's hand at the wrist. Micha glares at his hand in shock, then screams like a pig-tailed girl in a playground and drops harder than a dubstep beat. A spray of blood splashes Divinica's face. She starts but doesn't scream. It takes her less than a second to recover, then she throws her body in a low roll toward the weapon I just stupidly gave her. Her body is little more than a blur as she slices her bonds on the curved blade in one clean twist of her arms. Freed, she jumps to her feet and grabs the scythe's handle, reaching for the knife in her boot at the same time. I swallow hard.

Dread is the air I breathe. I've lived through so many variations of this moment. Angry, crazed, powerful Divinica. She turns on me, teeth bared. The blank rage in her confused eyes makes me boil, but her snarling lips are the straw that breaks my beaten back. In my quiet moments, I believe I've managed to hold it together pretty well so far. But right now, my heart thus destroyed, obliterated, and irreparable, I think I lose it a little. I move, prepared to grab her arms and shake some damn sense into her. Seconds before I reach her, Divinica lifts her arm with a practiced move to throw her little knife at me.

"Don't you fucking dare!" I shout. She's not listening. Instead, the corners of her mouth lift in a triumphant smile before she throws the blade with exacting precision. I watch it cartwheel toward my heart. Some part of my mind tells me to stand still and get stabbed. With any luck, the knife will slice straight through my heart and save me from experiencing this nightmare all over again.

Dayle forestalls my dark wishes by jumping in front of me less than a nanosecond before the blade sinks into my chest. He's using an old car door as a shield. The knife hits the metal with a sharp twang that echoes like the crescendo of a bad soundtrack in a cheap horror film, the forerunner of my approaching doom. It stabs the dirt instead of me. Divinica glares down at the knife, then growls like a lioness robbed of her kill. Her eyes meet minergty67u and the entire world does the strangest thing. It stops spinning as Divinica runs toward me, faster than a human should move. I blink, and she's in front of me, sharply gasping in the air rustled by her momentum.

I reach out my arms before I can tell myself to stop being an idiot. I'm angry, furious really, but all I want to do is hold her, drag her stubborn head to my chest, and run my fingers through her hair. The dark mass falls around her heaving shoulders, and it seems weaved with starlight and mystery, strung with a few crystalline drops of the fresh, falling midnight rain. Her cheeks are flushed a hot shade, and the rosy color brings out the steel and fire in her eyes. Her mouth is mere inches from mine. I stare her down, feeling my breaths deepen. I have no idea what secret power keeps me from forcing a kiss on those parted lips. A deep emptiness opens inside of me, a waterless chasm, a sinkhole to nowhere. No matter how bad I want to hate her for tearing me apart, I just can't. I know she's my truest desire, my surest destruction.

I keep my gaze locked with hers, and when she tilts her chin, I see a glimmer in her eyes. A look, a spark of something that a hopeful man might call recognition. I am no longer a hopeful man. I'm a mountain climber at the end of his fraying rope with miles of deadly sky beneath him. No matter, I am destined to fall because I know she sees the villain in me, not the friend. I'm not the good guy in this story. I'm a killer who will do what needs to be done and leave the broken pieces in my past. Somehow I think she knows it and hates me because of it. For a blasphemous second, I almost hate her too.

The affection for her that afflicted me moments ago retreats under her glare of disdain, leaving my soul bereft and frostbitten. I don't see her then, just some crazy chick looking for another weapon to shoot or stab me. "Stand down, witch," I snap, harsher than intended.

Divinica's stare is bold. "You're Valance," she says, and it isn't a question.

"At your service, darling," I say calmly, though I've no idea how I manage it. I am cracking on the inside, my mind exploding, my heart in bloody tatters on the ground, and presently being stomped into the dirt by the raised soles of her sexy black boots. I drop down into a little bow, so angry that my hands are shaking. Heat twines like a poisonous snake through my veins, making me dizzy. My body is tense, expecting another attack at any moment, and my brain is wondering if I'll put up a fight or just lie in the dirt, stare at the sickly moon, and let her do her worst.

Divinica doesn't move though, remaining still as one of her statues, a warrior queen from another time, fists clenched tight, knees flexed to spring. She's the Valkyrie from my imagination, strong and wondrous as a color-soaked nebula. Even though I outweigh her by roughly a hundred pounds, I know I couldn't hurt her. If she were intent on killing me, I doubt I would resist. I open my mouth to say something unbearably witty, but I'm shocked into silence when a strange, almost yearning expression twists her face.

Divinica takes a single, unsteady step back. Her hands open and close, once, twice, and then she links her fingers across her stomach. "Do I...have we met?" she asks, hesitant, tentative, nervous, wary.

My body feels encased in dry ice. I try to swallow the sudden metal-spiked lump in my throat. "Yes, Divinica, we've met," I say, my voice tight as the skin around an old scab.

"Why did Micha bring me to you?" she asks, as she has many times before.

"How do you remember his name?" I answer, same question, different answer. She's never remembered his name before. Normally just calls him "that asshole guy."

"I don't know." She steps closer to me, I try not to move a single muscle, try not to breathe. "Do you...are we...?" I never get to hear the rest of it. Rashid appears behind her. I was so wrapped up in her eyes, I didn't see him coming. He lifts a syringe and, before I can shout protest, sticks the needle in her arm and presses the plunger. Divinica shrieks in shock, spins, and lands a karate chop to the side of Rashid's neck. He takes a step back, stumbles, trips, and then falls on his ass.

"What the fuck!" I shout, the words popping out like a threat.

Divinica's eyes fly back to me, devastating emerald orbs drenched in betrayal and shock. She falls in what seems like slow motion. I reach out to catch her before her knees hit the dirt, but she knocks my hand away with fading strength. "It's just to help you sleep, he didn't hurt you," I say, going down on my knees beside her.

"Bastard...hate y...you..." she mumbles. I catch her head as it drops. This time, she can't knock me away. Then, she's out cold.

My eyes go to Rashid, who's in the process of standing up and brushing dirt off his pants. "Don't glare at me like that, cowboy! If I couldn't go through it all again, I know you sure as hell can't," he declares harshly before I can say anything.

"She was different this time," I say, all the fight in my soul draining away.

"You always say that, and she never is. It's all just repetitive variations of the same damn nightmare. I hate the fear in her eyes when she looks at me, hate the anger and confusion I know she feels. Now she's dreaming. Not great, but not worse. Let her sleep it off. I can't watch her pain right now, I just can't. You're not the only one who loves her, you know," Rashid says.

I don't answer him. I lift Divinica in my arms and take her into the ship. I look down at her peaceful face, eyes closed, lips soft and pursed, then think about her telling me to take her to my bed and just do it. I remember the way her hands shook as she told me she couldn't go through it again, that she wasn't strong enough, that she searches the white silence, missing something, not knowing it's me. I'm glad memories can't kill, because mine would obliterate me.

I set her sleeping body down on the small cot in the cramped quarters near the *Gravity*'s flight deck. It's the captain's quarters. I spent three years in this room, staring at the Earth through my window. I always thought the room was a rather miserable, lonely place. It hits different with her in my bed. I slide my arms out from under her, forcing myself not to lean down and kiss her. Cheeks, brow, and the tiny line of consternation between them.

I'm angry. The angriest I've been in a while, but I want her. *God, I want her.* She curls her fingers into my shirt until her knuckles whiten, then holds on, just for a second, but long enough for my whole body to light up like a firework. All at once I'm hot and aching, needing, hating her all over again. The barrage of conflicting feelings is a razor-sharp blade slipped between my ribs, and I'm gasping like an untried boy macking on his first crush.

I take a deep breath, then another, and another, just trying, hoping I can pull it together. The breaths are unsteady, and they break. I have to pull away from her, stand up and run my fingers through my hair to keep my hands from shaking, pace the small room to keep from shouting, screaming, putting the muzzle of a gun to my mouth, and swallowing a bullet.

I dodge the small metal table pressed up against the room's south wall, then knock over a lamp. Divinica doesn't flinch when the light bulb shatters in a thousand pieces. I stop pacing and look down at the mess, just one more broken thing I can't fix. My gaze flicks back to her. Divinica's eyes move beneath her closed lids.

I feel trapped, trapped by her, by this ship, by this Earth I once called home. The *Gravity* is months from completion. The electrical system got fried on our re-entry into the Earth's atmosphere. Rashid says our main propulsion engine is shot, our split rudder is shattered, and our orbital maneuvering system has taken life-threatening hits. Our right elevons are warped. A piece of the left delta wing is orbiting the moon along with the payload door. I was banking on the supposition that this ship could get us out of Germany, a place where none of us belong. I could use this ship that once took me to Mars to take her away from Styx, away from that lab holding hours of her pain. I want to take her off-world and find myself wondering if she would remember me in the endless, crowded, empty confusion of space. Will the spell break when so far removed from its point of origin?

"Running away won't help," says Rashid, walking into the small room and reading my damn mind. "Don't do anything rash. We need Divinica to break the spell. Regardless of what she means to us. Everyone's lives depend on it. We lost three more during the wave. Julian, Skies, and Clarence, and Clarence was only five."

My vision hazes as darkness presses in all around me, smothering, suffocating me. "I know how old he was," I rasp. "And we don't know if she can save them. All we have are stupid alien theories. We can make a damn documentary, but that doesn't mean we can save the world. Stupid, dangerous theories, for her. For all of us."

"You better not change your damn mind. I've been stripping wires for twelve hours," Rashid says, hand on thrusted hip, a storm cloud looming in the back of his hooded eyes.

"I don't know what I'm doing," I admit and kind of half fall, half sit on the narrow bed beside Divinica. She doesn't move. The regularity of her breathing steadies me somewhat. "All I know is that I'm staying with her until whatever you shot in her arm wears off. I want to be the first thing she sees when she opens her eyes. She remembered me a second before you stuck her with a needle, at least I think she did." I rest my elbows on my knees and rub my eyes with the heels of my hands. "There was something about the way she looked at me, something—"

"Sounds like wishful thinking, dude. She'll hate you, like she always does. Brace for the fall, that's all you can do."

I know he's right, but his words enrage me, and it takes real effort not to hit him. I can feel my hands clench. They want to punch something, anything. "Get the hell out before I forget we're friends."

Rashid shakes his head. "Fine, but only because I don't want to be here anyway. The energy in this room is extremely negative."

"No shit!" I shout.

Rashid smiles, there's so much kindness in his eyes, pity too, but I don't mind it. "At least she's beside you, safe, Micha didn't hit her, she didn't stab you, if you look at it in the right light, there's a few wins."

"Get the fuck out," I say, but I'm smiling, and all the heat is gone from my voice. Rashid flips me the bird, then scurries away while rolling his hips like some exotic dancer. I lie down beside Divinica, I know I shouldn't put a hand on her without consent, but I can't help it. She's lying on her side, knees drawn up. I drape my arm over her waist, then fist my hand so I don't cup her perfect breast. I move a handful of soft hair off her shoulder, then stare at the gentle slope of her neck, bite my lower lip to keep from kissing the spot just behind her ear. She smells like the cheap lavender soap I left on the doorstep of Styx almost a year ago, like clean skin and fresh water. She makes my heart melt.

What if the *Gravity* is fixable? What if it can take us to Stonehenge, or some other random place of power? What if we can break the savior device? What if it kills her? What if I save the world and lose the girl I love? My what ifs have answers, I know them all. The answers haunt the darkness that comes to smother me when she forgets. Darkness that grows in density and fortitude each time. I don't care about the world. I know it's horrible, but I wouldn't trade her life for anyone or anything. It would mean the end of my life. Not that it would matter. If she's gone, I'll turn to dust. Cry until my veins are rivers washing me over the edge of a cliff.

I bury my face in her hair and take a deep breath that I hold in my lungs until it burns. *She remembered me. It will be different this time. I know it. I fucking know it!* I think, then curse loudly. There's that pesky hope again, like murder in the night it stalks me, pounces, leaves me wishing for a salvation that won't come. I realize, quite to my chagrin, that I'm sobbing. Big soul wrenching tears that shake my whole body. I bite down on my lips to muffle the sound of the sudden cloudburst, but it hardly helps. It feels like the bed is swaying like a hammock in the wind while the spinning floor is falling out from under me. The feeling sucks and makes me cry even harder. The last time I cried like this, I was kneeling beside my mother next to the rotting pile of her brain.

I cry until the broken sounds I'm making turn to harsh rasps that startle me almost more than the tears. After what seems to be an incredible amount of time, the tears finally start to dry up, and my heart rate slows to a more normal, somewhat coherent rhythm.

I tilt my head up to wipe my wet cheeks with the back of my hand, and stare at her sleeping profile, perfectly viewed from my vantage. There's no sign of the warrior girl in the gentle lines and full slopes of her sleeping face, right now she looks like an angel who misplaced her wings.

I'm not some damn romantic, I've never seen the *Notebook*, and sat through just one showing of *Twilight*, and only because my mother made me. Said it was her favorite movie and a true piece of modern culture. I liked it fine, but it didn't make me want to rush out and find true love. My mom always dreamed of true love. I know that in her beautiful, kind heart, she believed in happily ever after—and look where that got her. Loneliness lane, and a date with a speeding bullet that she found at the end of the world.

A great queen once said that pain is the price we pay for love, a price I never wanted or intended to pay, but the second I saw Divinica, it was like something old and wise inside of me just clicked into place. I know it sounds fucking crazy, but what I experienced was more than love at first sight. I felt like I had been looking for her, waiting for her my entire life. I felt like she was mine and I was hers. It was a fact, an unshakable truth written into the cornerstones of the universe. That was two years ago. I've always had an obsessive, rather addictive personality—a trait I inherited from my father—but now it's out of control. She's my drug, her kiss is the fix I crave. When she remembers me it's the high of my life, passion-soaked trips fraught with kisses and whispered words. When she forgets, the withdrawals are worse than anything. Replete with cold sweats and a sense of emptiness so deep it seems fathomless.

I lie my head on the pillow beside her, bury my face in her hair again, and pull her closer, closer, closer still, until her heat is mine, and the cadence of her breathing commands the beat of my heart. We fit so perfectly together. I have that weird thought again, that unshakeable sensation that she was made just for me, her soul mine alone, forever, no matter what games time plays. It's agony and mayhem, but if it means I can keep her, I fear I wouldn't have it any other way.

Just as I'm starting to give into the pull of sleep, Divinica stirs, then mumbles a single word. "Valance." My name. Only that. She says it again and again. "Valance, Valance, Valance, Valance." The feeling of hearing my name on her lips kicks the air from my lungs and makes me lightheaded. *Shit! I've got it bad*, my mind wails, but I meet my approaching nightmares with a beaming smile.

CHAPTER TWENTY-FIVE

In this world, flashbacks are all the rage

DIVINICA

White light spears through a small circular window above my head shining a spotlight on my face. My cheek is hot in all the places where the light touches. My chest feels tight, like something heavy is lying on top of it. My ribs are sweaty and sore. I blink, trying to dispel images of the dream I escaped by waking up. I dreamed of a lab full of glass tubes, ink pots, needles, and a cold metal table. The room is haunted by the cringy sounds of my blood-curdling screams. Hecate makes little patterns down the front of my body using ink and a needle that glows like a captured star. I dreamed of pain, fear, and four walls that echo the sounds of my torment.

I also had another dream, a better dream. Same lab, same table, different occupants. No three headed woman with smug smiles, only a man. Tall, mesmerizing, mine. Time collapses, flows away, hemorrhages like a sliced artery. He's touching me, hard hands all over my body. The dreams snap between the two scenarios at will giving me whiplash in stages.

It takes me a few seconds to realize a muscled arm is lying across my waist. There's confusion in the realization but no fear. Sitting up and swinging my feet over the side of the narrow bed is easier said than done. I'm out of breath when the activity is complete. The arm was heavy, and the hand attached to it seemed deeply reluctant to let me go. When I stand, the owner of the arm stirs but doesn't wake. Still, I hold my breath until I hear his own steady, then deepen. I stare at his face with what feels like stars in my eyes. Full lips, chiseled jaw framed by hair so golden it strikes me as out of place in such a dark, cold world. I tear my eyes away from him and take a moment to inspect my surroundings. Small bed, small white table, and a single chair. On the wall directly beside the door is a skinny mirror with a white frame.

I walk to the mirror and stare at the girl reflected in the glass. A girl with dark, curly hair. Tilted green eyes far too large for her small, heart-shaped face. Dark skin, lips red as fresh blood. She's pretty and foreign. I know she's me, but I hardly know her at all. I do recognize her tattoos. Dark ink forming strange symbols that run down the front of her—my body. I lift my hand, moving like a sleepwalker, and touch the one in the center of my forehead. It stings when my fingers brush the thin black lines. As I touch it, it starts to glow. I remember it does that sometimes.

As I stare, my reflection begins to blur. In the murky glass I now see a circle of women, goddesses, hands linked, eyes glowing. I am one of them. A man is on his knees in front of me, there's a smoking black hole in place of his heart, he's swearing that he would rather die by my hand than any other. I can smell his burning flesh. I smack my own face, hard. First one cheek, then the other, and my own reflection makes its unenthusiastic return. I spin to glare at the man on the bed. *It's the same man,* I think. It was him for sure. I would recognize that jawline anywhere. He's alive. It must have been a dream. Just a dream of doll bodies and ancient spells, prison worlds and curses cast. If I'm awake, then who is he? I turn back to the mirror.

Who am I?

In the glass I see a younger version of me. My hair is pulled back in a tight ponytail. I'm sitting crossed-legged in a pile of Taylor Swift albums. *Taylor's version of course,* I think, and don't bother wondering why it matters, or how I know who Taylor Swift is. Midnight rain blares through the room. My body moves to the bougie beat. There are a dozen posters on the walls, bright and moody colors. One is of a dark sky flush with a million stars. I see everything in the mirror, it's as real to me as if I were standing in the room. *Lord of the Rings* is playing on the huge flat screen that hangs above my desk, and my iPhone lays in the middle of my bed charging. For a moment, I watch the green ring spin round and round. I remember this day perfectly.

It was a Sunday, three days before we flew to Germany. My mother, my father, my brother. Yes. I used to have those things. I remember being unreasonably angry about the trip. I was in a dark place, everything had all become so meaningless, my dreams handcuffed by social expectations, and the overwhelming pressure of academic achievement. In the mirror, I watch my younger self close her eyes, listen to Taylor's flawless notes. I was wondering what would become of my aspirations. Would I ever amount to anything? Was there a purpose to my life, or am I merely a speck of energy in a vast universe?

That girl wanted passion, fantasy, excitement, danger, a story worth writing. I close my eyes and when I open them again, she is gone. I am what remains, tattooed, battle scarred, and nearly unrecognizable. It dawns on me that my life can be reduced to a single admonition: Careful what you fucking wish for.

I scrub my hands over my face to wipe away the residuals of whatever the crap that was. The guy on the bed shifts, then rolls onto his back. I hold my breath, and stare at him like a cornered rabbit until he falls still.

His name is Valance. "Valance," I whisper, when I say the word, I know I'm right. He is Valance, and I'm Divinica. Skylord. My diary says I'm an idiot for forgetting him, and right now I feel like one. He looks like Apollo caught napping, tired of burning too bright. Or maybe Hercules grabbing some shut eye after battling a lion. I'm on the verge of walking over and shaking him awake when a blinking green light snaps my full attention to the center of the closed door. I hear a click, followed by a brief *whirring* sound, then the door starts to slide open.

I jump so hard I pull something in my lower back and hiss. My body is tense. My hands clench into fists as I prepare to punch whatever walks through that door. All the fight goes out of me when I see a thin boy with a riot of chestnut curls, fearlessly meeting my threatening snarl with a shy smile. He's got a bad bruise on his right cheek, and a split lip. He seems a little dazed, maybe disoriented.

Who fucking isn't? snaps my annoying mind. I sigh and lower my fists. I notice for the first time how dry my mouth is, my tongue is cotton and limestone, also, a spot on my upper arm hurts like shit. My head aches all over, and there's a bitter knot in the pit of my gut.

"I come in peace…uh…I think?" the boy says, staring at me like he's unsure whether to hug or attack me, maybe do an uneven combination of both.

"Me too?" I manage to croak.

"Uh, was that a question?" he asks, drawing out each word like he's speaking to someone with limited mental capabilities—maybe he is.

"No," I whisper.

"Who are you?" he asks.

I look for words, but they hide. The girl the mirror of memories showed me was poisoned by dreams of magic and grandeur. I don't know who the hell I am, but I know I'm no longer her. "Why?" I snap. "Who are you supposed to be?"

He shrugs.

"What are you doing in here?"

He shrugs again.

I roll my eyes. "Please leave, I have enough to deal with, and I've always been a shitty babysitter."

The kid folds his arms in a show of defiance. "Not that I'm disagreeing, you don't look fit to sit on any babies, but how do you know that? I mean, how do you know what you've always been?"

"I don't know," I say truthfully.

"Good thing I'm just making conversation, and don't really care," he mutters, then lifts his chin and squares his shoulders. "I'm running away from this place. Thought I might find something useful here. Found you, and that sleeping guy instead."

"Where are you running to?"

"Don't know, guess I'm gonna see where my feet take me." He flicks his chin toward the bed.

"Valance," I say, answering the question I know he's about to ask.

"What's a Valance?" the kid asks.

"Him, that's his name."

"Yeah, well he's giving me some *Alien vs Predator* vibes, emphasis on the predator."

"That was a movie," I say, as a bizarre looking creature flashes through my memory. I want to ask him how he remembers names, or movies, but I don't. I don't say anything.

"So, who is he?"

"I don't know him. Not really. But every time I look at him, it feels like my soul is a guitar and my heartbeats are strings," I finish, then blush, shocked that sentence actually came out of my mouth. I clear my throat. "Do you know what I mean?"

"No, but I stopped listening the second it got cringy." He makes a sappy lovelorn face at me, then jerks his thumb toward the door. "You coming? You can tell me more about your heartstrings on the way, I don't mind. I'm rather good at blocking out crap I don't want to hear."

"You're a little shit, aren't you?" I ask, my smile is saccharine.

"You know, I've heard that before, can't remember where exactly, but I think whoever said it to me was embroiled in a bit of a pot kettle situation."

I roll my eyes at him. "What's your name, anyway?" I ask as we both move quietly toward the door.

"Big guy, Dayle, I think, he said my name's Daniel. I have a sister I'm supposed to find. Her name's Divinica. What's your name?"

I pause in the act of shading my face against the milky rays of the sun and look him dead in the eyes. "Divinica."

No one stops us as I help Daniel onto Boogles's back. Boogles nudges his nose against my hand. He makes that muffled, trumpeting sound of his. I realize it's a sound I adore. I lean down and kiss Boogles right between his squinty eyes, then mount up. With Daniel's head resting against my back, reins in my hand, and wind on my face, I take the road it feels like I've traveled a thousand times. It's the road to the only home I have left.

When we finally see the imposing structure of Styx towering in the distance, Daniel sighs deeply, there's dread in the sound.

"I know, it's spooky, right?" I say, my voice holds a reverence I'm not sure I feel. The house is its own backdrop of horror. The way it rises from the ground like a prehistoric monster, covered in hundreds of tiny windows, watchful as eyes. Its four dark parapets look like dragon arms soaked in rust and lavender mist. It starts to rain when Boogles makes his way through the statues flanking what was once a driveway. Statues with missing arms, or three heads, all carrying artifacts like mine. *Like mine, just like mine, like mine.* The words repeat themselves over and over in my head until they start to mean something.

We ride the path that winds between the stone goddesses. I stare at each one as we pass it. My mind soaks in every minute detail. A shell, a vase of light, a peach, a bird with flaming wings, the braided crown of a Norse witch, the shield of a warrior. Resting on the pedestal of a decapitated statue is a head crowned with hissing snakes.

I take Boogles to the back of the first courtyard. Daniel and I dismount, then the three of us attack my stash of canned goods. Daniel and I eat until we're sick, Boogles exercises a bit more restraint.

"Not much left," I say, staring dejectedly at the three remaining cans.

Daniel glares down. "Yeah, they look pretty sad and lonely."

"We can search the east wing of this place. I haven't gone there much; the back rooms always scare me."

Daniel's head snaps up, he gives me a sharp, puzzled look. "How the hell do you know that?"

"No idea. Seems like I know a whole bunch of stuff right now."

He shakes his head. "That's crazy. I can't even remember…anything, it's all just…blank and scary."

"I know." I pause to wipe rain off my face. "So, are you brave enough to come with me?"

Daniel puffs out his slender chest. "Please, I'm the bravest person I know.

Well except for the blonde guy you attacked. Dude just stood there. Really thought he was going to let you stab him."

"I have a bad temper," I say by way of explanation.

"I think I do too, though I can't say for sure, since I can't remember my own name." He looks at me, rain drops splash his upturned nose. "Are you really my sister?"

"Yes," I say, no hesitation.

"What about our mom and dad?"

"They're dead." The second the words leave my mouth, I see a flash of my father's face, there's a smoking dot appearing right between his eyes.

"Crazy. I can't remember. When I try to think about anything, where I am, what happened, the way things used to be, it's all just—" he shrugs.

"White silence?" I offer.

"Yes. Loud silence, screaming silence," he says, dropping his head, but not before I see the glitter of moisture in his eyes. A beam of weak sunlight touches the few strands of auburn in his hair. It pours through the folds of his leather jacket like tiny rivers of molten gold when he stands and brushes his hands down his black jeans. The jeans are badly torn at the knees, and some of the little metal spikes dotting the numerous pockets are missing. I notice he's wearing thick silver rings on nearly all his fingers.

"Where did you get those rings?" I ask, weirdly drawn to the odd symbols on a few of them.

Daniel looks down at his hands like he's surprised he has fingers, much less wearing rings on them. He appears to think about my question for a few long seconds before he shakes his head. Dark curls fly everywhere. "I...I got them from a cardboard box I found in the old Rec room. It was full of papers and files. I think...I think I can show you," Daniel says, still staring at his hands, eyes wild and huge, shining like beacons in his pale face.

"Well? What are we waiting for?" I ask, then on impulse I throw my arm around him. He flinches again but doesn't pull away. We start walking, our sides pressed together, our bodies forming a slightly uneven heart. For the first time since I opened my eyes to find myself wearing a skin I can hardly remember, I feel a real smile touch my lips.

CHAPTER TWENTY-SIX

The thirteenth artifact

DIVINICA

Daniel and I sit on the chilly concrete floor of a dilapidated room surrounded by piles of paper, photos, charts, overstuffed cardboard boxes, and a plethora of scribbles and drawings I don't understand. The walls of the room we are in are clearly quite old, crumbling and strung with dust and spiderwebs, interlaced by peeling graffiti and splatters of white paint. I feel these walls are somehow still echoing the distant screams of misery harmonizing with whispers of trapped ghosts. Spiders with bright yellow eyes make their homes in the four corners of the slightly vaulted ceiling. Archways slope over the high cathedral windows, framed by tiles that were once a cheerful blue and white, but now are cracked and stained like everything else. The air is stale and smells like death. A giant hole in the roof lets in the rain and sleet. Chipped boards and bent, rusty nails hang down, dripping soggy brown water. The boards look wet and gooey. Like the house was once mortally wounded, and I'm looking at the guts that spilled through, and the black vines crawling all over the walls are exposed veins. Rusty hospital equipment and two dozen blood-stained cots furnish the freezing room. Blood spotted gowns that tie in the back are heaped in two piles near the door. Thorns, more vines, and dry leaves cover the floor. In this room at least, earth is reclaiming the land.

Wind howls through the broken windows, turning puddles of dirty water to ice, and freezing through skin to attack blood and bone. Daniel and I have been taking turns shivering. I gave him my cloak a few times, though he keeps giving it back to me. I want to use my tattoos to warm my blood, like I was somehow able to do...last night? Two nights ago? Who the fuck knows. I don't want to scare him by glowing, so when the cold gets too bad and the marks start to tingle and sting, I fight it. So far, I've won.

I busied my mind by looking through a bunch of the boxes, the majority of the content was gibberish to me. I felt like Sherlock Holmes—yes, I randomly remember who that is—digging for clues, trying to make sense of the nonsensical. Then, I reached some boxes that changed the game. What I found inside of them shocked me so badly, any excitement I felt died an excruciating death on the spot.

When I lifted a set of drawings with wet, curled corners, I froze and haven't moved since. The rest of the crap in here might not have meant much to me, but I understand these pictures perfectly. The one held loosely between all ten of my trembling fingers is pretty fucking clear. It's a visual representation of Stonehenge, or so it says at the bottom of the paper. Ink and paint skillfully laid show a bright red sun in the sky, partially covered by a full, blood moon. Its aura is maroon. Like someone stabbed the sun just to watch it bleed. In the center of the double stone circle is a square cut altar. On it is a girl. She's naked. The altar is surrounded by twelve artifacts. I recognize a few of them. Why wouldn't I? They're down the hall in my room.

In the image I hold, the girl has tattooed symbols that run down the front of her body; the tattoos are identical to my own. A spear of light slices through the gap between the two main stones and cuts straight into the girl's chest. The drawing is vivid and bloody. The girl is clearly dead. *Her limbs look like overcooked pasta noodles,* I think. My mouth promptly waters as it recalls the taste of pasta in all its wondrous glory. Hunger battles nausea.

I hear Daniel's feet shuffle. "Divinica, say something. You haven't moved in ages."

I try to smile, but only pull off a snarl. There's more writing at the bottom of the page. A part of me recognizes the writing, but of course I can't place it. I read the words aloud.

Must acquire 13th artifact for full functionality. Ideas for artifact: Sirius galaxy. Star/nanotech. Artifact will be marked. Attributes of artifact are: strength, ~~time travel?~~ Star travel. Flight? If sentient, they will be a linguaphile. If digital N/A. Will possess unparalleled power. Mythmarked? NOT HUMAN!"

Time stone. Time circles. Seven major stone circles known on Earth. Stonehenge, perhaps? Soul will be split in ~~12~~ 13 pieces and sent through time? ~~Soul will be demolished. Cannot survive time.~~ Souls are matter, matter can only be created, never destroyed.

I turn the paper over, but there's no more writing, only a small smudge at the top left-hand corner of the page that might've been something once. More renditions of this strange, detailed drawing are slotted into the surrounding piles of paper, all depicted from a slightly different angle.

Horribly, this drawing isn't the worst thing here. There are also hundreds of photos, maybe thousands. Photos taken from the neck down show the headless torsos of too many young girls. All of them are lying on the metal table which features in my lab of nightmares. All of them are topless, and all of them have tattoos running down the middle of their bodies, exactly like mine. Exactly like the drawings. All of them are wearing autopsy scars with chunky stitching. Some of the photos are so old, they seem to pre-date color, some are grainy, others are crisp and bright, lit by a light so cool it has a blue sheen. On the back of each photo, in strange, curling handwriting is a name and an age. The numbers range from thirteen to eighteen. It's sickening. All of it. I finally glance up and meet Daniel's eyes which are soaked in genuine worry.

"Dude, you good?" Daniel asks.

"No. Why am I alive?" I whisper.

"You're asking me? I don't even know what 'alive' means."

"No! I mean, why me? When so many others are dead. Why did I live?" I wail. "Look at this one. Alyssa, fifteen. Here's another. Daksha, sixteen. Rachelle, thirteen. Abike, thirteen. Mei, seventeen. Tanya, fourteen. Oh god! I think I'm going to be sick."

Daniel makes a pious face. "Ugh, bean vomit. Gross. Kill me now. If you hurl, I'll hurl. It will never end." Daniel stands up, moving like an old man. He even groans a little, and I hear something pop in his left knee. "Well, you keep sitting here freaking yourself out. I'll leave you to your internal monologue. I feel like I remember this place. I'm gonna walk around a bit."

I drop my head to stare at the photos again. "Okay. You live in the south wing," I say without thinking.

The look Daniel gives me says he thinks there's something deeply wrong with me. "You say weird stuff, Divinica."

"I'm weird, so it's okay," I assure him, happy to see a smile on his face as he turns to leave.

Time fucks with me on the reg, but it can't be more than five minutes before I hear footsteps. I don't look up from the photo I'm holding. Kathryne, thirteen. She's so young, she barely has breasts. *Why not me? Damnit! Why?!* The question batters my sanity. The footsteps grow closer. "Daniel, did you not find what you were looking for?" I ask absently, reaching for another photo.

"Actually, I found exactly what I was looking for," says a deep, angry voice.

My eyes snap up. His face is cast in harsh shadow, but I know him. "Valance," I breathe. The photo falls from my numb fingers. It flutters to the ground. His rumpled, checkered shirt is untucked and unbuttoned. The laces of his sneakers untied, he's not wearing any socks, in fact, it appears he barely managed to fasten his jeans. The zipper's halfway down. He looks beautiful, compelling, dangerous, and kinda like he wants to kill me. Words—as they do when I need them most—abandon me. Valance takes three massive steps and stops when he's towering over me. I continue to stare up at him, jaw dropped.

His aura crackles with fury.

"Are you trying to get yourself killed?" he asks through his teeth; his voice is a thousand shades of radiated rage.

I flinch. "What the hell's your problem?"

His eyes bore into mine, saying more than words ever could. Finally, after a long moment, he sighs and his shoulders slump. Some of the tension he carried in with him visibly flows away. "You, Divinica. You are my problem."

I drop my eyes before the ticking, twisting thing in my gut detonates and brings about my untimely demise. "Well, no one asked you to come storming in here," I snap, trying to find busywork for my hands, they settle for picking up the photo I dropped.

"I would've been here a hell of a lot sooner, but Cloud raiders attacked. You and Daniel missed them by seconds."

"Good on us," I retort, keeping my eyes on the dead girl in the picture so they don't stray to him. I don't have the headspace right now to try and dissect why he affects me the way he does. I want him. That's all I really know. I want to run to a place where fear doesn't control me, a place where I trust myself, and shadows don't rule. I want to run to him. My fists clench, wrinkling the corner of the photo I'm still holding.

Valance hunkers down beside me, arms slung over his knees. His smell is so intoxicating, it sparks something in my tired brain. The rushing pictures that come with that smell flay me. Us. Always us. My hands in his hair, his name on my lips, a scar on my soul.

"What are you looking at?" The proximity of his voice makes me jump, it takes everything in me not to lift my gaze and meet his eyes. He moves a little closer, and holding my breath becomes an exercise in absurdity. It's like my very skin absorbs his magnetic energy, creating an unbreakable connection I don't think I'll ever stop feeling.

"Daniel found this box," I say and point to the old cardboard wreck beside my leg. "These photos were in it, along with tons of assorted jewelry that I'm guessing once belonged to a bunch of dead girls. There are probably about twenty odd boxes here. I haven't looked through all of them, but the ones I opened were full of paintings, crystals, and a shit ton of mathematical equations far too advanced for my brain. Research that seems to span centuries. I don't understand half of it."

Valance reaches past me to lift a photo from the top of a stack of them. His arm brushes mine. A sharp spark of electricity jolts through me, through us. I know he feels it. I can see it in the widening of his eyes just before he drops them. He clears his throat, then stares at the photo. A beat of silence passes. I can almost hear the gears of his mind grinding as it tries to comprehend what it's seeing. When understanding dawns, his whole body goes rigid. Deep shock and revulsion twist his handsome face. He sets the photo down on the cold concrete floor, and grabs another, then another. "What the fuck is this?"

"My predecessors, I think."

Valance hardly seems to hear me; his eyes are riveted on the photo. I know who he's looking at. Mei, seventeen.

"My god," he bites out. "This is fucking horror."

"Yep, I guess save for the grace of all the freaking gods go I," I say. My attempt at humor falls flat and hollow. He doesn't speak, but I see that his hands are shaking as he places Mei atop of the pile of so many others. I pick up the drawing with the blood moon and dead tattooed girl.

"Divinica." He leans closer, I feel his breath on my ear. Gods, he smells like memories. *On the bright side, I'm not fucking cold anymore,* I think and watch his face as he takes in the full scope of the creepy drawing. I shift uncomfortably when I look at those sprawled, wet-noodle limbs of the girl with the beam of light burning a hole through her tattooed chest. I exhale raggedly. I'm terrified of such a future, but some reckless, deeply disturbed part of me is fascinated.

"May I?" he asks, holding out his hand for the drawing. I give it to him. He brings the paper close to his eyes, then squints. "This is your father's writing."

My body jerks. "How do you know that?"

"I've studied his work for two years. He came here with the majority of his research. Dayle and I found it in the trunk of his car after he died. It was the first time I came here looking for you. He parked just past the statues. I saw an abandoned car, but no bodies in sight. Your tracks stopped here, but the damn house was invisible." He turns the paper over in his hands. "The tattoos are—"

"Exactly like mine. I think she is me, or at least a visual representation of what will happen to me when I get all thirteen artifacts. I assume it's thirteen because I have thirteen tattoos, even though I only see twelve artifacts in the drawing, and there were twelve goddesses. Whatever. I guess I don't make it out of this alive," I say, astonished at how calm I sound. "It's a shame. I want to see who my brother grows up to be. I bet if he lives, he'll do something amazing. He's pretty cool."

"Divinica—" Valance's voice snaps over my name.

"It's okay. I read some of the writings in my diary. I know about the waves. I know you think I'm somehow connected to it all, and this proves it. I have the same symbols on my body, and some of these artifacts in my room, and I know how to get the ones I don't have." I point to the drawing. "This horror circle might put a stop to the red waves. No?"

"No," he says, too quickly.

I give him a weak smile. "Liar."

Valance's eyes catch fire. He waves the drawing in my face. "I don't fucking care about the damn world. We're not doing this. Not a chance in hell," he shouts.

"Fine with me. Let's think of something else. I have no desire to die for something I can hardly remember." My voice drops. "Honestly, the idea of a brutal death isn't what's bothering me. I want to know why I lived. Why me? Were we just picked at random, or was there some sort of plan?"

"I don't think a witch who's been around since before the dawn of time does anything random," Valance says.

"Hecate," I say, remembering. "She's the one who did this to me, to all of us. Do you know her?"

The ghost of a smile cracks his agonized expression. "No, and I don't fucking want to. I bet we'll run into the bitch before all this is over. My mom would slap me upside the face for saying that word, but—"

"She is a bitch. I saw her in my dream. Three heads, a dress that moves like storm clouds, eyes black all the way through." I whisper, remembering the way the Celtic prince died in my arms.

"It wasn't a dream, Divinica."

"Well, that's good news, because I hit her with a lightning bolt right before she killed you."

Valance's eyes meet and hold mine. "That's my girl," he whispers.

My mouth goes dry, but I manage to force words out anyway. "Am I? Am I your girl? I remember kissing you," I say, and hear him curse under his breath.

"I shouldn't have said that," he quickly recants. "You're not mine. You never have been."

I flinch. "But I—"

"Don't think about it, Divinica. Don't think about us. I know I sure as hell can't. Let's just get out of here, yeah? We don't need any of this crap. I don't care about some old drawing, or a bunch of cursed, probably possessed artifacts. I'm not going to let you die. I'll find another way."

"What if there isn't another way?"

Valance's nostrils flare. "There's always another way."

"What would I even be saving? What was the Earth like before all this started? Is bringing it back worth my death? Do I even have a choice? Why do I feel like I can't run from this?"

Valance lifts a brow. "That's a lot of questions, love. Let's see, the world was hurting. Your Dad thought all the viruses that started attacking humans around 2020 were the Earth's way of fighting back. War ruined us. The nuclear battle between America and Russia nearly ended it all. Bringing it back is not worth your death. Nothing is. You always have a choice, and if you run, you better take me with you."

"So, what are you saying?" I ask, tearing my eyes away from his to skim through more photos of mutilated dead girls. "This is Vivian," I tell him, "she was eighteen. She had a small hummingbird inked just below her collarbone. Blue beak and bright rainbow feathers. She died in a madhouse. Her life prematurely snuffed out to serve a greater good. Death to fight death. An infinity of darkness. How long have we been living like this, Valance? How long have we known each other?"

Valance sighs deeply and rubs his eyes. He drops his hand, and his hard features smooth into a mask of impassivity. "Seven hundred and thirty-three days. Seventeen thousand, five hundred hours, or one million, and fifty-two thousand minutes, give or take," he says.

"Oh," I mutter. I pick up another picture. Jane Doe, age unknown. I feel kinship with all these dead girls. They're my sisters through torture and tragedy. "We can leave, but I'm taking all these photos with me. They don't deserve to be forgotten. These names should be on your memory wall if nothing else."

Valance narrows his eyes. "My wall—god, Divinica. What do you actually remember?"

"Enough," I say. He moves closer. My pulse skitters. "I remember you."

I hear him sharply catch his breath. Warmth spreads through me at the sound. "Do you?" he asks.

"Yes…I do. I have a memory of wrapping my legs around your waist. You're kissing me, and my fingers are buried in your hair. It's so hot between us, I can't breathe—I can't—"

"Fuck, Divinica. God! Will you please shut up before I do something stupid."

His tone makes me immediately want to disobey him. I open my mouth to keep firing words, but he moves so fast, he's looming over me before I can say a single thing. Fists clenched, my exhale is ragged. I lift my chin and meet his turbulent eyes. "Stop asserting your dominance by towering over me, I'm not afraid of you, Valance."

"That makes one of us. I'm terrified of you," Valance says, but his voice has turned to honey. His hand brushes my cheek. He draws his lower lip between his teeth, then his gaze falls to my lips. He stares at me, and I realize the panting sounds ripping through the room belong to me. I can't take my eyes off him as his head lowers. My whole soul engages in the waiting, the needing. I part my lips and close my eyes. Suddenly, he jerks and drops his hand like my skin is lava. My eyes snap open. He turns away and starts rifling through the box by my leg. "Do you know what the Lycurgus cup is?" he asks, not glancing up.

I don't say anything. I'm catching my breath as my heart thumps erratically against my ribs. I'm so busy trying to collect myself, while also shooting daggers from my eyes at his strong, flawless profile that I almost don't hear his question. When it registers, I scrunch my nose forgetting some of my rage. "No, should I?"

"Not necessarily, but your dad may have mentioned it to you at some point."

"If he did, I don't remember."

"But you remember me?"

"Yes, almost."

"Almost isn't good enough," he says.

"Fuck you, Valance. Why are you talking to me about a damn cup?"

The corner of his mouth ticks up in a smile, showing a dimple that makes the butterflies in my stomach melt and die. "It was made sometime in the fourth century. It changes color depending on the direction of the light hitting it. When the light is coming from behind, the cup glows jade green, from the front it's blood red."

"Sounds beautiful. What's it made of?"

"For centuries, that was the million-dollar question. During the late 1990s, a group of researchers discovered the cup was made using an ancient form of nanotechnology. Craft workers ground up particles of gold until they were about fifty nanometers across, then used the material produced to create the cup. The precision of the design and execution proves the artists were masters. It was tech that wasn't supposed to exist back then, but the cup proved it did. My mom thought it was the holy grail. Maybe she was right. The secrets of ancient technology are all wrapped up in a pretty cup." He lifts a piece of paper covered in black numbers, strange sloping graphs, and curling letters, then waves it at me. "The math on this page calculates the foundations necessary to understand the mechanical, chemical, thermal, and electrical functions that characterize materials at the nanometric scale, using mercury instead of gold. I think it's the mercury that takes it from nano to star tech."

"The chemical, thermal, nano, starry, what?" I ask, mouth agape.

"Your dad mentioned the term in his research. Star tech. Even you talk about it sometimes, right after the wave before—"

I cut him off. "I do?"

"Yes, Divinica, you do. Anyway, I've never heard of nanotechnology used on humans before, not even with gold, but mercury? That shit's toxic as fuck," he says almost absently.

I can feel my eyebrows furrow. "What are you saying?" I ask but have a feeling I already know. Dread blossoms in the pit of my stomach.

"I'm fairly certain Hecate used this nano/star tech on you, embedded it in your tattoos to make you something more than human. Most mortal bodies would reject that kind of primal cell manipulation. You're different somehow. Special. It killed these other girls and made you a time walker."

My eyes fall closed. I see a tree strung with glowing planets, hear the rush of wind and exploding light. The dread in my gut turns to anger. I lift the creepy drawing and stare at it once more. My throat tightens as I look at the graphic, the splayed limbs of the girl who is me. "This is what's going to happen when I get all the artifacts, isn't it? Why are there only twelve artifacts in the drawing? My dad's notes say the spell needs all thirteen."

Valance's gaze meets mine for a second, then flicks away. His eyes rove over the paper again, and he looks sicker by the second. "I think you only need twelve," he says hoarsely. The words sound like they cause him physical pain. "Oh god, this is so fucking insane!"

"But…I have thirteen symbols on my body, and so does she," I say, pointing to the drawing.

Valance turns away from me and starts rifling through the box again. A few seconds later, he hands me a piece of paper with the word *Ophiuchu* written in the same curling script as the ink writing on my arm. Beneath it is a symbol painted in gold. It's a thick Y with a slender, vertical pedestal in the center dotted by a single flame. "Is this symbol the same symbol as the one tattoo on your body that I haven't seen?" he asks.

I swallow hard and nod.

Valance's countenance hardens, and his eyes narrow thoughtfully like he's confirming a private theory. "It's also the same shape as the candle in your room," he says, almost to himself.

"What symbol is it? Do you know?"

"Yes. It shows up all the time in Aramaic and Celtic mythology. It's the thirteenth star. The lost zodiac sign."

"What does that mean?"

Valance drops the papers he is holding and turns to face me. "Divinica, I think the last symbol belongs to you. You carry a piece of each goddess; those pieces have made you something more than human. They made you a goddess. More powerful than any of the ones you travel to, because they gave you the best of all of them. Ophiuchu is yours. You're the thirteenth artifact, baby."

His low words resonate in my ears. The knowledge is chaotic, the very crux of madness, but somehow, I know he's right. I can feel the fury radiating off him, merging with the hot waves of my own. I watch his face as the harsh realization breaks over him, and I swear I can literally see all the pieces coming together in his mind. The hard set of his jaw and snarl twisting his lips tells me he doesn't like the picture they make. I assume it looks a lot like the one in my hand. Bloody, broken, dead, magical.

CHAPTER TWENTY-SEVEN

Goddess rest my soul

Valance leans his forehead against his fist. "None of it matters, Divinica. For once, I want you to forget. You're not going to die. That can't be how this story ends for us. If you staying alive with me leaves humanity no hope, then so be it. I can live with that. I can't live without you."

He's so real for saying that. I don't know why I feel the same, but I do. I do. I do. I pick up more papers covered in my father's messy scrawl. Numbers, shapes, and symbols that look like the remnants of a dead language. "Do you know what happened to my dad?" I ask.

Valance nods absently. "Yes. You've told me a dozen times. I could describe it to you if you want?"

"No, don't bother. Do you think my dad knew he was bringing me here to be tortured and groomed to die?"

"I don't know. It's possible he suspected. All I know is that he came here, to the Hadamar, chasing a theory. He was tracking solar flares and geometric storms." Valance casts a glance around the drafty rec room, then says, "Not sure he would be doing a happy dance that he was right."

"I hate thinking that he knew what he was getting me into," I say, then dismiss the thought. "No, he loved me, I know he did, I mean I can't fucking remember, but I feel it in my heart. He loved me, Mom did too, our lives were happy. Golden sunlight. Laughter. And if he did know," I shrug, "I can't fault him. He was trying to save the world, who's to say either of us wouldn't have done the same." *Or will do the same,* clarifies my unhelpful mind. I pause on that thought, then, "Valance? Will you take me to Stonehenge? I want to be there before the next wave hits."

"That was the idea, but now, fuck no! That's the last place in the world I'm taking you. I'd rather go to the pyramids and try our luck with portals. If I can get you off world, maybe the spell taking your memories will break."

I lean back on my hands to look up in his eyes. "Off world?"

"Yeah. Mars, maybe further. I'm an astronaut, remember?"

"Yes. I do, actually."

One of his brows rises in a sardonic tilt. "Do you now?"

"Yes. You weren't here when the first wave hit, so it doesn't affect you."

"Did you read that in your notebook?"

"I don't think so. I just remember you saying something along those lines once."

"I've told you more than once."

I shrug. "What about all the people we leave behind?"

Valance smiles a wicked smile. "Fuck 'em. All I care about is you."

I sit up and lightly punch his shoulder. "You don't mean that."

He curls his fingers around my chin and tilts my head, so I'm forced to meet his devastating gaze. His eyes are burning blue ice. "Don't I?" he breathes. My heart turns over at the look on his face. I think he's going to kiss me. The way his eyes drop to my lips and stay there tells me he thinks so too. Then his hand falls in slow motion, and he turns his back on me. "We had our chance with this planet, and we failed. Let the Reptilians have it. They seem to want it more, and I bet they'll do a better job taking care of it. Besides, the radiation from the waves slowly, painfully killing every person doesn't seem to affect them."

Valance spins back to face me and takes my hand. "You and me baby, let's get the fuck out of here."

"And Daniel," I say.

Valance tucks a strand of hair behind my ear with his free hand. "That's a given, love. I'd never let myself go anywhere without that little critter. Kid's got a way of crawling into your heart and staying there."

For a wonderful moment I let myself imagine running with him and finding a spot far away where I can give him all my sunrises. The moment is fleeting. When it fades, I sigh at its loss. "I don't want to keep living like this. Remembering some but not all. It's like I'm being constantly poisoned to death and never dying. I get randomly thrown through worlds and times where I die or kill the people I love. I can't take it."

Valance doesn't say anything. My knees are beginning to throb. I shift uncomfortably, bristling under his unwavering stare. The look in his eyes makes me want to run for cover, but I don't because his hands have made their way back to my waist, and it feels too good when he holds me. I settle for grabbing a handful of my hair and tugging it over my shoulder, then twining the strands nervously through my fingers.

"I want my memories. All of them. From the way you can't stop glaring at me, I know there's something between us. The air quite literally crackles when you touch me. My dreams of you are wild and breathless. You're always touching me, always kissing me," I say.

Before the last word falls, I'm in his arms. "They're not dreams, Divinica. They're memories. Yours and mine, we are—" He hesitates, staring down at me with an indefinable expression on his face, then he sighs deeply as if the weight of the world is wearing him down. "I'm probably going to regret this," he whispers, sweeping the pad of his thumb over my lower lip. I have to fight the urge not to flick out my tongue and taste his golden skin. His aura is almost blinding now, the hot light intensifies by the second. My tattoos drink the glow and shimmer.

I sink my fingers into his hair, that way I know I love to do, then drag his head down to mine. He capitulates to the pressure of my hands with a groan.

"We shouldn't do this, not again. I can't go through this again," he says, but dips his head slowly. His eyes are sapphire lightning. His lips brush mine and bring the thunder.

We are the storm. The kiss is chaotic. Blindly, gasping, needing, we fall into madness together. Our tongues lock and linger, our teeth bite, our lips worship. This old gothic room filled with the pictures that broke my heart just fades away. There is no red wave, or slanting, freezing rain. No savior device or white silence. No blistered humans or murdering, sentient creatures. No plots or goddesses with their deceitful tales of grandeur and destiny. Nothing to intrude on our sultry silence. There's only us. Always us. Forever us. A pair of fated lovers who managed to find each other somewhere in the confusion of time. In this hallowed moment, we are Valance and Divinica, the only two people in the world.

In the back of my faltering brain, I fear this moment of fire and passion is counterfeit, and I will pay dearly for spending so wildly. I don't care, I will take it, whatever the price. All I care about is him. Us. Fire and thunder. His hands cup my hips, then find the curve of my ass, he squeezes tight, then lifts my body closer so his mouth can kiss and ravage.

Valance slants his head and makes a deep, shadowy sound in his throat that turns all my joints to mush. Not breaking the kiss, Valance sits back, then drags me onto his lap. He cradles me in his arms and uses his lips to tilt my head further. My hair pours over his bicep, flexed and hard as granite under my cheek. His kiss turns desperate, like the taste of my lips is necessary to him on a visceral level. His mouth steals my sanity, changes my reality. My pulse pounds with dizzying ferocity. Hands in my hair, he drags me even closer, erasing the intruding air that dares put space between us.

His fingers find the slider on the zipper of my romper tucked between my breasts; I can hear myself panting as he slowly retrieves it. His hand pauses and looks at me. His smoldering stare is the whole focus of my soul, and it makes me ache everywhere. My lips, the tips of my breasts, and between my tightly pressed legs. Gently, he tugs my zipper down.

Valance reveals one tattoo at a time, kissing each in turn as it's uncovered. He breathes on the tattoo between my breasts, then his lips move lower, lower still. "This is going to fucking kill me," he whispers as the zipper parts the cloth until it can go no further. He slides his hands up my naked torso, then peels the romper over my shoulders and down my body. Cool wind and errant drops of icy rain brush my skin. I shiver, but not from cold. Far from it. I'm burning,

Valance pulls back to stare at me. "Goddamn, Divinica, you're so fucking beautiful. This feels like a dream I've had a thousand times. Sometimes, I sleep just to be with you," he says, then his lips lock around the tip my breast.

Sight and sound desert me. I taste starlight. I gasp and arch; twist almost mindlessly against his scorching mouth. My touch turns frantic as he licks and bites my nipple, first one, then the other. I'm gunpowder and he's a match. I'm the dark horizon and he's the rising sun. I grab his head and hold him close as his lips drive me wild, his mouth is the pyre I wish to die on. A reckless thing inside of me is building, pulsing, straining for something unknown. Valance tears his mouth away, then blows lightly on the tips of my breasts, still wet and glistening from his kiss. It's a waft of hellfire branding me.

"I want you, Divinica. More than I've ever wanted anything! Fuck me, desire like this is a death sentence." He kisses my throat and tugs the crumpled romper to my hips. Following some invisible, sensitive line, he trails his left index finger down the center of my body until he reaches the top seam of my thin black panties. He strokes slowly back and forth. His fingers skim over my final tattoo, still hidden by black cloth.

I know the symbol's glowing. The soft light illuminates the harsh planes of his face. "

I've never seen this tattoo, not once in two years," he whispers against my throat. He nips at my bottom lip, then sucks it into his mouth. I turn my head, trying to deepen the kiss, but he pulls back. "Show it to me?" he asks, his voice is gravel and passion.

I give him a slight nod of assent.

"Say it. Say yes. I want the word," he demands.

"Yes," I snap, twisting, arching. "Damn it, Valance. Do whatever you want. Just…please…please—" I don't even know what I'm begging for. I just know I need it more than sight, air, or sound. This feeling he invokes with his ruinous touch is all.

He stares at my face as he slides two fingers beneath the cloth. My arms twine his neck as his large body urges mine to the ground. There isn't even a flicker of hesitation on my part, I move with him, yield to the pressure of his hands. He spreads my cloak on the ground and lies me on it, his fingers never losing contact with my final tattoo. The weight of his body as he settles between my legs is another layer of torment and ecstasy. He rips his T-shirt off with one arm. I don't know when the checkered shirt was discarded, only that I'm glad it was. Valance is flawless. Each muscle, dip, and ridge are touched by my light. He's a Grecian god dipped in Olympian gold. My tongue flicks out to lick my suddenly dry lips.

"If you keep looking at me like that, this will all be over way to fast," he says.

"That's a confusing sentence that sounds like a warning. I can't help how I look at you. You're right, this feels surreal. Are you sure we're not dreaming?"

"I honestly can't tell anymore," he breathes and moves his body over mine, the bare skin of his chest is hot as an open flame against my breasts. "And I know it's cliché, but I hope I never fucking wake up," Valance says, his voice is harsh, but his kiss is soft and drugging. My left leg links around his narrow waist, and he flexes his hips into mine. He breaks the kiss and tugs my panties down, past the last symbol. "I'll die if I don't taste you," he says, then his tongue swirls around the tip of my breast before he draws it back into his infernal mouth. I arch and cry out. He covers my mouth with one hand while the fingers of his other move over my stomach, then lower, gods, lower still. My hips jerk off the ground as he slides a finger inside me. My whole body goes taut.

"You feel like silk, Divinica. So wet, and hot—" His voice thickens as I buck my hips again. There's some pain, a slight burn, but pleasure is there too, pleasure is everywhere. I watch a muscle twitch in his clenched jaw as Valance moves his fingers, staring at my face as I cry out again. His touch is relentless. I dig my nails into his skin, leave furrows down his back. I can feel him, straining against the barrier of his jeans hard as iron against my inner thigh. I reach down and trail my fingers up his leg, wanting to touch him.

He grabs my hand and locks it above my head. "No, if you touch me, I'll take you. I won't be able to control myself." His hoarse voice barely sounds human.

I tug at his arm; my digging nails make indents in his skin. "Please—please. I want everything."

Valance smiles like a villain. "I know what you want. I don't want to hurt you. You're so fucking tight—" his words break off.

"Hurt me? I'm not a delicate flower. I don't care about pain. There's more right? I know there's more. There has to be more—"

He bites my neck, hard enough to leave a mark and make me flinch. The slight pain adds to the madness. "Yes, Divinica. There's more. I want to show it to you. All of it. God, I want your first time to be with me. I want to keep you in bed for days, rule all your nights. Not let you go until your skin imprints on mine." His fingers press deeper. Vision is replaced by wave after wave of brilliant sparkles. His hand moves, slowly at first, achingly gentle. He touches me like I'm the most precious thing on earth. It feels incredible, but I don't want it.

I smack his shoulder again. "Valance! Please. I'm the furthest thing from fragile."

"I know. You're the strongest girl I've ever met. I just...I can't believe I'm really touching you like this." He withdraws his fingers to trace them over the most sensitive part of me like he's memorizing every line. "So beautiful," he whispers, reverence in his tone.

"Valance," I demand.

"Fine, have it your way, I can't take it anymore either," he murmurs, then he slides down my body and his lips replace his fingers. My cheeks go up in flames. My voice breaks on his name.

"You taste like an angel," he whispers, raking his teeth over the glowing ridges of my thirteenth tattoo before his lips move between my thighs. The way he kisses me then changes all the colors of my world. His tongue twists wild, frantic sounds from me. My tattoos start glowing in earnest, bleeding golden light that pools around us and heats the air. I listen to myself gasp and pant as his lips find a maddening rhythm and my legs part helplessly.

His hands are all over me, his fingers stroke my thighs, pinch the aching tips of my breasts, then skim down my torso before he presses his index finger inside me again. He's not gentle this time. My hips rock with each thrust that seems more powerful than the last. I writhe, and he moves with me for a time before his free hand clamps down on my hip to keep me where he wants me.

I open my eyes as the pleasure turns piercing and glance down at the top of his golden head, just as he looks up. Our gazes lock through the brilliant light of my tattoos. "You're too perfect like this, all flushed and wet from my mouth, so fucking gorgeous. Come for me, Divinica," he says, then kisses me again and the world explodes. Breath leaves my lungs in a shattered scream as my body is lifted on crashing breakers of undiluted ecstasy. My back arches off the ground, and I twist my fingers into his hair. Eyes closed, I see stars and whisper his name in tones of shock and awe. The pleasure crests and ebbs for a long time, and when my body finally goes limp under his lips, I'm senseless, unraveled, changed.

CHAPTER TWENTY-EIGHT

A deadly difference of opinion

VALANCE

Divinica. My Divinica. A red-rose flush infuses her cheeks adding to the fairytale aura she wears. It's giving Snow White seconds after she's kissed back to life by the jaded prince. Her silky skin is damp, shining like an underwater flame. Her broken breaths are a siren's song. I'm captured by every note, I can't take my eyes off her.

We're magnets with opposing poles, our atoms lined up in the same directions, so they are forever, irresistibly pulled together. I'm fairly young, but I still understand that I'll never love another girl the way I adore this one. When you know, you just know. When I wasn't looking, she stole a giant part of me I'll never be able to reclaim. It's her bravery. Her fight. Her honesty. Her fucking erotic eyes. Right now, she looks otherworldly with all her tattoos glowing. Their inner light creates a sphere of gold around both of us, shielding our kisses from the harsh outside world. I lick the moisture collecting in the hollow of her throat. It kills me to do it, but when her soft screams taper to gentle gasps, I slowly drag my hand from her body.

The inner battle I fight is epic. I want her so damn bad. I genuinely have no idea how I haven't fucked this girl yet. I'm not a nice guy by nature. I have an explosive temper, and I'm fundamentally selfish, traits I inherited from my father. I'm not usually in the habit of doing things and getting nothing in return. This treasure in my arms has warped all the rules. This magical creature who is too sexy for words begs me to go to bed with her on the reg, and somehow this is the most action I've had in two years. For a guy who spent the last three years of college with a different girl every week, my recent restraint should be considered the stuff of legends. Divinica's turned me into a bloody saint. Right now is no different. I have to take my hands off her. I know when I do, it will feel like ripping off my own skin.

My cock's so fucking hard right now, I'm afraid I'll crack in half if I make any sudden movements. I don't know how much longer I can fight this. I'm mere seconds from snapping. From ripping the rest of her clothes off and seeing just how bright I can make those damn tattoos glow.

Her lips part like she wants to say something, but she doesn't, she licks them instead. I barely manage to bite back a groan. Eyes like sun touched jade roam over my face. I wonder if she sees my need and understands how close I am to doing something she can never take back.

Her lashes flutter, before her lips part on a sigh. "Valance, have you ever done that to me before?" she asks in a shy, adorable whisper.

"No," I say, sounding pissed about it.

"Why the hell not?"

"Because—Because I'm a stupid, stupid man."

"But you didn't—? I mean what I felt at the end, you didn't—?" her words break off, and she rolls her eyes violently.

I lift my brow. My smile takes over my face, and I can't help winking at her. "Didn't what?"

She smacks my chest again, not so playfully this time. "You're still very hard."

"You don't say?"

"Valance!"

"No, I didn't. It's okay though, I'll live. I think," I say. There's a melting look in her eyes, like she just had a cocktail made from the color found at the end of a rainbow. I didn't think it was possible for me to get any harder, but the way she's staring at me makes my tenacious body prove my mind wrong. I drop my head, let my forehead rest against hers and pant, trying to reclaim my sanity. She purrs low in her throat, her slender back arches. The movement presses her hips tightly to mine. "Hold still," I breathe.

"Please—" She squirms again.

"Divinica," I warn.

"I can't help it. Valance, I want to—I need you too—can we please—?"

"Divinica—" my voice sounds like the last breath of a tortured man. She purrs again, surging against me. I roll fully on top of her and brace my hands on either side of her head. Her nimble fingers undo the buckle on my jeans. I lock my jaw as I hear the metal teeth of the zipper retreat. Her hand slides over me, then she touches, squeezes, and runs her nails down my aching length. I can't stop it. It's going to happen now. I'm gonna fuck her, then she's going to regret me. I know this, and I don't care. I need her. Just as I lean down to take her mouth, then her, I hear a high-heeled set of footsteps. The familiar sound acts like a bucket of ice water.

"Valance? Divinica? I'm assuming those intertwined silhouettes belong to the both of you. I don't need to ask what you're doing. It's a good thing there's a freaking golden shield around the both of you—what the fuck is that, by the way?" Rashid asks in a high, slightly annoyed voice.

I don't need to turn to know he's standing about ten feet behind me. There's no time to react anyway. Divinica makes a strangled, stressed sound that triggers a frenzy of odd movements.

"It's okay, Divinica. He can't see us," I say, but I'm not sure she hears me. She sits up so fast that her forehead smacks into my chin. I don't even think she feels it. She starts squirming, trying to tug her cloak out from beneath us, while struggling to locate her zipper at the same time. Her fingers are all operating like backward thumbs and success eludes her. I sit up, rubbing my sore chin. She's making a bunch of adorable, embarrassed, frustrated sounds, actually snapping her teeth at me when I don't move my knee or lift my hips fast enough to suit her insane tugging of the cloak, while at the same time moving my body to try and shelter her from any further embarrassment.

Finally, her fingers find the slider on the zipper, and she gives it one good tug, then starts fighting with her breasts. One hand holds the slider, the other tries to stuff. I grit my teeth but can't help smiling at the flustered picture she makes. Green eyes all hazy, hair wild, face flushed. "Honestly, how do you zip that thing up on your own every day? I really should put a camera in your room."

Divinica gives me a withering look. "You're not helping."

I can feel my smile turn wicked. "Darlin,' helping you put those beauties away is the last thing I'm trying to do."

Divinica shrieks in frustration, and Rashid starts laughing so hard he has to wrap his arms around his stomach and throw back his head. I can't help but follow suit.

"Laugh all you want," Divinica snaps, giving up on the zipper and reaching for the cloak. "I can cover up, but there's no way in hell you can hide that," she says pointedly.

"It'll go away," I say, but I've never felt less sure of anything.

Divinica purses her pretty lips. "If you say so. Maybe you can hang your shirt off it," she suggests.

Her whisper is so sexy, I almost grab her again. I can't help leaning in to steal one last kiss. She allows it for a second before pulling away to wrap the cloak tightly over her torso. That piece of cloth she wears is scrunched around the flare of her hips. It's not going anywhere without some sincere effort. Now it just looks like a pair of shorts, a little too short for my sanity.

When she's fully covered and sitting a safe distance away from me, the glow of her tattoos begins to diminish. The pale light still drifts toward me and shimmers under her silver, repurposed emergency blanket, but slowly our shield against the outside world fades. I grab my shirt from where it fell and tug it on. My breathing is not at all steady, but as the final bits of her light dissipate, I see that Rashid has stopped laughing and is now glaring at the drawing of Stonehenge, a blood moon, and a dead girl. He's turning the paper over in his hands, bringing it close to his eyes, then drawing it further back. "Valance, what the fuck is this?"

"Nothing," I snarl, jumping up and snatching the drawing from his hands. "Nothing that matters."

Rashid hardly seems to register my overbearing, looming presence. He ignores me and turns toward the first stack of photos, lifts one, then another, and another. "Shit! This is so messed up!" he says, voice hushed. His eyes snap to mine, wide and terrified. "You were right. The tattoos are nanotech." He picks up the paper of equations Divinica discarded when I started kissing her. "This math is old. Mercury instead of gold." Rashid's gaze travels to Divinica, and my heart stops dead in my chest.

"Don't look at her. Don't you dare look at her! None of this means anything!"

"She really is the key," Rashid says. "This can actually end. All of it. She only needs seven more artifacts."

"Six, actually," Divinica mutters.

"It will *kill her!*" I roar, physically unable to stand it for one more second.

Rashid shakes his head. I watch moisture flood his eyes. He sniffs loudly, then wipes his powdered nose on the back of his hand. "One life in exchange for thousands," he says. I have to fist my hands to keep from reaching the short distance between us and outright strangle him. "Valance. This is meant to be. This is what she was made for."

"But not why she was born! She has a choice, just like anyone else, and so do I!"

"You don't know that. She could've been—"

"Stop it!" I shout over him. "Stop talking about her like she's some faceless casualty. It's Divinica. Our Divinica! You're talking about killing the girl I would die for."

Two tears slide down Rashid's cheeks. They enrage me. How dare he cry for and condemn her to death in the same breath. "Valance, have you even asked her what she wants?"

"I don't care! It's in her nature to go all noble. I won't have it. Do you hear me? *I won't!*"

Rashid leans back and holds up his hand like a squirrel about to play dead. "There's no need to shout. I, more than anyone, see your point. Horrible as it may be, there are things to consider, you know there are."

I didn't know I was shouting, but I'm not sorry. I'm sorry I haven't knocked him on his ass. Divinica's quiet voice forestalls any violent action on my part. "Can you guys stop talking about me like I'm not sitting right here? Rashid is right. It's my choice. If I decide I want to die, hell if I decide I want to stick a knife in my heart and float down a river on fire, there's not a damn thing either of you can do about it. Stop pretending like there is."

"Divinica—" I start. She waves me to silence with a flick of her hand.

"No. I need to think about all of this. Somewhere without the two of you shouting."

Rashid gives her a pretty pout. "I wasn't shouting. Yell at Mr. Testosterone over here."

The corners of Divinica's lips lift. "I was."

"What if it doesn't work? What if we get the time, or god forbid, the math wrong? What if we kill her for nothing?" I ask, my voice a single decibel below an all-out scream.

"It's a horrible thought," Rashid says, idly running his fingers over a photo. Another dead girl with a particularly bad case of mercury poisoning. The little jagged lines are running down her arms and past her navel. "Really horrible. But we're all monsters if we don't at least consider it. Do you know how many bodies I've burned these past two years? Mothers, children, babies, family, friends?"

I don't answer. I can't. Rashid's words make me see red. Before I can stop myself, my arm is snapping out, my hand grabs the collar of his cropped red-leather jacket, and my fingers catch in the fishnet of his tight shirt. He makes a small squelching sound as I shake him like a child's rattle. "You don't have to fucking tell me how many people we've lost." I shake him again until I hear his teeth click, hear his throat work on a swallow and fail. "Damn it, Rashid! You want to save a life by taking another. You want to kill that girl right there!" I yell, pointing to Divinica.

"He doesn't want to kill me," Divinica says, shooting me a nasty look. "All he's saying is—"

I cut her off sharply. I can't hear it. "Enough, both of you. I'll figure something else out. I'm the smartest person in the world, remember?"

"Oh, I remember, since you can never shut up about it," Rashid says viciously, wrenching his clothes from my grasp. "You are not the right person to discuss this rationally. You should leave and let cooler heads prevail."

"No! There's nothing to talk about!" I spit.

"God damn it, Val! You can't let the world burn because you want to get your dick wet," he says crudely. It's too much. Rage in its very worst form is all consuming. I don't think. I draw back my arm and let it fly. My clenched fist finds his jaw with bone shattering force. It's a knockout. Divinica makes a sound like shattering glass. I don't turn toward her; I don't want to see the disgust I know is stamped on her face. I stand there over Rashid's body, panting hard, fists clenched and stomach roiling. It's a long time before I realize Divinica left me alone to wait for my best friend to regain consciousness. Alone with the consequences of my actions and sickened by the bitter taste of guilt.

CHAPTER TWENTY-NINE

Sometimes the truth really hurts

DIVINICA

I strip down to my panties. I can't put my jumper on again, it's filthy, and there's a patch of something on the collar that looks suspiciously like blood. I stand naked in my bedroom just staring at nothing, cold as hell, then in a strange moment of inspiration, drop to the ground and look under the bed. I think dreamed I left a purse under here once. I don't find the purse, but in the mess of broken tiles and cobwebs, I find a soft duffle bag. Inside is a pair of dark pants, and a small, pink shirt that looks like it might've been part of a nightgown set once. Not ideal items in which to face the apocalypse, but better than a pair of black panties.

I set the clothes on the badly warped lid of my small toilet. Cracks line the base of the bowl and crawl up the sides, with a few black vines which have managed to make their way through the narrow spaces in the old stone wall. There's a much-depleted bar of lavender soap sitting on the rim of the sink where I left it last night. I grab it and step in the shower with my panties on. The water is freezing, but miraculously, the pressure is magnificent.

When I finally turn off the valve, I'm shivering to the bone, and I can still smell Valance all over me. I'm angry at him for being an unreasonable tool, but it felt good to be protected, also I think I might be obsessed with him. Literally can't think about anything else. The way he kissed me, the way he touched me was food for composers. I don't care what I experience for the rest of my life—however short that might be—because with him, that was fucking epic.

Cast in the glow of my tattoos and his own celestial aura, he really did look like a fucking Skylord. A Seraph on a mission. A Nephilim with a cause, come to change the fantasy scripts for the daughters of men. I pull on the black pants which are surprisingly soft, stretchy, and tight as a second skin. The shirt is silky and moves like water when I spin. I don't have much time for spinning though. The events of the day are still fresh in my mind. I have to write them before they fade. I grab my diary from where I left it on the floor near the window, then sit at the edge of my bed, and start writing before I even know what I'm going to say.

Oh, my gods, oh my gods, oh my gods, oh my fucking gods! Important! First, if Valance says that the two of you never kissed, he's a damn liar. Also—he's incredible. It was so amazing with him you want to die. Seriously! Lie down on the ground and just end it all because nothing else will ever be so fucking spectacular.

In other, less swoon-worthy news, you're most likely going to need to die to save humanity, which is very Jesus of you. You're proud of yourself for having the bravery of a messiah, if dying is what you decide to do. You're also proud of yourself for remembering who Jesus is.

The red wave takes away what matters. Love, friendship, family, home—if you don't love, you can't hate. Yin and yang, dark and light. Take away the light and there is no more possibility of getting lost in the dark. In theory, it sounds like a clever idea. In reality, it sucks. Remember this. Focus on what you know. Don't think about the rest. It will come.

I'm still scribbling nonsense when Rashid gives my open door a perfunctory knock, then walks in before I have a chance to say anything and sits on the bed beside me. I glance up at him then freeze. His jaw is a study in the varied shades of red, yellow, green, and blue. "Rashid! What the hell?" I gasp, horrified. "Valance is such an asshole. I can't believe he did that. I can stab him again if you like."

"I'm thinking about it," Rashid says, leaning back against the paint splattered headboard and closing his eyes. "Not the first time that pretty boy decked me. It's easy to push his buttons when he wears them all over his checkered sleeve. I mean, damn. The torch he carries for you burns so hot it could set fire to the rainforest—or what's left of it."

"Where is he?" I ask, glancing back down at my scribbles, because I don't want Rashid to see the light of my own hefty torch blazing in my eyes.

"Don't know. When I finally came to, he was looming over me like some ancient conqueror, really taking up all the air in the room, if you know what I mean? I told him he had to take a walk and cool down before he was allowed to speak to me. He was riddled by enough guilt to obey. Honestly, if my jaw didn't hurt so damn bad, I would've felt sorry for the guy. He looked like a freshly kicked puppy."

"I can't blame him. If you were trying to convince me Valance needed to die, I wouldn't be proud of it, but I'd probably try to rip your head off."

Rashid takes a deep gulp of air. "I know. Fuck our lives, right?"

I almost smile. "Right."

"I hate that it's you, Divinica. I don't want you to die. You believe me, don't you? Please tell me you—"

"Of course I do. I don't think you want anyone to die."

Rashid unfolds his arms and pushes away from the wall. He takes my hand, silencing whatever gush I had been about to spill. "Why are you looking at me like that?"

I sigh and shift. "It's nice to have a friend, let's just leave it at that."

Rashid makes a pained face. "A friend who's trying to kill you."

"You know what's crazy? When I was young, I wanted to be a superhero. I would daydream about saving the world. Using mind control on all the filthy politicians and warlords. Now—" I shrug. "I can't remember what matters. I don't care about all the people left in this world, I know that sounds horrible, but in my mind they're only shadows. Non-player characters in this messed up game of life. It's hard to consider selfless sacrifice when you don't know what it is you're trying to save."

"Yeah. I feel that," Rashid says. "I don't judge. Also, side note. Where the fuck did you get this crown? It's such a fashion moment. So bold. The detail of this metal work, the curved precision of these little branches is amazing. The way the metal moves is pretty weird, almost mercurial."

"I know. It's gorgeous. I stole it from a Norse goddess."

Rashid's eyes go even wider. I can see little bits of aqua glitter clinging to his thick lashes. "You traveled to Freya, I don't know what it is about that goddess, that whole era actually, it really revives the Viking-nerd boy in me." He reaches his hands toward the crown, then stops abruptly. "I'm not going to like, blow up or disintegrate if I touch it, am I?"

"Sure hope not. I already had to clean some burnt bones out of this room when I first moved in," I say distractedly, staring at the small flowers that weave like moss around the crown's twisted band.

Rashid makes a scratchy little sound in his throat. "Divinica," he wails, and my heart stutters as I realize what I just said.

"Oh shit! Good for me. Finally, I managed to find a single, random memory that helps no one. Awesome."

Rashid's eyes go as soft as his smile. He lifts the crown and turns it around in his hands. "It's *that* you managed to remember, not *what* you managed to remember."

"Actually, I remember a bunch of stuff right now. It's weird. I remember Valance so much I feel like running after him. I remember you, and how horrible you were to me when we first met."

Rashid drops the crown and fashions his pointer fingers into a cross, then holds the symbol in front of his face. "My mother taught me to fear all witches, especially the beautiful ones."

"Awe, Rashid." I flip my hair. "I think you're pretty too," I say, but the foolishness in my voice fades as I realize it's not a joke. I do know him. "Rashid," I gasp. "Oh my god. You're twenty-seven, a Scorpio from Iran. You love warm beer and hate snakes." A harsh breath feels like it's punched out of me. "Holy shit! I remember—a lot," I say, jumping to my feet and swaying a little. I stumble back a few steps, and my moment of bright clarity suddenly darkens, like some unseen hand flipped off a switch in my mind. I retrace my steps to the bed, and the brightness returns.

"It's the crown," Rashid says reverently. He lifts the thing higher, then stands and places it gently on my head. Instantly, my mind feels lit by a thousand torches. I almost crackle with power, the kind that can end realms and erase eras. I feel like if I close my eyes and raise my arms, I could fly. If I opened my mouth, I could exhale a breath that would poison the earth. Memories come then, like a galloping battalion of warriors from all lives, all times. I'm momentarily completely overwhelmed. I'm afraid if I open my mouth, I'll spit flame or scream until my lungs explode as I remember with perfect, exacting clarity every single moment leading up to this one.

My voice is three octaves higher when I finally manage to force out a sound. "It's too much. It hurts—"

"Does it hurt as bad as the waves?" Rashid asks, and I fall silent. Nothing hurts worse than that electric, burning insanity.

"You can take it," he says, sounding sure of me without a cause. Pressure pierces my eyes, implodes behind the bridge of my nose, attacks my temples. It's a crown of assaulting thorns, poking deep. I feel the power spearing through my mind. The moment is transformative. I don't just remember Divinica's life, I recall all the lives of my soul. Time immemorial stretches around me. Loops like the eternal eight. Infinity. What has been, is, and will always be.

"I don't know how you're doing this," Rashid says.

"What?! You just said I can take it."

Rashid shrugs. "Manifesting the desired outcome, dear. Just manifesting. The little silver branches are star tech. I think. They're moving. Your hair is moving too, by the way. It's wrapping itself around the crown. The silver branches are stabbing into your head—"

"Oh, you don't say?" I snap as fresh pain rushes through me like chills.

"Satan's balls, Divinica. You should see yourself right now. You need your own montage. *Annnd* now you're hovering. Great. You're going to turn into something hideous and murder me, aren't you?"

"What? I'm hideous?"

"No. You're fucking gorgeous." Valance's words low and deep, find my ringing eardrums and imprint themselves there.

My head snaps around and I see him, standing in the frame of the open door, arms folded, expression thunderous. Rashid tosses his head in a marked snub. "Uh, Divinica and I are having a moment. I'm still not ready to talk to you yet," he says.

Valance doesn't say anything. He keeps staring, his gaze moving from my lips to my eyes, to the crown playing havoc with my hair. Shivers curl through me, rushing from my pointed toes to the top of my head. A part of me is utterly bewildered by whatever is happening, but the rest of me seems to know exactly what's going on. Somewhere in time, I've worn this crown before. Felt this piercing agony before. I'm surprised how well I'm managing the pain, molding myself to it, understanding it, and slowly losing the fear it invokes.

Valance drops his arms to his sides, then starts to walk toward me. Power surges until it's a swirling tornado inside of me. All at once it's too much. I taste rage. Fear returns with a vengeance, so forcefully it overrides my ability to bear it. Fear of dark things lurking in suffocating shadows, fear of dead people I loved who took parts of me to their graves, fear of loss, fear of extinction.

I recall all the things Hecate told me while she threaded the star tech into my skin. It took over forty hours, and she talked incessantly for all of them. She told me of her home in the Sirius constellation, how the other worlds had watched Earth form and called her little sister. How the beings of all surrounding planets had promised to protect this new realm of magic and endless possibilities. She talked about humans like they were a plague. How she had watched their creation with disdain. How she would kill them all if she did not fear the circle of goddesses who would surely slay her. How she didn't care if I lived or died. She was secretly pleased when the bodies of her subjects rejected the mercurial nanites.

I bring up my hands to cover my ears as if that will somehow stop the voices in my mind. *Breathe in, breathe out,* my mind softly chides. My body can't comply. Resistance builds in my chest. Tangy anguish and hopelessness at being forced to live out a destiny that will surely end in my death. Disbelief as the reality of my situation truly settles over me. I drop my hands and link my fingers in front of me, then lift my head and meet Valance's eyes. The intensity of his stare scalds me, but I stare right back, knowing him as well as I suddenly know myself.

Rashid catches my fingers and holds them to his chest. "Fuck, Divinica! You're really glowing," he whispers.

I know I am. I can see my light reflecting on their stunned faces. The floor feels like it's trembling, the four yucky green walls are shivering, collapsing. I hear whispers and songs in the whistling wind squeezing through the cracks in my room created by the earthquake in my mind. I can almost feel the fabric binding all dimensions together, almost taste the barriers of reality. Suddenly, I think star travel might be the least of my powers.

"Alright, queen. You're freaking me out. Come back to Earth now," Rashid says in a light tone, but there's a real tremble in his voice. Valance knocks Rashid out of the way with barely leashed violence. Rashid levels a scathing glare at Valance's oblivious back but doesn't fight the shove. Valance pays no attention to anything except for me. He grasps the tops of my arms and pulls my feet to the ground.

"Time to come back to Earth, baby," he says. I want to smooth away the worry lines marking his brow with my fingertips. I want to run away from my destiny and find an abandoned beach in the middle of nowhere, then watch the last sunrise from the safety of his arms. Kiss him as the red wave burns the world to ash. Suddenly, I don't care about his brutal temper, or split, bloody knuckles, this is Valance. The hero in all my plotlines, with hands of fire and mysterious eyes filled with uncharted stars. I remember all the lives I've loved him, and also the times I've killed him.

My voice is soft as I step toward him, stopping when our bodies are touching from the waist down. "Heya, cowboy," I whisper, going up on my tippy-toes and pressing my lips to his.

Valance's surprised gaze flicks over my face. His body is tense as stone, and he flinches when I lightly bite his lip. I sink my fingers in his hair and feel his resistance break. He wraps his arms around my waist and buries his face in the curve of my neck. All too soon he lets me go with a reluctance that is almost palpable and takes a step back. My hand on his cheek, we let the seconds pass. He brushes back a strand of hair that's fallen into my eyes. There's so much to say to him that I can't say anything at all. I drop my hand and walk past him to my bathroom.

Rashid rushes in behind me, slams the door and throws the slender bolt. He leans back against the door as Valance thumps on it. Their theatrics happen in my peripheral, the mirror has my focus. The slender branches of the crown have embedded themselves into the tight skin of my brow, tearing into it like claws. Streamers of blood run down my forehead from each angry puncture wound. My hair is wild. My eyes are as bright as I've ever seen them. My skin is glowing, like every atom is individually lit from within. There's something older about me, like this crown is a symbol of past, greater times. *Horror kills youth,* I think, then I feel sad all over again.

"Nothing about this is fair," Rashid says, meeting my eyes in the mirror. "Nothing at all, but right now you look so—"

"I know," I whisper.

"Maybe you won't die," he says.

My smile is sad. "You can't possibly believe that."

Rashid closes his eyes for a second, when he opens them, the mirror's reflection makes the tears in his eyes sparkle. "Daniel is dying. The wave is killing him. I held him when the last one hit. I don't know if he can take another, I don't—" His words break off, and he throws up his hands. "He has some immunity to it. The Prussian blue that Valance's been injecting him with for two years to treat the killing levels of cesium and thallium that the wave leaves in its wake were working. But a few months ago, his body started building a resistance to the drug. If that happens and the poisoning continues, it's only a matter of time."

"You told me about this six months ago," I say. "I remember the day perfectly. I called you a liar, then cried for two days. I was happy when the red waves came for me that time. Happy to forget."

Rashid's gaze is openly pleading. "If you do this, you can save him, you can save everyone."

"I know. I knew it the second I put on the crown and got my memories back.

I was wrong in what I said earlier. I don't have a choice. Maybe I never did. Hecate took that choice from me when she put these tattoos on my body."

Rashid's expression tightens, and his voice is wretched. "For what it's worth, I'm sorry."

"Me too. I would've liked to see Daniel grow up."

"If you do this, then at least he'll have a life."

"I know. What's it to you, Rashid? What are you trying to save?"

Rashid purses his lips; his voice is deceptively airy. "Nightclubs, festivals, you know?" His face falls, his tone is lower, sadder when he keeps talking. "Roaring fires at Thanksgiving, family vacations where everyone argues and never forgets the slightest thing. Birthdays. Laughter. Maybe I'm just being selfish. I know I'll never get it back the way it was, but—"

"Valance will fight us, fight for me. He won't let me go easily," I whisper. I turn around and take Rashid's hands. "What are we going to do?"

"What can we do? The next wave is in eleven days. The *Gravity* is shot. I have a truck, it might make it a hundred miles or so, but Stonehenge is over five hundred miles away. We'd have to go the rest of the way on foot, or with the Rades, if we bring them with us in the truck. It's an old Amazon vehicle. I think they might fit. It will be hard. Munich and most of the coast is overrun with asshole Reptilians and starving humans," he says before he reaches out to untangle the crown from my wild hair.

I grab his arm. "No, wait. I want to talk to Valance first. Like this, with all my memories. To be honest, I might never take this off again."

"We don't have time—" Rashid starts, but I make a pleading face, and he falls silent.

I drop my voice to a whisper, hoping Valance can't hear me through the door. "Let me be with him tonight, I'll figure out a way to leave him in the morning. When I'm gone, you can tell Valance whatever you want, but tell Daniel I love him, and when it's all over, tell him I did it for him."

Rashid flips his hair and shakes his head. "No way, girlfriend. You'll have to make someone else your messenger boy. I'm obviously coming with you."

"If you do, you'll probably end up dying too."

"Oh please, I'm an Iranian gay man. I was born in the middle of a two-thousand-year war. I've been fighting since I could walk. I laugh in the face of danger."

"Alright, simmer down," I say, smiling. Hearing him quote one of my favorite cartoons reminds me of better times. Times of ignorance and bliss. Where I didn't know about old angry powers and all the repercussions of killing our Earth. Now, knowing what I know and what I have to do leaves me with a feeling so vast it echoes like thunder rolling over the Alps. "I have the beginnings of a plan. Give me tonight, just be ready to leave at sunrise."

I stop on the verge of running my hands through my hair and link my fingers behind my back instead. "This is so crazy," I say, more to myself than him.

Once the words are out, I listen back, then think they might be wrong. With the crown of star tech thorns on my head, none of this seems crazy at all. Crazy, insane, impossible are suddenly silly human words that mean nothing. This path I walk is older and bigger than any of us. I take a deep breath and realize I like the taste of peace that comes with accepting one's fate. "There are more things in heaven and earth, Horatio, than are dreamt of in your philosophy," I quote, still whispering.

Rashid's brows race for his pink hairline. "Hamlet, really? How very macabre of you."

I shake my head. "It's just something my dad always used to say."

There's another loud volley of thumps on the door and Rashid rolls his big eyes. "We good? I better let this cowboy in before he breaks down the door."

I nod. "We're good. Go to your sky base, but when you come back tomorrow, I need you to bring some more of that tranquilizer you shot me with a few hours ago. It will give us a head start if nothing else."

Rashid's sigh is long and heartfelt. "The truck's a sixteen-wheeler, electric, but still, it's big and loud."

"Then you better bring two syringes," I breathe. Rashid nods and unlocks the door.

"What the fuck, Rashid?" Valance roars.

"I don't forgive you, but I understand why you hit me. This sucks," Rashid declares.

In the mirror, I see Valance's eyes narrow as he bares his teeth. "I didn't ask for your damn understanding or your forgiveness," Valance says as he shoves past Rashid. I hear Rashid's sigh as his footsteps retreat. Valance storms into the bathroom, instantly taking up all the space, our gazes meet in the glass. His pupils dilate, and he shoves his hands in his pockets. I can tell he's exercising physical restraint in not putting a fist through another wall. He takes a step toward me, and I brace myself for his touch.

"Divinica, fuck...you look...fuck..."

I smile at him, still spilling glow from all my pores, like someone painted me with undiluted starlight. The crown has completely fitted itself to my skull, its colorful leaves and flowers multiplied. They run down the length of my hair, twining themselves through my wild curls. My hair looks like summer unleashed. "It's kinda amazing," I say, watching in the mirror the way the colors of my aura merge and mesh with his. I love it when they do that.

Valance takes another step toward me. His voice is rough. "Please tell me you're not seriously considering this."

"Considering what? Saving everyone from a slow, horrible death? Saving my brother? Yeah, I'm considering it. I'm surprised you're not. You care about people more than anyone I've ever met."

"And I'm surprised you think I would be down with any plan that involves killing you," he retorts. "Come on, Divinica. There's another way. There has to be, all I have to do is find it. I just need time."

"Daniel doesn't have time," I whisper. I swallow the lump in my throat, and it burns on the way down.

"The next wave is eleven days away. Give me those days. If I don't figure something out by then, I'll help you go all sacrificial lamb."

I don't break his gaze in the mirror as his hands fall to my waist. The silky pink shirt slides against my bare skin, and I hear his breath hitch. He dips his head, still never taking his eyes from mine, and kisses my shoulder, the curve of my neck. "Please, Divinica."

I close my eyes and lean into him. "I won't make a promise I can't keep," I say. My eyes fly back open and watch him in the mirror, properly fixated, like I need to look at him or I'll die. I stare at the way his golden hair tumbles to his jaw; his face is all sharp angles and enticing shadows. "Valance?"

"Hum?"

"Do you remember almost two years ago, right after the third time I stabbed you, you cuffed me, and I slept on the red bean bag? You told me one night when I wasn't so angry you would take me stargazing."

"Holy shit," he whispers, and his eyes fly to the crown, giving it a look of newfound respect.

"Yeah, cool, right? I'm like an old lady with Alzheimer's. One moment you're the apple of my eye—" I reach my hand behind his head and sink my fingers in his cool hair. "Next, I will forget you entirely. It's kinda nice, less accountability for me if I do something embarrassing or stupid."

"You're never stupid," Valance whispers against the curve of my ear. A little of the built-up tension leaves my chest. "But you do embarrass yourself all the time."

I giggle. I actually giggle. I can't help it. Despite it all, at this moment, I'm happy. "Come on, cowboy. Let's go gaze at some stars."

CHAPTER THIRTY

Truth in the stars

Hand in hand, Valance and I scale the ragged, crumbling walls edging the old north tower. Mist clings like skin to the moving sky. Icy dew infuses the air with the scent of sleet. We find the old metal stairs built in a serpentine twist, soaked in rust and sharp black vines. We clutch at the vines, carefully avoiding the grasping thorns, and find our footholds in the places where the red bricks have given way to dust.

When we reach the trellised tiles hanging onto what remains of the roof, I realize this old house which has kept me these last two years is better seen from above. The Hadamar. That's the name of this place, but the darker side of history knows it as 'The house of shutters.' My dad was the person who first called it Styx because it was once one of the six sites for the T4 euthanasia program, which performed sterilizations and mass murder during Hitler's reign of mayhem and terror. My dad told me the centers were responsible for over two hundred thousand deaths. It was also, apparently, a safe place for Hecate to go under an assumed name and play with mercury, child death, and ancient magic.

Valance and I continue climbing to the summit of the crematorium, which is situated directly above the old gas chamber, or as I recently like to call it, Hecate's lab. This section of the roof is mostly flat and nearly overrun with more black vines that cover the cracks in the old concrete like a spiky blanket.

It takes a moment, but we find a spot relatively free of debris after Valance kicks a few broken metal pipes and a pile of glass out of the way. He turns to stare at me in that way that robs the earth of air, then he crosses his arms as a cool smirk takes possession of his lips. "Divinica, where the hell did you get those pants?"

I look down at my legs and see nothing out of place. "What? Once upon a time these were my favorite pants. What's wrong with them?"

"They're tight as fuck. I think you better sit down before I attack you."

"Promises, promises," I sigh, and spread my cloak on the ground, then sit cross-legged facing the rising crescent moon. Valance sits beside me, arm slung over his drawn-up knee. I lean against him, and he wraps his other arm around me.

Silence ensues, but it's warm and comfortable, the silence of best friends. I could sit here, with him, like this, forever. Him and me, with a thousand memories warring between us. No barrier of forgetfulness to dull the sensation of just being near him. Here, alone. Both touched and changed by this eerie, horrifying place.

My voice is scratchy as hell when I finally use it. "A few days before we left, my father told me we were coming to Germany. He told me all about this place, actually. I Googled it. The house of shutters. Just the name is scary. He was coming here to meet with a renowned German scientist, or ancient immortal, star powered witch depending on how you look at it. She was evidently fascinated by his work. His eyes used to sparkle when he talked about her. She said she had information that might further his cause—"

Valance grunts. "Boy did she ever."

"She never had a chance to tell him anything. The wave hit, and then she was too busy shooting him right between the eyes."

Valance lets out a short bark of laughter that shakes his body. He sobers quickly, looking instantly contrite and downcast. "Sorry. It's not funny."

I face him with a sad smile. "It's laugh or cry, right?"

His face falls dramatically. "Oh baby, how is anyone ever going to know how ridiculous and hilarious and perfect you are if you're dead?"

"Word of mouth?" I suggest.

Valance doesn't say anything at my lame attempt at humor. The moon calls his eyes, and I watch the light play over his face. After nearly a minute of silence, he turns back to me, his voice is so low I almost don't hear it. "You really are made of magic and resilience. You're the bravest person I've ever met."

"No. I just love more than I should. More than is safe. Now that I remember everything, I almost see the value of forgetfulness. There's so much less pain in the white silence."

"Not for me. Your white silence is my red agony," Valance says, and I hear a wealth of unspoken anguish in those words. "I mean, when you're a kid, they tell you love's gonna be hard, but this goes years beyond hard. Soul wrenching, miserable, unquenchable, disastrous, those are just a few of the words that come to mind. Loving you has been the torment of my life." He buries his head in his hands and tugs handfuls of his hair. His voice is broken. "Losing you will end me."

I touch his shoulder lightly, stroke my fingertips down the center of his tense neck and watch him shiver. My voice is wistful. "You know, I think I spent most of high school and my senior summer willing you into existence. I didn't know at the time that I was fated to find you, but I always saw you in my mind when it conjured visions of my dream man."

"I used to close my eyes and see you too. I would see your eyes in the faces of the girls I slept with. I would look for you in crowded rooms, on empty streets," Valance says, voice muffled by his hands. "Please tell me how any of this is even fucking possible."

"You haven't figured it out yet? Why not? You're the smartest man in the world after all."

He shakes his head. "That's all a front, I'm just as lost as the next guy, trust me." He turns to meet my stare, his eyes flash quicksilver. "So, what exactly do you remember?"

"Everything from the time I was about four, when my parents moved from Riverside to Huntington beach, it gets spotty before that." I fall silent for a moment to study the dirty maroon mud caking my naked toes. I didn't put on my boots. It didn't feel like I needed them. The crown is doing strange things to my mind and body. I feel stronger, almost impervious to the elements which have been my steady persecutors these past two years. "I remember you. Not just in this life. I…I remember—" I throw up my hands, abandoning that line of thought. It's a confession I'm not yet ready to make, so I settle for something that needs saying. "Thank you, Valance. For everything. Daniel and I would've died two years ago without you. There was no reason for you to be so…kind. Especially after I kept attacking you."

Valance laughs, it's a harsh, dark sound. "Kind? I swear no one's ever accused me of that before."

"I see right through the muscled cowboy routine. Your mother was right, you've got a heart of solid gold lurking somewhere under all that brawn."

"I would do anything for you, Divinica. You're the only thing that's kept me sane. Ever since the crash, nothing's made sense except for you. If you die, I'll spend the rest of my life getting over you. Falling in love with you was as easy as breathing."

My heart stops, restarts with a gallop, then races off, buoyed by nerves and terror of what I'm about to say. I clear my throat, then cough, it sounds like a muted shriek. "It's just a curse. You love me because when I was connected with that part of me that belonging to Freya, I cursed you, cursed us both I think. You were Freya's lover, and the goddess circle was going to kill you. Freya was just going to let it happen. I kill you in so many lives, and I guess...I guess I just rebelled. I didn't think. I was angry. I cursed you to always find me, in all my lives, in all times. Me. Divinica. Not her." I close my eyes as the words stop flowing, unable to take the weight of my dark confession.

Instead of the anger I expect, he cups my cheeks in his big hands, and I hear a smile in his husky voice. "That's my girl," he says and kisses me softly, just once. A brush of the lips scarcely felt but wholly absorbed. He sits back, eyeing me quizzically. "Maybe it wasn't a curse. Maybe you gave me a form of immortality."

"In some of those other lives, I kill you."

"Well, in all fairness, you tried to kill me in this life too."

"That's true. Maybe you're the problem."

Valance moves closer. My blood thrums in my ears. "Curse or gift, I feel it. It's a living thing inside my chest dragging me to you." He catches a strand of my hair between his fingers, twirls it slowly, then tucks it behind my ear.

"Valance, you don't understand. It's not real, what you feel for me is just a spell. It's not rea—"

Valance catches my chin and tilts my head, demanding I meet his eyes. "It's the realest thing in my life. Everything is dust and death, Divinica. You are light and breath. It's not just the star tech, your soul was rare at birth. You're the perfect heroine. Much as I hate it, I know why they picked you. Strong heart and mind. Pretty much all anyone can ask from their heroes."

"What are you talking about? You know what a mess I am! The crazy shit I've done over these last two years, to you, to myself...it's pretty fair to say I'm completely mental."

Valance laughs. "All good heroines are."

I shake my head. "The funny thing is you're probably right, but doesn't that just make it all so much worse? This world isn't that bad if you look at it in the proper light. Sure, the butterflies and green things are gone. Lava and ice have covered all the roads we were once so proud of, but at least in this world, we're not harpooning dolphins, shooting children in their pre-schools, or murdering women who decided they should be masters of their own fate. Was it really better before or is life just a loop of constant horror better left unlived? If it was up to me, I would've activated the savior device a long time ago. Maybe around the Inquisition or the First World War."

I stop talking and lift my face to see him listening in the way he does. Head tilted a little to the left, lower lip held tight between his white teeth. "Maybe if I can find a way to keep you alive, you can figure out which artifact heals and use it on Daniel, then the world. We might stand a chance."

"What if instead of breaking the savior device, I implode the world?" I ask.

"Then so be it," he declares. He moves to kneel in front of me, gripping the tops of my thighs, and dragging me close, stopping only when my knees are clasped between his. He grips the back of my neck with his left hand and applies enough pressure to tilt my face toward his. "You don't have to do anything, Divinica. You still have to get all the rest of the artifacts and that will take some time. And we have time, at least a little. I want your promise. Swear that you'll give me eleven, no ten, just give me ten days before dashing off to do something noble and stupid."

I shake my head, trying to drop my gaze and break away from his searing, blistering stare. His grip tightens, holding me where he wants me. "Divinica—"

"I can't," I say, sounding and feeling on the verge of tears. The truth is, I would do almost anything for him. Of course I would, but— "Valance, I can't. I don't want to lie to you."

"Then don't! I know how much a promise means to you. I've seen the way you've tried to keep the ones you made even when the waves took your truths. Give me your word, and I'll trust it."

I suck in frigid air and shake my head, letting my eyes fall closed. I can't bear seeing his pleading desperation. "Valance please, don't ask this of me. Daniel is dying…everyone is dying. I have to try."

"I would never let anything happen to Daniel. You have to believe that. Even with all your memories, you can't know how horrendous these last two years have been for me. Divinica, you owe me this. For all the times I've saved your life, and Daniel's life," he says, pulling out all the stops. He's right. I owe him this and more.

My whisper is as hollow as a paper straw. "Hecate said it's my fate. No matter what I try to do, I'll die. It's my destiny."

"Well, your little curse made it mine too. We are linked. You get cut, and I do the hemorrhaging. If you kill yourself, you'll be killing me too!"

Pressure clamps down on my chest, twists my heart. Bile climbs up my throat, I swallow a mouth full of unshed tears. "Why do you even want me? All I do is hurt you."

"Then swear this to me and start making some of it right. As to your other question, the answer is inexplicable. All I do is want you," he snarls. His eyes flick to my lips and it's all the warning I have. His mouth crashes down on mine. Desperate, devouring. Every emotion: fear, desire, rage, anguish is prevalent in the taste of his kiss. It's a kiss that forever brands the very heart of me, and I respond without fear or thought. I wrap my arms around his neck and press my body close, and our tongues battle. There's no gentleness in him now, only unfettered intensity. He kisses me until my breaths are his and the thrashing beats of our hearts intertwine.

My hands skate down his shoulders, I dig in my nails, then try to drag him closer, but only gasp as he tears his mouth away. "Swear it, Divinica. Give me time, please. I promise if I can't figure it out before the next wave, I'll tie you to the altar at Stonehenge myself and let fate have its way. I'm begging you goddamn it!"

My heart stops as his punishing, glorious lips descend again. This kiss makes me dizzy. Words and thoughts scatter. He bruises my lips and steals my air, and I pull him closer, closer, close enough to steal my soul. Wind screams and icy rain falls, yet steam rises off our straining bodies. When I think I might faint, he breaks the kiss. My mind is cartwheeling, but my body is twisting, needing him. I try to drag his mouth back to mine. He resists and it's like trying to move a brick wall.

"Divinica," he says deeply. Fire skates down my spine as he slides his hand under my loose shirt.

I want him. I want to take the agony from his eyes. Who cares if I'm a liar? It's not like I have a date with a firearm tomorrow. There's still the matter of the five hundred some miles that must be traveled to reach Stonehenge. I might be able to keep my word. I lie back on my cloak and pull him down on top of me. He braces his hands on either side of my head. "Kiss me," I plead, tugging on his hair. He does. Oh, so skillfully. His lips are a scalding, a contrast to the freezing, ice tipped wind. He's a magician with his mouth and tongue. This kiss is slow, he takes his time making me writhe. When he finally lifts his head, I'm so fucking lost in him, I think in that moment I would've promised him anything. "I swear it," I breathe. Praying I'm not telling a lie, praying he figures something out in time, so no one has to die, praying there's someone kind and fair out there who still listens to prayers.

The words are acid on my tongue, but Valance's smile is bright as the sun. His perfect dimples and sparkling eyes change his face from ruggedly handsome to absolutely devastating. The rush of raw emotion he invokes threatens to swallow me. "Thank you, baby," he whispers, and I feel like the very worst of monsters.

My mother used to say that lying darkens the soul, and at this moment, I know she was right. Pure black, the inky, sticky kind, intrudes on my brilliant moment. Tears burn my throat, tingle my eyes. I blink them away, so he won't see as he leans down to kiss me again. The kiss is still everything, because it's him, but my golden moment is gone, it's oversaturated by the scarlet colors of my guilt. He trails his lips across my cheek, down my throat. His voice glances off earth and sky, echoing forever. "I love you, Divinica," he whispers, and my tears start to fall. Hot liquid runs from my eyes into my hair. I pray he thinks it's rain.

CHAPTER THIRTY-ONE

Betrayal

My head rests on Valance's chest, his arm is slung around me, and the sound of his steady, sleeping breaths are hypnotic. We kissed and talked for hours about everything and nothing. I told him about my childhood, all the things I had never been able to remember before. He told me about a boy named Chad Preston who had tormented him all through middle school. How good and horrible it felt to finally kick his ass in senior year. In whispered tones, I spoke of the first boy I kissed, how awkward and embarrassing it had been. He talked of the girl he had a crush on at sixteen who slept with his best friend, and how he had sworn never to love again. We laid there, fingers intertwined and told each other all our secrets. He fell asleep while I waxed poetic about my favorite albums and the lyrical goddess who sings them, then I held perfectly still and listened to him breathe until pale and spiraling streamers of mauve light spread their fingers of doom across the sky.

Now, the crown jabs cruelly into the side of my head, but I don't move. I don't care about the obnoxious discomfort. I'm afraid if I leave his arms to do what I need to do, I'll never be held in them again. I wait until the very last moment, then slowly, carefully, and dragged down by the deepest reluctance anyone has ever felt, I disentangle myself from the warm safety of Valance's arms. When it's done, I sit and stare at him until the sky is burning pink at the edges. Finally, I stand on shaky legs, sighing. I force myself to turn away from him and climb back down the crooked, broken bricks, dare to descend the twisting, rusted staircase, then sprint across the courtyard to where I know Rashid is already impatiently waiting.

He's right where I expect him to be, flanked by Dayle and… "Daniel! Daniel! What the hell are you doing here?"

Daniel shrugs his leather clad shoulders, the very soul of nonchalance. "I know you're about to find a way to save the world. I assume it's probably going to kill you. I thought I should give you the pleasure of my company in your final days."

I eye him wryly. "Uh, thanks? But you can't come."

Daniel frowns. "Rude. Well, you're going to have to use those tranquilizers on me, cause that's the only way I'm staying."

"He's just as safe with us as he is anywhere else," Dayle says.

Rashid holds out the syringes. "We're wasting time. Here, use both. We need whatever head start we can get. Valance is a pretty scary, resourceful guy."

I stare at them all, my heart thumping so hard I can feel the unsteady beats in my temples. "No one has to come with me. We're honestly probably all going to die," I say. Staring at them, I realize my words are true. Here are three of the four people in the world who care if I live or die, and I am about to take them on a death mission. The other, the cowboy I left sleeping on the roof, is seconds from feeling the literal sting of my betrayal. My allies are few, and soon to dwindle.

"Fine, come if you must, Daniel," I say sternly, holding up my hand to forestall his triumphant smile. "You have to swear to listen to every word I say. If I tell you to run and save yourself, under no circumstance does that mean to rush in guns blazing."

"I promise," Daniel says glumly, and a little too quickly. I fear his promise holds as much weight as the one I gave to Valance.

I turn my attention to the Rades, saddled and ready to ride. "What about the truck?" I ask, going up on my toes, trying to see through the thick mists obscuring the courtyard and beyond. It's going to snow. I can smell it in the air.

"I parked it about a mile away," Dayle says. "It'll fit two Rades, Boogles and Rashid's, Donner. Daniel can ride with me, Rashid with you." Dayle shades his eyes and turns to face the weak sunlight bleeding into gray dawn. "If we're trying to reach Cologne by tonight, I'd say you have about ten minutes to make sure your man doesn't follow us."

I grit my teeth and take the syringes from Rashid's outstretched hand. His voice is pitched low, for my ears only. "Don't think about it. Just do what you need to do."

"He's never going to forgive me for this," I say, staring down at the capped needles. My despair is sharp as the ice capped wind.

Rashid puts a hand on mine and gives it a comforting squeeze. "That's tomorrow's problem. You're doing the right thing, Divinica. For all of us."

I turn away from then, tracing my steps back to Valance.

"Maybe put on some shoes, sis. You look like a Hobbit," Daniel calls loudly after my retreating form. I don't turn to ask how he knows what a Hobbit is. *Lord of the Rings* was my family's all-time favorite trilogy. Daniel had always loved Hobbits the most. He argued that they were Tolkien's bravest creation, and ultimately the saviors of Middle Earth. He had been standing close to the crown, who knows what this thing retrieves from the silence. Hobbits apparently. I shake my head as I continue walking away. At least Frodo got to spend almost a year enjoying the world he rescued before the Elves whisked him away. I suspect, fear, and deep down somehow recognize I will not be so lucky.

I go to my room first. I'll need my artifacts, my weapons, and my boots. When I walk in, Valance is sitting on my bed, hard eyes trained on my face. His voice is raspy from cold and lack of use. "Where the hell were you?"

I turn to close the door and hide my face while I try my best to school my expression into one of innocent confusion. "Nowhere. I went to check on Boogles."

Valance looks like he believes me about as far as I could throw him. He keeps his unflinching gaze on me, and it takes actual effort not to nervously shift my weight. I almost break right then. The real truth is I don't want to go anywhere that takes me away from him. I don't want him to hate me, but more than anything, if I'm going to die, I really want it to be in his arms. I walk to him slowly, faking a calm I'm years from feeling. I don't have to fake the desire flashing in my eyes, or the tremble in my hands. I sit on his lap, facing him, draping my legs over his iron thighs. Some of the distrust fades from his eyes replaced by naked lust as I link my fingers behind his neck and drag his head to mine. I didn't know much about kissing before this man crashed into my life. I take the tricks he's taught me and use them on him, rubbing my body against his. The kiss is so wild, I'm in real danger of losing myself to it and forgetting the mission.

He says my name as his hand slips under my shirt. My cold, tired body is suddenly a bundle of burning nerves as I reach for the first syringe. There's a slight tensing of his muscles before his eyes fly open, and he starts to pull back from the kiss.

He knows! He knows! screams my unhelpful mind. I clutch handfuls of his damp hair and use real force to keep his lips locked to mine, then I grind my hips into his. Undulate against him like some exotic dancer. I don't believe he falls for it completely. I just think he doesn't want to stop kissing me as much as I want to keep kissing him. He whispers my name again, licking at my lips as my fingers find the syringe hidden in the thick waistband of my pants. I snap the cap off with a single flick of my thumb, bite his lower lip, and stick the needle in his arm, jabbing it to the hilt as I shove the plunger down.

Valance's body jerks, he rips his mouth from mine, then leans away to look at me full in the face. It hurts that there isn't more shock in his eyes, all I see is bleak, freezing rage. Cold as extreme as the Alps' summits in winter. "I'm so sorry," I tell him, knowing perfectly well my words are meaningless, understanding that in this case, 'sorry' fixes nothing. I'm barely holding back tears. If I tell him how much I love him, I'll break down, and beg him to bed me, beg him to save me. I blink my burning eyes, his face blurs, wavers. I blink again and the tears almost roll. I wonder if this is what a breaking heart feels like, where each breath is made of jagged metal shards and flaming knives.

"Fuck you, Divinica," he snarls harshly, spacing every word for a dramatic emphasis which I feel deeply.

"You didn't give me a choice," I say. I can't bring myself to meet his eyes.

"Please." His voice cracks like a whip. "Do you really think this is going to work? It's gonna take more than that to stop me. It's gonna take—"

I don't let him finish. My eyes flick to his, and I hold his gaze for a split second before I stick the other needle in his other arm.

This time, his roar of rage shakes the rafters. He throws me off his lap. I go sprawling, getting some serious airtime, before the back of my head has an uncomfortable meeting with the hard floor. I lie still for a second, dazed, then shake my head to clear it. He's standing over me, fists clenched, teeth bared. For a horrible moment I think he's going to hit me. I truly feel like I deserve nothing less. He takes a menacing step toward me. I scramble backward. Spider crawling until my elbows encounter the wall and I can't go any further. I hold up my hands, defenseless. "I have to do this," I say haltingly. "This is my choice. Not yours. Not anyone's. Mine."

Valance looks like he wants to say something, but he never gets a chance. His eyes glaze over, and he crashes to his knees. Toppling in the way a mountain might fall. "Fucking…knew it…liar…shouldn't have trusted…those goddamn eyes," he says haltingly as his body crumples. His face hits the floor with a thud, then he says no more. Everything that follows is a blur. I hurry, but my movements are wooden. My heart and fingers are numb as I run to the silo, grab the first duffle bag I see, plus two pistols and three boxes of ammo. A bulletproof vest for Daniel, my favorite bow, and enough arrows to bring down an army. In my room again, I step over Valance's sleeping body to collect my artifacts and tug on my socks and boots. The firebird creams at me and flaps his huge red wings. Valance doesn't even stir. I quickly abandon the idea of attempting to drag him over to my bed and settle for placing my pillow under his head. I kiss his brow. If he were awake, I know there's no way in hell he would let me kiss his lips, so I don't allow myself to take advantage of his comatose state. Instead, I brush away the golden curls which have fallen across his face, and stare at him for a collection of breathless moments that end in no time at all. I don't know when I started crying, but tears rush down my cheeks as I grab the candle and my notebook, then stuff both items in my bag. I leave my room with stomping feet and don't let myself look back. If I look back, I will stay with him forever until I die.

Monsters of misery sink their fangs into my skin. How did I go from a carefree girl frolicking on a beach, always drenched in music, laughter, and sunshine, to this horror I've become? My breath hitches as I walk away from him, my exhale is splintering glass. There is no sunshine left in my life. My generation was the generation of dreamers and now that dream is dead. I march back to the three guys who I believe will be my companions until the end. Wind slaps me in the face, the ice is a thousand needles stabbing my skin. Flakes of snow ride the morning breeze, streaming from the distant mountains. I don't see their rugged beauty. I get angrier with every step I take. I was wrong. The goddesses were wrong. Evil may have existed, but humanity as a whole didn't deserve this. Valance was right to hope, Rashid was right to fight. There had been so much good. So many beautiful souls that woke up every day to do their best. Now? How many of us were left? Thousands? Maybe hundreds? The innocent had been punished with the guilty, and not to sound entitled, but it wasn't fucking fair.

My skin, blood, and bone feel iced over as I reach the courtyard. Statues waver in the morning mist. Goddesses lost to time. Hecate told me they were sleeping. She said that if I failed in my mission, as she hoped I would, I was on my own. She would watch from afar, then laugh as we burned. Suddenly, horribly, I'm sure a part of those wicked goddesses lives inside of me. Stitched into the ink that glows under my skin, bright as a star captured in a glass jar. I want to claw at my chest to rip them out, dig my nails into my tattoos and tear at their essence. Bloody, red rage clouds my sight. Anger is my entire world. Who cares if stories, songs, and cults are formed on the power of your name? Being a hero sucks.

CHAPTER THIRTY-TWO

Bone cold

DIVINICA

Four days of unpassable roads and freezing cold. Three nights of wet socks and stinky clothes. Of sleeping between two Rades who have a propensity to fart when they dream. Flatulence that increases in volume, temperature, and a smell so overwhelming it boggles the mind. Four miserable nights of searching for bathrooms in abandoned homes and malls with shattered windows and praying they flush. Four endless nights of caving in, breaking down, and peeing in parking lots. On top of all that, the state of the world is shocking. I knew it would be bad, but nothing could've prepared me for all the bodies. It seems at the end of the world all we are left with is piles of rotten bodies, old buildings, and millions of broken-down cars. The roads leading in and out of the main cities are overrun with people and their cars, all in various stages of escape. Their decomposing faces are frozen in the final throes of unmitigated agony. All the cars, regardless of what lane they occupy, travel in the same direction. Out of the cities. Into the mountains. None of them made it. They died in the agony of the waves, as so many did. Smashed their heads through the windshields of their cars or clawed the skin from their faces. I learn more each mile of how imaginative people can be when they just want the pain to stop.

The smell of the cities lingers in my nightmares. When I wake from them screaming, I'm possessed by the feeling that I've somehow been contaminated.

In my quiet moments, I wonder what Los Angeles looks like, and how fair the beaches of home? I hardly dare imagine it, but whatever its state, I know it's the city of dead angels now.

On the morning of the fourth day, we reach Brussels. Previous population two million, current population, I don't know, but it can't be more than a couple hundred. The city looks like the site of a genocide. Millions of dead, lying where they fell. In their houses, shops, in quaint cafés, on the floors of renowned museums, and all throughout the grand hotels. On day two, we found a single solar charger just beyond the city limits of Maastricht. It bought us another three hundred miles. This old truck has done its part. Amazon for the win, as always. It was also at that gas station where we saw our first Reptilians, or as Daniel likes to call them, the Lizard Lords. These were different from the ones I fought at Styx. They were mostly human in aspect, only taller, faster, and scaled in places with bright yellow eyes. They watched me as intently as I watched them from the truck's small window. Dressed like a biker band, their leather chausses made their slightly bowed legs look like sheathed scythes. They were our only encounter. In the cities, the few survivors we saw traveled alone, poisoned by the consistent radiation, dazed, still lost in the onslaught of the recent wave. Blank stares, empty, vacant eyes that see everything and nothing. Bits of skin and open sores splattering their skeletal faces. Daniel says they're not even good for eating anymore. I punch his shoulder but secretly agree.

Today, in Brussels, we found an abandoned mall. Mercifully empty of starving, confused humans and mythical creatures who shouldn't exist. Outside, the sky is gun metal gray, and the weather is icy, wet, and abysmal, and I am grateful for a mall in a way I never thought I would be. Daniel and I found two mostly intact clothing stores. We don't care at the moment about the monsters and riotous elements—we're lost in the wonder of new loot. Daniel scored a pair of sturdy brown shoes with thick soles. His own were full of holes. I also found a pair of shoes that fit well, but I can't bring myself to give up my birthday boots. They're a symbol of better times. I settled on a pair of black pants, similar to mine, only made for German winters and not Cali summers. I also grab a black turtleneck that might be cashmere, it's the softest thing I've felt in years. I put it on immediately, along with a lavender, shag faux-fur jacket that smells like cigarettes and old ladies. I love it on sight.

Daniel holds up a pair of corduroy Empires with huge pockets decorating the sides. "What do you think?" he asks, running his hand over the fabric and looking wistful, like he too might be thinking of better times. Daniel's memories are fairly good when he's close to the crown. Close to me.

"Imagine what they'll feel like soaking wet, or caked in ice and snow," I say, and watch his face fall. "You know what? Just keep em.' Who knows? Maybe we will manage to find a dry spot somewhere in this muggy, wet, and let's face it, god awful place."

"Yeah, this place sucks the big one," Daniel says, walking over to a rack of beanies. He picks out two, then reaches for a pack of socks.

"Hey, throw me one, yeah?" I ask. He grabs a pink pack and tosses it over his shoulder without bothering to see if he makes the shot. He does. It's perfect. My catch is pretty flawless as well. "Badass throw. Thanks." Eyes on a stack of shiny belts, Daniel gives me a thumbs up. *Just like old times, with Mom at the Galleria,* I think. For a beautiful, horrible second, everything feels unnervingly normal. We're out shopping like we've done a hundred times. Mom and Dad are waiting in the car. Daniel's going to make me buy him ice cream. I'll say no, and he'll threaten to throw a monster sized fit, and I'll curse at him, then give in. I spin around as if I can run from my thoughts and catch my own eyes in the floor length mirror near the fancy mannequin display. I see the crown of moving mercury thorns on my head, controlling the way loose curls fall over my face, and realize normal died a painful death in the fires of the first wave. Perhaps long before that, maybe it was the night a group of goddesses decided to destroy and reform the world. With the fluffy lavender coat falling to the tops of my boots, shaggy as a soft carpet, I look like a woodland nymph from Aphrodite's time. Even my face is changing. Hardening.

"Like what you see?" Daniel asks from behind me, he meets my eyes in the mirror.

"I don't know. I'm not sure how I feel about it. I'm sure it's only gonna get worse," I say, watching the way my pale lips move in the glass.

"Comforting, sis. Hey, remember when you used to tell me you were a queen, then make me do all the fucking dishes?"

I smile. "Yes."

"Guess you were right."

"Guess so," I say, looking down at my dark, nondescript clothes beneath the wild jacket better made for robbing banks at night than commanding subjects. "I don't feel much like one though, just a cold, lost girl, way too far from home." My eyes wander the store, searching for trouble, hoping for a few more seconds of this slice of normality and peace. Beyond the mirror's fresco frame, on the mannequin closest to me, sits the prettiest white dress I've ever seen. The bodice is tight, a modest, off the shoulder design. Elasticized lace from the look of it. The skirt falls from the high waist in a straight, simple spill. Layers atop layers of a sheer material dotted with tiny diamonds that wink and sparkle under the flickering neon lights. Pieces of cloth each lying atop the other like a waterfall of delicate butterfly wings. Each piece ends in a sharp point tipped with more lace. There's no place on Earth to wear a dress like this anymore. I know this but take it anyway. If it's my fate to give my life for a bunch of people I don't know, and let's face it, would probably try to kill if they came right at me, then the universe should at least extend me the courtesy of being able to die in a pretty dress.

Daniel gives me a questioning look as I stuff the dress in the duffle bag, but he doesn't say anything which makes me grateful and sad. In the old days, he would have certainly had an obnoxious comment or three. I miss the hell out of my annoying little brother, but I'm proud of the fearless guy he's become. He leans over to shove another pack of socks in his back pocket, then sways on his feet when he straightens.

I reach for him. "Daniel, are you okay?"

Daniel smacks my hand away. "I'm fine, just stood up to fast. That's all."

I nod like he isn't lying. "Alright."

"Give me a gun," he says, reaching past me and beginning to rifle through the duffle. "In case the Lizard Lords come back, I should have more than a knife, serrated and cool as it is."

I sigh and reach for the .22 pistol I stowed in the bag's side pocket. "Sis, hand over the .45, and I won't say a word about the dress, not even when you're having a 'me moment,' and actually attempt to wear the thing," he says, all cheekiness and twinkling eyes.

I make a sour face at him but grab the .45 and check that it's loaded, then hand it to him. "Sweet," he crows, hoisting the piece high. "Do you think they're going to come back?" he asks, voice lower than it was a second ago.

"Yes," I say, because it's true.

Daniel nods. "You saw one once before all this started. I remember. We were camping with Mom and Dad at Joshua Tree. You were freaked. None of us believed you, well maybe Dad did a little. Mom wanted to give you Nyquil. Help you sleep it off."

"Yeah, I remember."

"We should've believed you," Daniel says, eyes downcast, feet shuffling.

"I don't blame you all, it was unbelievable. I had the strangest feeling that it was looking for me. I thought I'd never forget those fluorescent yellow eyes. They blinked vertically, that's how I knew it wasn't human—that, and it was about eight feet tall. Fuck! It was terrifying."

Daniel laughs, a hard, old sound. "That was, of course, before you knew what terror actually was." He sits down on a pile of pants and crosses his arms. "Do you think they've always been here? The Lizard Lords? Hiding underground, just waiting for humans to die?"

I don't even need a moment to ponder. "Yeah. I do. I think there's a lot of things on this planet with us that we've been told our whole lives don't exist. We believed liars, called reality conspiracy, and history myth."

Daniel shakes his head. "Dangerous lies. While we were getting blinder, the Lizard Lords were getting stronger."

I open my mouth but never get a chance to speak my mind. A huge, grinding crash, sudden as a crack of thunder on a sunny day, splits the silence, and makes us both jump hard. Daniel and I spin in time with each other, both pointing the muzzles of our guns at the sound.

I put my forefinger to my lips, telling him to keep quiet. Daniel violently rolls his eyes, then gives me a different finger. "I'm not an idiot," he mouths.

"Sorry," I say in the same soundless voice. I crouch slowly, not taking my eyes off the possible distant, unseen danger, and sling the duffle over my shoulder. "Back to the truck," I whisper. Daniel nods and leads the way. Beyond the sliding double doors, the world is a snow globe tilted on its side and shaken well. The wind is a clenched fist made of razor-sharp shards of ice; it punches us both in the face. We stagger back, then duck our heads and press forward. Each step is a battle. My fingers are a collection of clumsy, disjointed icicles when I finally manage to pry open the door on the passenger side of the truck. I crawl inside the safety and warmth of the cab, then turn back and reach out my hand to help Daniel up the steps. He knocks my hand aside, and hoists himself up, giving me a dirty look all the while. Snowflakes cling to my lashes and clutter my vision as I swing my legs over the center console, then jump over the fifth-wheel coupling and down into the detachable closed cargo space. As I find my feet, I see that Rashid has carefully organized what looks like half the mall's contents into neat stacks. Food, clothes, toiletries, make-up accessories, and an assorted collection of weapons they brought from Sky base.

Rashid smiles when he sees me, but it doesn't reach his glitter-soaked eyes. Apparently, he found a salon in the mall and made effective use of it. His brows are recently waxed and perfectly shaped. His hair is freshly dyed a deep, electric green. He's wearing a tight, black, long-sleeved undershirt that looks military grade. Over it, he has a blue knit turtleneck. The sleeves come to a wicked point, with little loops that hook over his middle fingers. The outfit is completed by dark jeans and ankle boots sporting thick, shiny, Mary Jane buckles.

"Your wardrobe is on point," I say, smiling, "Very apocalyptic chic."

Rashid winks at me. "Just because you can't pull it off, doesn't mean you can hate."

I raise my hands. "I wouldn't dare."

"You're not too off base, yourself," he says, giving me a quick head to toe inspection. "You look warmer. I like the jacket. That crown is fucking something else. It's like I'm watching a player in a game. *Destiny* or *Diablo*. You're leveling up. Every artifact you've collected so far seems to increase your XP. It's fascinating to watch."

"Thanks," I say caustically. I sit beside him, drawing my legs into my chest and resting my chin on my knees.

Rashid gives me a hooded look, but I hear compassion in his voice when he asks, "You miss him, don't you?"

I don't have to ask who he's talking about. Valance. Always Valance. "Every damn second of every damn day. I keep going over everything in my head. The last two years are playing on a loop. He's lost me so many times. I've given him so much hate, hurt him so badly, but he's never stopped caring, hoping, fighting. If our tattered love story ends in my bloody death, it's really going to suck."

Rashid scoots closer to me and slings his arm around my shoulder. "If you think about it, most great romances end in death. Romeo, Heathcliff, Kathy, and Juliet."

I press my nose between my knees and sigh. "Thanks, Rashid. That's super helpful."

Rashid reaches across me, then rustles through a box near my foot. Seconds later, his hand emerges with the most glorious of all treasures. Cup of Noodles. I shriek like a crazy lady and snatch the Styrofoam from his hand, then start tearing into it like a starving wolf on a fresh carcass. When it comes to ramen, Divinica waits for no man.

Rashid chuckles. "Uh, easy there, dear. There's some hot water in that thermos over there. Unless you want to just—oh, yep. You're just digging in, perfect. Eating those noodles like a cracker. Attractive."

"I won't wadder," I say over a mouthful of dry noodles and msg. Still, this was by far the yummiest thing I've put in my mouth in two years. Two more bites and I make it to the thermos. It's a painful test of sheer will to wait the three minutes for the damn thing to cook. "Tell me about Mars," I say, sitting down on the truck's cold floor, and resting my back against Boogles's rumbly tummy.

Rashid's eyes flick to mine, his mouth opens to say something, and I'm busy being jealous of how well he can pull off a red lip, when the driver's door is flung open, startling me, and letting in the ice and screaming wind. Dayle grabs the hand guard and hoists himself into the truck. He closes the door quietly, casting a soft glance at Daniel curled in the passenger seat, huddled deep in a pile of blankets and coats, then climbs over the center console. He's so huge that the whole event looks a bit like a bear straddling a dollhouse. His movements are slow, he's careful not to wake Daniel, or jostle him in any way. He narrowly squeezes his bulk through the metal-mesh divider, then jumps down, unscathed. He takes a lusty sniff of the air, and makes a deep, pleased sound. "Nothing like hot ramen on a snowy day," he observes.

"How about lukewarm ramen in a blizzard?" Rashid offers.

Dayle laughs, and my fire bird screams like someone plucked out a tail feather. I jump again, then throw the bird an angry look, which doesn't have the desired effect. If anything, my glare strengthens his vocal cords, because he screams again. Louder. Daniel stirs and Rashid sticks a finger in his ear, making a pained face.

Dayle sits cross-legged in front of me and cracks his neck and knuckles until I'm cringing. "Walked about two miles south," he says, "Roads are a bust. It's all just bodies, water, ice, and mountains. Looks like some faulty dams met some angry rivers. We're gonna have to take the Rades the rest of the way. This truck isn't made for off roading in the Alps. We'll wait until the storm lets up." He cracks the knuckles in his thumbs and sighs, eyes on Daniel's sleeping, adorable face. Dayle's hooded expression softens, turning his dramatic features from menacing to cuddly. "Kid won't make it much longer. He's strong, but—" His voice breaks off. He doesn't have to say it. Daniel is dying. Rapidly. Right in front of my eyes.

My sigh is broken, my voice is a scratchy, threadbare sound. "I've seen it. I haven't wanted to think about it. If I do, I'll scream. If I do, I'll go into the past and slay the goddesses where they stand," I drop my head in my hands, "if I do, I'll abandon my fate to find Hecate and slit all three of her throats," I say, sounding as vengeful as the creatures who did this to me. I'm already on my way to die. What else can I do? Nothing at all save watching the healthy pink in his cheeks fade to a grayish blue. Drop my gaze when he tries to catch it, so I don't see that the whites of his eyes are turning yellow as spilt yolk. Cry and fear in silence as his movements grow increasingly sluggish. *Don't hate on your brother,* my mother used to say. *In the end, family is all you have.* My eyes rove over each of the truck's passengers, and I realize in this she was also right. Right and wrong. Family is blood, and it's the people you choose. Souls that link and mesh with your own. Friends who will stay by your side when the sun shines or the sky storms, fight for you, and if necessary, die for you. Just as you would die for any of them. *Will die,* my stupid mind clarifies, and the taste in my mouth is acid and rain.

Dayle shuffles to the side, takes a metal comb from his back pocket, and starts attacking his wet hair. "You know," he says, eyes still on Daniel, "when they used to dramatize the end of the world, no one ever talked about all the dead kids. Kinda takes the wind out of the glorified dystopian fantasy's sails." I watch Dayle's eyes glaze over, and he doesn't bother to blink at the gathering moisture. I know he's thinking about his family, about the daughter he lost. Nearly two years ago to the day, Dayle went to find his family in England, where he had safely left them. He returned a month later, bloody, alone, changed. Two nights after he got back, Valance told me what happened. I cried until I forgot. Dayle's wife had shot herself sometime between the fifth and sixth wave. Their four-year-old daughter had died of starvation and neglect a little under a week later. She died in her bed holding the pink-haired Bratz doll Dayle had given her the day he shipped out. He cried, cursed his god, and buried them with his bare hands in the garden his wife had once planted. When it was done, he put a gun in his mouth and sat in the center of the life he had lost. He never pulled the trigger. I know when he looks at Daniel, Dayle thinks about all the kids he's buried since.

"Mars is hot and red, since you 're asking," Rashid says, breaking me from my thoughts by cleanly changing the subject and taking some of the sadness from the air. "It's also pretty fucking magical. Not just a lost civilization, but a lost world. I stood in the ruins of a red pyramid older than time. Fixed a rover named Spirit who's been up there sleeping for decades. The governments of the old world say it was a barren place, void of life, but—"

Dayle interrupts with a sneer. "Give me a fucking break. They also said Reptilians weren't real. In the last two years, I've killed enough of them to form my own opinion."

Rashid waves his painted nails in some general dismissal of it all. "Smoke, mirrors, and hoaxes." He shakes his head. "Politicians. Fucking liars, the lot of them."

"Sometimes, I think the red wave was first used on Mars. Only something went terribly wrong," Dayle says.

Rashid snorts derisively. "Wrong?" He flings up his hands to gesture at the stunted finery of our stuffy, metal hovel. "Worse than this?"

"Yes," Dayle says flatly.

No one says much else after that. I make sure Daniel is well covered, tuck the blanket under his feet, then push the dark spill of hair off his face and kiss his cool cheek. "I love you," I whisper. Then, on second thought, I dig through my duffle for Magu's peach. The thing is glowing like a halogen bulb. In the truck's dark interior, the light seems to be alive. I remember in Magu's world, she died to save a child; the tree of life that grew from her body gave me this peach. I set the thing in Daniel's lap and cover it with a blanket, so the light doesn't bother him. When I assure myself that he's sleeping as peacefully as possible, I lie down beside Boogles and snuggle into his warmth. I'm asleep in seconds. The dreams come, and in sleep, I can no longer run from the memories. They charge at me like the four horsemen of the apocalypse. They carry me away to the lands of oblivion.

CHAPTER THIRTY-THREE

Where's a cloaking device when you need one?

DIVINICA

My dream takes me to the recent past and straight into what feels like a memory. I'm sitting beside Valance in his throne room watching the way evening light smooths the harsh expression on his face. I remember everything as perfectly as if I'm living it all over again. I remember being chased by shadows and running into his arms, then there was the fight.

Valance had whispered in my ear. It was the first time he made my tattoos glow. It was also the first time the Reptilians had come for me. Now blood is everywhere. Dark as ink, it stains Valance's hands, threads through his golden hair, smears his bare chest and drips off the tip of his straight nose. His eyes are vast, barren plains of raw emotion, watching me. I stare at his lips. I remember that I've wanted to kiss him for so long.

Buried in the blood smearing his cheeks I see scales; they glimmer and shine as he moves. My wide-eyed stare drops to inspect the blood puddles on the floor. There, I see more scales clinging to severed fingers too long for a human. Still more all over the decapitated head of a Reptilian lying where it fell near the base of Valance's throne. I look into the head's sightless yellow eyes. Its lolling tongue is split down the center like a viper.

Valance follows my line of sight. "I'm afraid they'll never stop coming for you. I think the way you glow calls to them. They can find you here, away from Styx. I have to take you home. There are so many moths and one fucking flame," he says darkly. I shake my head. In this memory, I have no idea what he's talking about. How can I decipher the mystery of 'they' when I have no clue who I am? I open my mouth in hopes of saying something witty and intelligent, but all that comes out is a breathy, "Why?"

"Because of who you are," he says. He cups my cheek in his bloody palm. The touch of his skin is so real, so vivid.

My breaths accelerate. "Who am I?"

"Something old, something strong, something they want to kill. So many moths, one fucking flame." I watch him wipe a handful of blood off his face. It's dark, oily, and splatters like a bursting water balloon when it hits the ground.

When he sees me staring at the way the droplets roll, he says, "Don't worry, it's not all mine. I'll never let them hurt you. I don't care who or what you are. I'll die before I let something take you from me. It will never happen, never." He speaks in a vow that tempts me to believe.

I gaze up at him mutely. My breath's all tangled in my lungs like a ball of confused string. He lowers his head. His strong arms, his touch, his sensual voice take away the fear of forgetfulness, abolish the darkness, and erase the blood. All else fades, the dying world, and this broken dream. For a moment the universe is perfect, and it's only ours. The way he stares back at me ignites something low in my stomach, a thing forbidden, hot and desperate.

I twirl my fingers through a few gold curls hanging over his ear.

Valance closes his eyes; his groan is heartfelt. "One day, Divinica, I'm going to kiss you. When that day finally comes, I don't think I'll ever be able to stop."

"Kiss me now," I say with a bravery I'm far from feeling. His hands slide to my waist, then he sits back on his throne, pulling me firmly onto his lap, and rests his forehead against mine.

"Don't tempt me," he says, brushing a finger across my throat. "Divinica, kissing you is a crime."

I sink my fingers into his bloody hair. "Valance, kiss me. There are no more crimes at the end of the world."

"Careful, Divinica. If this happens between us, you can't take it back. This game is dangerous."

"I don't care. Show me what it feels like with you. Please."

Valance places a single finger over my lips to halt the flow of my tempting words. "No. I can't. I've wanted you for too long. I don't trust myself to stop with a single kiss."

"Then don't stop!" I say harshly. "Valance, please. I want everything with you."

His entire body shudders hard. "Fuck me! What are you trying to do to me?"

"I want you, damn it!" I say again, my voice rising in desperation. "Valance, I think…I'm in love with you…I love you."

"You're too young to throw around a word like love," he says brutally, making me see red.

"And you're too stubborn to deserve it, but here we are."

"I've survived a lot in these past two years, but I don't think I would survive you regretting me."

"Never!" I whisper. "I could never regret you. Not even when I forget you."

He shakes his head. Blond curls fly, bloody and brilliant. "You don't know. You can't say that. After the wave, you always hate me. Hate the darkness you see in me. If your memories come back before—I…Divinica, I couldn't bear it."

"Hate or not, I bet I'll still want to kiss you. It's probably why I keep trying to stab you. I ache when I look at you. It's confusing; it makes me hot and restless," I tell him.

"How can you be so goddamn seductive without even trying?" Valance asks through gritted teeth. His hands stroke my cheeks, pushing my hair from my face. His eyes lock and hold me to him. "Divinica, if given half the chance, I would devour you. Taste you, kiss you until you forgot what it felt like to be alone. I would take the innocence from your eyes. God, I want to ruin you for anyone else."

"Do it!" I challenge, then tug hard on his hair, scratch my nails over his scalp until he hisses and groans. His head lowers, his lips brush over mine. A single spark, white and hot ignites the breath of air between us. I feel the sting of it on my bottom lip, sharp as the snap of a rubber band. We both jump and stare into each other's eyes until the world stands still.

"Don't you dare stop," I demand, and Valance capitulates with a hiss of air between his locked teeth. He kisses me and the spark happens again, but we're prepared and neither of us flinch. The air crackles, and it feels like lightning strikes my heart. Everything goes dark. There's a sharp ringing in my ears as his tongue finds mine, suddenly it's raining starlight. The kiss is carnal, deep, and altogether intoxicating. I'm making little frenzied sounds in my throat, twisting in his lap, trying to get closer, closer, so much closer. We both pant when he tears his mouth away. "Divinica." His voice echoes as the room around me starts to spin and change. The blood on the floor turns to a boiling fountain that makes a rushing river. The roof above my head with its little halogen lights is gone. The sky is boiling black lava. "Divinica," he says again. I meet his eyes. They are red as a sailor's dawn. "You need to wake up!"

I shake my head. "No, no, no, no, no," I moan. Just no, forever no. Let me exist only in this memory and die in this dream, let me stay in his arms eternally. *"Divinica!"* he shouts. "Wake up! *Now!"* Flames explode in his eyes as his face morphs into the snarling visage of Hecate. Then Valance is completely gone, and I am alone with her. Hecate is holding me in her arms, we are standing on the edge of a black, endless cliff and blood is the entire world. As I stare in her obsidian eyes, two more heads sprout from her slender neck. Lightning crackles and thunder booms. Hecate throws back her heads and screams like a dying hyena at the torrid, blood-red sky. I scream with her. I can't help it. I wake up still screaming.

When I open my eyes, I find that all of them are staring at me, mouths dropped, eyes sleepy and scared. I want to stop the screams tearing my throat to shreds, but I'm powerless, the screams have gone supersonic. I sound like a hurricane devouring a city. My tattoos glow so bright, it looks like a mini sun is rising from between my breasts.

Rashid meets my eyes, his voice is shaking badly as he puts a finger in both ears and says, "Shit, girl. Way to take up all the space in a room."

I can't respond. Everything is burning, sharp and biting like iodine poured over a bloody wound. I draw in a breath, gathering force for the next traumatized sound about to rip its way out of me. Daniel puts a hand over my mouth, and I stop fighting. There's a smear of blood under his nose, a gruesome frame for his trembling lips, white as fresh fallen snow. His tone is one of frustrated awe. "Uh, sis? Did you know you're a fucking glow stick right now?"

Valance's dream words are a red flare cutting across the night sky of my mind: *Something old, something strong, something they want to kill. So many moths, one fucking flame.* I scrape and scramble to my knees. "Make them stop!" I gasp. "I have to make them stop glowing." I scratch my chest, pound at the marks, I want to rip the skin from my bones and the hair from my head. "How? I don't know how!" I wail, my voice climbing with my rising hysteria.

"Do you know what she's on about?" Dayle asks no one in particular.

"Yeah, Val has a theory," Rashid says. "And I think it's already too late. They're here. Dayle, now might be the time to push that little start button by the steering wheel and floor this bitch. Otherwise, I think we're in for a bit of a fight."

"Just calm down and breathe, sis," Daniel tells me, kneeling and squeezing my arm. "In through the nose, out through the mouth. No—not like that! Through the nose, out the mouth. And Rashid, what the hell is Valance's theory?"

"He thinks her tats are some kind of homing beacon for the Reptilians," he glances at Daniel. "Sorry, Lizard Lords," Rashid explains, leaving his post at the window to pull on an armored gauntlet. Standard issue formation, steel teeth at the knuckles, and thick retention pins great for cutting deep into rock, also great for slaying bad guys.

I try to cover the tattoos with my hands but the light pierces through my fingers and seems to grow brighter by the second. "My tattoos used to glow all the time at Styx. They never attacked, just that once." My voice breaks away as I try to wrack my brain for any other instances.

"Cloaking shield. That device you broke when you were fighting the Djinn in the lab. Valance thinks it's what kept you and Daniel relatively safe. That, and the symbols around Styx, or protection wards, as he called them."

"Less than three hundred yards and closing fast," Dayle says. Climbing up front, he fires the ignition. The truck's still holding a solid charge and starts with an angry roar. "Hold on," Dayle commands, then slams his foot down on the pedal. Nothing happens. The wheels spin. The truck whirrs and grunts, but we go nowhere. Dayle curses violently, giving the steering wheel a good hit. "Sack of hairy balls! We're snowed in. I've gotta dig us out."

"Not a great idea," Rashid sings, nose pressed against the window once again. "You're strong, huge, hot, and I know you single-handedly fixed the *Perseverance*, but there's thirty of them and one of you. Go out there, and you're fixing to get your ass handed to you on an ugly platter. Keep trying. We've got some frag grenades and smoke bangers. Divinica and I will do our best from down here—"

"Hey!" interrupts Daniel, sounding put out.

In the middle of it all, Rashid has enough in him to give my brother a smile. "I didn't forget about you, dude. I need you to go up front, take these, and open the window," he says, handing four grenades to Daniel. "Pull the pin when I tell you, then start throwing. Not too far mind, but not too close that shrapnel hits the truck. Good?"

Daniel nods, more man than child. "Good."

A projectile strikes the side of the truck with a metallic twang. None of us react, we all just look at each other for a tense few seconds. I've managed to pull it together somewhat, swallowing the screams and sobs clawing at the back of my throat. I dive for my bow.

"I've got some hydrogen arrows," Rashid informs me, pointing to the right far corner of the cab where I see a bunch of them are neatly stacked. "A bit heavy on the draw, but they have a detonation radius of about ten feet. A direct hit anywhere is lethal."

My eyes make a pass over all the weapons. "Fuck guys, it's like the love child of Hawkeye and Batman's dorm room."

Rashid laughs as he tosses a 16-gauge shotgun at Dayle, who catches and cocks it in one big hand. We all jump this time when something lands on the roof, denting the metal. Footprints seen in reverse. Daniel points his gun at the spot. No hesitation. He pulls the trigger. Three shots, one hit. The thing on the roof screams. Rashid unlatches the window and hollers, "We're armed, cold, knackered, a little hungry, and a lot angry. I'd fuck right off if I were you."

The screeching sound of the windshield shattering in a million connected pieces is our only response. Bitter cold instantly seeps through the cracks in the double tempered glass, winding through the deep fissures in the laminated poly-vinyl between them. Over the howling gale, I hear the heavy beat of rushing footsteps.

Daniel throws Rashid an askance look, finger hovering over the grenade's little pin.

"Wait for it," Rashid says. He holds up his right hand with all five fingers splayed, then folds one finger at a time. We all count down with him. None of us breathe. One...two...three. "Wait for it," Rashid commands again. The last finger falls. "Now, Daniel!"

Daniel rips at the pin, then tosses the grenade out the window, peeking his head up to see where the grenade makes landfall. He ducks almost immediately, a foreboding expression on his face. "Holy shit! There's a lot of them."

Rashid faces me, and I know the grim light in his eyes is reflected in mine. "Take your aim, Divinica. I'm going to open the tailgate, and I want you to start shooting. Go for the kill. I'm not losing you to a bunch of talking lizards today. Besides, if I manage to survive whatever kills you, Valance will maim me and smile while he does it. Ready?"

I nod once. "As I'll ever be."

Rashid tugs hard on the metal latch to the right of the wide, paneled back door. There's a click, followed by a slow, motorized whirr, then the tailgate flies open, and I see them. Shadows in the snow. Daniel's right. There are a fuck ton of them. Behind me, I hear Rashid yell, "Divinica you want a cup of tea first? Shoot, goddamn it!"

I obey with a grimace. My arrow is already nocked and ready. I let it fly, loving how the arrow's synthetic feathers feel as they slide through my fingers. Seconds later, I hear a thud as my arrow strikes flesh, instantly followed by an explosion that leaves a fluffy blue cloud in its wake. Something screams in the distance. I grab another arrow, pull back my arm far as the string will go, then let the arrow loose. Another explosion, another scream, another fluffy blue cloud. The carnage my arrows wreak seems meaningless. The shadows advance quickly. I fire another arrow, then another. "There's too many of them," I shout, trying to be heard over the howling wind.

"Fire in the hole," Rashid says jovially and throws two frag grenades over my shoulder. The shadows scatter. Snow falling like a winter blanket makes for spotty visuals. I nock another arrow and take aim. A dark thing flies at me from the wall of white, fast as a speeding bullet. Before I have time to blink or react, a blow to the gut sends me flying. My head strikes the cab's metal wall. The sound my skull makes on impact is terrifying. I roll to my feet before the spots clouding my vision fully clear. I blink long and hard, and when my eyes refocus, it's to see Rashid in hand-to-hand combat with the creature who attacked me. The creature has the upper hand, Rashid brought a knife to a flaming sword fight. The sword the creature wields is bathed in electric green flames, bright as if the blade were dipped in some irradiated cobra venom. Rashid is quick, moving like a dancer. The creature is quicker. The aqua light pouring from its sword illuminates its face. It's a she—tall, lithe, and stunningly beautiful. Huge eyes that tilt like a sphinx with irises of pure amber. Her body is human, slender, naked, and drop-dead gorgeous. She looks directly at me. Her mysterious eyes glisten rage, and something more, something strong, impossibly determined. Like every action she ever makes is fueled by belief or inner purpose.

They're not just attacking for the hell of it, Valance is right, they're here for me, my mind states bluntly. For a wild second, I imagine my tattoos are speaking, I can almost hear them whispering in my ears.

Teeth bared and my own variation of a war cry on my lips, I charge at her. My blind attack gives me the element of surprise. She lets out a high-pitched scream as I barrel forward full throttle. The top of my head smashes into her solar plexus. She grunts as we fall out of the back of the truck and hit the packed snow below with a bone-jarring thud.

CHAPTER THIRTY-FOUR

Flying isn't for everyone

DIVINICA

This week really blows, I think as I roll to my feet and unsheathe the knife in my boot before turning to face her, blinking big flakes of snow from my eyes.

"You're shorter than I expected," she says in a language I know isn't English. It speaks volumes for my mental state that I'm not even surprised I understand her perfectly. She continues in a voice made for bedrooms and candlelight. "My name is Xola. I think every goddess should know the name of their killer."

I raise my knife higher. Snow makes a funny pattern on the slightly hooked blade. "Are we going to introduce ourselves, or are we going to fight?"

Xola's pretty face breaks into a cool smile that freezes my blood. "Oh, we're going to fight," she says, then she's a blur again, flying at me. This time I'm ready. I feint right and throw my body in a forward roll. Snow sticks to me like glue, falling in a cylindrical shower of white as I find my feet. Xola spins, flaming sword leveled at my throat. I manage to dodge death, just barely.

Xola laughs, a deep, pleased sound before she takes another swing. I duck, but I'm too slow. The flat of her blade whacks my back. White hot pain explodes. It feels like I got hit with a baseball bat, and it's a home run. Breath leaves my body in a rush. I fall, rolling onto my back, arching, gasping. I look up to see her standing over me, sword lifted high. Green fire illuminates her face. There is a light smattering of scales on her high cheekbones, and a few more dust the tip of her slender nose. She brings the sword down with a holler, the blow intended to split me in two. I roll away at the last second. She kicks me hard in the back, again in the stomach, thigh, then steps on my ankle. I scream as something there snaps. The heel of her flat foot strikes my jaw. My head snaps back, reality ripples. I get to my knees as she swings again, my exposed neck her easy target.

"No," I say. My voice sounds nothing like my own. It's low and thunderous. I catch the sword inches from my jugular. The razor edge of the blade slices deep into my palms. Blood rushes down my arms and splashes the snow. Big drops that look like fallen rubies. Pain is everywhere. My body is torn and screaming, but I'm not afraid. The pain is a miracle. It centers and strengthens me. Xola shoves at the sword. It cuts deeper, deeper, deeper into my palms, nearly severing my artist's hands. I hear Rashid and Daniel yelling my name, but I can't focus on them. I can't think about anything. Only her. Only the strengthening pain. Only this kill. Like in Kali's world, I taste the bloodlust on my tongue, sweet and tangy. Beautiful. I focus on the blood running down my arms like rain, on the rush of wind humming in my ears, on the beats of my steady heart.

Vines, black as graphite dust and just as defused fly from the centers of my bloody hands. They twist and twine around each other, increasing in size and density. They grow sharp thorns that stab the packed snow. The vines rocket toward Xola, then wrap around her body like a boa constrictor ready for the kill. *Freya,* I think. I can taste her magic, and I know at this moment, it's her tattoo that sheds the brightest glow. Xola fights the restraints, but the thorns dig into her skin, and I smell the unusual flavor of her cold blood.

I sense two others behind me. I hear their erratic heart beats and press my palms to the earth, then think about a full moon and the silver wolves who howl at it. I think of the goddess Nokomis and how she ran with warriors, empowering them to do what mortals can't. *Empower me,* I think. I pray. I know she's listening as darkness begins to pour from my fingertips, black froth that bulges like heavy storm clouds. The darkness bleeds from my eyes, ears, and mouth. It changes the molecular density of the air we breathe, sucks the meager moonlight from the sky, and blinds my approaching attackers. I hear them stumble and curse, then I smile a wicked smile. I close my eyes and revel in the sound of Xola's screams. I feel the crown on my head sparking, see the light that spears from the twisted mercurial thorns digging into my skin. I understand the threads reaching into my mind and waking the powerful places that sleep.

My body starts to rise off the ground. Black smoke and thrashing vines hold me suspended in the air. From my vantage, I can see Dayle and Rashid in hand-to-hand combat with two more towering creatures. These have tails. Daniel has run out of grenades. He's using the gun I gave him and whooping like a cowboy in some old Western movie. I rise higher. My eyes can see through the snow now. I am the embodiment of precision and focus. I am raw power and deadly flame. I lift my hands and point them at my friends. Artemis's golden arrows fly from my torn skin. They soar like flaming fireworks and strike the two Reptilians who dared to attack the people I love. The creatures drop dead where they stand. I fly back to the truck, loving the way the icy wind brushes my cheek, and how for once, I'm not fucking cold at all.

When Rashid notices me hovering over him, he puts a hand to his heart and screams like a little girl. "Holy fucking shit, Div! What the fuck!"

I smile down at him. "Always so eloquent when it matters, Rashid. I like that about you."

"Divinica, your hands need medical attention. That's a lot of blood on you," Dayle says. He's wearing a brave face, but his voice trembles.

My smile gets wider. "Don't worry, most of it is mine. I'm fine though. I'm gonna give this truck a push and get us the fuck out of here. I don't know how much longer I can keep flying around like this. I don't really know how I'm doing it right now to be honest."

Dayle shakes his head but doesn't move. "I thought the pyramids on Mars were unbelievable, but this is fucking wild. You bossed up, girl."

I smile. A real one. "Thanks, Dayle." Beyond his shoulder I see Xola, she and her wicked sword have almost cut through all my vines holding her tethered to snow. The others are fighting my cloud of darkness, but are still advancing. Rashid grabs the handrail and pulls himself back into the still rumbling truck. I press my torn hands to where the lip of the roof meets the edge of the tailgate door, grit my teeth, then shove with all my strength. The truck shudders and moves. I let out a glad cry, only now able to admit to myself that I half expected it not to. More plumes of ebony explode from my eyes as I give the truck another shove.

"She's free!" Dayle yells. "Divinica, get your magical ass in here."

"Just a sec," I call and land in front of Xola, who stops struggling with my vines to meet my eyes with a rage-fueled glare.

"I'll be seeing you," she says, her smoky voice a study in malice.

"I hope so," I say, then punch her directly in the face and take her sword on impulse.

Back inside the truck, Daniel throws his arms around me, burrows in like a tick, cheek pressed tight against my shoulder. "We didn't die," he says weakly. "Go us."

I kiss his sweaty brow. "Yeah, go us."

Daniel pulls back momentarily to stare down at my hands. "I saw her cut you, I screamed but you didn't hear me."

I look down at the wreck of skin, bloody severed nerves, sliced tissue, and tendon. "It's okay," I say, because it is. The tattoo on my forehead is starting to glow now, brighter than all the others. I feel Aphrodite's power surge through me. Both Daniel and I watch in shocked wonder as the skin on my hands stitches itself back together with such flawless precision, I know it won't even leave me any sick scars I can wear as symbols of my badassery.

Daniel sniffs loudly, then wipes his nose on the back of his hand. "You're scary as fuck, by the way," he tells me over a yawn that moves his whole body. "But I guess you always have been. Remember when you convinced Mom I was the one sneaking out of *your* window. She clocked me on the head, and I had a headache for a week."

I pull him closer. Hug him tighter. "Yeah, I remember. I'm sorry. I'm honestly the worst."

"You're alright." He yells his way through another yawn, then looks up at me. "I love you, sis. If I was going to be stuck with anyone at the end of the world, I would've picked you. And that was before I knew you could fly."

Tears sting my eyes. I don't blink them away. Seconds later, I feel their wet heat on my cheeks. I gently stroke the hair off his clammy brow and kiss that soft spot right between his eyes. "Oh, Daniel. I would've chosen you too," I whisper. I hold Daniel close to my chest, cup his cheek in my hand, and stroke his soft, knotted hair. Dayle drives like the hounds of hell are nipping at our heels, and Daniel falls asleep in my arms.

CHAPTER THIRTY-FIVE

The deadly danger of true love

I wake to the taste of betrayal. Let me state for the record that it is bitter as fuck. I spring up like a cranked Jack-in-the-box, rip one needle out of my arm, then another. I stare down at two syringes for a few beats confused as all hell. My mind is like a Kentucky mud puddle, moving but opaque. Standing up and shaking it off becomes my first priority, but I'm actually panting when I get to my knees. If there's something worse than shit, that's what I feel like. I have no idea how long I've been lying in this room where Divinica left me to rot. My head feels like the morning after a recovering alcoholic fell off the two-year wagon, and I smell like a three-day road kill.

My head falls to my hands, my groan sounds like it comes from my soul, "Ugh! Fuck me until I die." I'm an idiot for trusting her. Well, truthfully, I'm an idiot for a lot of reasons, but trusting Divinica and her soul-bending eyes has always been my flaw numero uno. Standing makes my head spin. I stumble to her awful window. It's dark outside, I've lost a full day, maybe more. "Fuck!" I groan again. I'm burning moonlight indulging in self-pity, but all of a sudden, I'm so angry I can hardly see straight. Goddamn me for believing her. Goddamn her, too, for leaving me here, alone, with morning wood that could battle iron, and an ache in my chest the size of Texas. I wash my face with brown water from her gurgling tap, stop to stare at her bed and imagine myself there, with her. Inside of her arching body. I would lick my name off her lips and take her a dozen times, in a thousand diverse ways.

There's no improvement in my mood when I find the weapon silo, and a long-sleeved Kevlar jacket that fits like it was made specifically for me. I'm still breathing erratically. All my training and mental fortitude escape me as I try to bring myself under control. Everything in me wants to abandon ship and go after her. Wrap my hands around her pretty little throat and throttle her, then pull her down to the ground with me and give her what she's been asking for. The pain of her is second to fucking none. I'm addicted to it. I'm tired of it. She tears me up over and over again. She's the rack, and I'm the traitor. The laughing gods are torturing me for information. I would give it if I knew what they hell they wanted. Divinica is my refined agony. One minute she's in my arms, my fingers on her body, her every trembling breath in the palm of my hand, and I feel strong as a god. Then comes the inevitable shift and I understand what it means to be *only human*.

Still, after everything that's been taken from me these past two years, her siren song calls me. I'm a willing victim to the spells her eyes cast on me. Even knowing I'm swimming toward oblivion and death by drowning, I can't shake this need. This overwhelming desire to be next to her, touching her always. It fucking sucks.

The only thing keeping me from dashing off madly to who knows where is my people. If I leave, there's no hope for them. I go to her, and they die. I genuinely don't know if I can shoulder all that guilt along with my other baggage. If I don't leave, if I stay and help them after the next inevitable wave, then Divinica is going to voluntarily self-destruct, taking every single thing I care about in this world with her to the grave. The choice is simple. Horrible, but simple. If it were a question of her life or death, I'm afraid I would slaughter them all with my own hands. I know it's a monstrous thought, but it's good to be honest with oneself, especially in matters of massacre.

My every feeling is controlled by the emotion on her face. I belong to her, heart, and soul, and it's killing me. I have to break away from the spell she weaves. I have to save myself from this torment, but I can't. I fucking can't. She's the air in my lungs.

While I change into a pair of black camo pants, my watch falls out of my back pocket. The sound I make as I catch it before it hits the ground can only be described as a cry of joy. I instantly note the date and time. Red splatters my vision. I smash my fist down onto the ammo shelf, and the structure crumbles with a whine. "Fuck! Fuck this! Fuck her!" I was out for almost twenty hours. "Two shots, really?! Motherfucker!" She has a hell of a head start. I should leave right now, but the faces of my people torment me. Nigari is turning thirteen tomorrow, her brother spent all week re-learning how to bake her a cake. The kid's mad-talented. The pair of them don't have much longer. They're both extremely anemic, the wave's radiation is killing them quickly. Without the iron shots, and my remaining supply of Prussian blue, this wave may very well be their last. Jackie, he lost his leg eight months ago. A scarred, now dead member of the Burning tribe cut it off and ate it while he watched. Jackie is glad of the waves. He just learned how to walk with the metal leg Dayle fashioned him out of an old vacuum cleaner. Lesa who remembers her dreams, but never her name. Paul, who loves Lesa, even when he forgets. And two hundred others under my care are now about to die because Divinica refused to trust me. Even with her memories intact, she made a choice to stab those fucking needles in my arm and walk away. Not gonna lie, knowing she could do that to me, even after remembering all we are to each other, really hurts.

The way I see it, I only have one course of action available to me if I want to save everyone. I have to find her, capture her—which in my experience is easier said than done—then get back here before the next wave hits. According to my watch, I have about nine days and six hours to accomplish this feat. Not to come off as a guy with an overinflated sense of self-importance but if anyone can pull it off, it's me, besides, finding her won't be that hard. I tap on a tracking app I installed a year ago on my watch, and a little red light starts blinking. I put the little attaching node on her crown when she was on my lap kissing me—what was it, yesterday morning? I wanted to trust her, but precaution saves lives. An idea, one I've been toying with for the past few days, is making my fingers itch. Even with all my rage and survival training, I'm going to need help, and this asylum of murder which has been my bane is going to give it to me. That is, of course, if I'm smart enough to fix what's broken.

Divinica. Present day.

Dayle kept his foot on the pedal straight through the night, and well into the morning. Right until the old truck gave up its mechanical ghost on the outskirts of Bruges. Now the English channel looms before us like the river Styx. Uncrossable without the boat man. The stormy waters of the channel lap at the truck's front wheels, and the four of us sit in the drafty cab locked in a staring event rife with screaming silence. Our collective eyes are glued to my V-shaped candle holder and the little burnt wick currently absent its flame.

"Okay," Daniel finally pipes up, voice scratchy from the cold and lack of use. "No one's said anything in ages. It's starting to get awkward."

"This whole thing is awkward. Only Valance has ever seen me travel." Saying his name kicks me in the chest and the rest of my words dissolve on my tongue.

Dayle chucks me on the shoulder. "That's all good, girl. This is a safe space. We've climbed the trust tree. From now on, you do you, boo," he says in his gruff, comforting voice.

I nod and let my eyes flick up to Rashid's face. I want to know his take on all of this, want to know if he will look at me differently after he sees the star door in action. Busy biting his nails, he doesn't notice my insecure scrutiny. I can tell the moment he feels my eyes on him because his shoulders stiffen, then he looks at the weirdly shaped candle holder instead of me. "Let's just get this over with," he says in a monotone most commonly used at death beds.

His attitude and tone sting my raw feelings. "What the hell, Rashid? Why do you look like there's a gun to your head? I'm the one who's about to throw themselves through space time and become a decapitated snake. As my mom would say, kindly keep that scowl confined to the back of your head where it belongs."

Rashid rubs his hand over the thick stubble on his jaw. "Who says you're going to die?"

"Please. This is me. You think I'm going to go back and relive Medusa's happiest memory? Not really my style. It's either rape or beheading. With my luck lately, I'm guessing it's the latter. Nothing for you to be mad about. It's my neck."

Still not meeting my eyes, Rashid mumbles, "It's not that. I just can't shake the feeling this was all a horrible idea."

"What was? Running?"

Rashid nods, eyes still downcast. "All of it. Valance will already be on his way. He'll find us soon, and when he does—" Rashid shrugs. Suddenly, his head snaps up as his eyes widen dramatically. "Are you wearing anything right now that you were wearing the last time you saw him?"

Unconsciously, I touch the crown, wind my fingers into the hair curling around and through it like ivy on an old castle wall. "Just my crown, why?"

Dayle loudly clears his throat, then says, "Tracking device." As if those two words were explanation enough.

Rashid nods once. "Yeah. I'd bet my life there's one on her right now."

"What?!" I reach for the crown but pause in the act of ripping it off my head.

Without it, the white silence looms like a monster. I ball my fists. "Somebody check!" I holler.

Daniel snorts. "Seriously, sis. Have you seen yourself? Your hair—which, let's face it, has always been a whole thing—and that crown have both taken on a life of their own. You're gonna need garden shears to hack through that mess."

A shudder works its way down my spine as my hands fall dejectedly to my lap. I swallow what feels like a ball of black poison. "He didn't trust me. I gave him my word, and he didn't trust me. He didn't trust—"

"Valance doesn't strike me as someone who trusts anyone," Daniel says, placing a consolatory hand on my arm.

"He knew I was going to betray him. He knew the entire time," I say, tone hollow as an old, rotting log. My head is cheap tissue paper, and that knowledge is hot water poured atop it. I'm shredded. Dissolving from an internal bleed that will never clot. I clamp my hand over my mouth to hold in a squelched sound of hurt. He was right not to trust me. Wrong to love me. I'm the real danger. I've never brought him anything but misery and death. Fate is having a laugh at the expense of our hearts. "Just light the damn candle," I whisper through my fingers. I've fucked up with him so many times, I don't think he'll find it in himself to forgive me this time. Pain shrieks through my chest. I did it for Daniel, for all the people he's cared for, but that won't matter. I didn't trust him. That's all he's going to see. "This sucks monkey balls!" I say, pulling back the fluffy sleeve of my jacket and staring down at the words inscribed deep in my arm. Words I'm beginning to loathe.

Rashid strikes a match and places the burgeoning flame against the still wick. It lights with a bright spark. I close my eyes. Thousands of flickering candle flames dance behind my lids.

"Now what?" I hear Daniel ask. He's gripping my upper arm, but I sense he's using the touch to settle himself instead of me.

"Now I read these words out loud. Somehow, they activate the star tech," I tell him. Eyes still squeezed shut, like if I stay blind, I won't see or experience what's coming.

"Like voice activation?" Daniel asks.

I nod. "Yeah, I think so."

"Then what?"

I shrug. "Then, shit gets wild. Since my Medusa tattoo is currently trying to out glow a star, I suppose that's where I'm going. To her. The first priestess. I read about her in the first year of high school. The unkillable monster. I always felt sorry for her. Her rape and death both orchestrated by gods. Should be great. Loads of fun, really. Can't wait."

Daniel lifts a sharp, dark brow. "Sarcasm?"

I smile into his frightened eyes. "Thinly veiled. Don't worry, love. I'll be alright."

Dayle takes my hand, forcing me to meet his gaze. "Will you, really?"

"Yes. If I die in these other times, I don't die in this time. It happened with the goddess Magu, she just laid down and died...and I—"

"That sounds like it was peaceful. This will be violent," Rashid says, finally having the bravery to meet my eyes.

"Rashid, This isn't your fault. You did the right thing by bringing me here. You did the only thing. Don't beat yourself up for it. It's not good for your psyche and also, you're pissing me off."

Rashid looks downcast, scuffing the toe of one boot against the other. "Sorry."

"Told you we should've trusted him," Dayle remarks.

A snarl twists Rashid's painted lips. "Why did you come along if you thought it was such a bad idea?"

Dayle laughs. "Boy, I wasn't about to let you go alone. You three are all the family I've got left."

"Well, you'll be minus one when Valance snaps my neck," Rashid grumbles.

"On that happy note—" my voice breaks as I look down at the writing on my arm. Daniel squeezes my hand. "Here goes nothing. Brutal death by decapitation here I come."

"Sarcasm?" Daniel asks again.

I shake my head. "No. Premonition."

CHAPTER THIRTY-SIX

Medusa. The first victim

They're coming to kill me. I hear the pounding of their feet, it's the drumroll preceding their deaths. So many have come, so many have fallen. I make my bed with their bones. Decorate necklaces with their filthy teeth. My world is a graveyard of stone statues, tributes to warriors who tried. I am a creature of nightmare, and they are merely human men who piss themselves when they look in my eyes.

They're closer now. Each terrified breath they take is music to my ears. I can't wait to tear into their veins and taste their fear. I do love my collection of statues, but on days like today, I want to feed. Their blood gives me visions of the outside world. I exist, alone in this cave, saved by their memories. I taste their sorrow and joy; their death is my pleasure.

Hurt people, maim others.

I should know better than anyone. Years ago, I was young and beautiful. My hair was long. Red as sunrise. The strands didn't hiss and sink their fangs in my neck when we were hungry. I walked on long, shapely legs and never once slithered. I was a priestess initiate. My eyes were full of dreams, my mind ever possessed by thoughts of grandeur. I once harbored such hopes for my life. I craved a great love and desired immortality. I have since learned to beware of the heart's desires. Now, I fear history will remember my name forever. Dreams have turned to nightmares. Now I am the hunted. The treasured kill. Taking my head will make a man a god.

I was a virgin and a child. I said my prayers at sunset, washed my face and hands in rose water and laid my soul daily on the altar of my goddess. Pallas Athena, Olympian. Virgin queen of the feminine divine. I was her favorite, and I loved her from the moment my eyes touched her face. In the dark, she owned my thoughts. I lived for the sound of her voice, the feel and smell of her chestnut hair. We shared long looks in silent halls. Her true smile was mine alone. My days were light, laughter, and love. I thought they would never end. Then came Poseidon, sniffing about for a fresh-faced maiden. To my eternal misfortune, his eyes landed on me. Athena commanded purity, and I more than any other was forbidden to him.

However, Poseidon was on the hunt and the scent of me was strong in his nostrils. I repeatedly told him no, I fought, I ran—in the end I wasn't fast or strong enough. Poseidon raped me at the foot of the altar where I once recited innocent prayers. He was big, I was small. There was blood and pain. Agony and regret. He took me over and over again. It lasted for hours. In the end, I was pliant, waiting for a blessed death that never came. When he was finished, he left me lying in the carnage of my chastity, drowning in a frigid river of useless tears. Afterward, Poseidon boasted of what he had done. He told Apollo that I had begged for it and only after much persuasion did he finally relent and give me what he said I wanted. He told Bacchus that I moaned like a whore. In the following dark days, I tried to protest my innocence, but Athena believed his lies.

"You have the soul of a viper," she said, "now you will slither like one." I knelt. I begged, but my heartfelt pleas were ignored. She was true to her word. My beautiful locks of hair morphed into venomous cobras, and I was forced to flee the home of my birth and take refuge in this cave where I have survived these last hundred years. There is loneliness but no boredom, my would-be murders keep me well entertained. In the early days, men thought I would be an easy mark, but I proved them wrong in this cave of traps, mazes, smoke, and mirrors. It's feeding time, and I like to play with my food.

Three men approach, quaking in their sandals at the mouth of my cave. There is one warrior whose heart beats stronger than the rest. In his veins, I smell the blood of the old gods mixed with the human scent I've learned to crave. I know him. He's the one my gorgons have so often spoken of. They say he needs my head to slay a son of Poseidon. A monster of the deep. The Kraken most foul. The Olympians have given him a sword with which to take it. Gossip claims he's beautiful and brave. I believe, for once, the whispers are true. I can smell the fear of his companions but catch not a whiff off him.

It could be bravery, or painful stupidity, either way, his end will be the same. I will rip off his head and paint my rocky walls with the color of his blood. My snakes hiss and bite at me. They're thirsty. I shriek as they sink their fangs in my neck and shred the soft skin on my shoulders. The men gasp and scurry for cover. The sound of my harsh laugh creates a grating echo that lingers. I slither through my mounds of treasure all brought to me by the men who sought my death. Gold coins sparkle like tear drops of the sun, winking at me from beneath the glassy surface of the river that cuts through my cave. The river is my secret weapon. It's a powerful mirror that has kept me alive these many years. In it, I see the men. Their faces reflect on my wet walls. Snarls and fearful grimaces forever memorialized in the numerous puddles that collect between the sharp rocks. Nothing escapes my sight. One of the men, a Andromedin soldier, carries a war hammer. Its spiked ball looks as thirsty as my snakes. The other, a Greek hunter, holds a short spear. Good for pinning targets to cave walls. Last, the man with the powerful heartbeat grips a golden sword in his left hand. On his right arm he wears a shield emblazoned with the insignia of the goddess who cursed me to this fate. Athena. The name is raw poison on my tongue.

I exhale a deep breath that extinguishes their torches. The darkness that follows is a powerful thing, but my yellow eyes are designed to see through the blackest shadow, and I'm unafraid.

"Death is coming," I tell them, running my hands along the wet rock walls, laughing all the while. I toy with them and chase them for a time. I imagine each of them wears Poseidon's face. It makes the kill that much sweeter. I twist and weave, slither over walls, crawl above their heads. They shout and swing their weapons. I'm too fast. I've been hunted for too long. Terror was my teacher, now I am untouchable.

The Andromedin swings his ball and chain. He's a skilled warrior, he's lived through many battles. He and I both know he will not survive this one. The spiked ball narrowly misses the tip of my tail. I throw my laugh, knowing how it will bounce. The sound confuses and frightens. In the dark, I'm a monstrous thing. He spins in silly circles, looking for me.

"You thought to come here and kill me in my own lair?" I laugh and laugh. I cannot be too cross. I'm grateful for the entertainment. The hubris of men is my constant source of amusement. The Andromedin spins again. I spring from the shadows and back hand him, then cackle as he goes flying. The Greek shouts his companion's name, "Perseus! Now!"

The warrior called Perseus unslings a bow from his shoulder. I did not see this weapon; I have reason to believe it only just appeared. He nocks the arrow and draws the string taut. The river shows me which way the arrow will fly. I see a flash of silver in the corner of my eye and dodge the projectile with less than a second to spare. The golden arrow stabs into the rock face at my back, like the granite was made of flesh. It's the arrow of Artemis. Olympian made, designed by Hephaestus himself. This enrages me. Haven't I suffered enough from this family that loathes me? They have cursed and harassed me. Now they send their golden warrior to kill me.

Through low tunnels and across the wet rocks I slink, fast as flowing water. I wrench the spear from the trembling hand of the Greek and run it through his heart in a single, clean stroke. I never let him see my face. He's not worthy. The one with the hammer gets my gaze. He swings blindly, but I loom behind him. I let him feel my presence, see the hairs rise on the back of his neck. When he turns, his jaw drops in horror, and snakes hiss and cackle. I laugh with them as he turns to stone. I will not keep him in my collection. He performed no great feat. All his years of training counted for nothing in this cave. In the end, he died, shocked and sloppy as the rest. I punch his face, and he crumbles like sunbaked clay. Perseus shouts as his friend turns to a pile of chalky dust.

I shriek and spin when he lunges for me. "Your weapons won't save you here, young warrior. Even if they are Olympian made."

"I must do this," he says in a strong, beautiful voice that gives me pause. "If I do not take your head today, Poseidon's monster will slay a city."

That name makes me scream. My snakes hiss and writhe. "You carry the sword of his brother and the shield of his niece," I accuse.

"I did not wish to. These weapons were forced on me. This fate is not of my design."

"They are the weapons of my enemies, and you will die today wishing they could save you."

He lifts his strong chin. "I have no fear of death, my lady. Not my own. I fear only the death of children, mothers and babies subjugated to the will of cruel gods."

"That is their fate. You are here, sword in hand to discuss mine," I whisper and glide closer, silent as the rising moon. His voice and stance compel me. I feel as if I know him. As if killing him would be a more monstrous thing than I. The river ripples, slightly disturbed by my passage. His reflection again catches my eye. The water shows me his broad, naked back. Only a strap of leather across his chest holds his sword belt in place. His britches are torn at the knees, and his legs are made for running. His arms are cut and corded; his bronze skin covered in a sheen of sweat that makes him look like a statue dipped in gold. His hair is the color of wheat and blows around his face, showing me his full lips but not his eyes. Feet evenly braced; his stance is perfect. His chin is dropped low, I see him staring at my face mirrored in the polished surface of Athena's shield. The image he sees is deceptive. It's merely a reflection of a reflection cast by the clear water. He's brave and handsome as Apollo, but not, I think, overly bright.

"What of all the people?" he asks, "Will you not help me save them?"

"What of me?!" I scream. "What horrible crime have I committed to deserve such an ignominious death?"

"None, my lady. I believe you were wronged. I do not wish to kill you. I simply have no other choice. I am trapped in this, same as you."

"Not the same. I cannot leave this place, but I will let you walk out of here unscathed. A courtesy I've extended no other man. There is a touch of destiny about you, and I do not wish to be the one that cuts your thread."

Perseus turns to the sound of my voice. His eyes are downcast. "Come with me, Medusa. Kill the Kraken, take your vengeance on Poseidon."

"I—" my voice breaks for the first time in years. "I cannot leave this cave. I will die if the sun touches me."

His shoulders droop in a deep sigh. "Then we must fight. If you win, take my sword, and somehow find a way to kill the gods who did this to you," he says slowly lifting his head, and in the water, I see the reflection of his bright blue eyes. I jump hard. My back slams into the rocky wall, and my snakes hiss and bite at me. I hardly feel the stinging pain, all I can hear is the voice in my mind screaming a name. A single, beautiful name. *Valance. Valance. Valance.* The voice in my mind grows stronger. I dissect myself from it. Understand it. She is not me. I am not her. I am Medusa. She is Divinica. I am Divinica. I traveled here and lost myself in this cave of death and tarnished souls. I am Divinica and this is Valance. I don't care what time we're in. I won't kill him again. Not in this life. Not in any.

I slither forward, move from the shadows of the rocks, and show him my face. I don't let my eyes hurt him. I love him. Always. Medusa fights the hold I have over her mind. She wants his blood. I won't let her have it. Not today. Divinica's premonition was right. I came here to die, and I'm ready.

"I'm sorry," he whispers, and I forgive him. Then he pounces; I watch the way he moves. There are no slight differences to trip me up as there were in other times, this man in front of me is Valance through and through. I see my reflection in his eyes, the same as always. Same as forever. He lunges again, I don't advance or retreat. I am still. I wait to die. His sword sings as it cuts the air and slices through my neck in a clean, swift stroke. My body writhes, my snakes scream. I don't feel the pain. I'm still looking in his eyes. In the last second, my hands reach out and catch my falling head. Then, I am the one falling backward through space time to the realm of nothing and the silence of the in-between.

"Cover it!" I hear Daniel shout.

"Don't look in her eyes," Dayle yells. The sound of hissing snakes fills my ears. My eyes snap open. I sit up, then take off and toss my jacket over Medusa's head in the same smooth move. The snakes writhe and spit under the cover of the fuzzy purple cloth. One of the vipers sinks its teeth into my leg, and I almost scream. I shove the head from my lap and jump to my feet. "Holy fuck!" I rub my hands over my face. "Valance, it was Valance who killed me," I say, my hand going to my throat and staying there. I feel exposed, vulnerable. I can still feel the cringy slice of his sword. "He was Perseus. Oh my god. I literally can't stress how much I hate my life." I sink to my knees as my legs give out with a shudder.

Rashid takes my hand, holding it tight between both of his. "Dayle, light the candle. Divinica. There's literally no time. You have to travel again."

My vision blackens. "Are you fucking kidding me?"

Rashid shakes his head. His eyes are full of pity I don't want. "No. I'm serious. Dayle's going to leave us here and look for a boat. We have until he gets back to collect the rest of the artifacts. You're glowing, Divinica, which means—"

"They're coming for me," I whisper, remembering the hate in Xola's eyes, I start to tremble. "It's too much. I need a moment to—I need a fucking moment!"

"No," Rashid says again. He drags the lit candle closer. Blindly, I start to fight his hold.

"I just died. I can't even breathe," I wail.

"Divinica," Rashid almost shouts.

Daniel makes a small sound of protest; my head snaps up, and I meet his eyes. There's blood under his nose again, smearing his upper lip. The fight in me dies. He wraps an arm around my shoulder and squeezes tight. "Rashid, I won't let you do anything she doesn't want! Can't you see what this is doing to her? You're hurting her. She can't be a superhero if you kill her!" Daniel shouts. He's using that big-boy voice of his. Strained and tight but incredibly determined. Feelings, so many feelings well up in me. They almost break me. I lost him for so long, and now, with his slight body hugged against mine, I know I'll do anything to keep it this way, travel to any world, die any death.

"Fine, Rashid." I wrench my hand out of Rashid's hold, Daniel squeezes me tighter. Rashid backs away, a deep frown pulling his brows together.

Daniel puts a hand on my arm. I can feel his fingers trembling. "You don't have to do this. We're just two kids from Cali. It's not on us to save the world. I mean, let's face it, you never liked people that much. I remember your rants on social."

I turn the underside of my arm toward the flame. The skin starts to burn. I'm afraid of the pain that's coming. The fear makes my movements slow and clumsy. I take a deep breath for bravery. "I'm not trying to save the world. I'm just trying to save you."

Daniel squares his shoulders. "Divinica, you're my sister. I'd rather die with everyone else than lose you again. I want to save you too."

I smile at him. A real smile. "You already have. Even when the wave took everything, and you were just a name in my diary, just a name. Daniel. Sometimes I thought that name alone would keep me from going crazy, but then you would become an idea, a thought…a hope—" My voice breaks. I clear my throat harshly. "I love you, Daniel. I love you so much. I didn't tell you that enough…you know, before."

"Do you think…?" He pauses. His eyes scan the floor until they come to rest on our hands, which have somehow linked together in the last few moments. His voice is hesitant when he tries again. "Do you think Mom and Dad are watching us? Do you think they know that we're still alive? That we have…each other?"

I shake my head until my hair tumbles in my eyes. I leave it there. Still, through it, I can see in Daniel's face what losing them has done to him. If I die now? I don't think he'll survive. I know I couldn't, wouldn't survive the loss of him. "I don't know. I hope so. Daniel, if this works, we're going to be all right," I say. I don't think I'm lying. "The goddesses are powerful and wild, but I don't think they're evil. Even Hecate—"

"The girl with three heads who shot Dad," Daniel says quietly.

"Yeah, her."

A frown notches a narrow crease between his eyes. "She's not evil?'

"In our perception, yes, but to her—" I shrug. "I don't know if she knows what evil is. They're purpose is to save the earth—humans are just a virus."

Daniel leans forward, his eyes intent on my face. "So, you're saying they might be the Devil, but they're the devil on our side? Is that it?"

"I guess. I think, in their own way, they're fighting for us. They set this up thousands of years ago."

"Set you up, you mean?" he says.

I laugh. "Yes. They set me up. Just in case—"

"Just in case…you know? Life," Daniel finishes. "Well, you didn't need to be some scary-ass three headed witch to know the world was gonna—" Daniel makes an exploding motion with his free hand, and a thunderous, grinding noise behind his teeth. "Social media was constantly throwing up warnings."

I nod again. "We were all too stupid to listen."

"Not Dad. He knew."

"Yes. He knew." *Look what knowing got him,* I want to say, but I don't.

"I wish I could do something," Daniel says, his grip on my hand tightens. Emotion rolls in his face as he searches the dark interior of the cab. His eyes stop on the candle. "I won't leave you. Not for a second."

"I know."

"I love you, sis."

"I know. I love you too." I look down at my arm once more. At the words that seem to be some sort of code. "Here we go again," I say.

Daniel takes a deep, bracing breath. "Here we go."

I read the words. "Misplaced powers scattered through time; I travel through firelight to make them mine." Icy chills pimple my skin as the letters start to flow off my arm. Shivers wrack my bones and chatter my teeth. I'm so tired though, so weak, like my bones are made of silly putty and chewed gum. I guess getting beheaded by the love of your life is exhausting. Who knew?

I travel four times. First to the Fates where I battle with multiple personality disorder and steal a gooey eyeball. I almost vomit when Daniel pulls a long corpse hair off the twitching cornea. Next, I go to Athena, and fall screaming into the exact moment she watches her library of Alexandria burn. I steal a book from the inner sanctum as flames raise it to the ground. The book is titled: *The Hypothesis of Space Opera.* It has a bright blue insignia on the front in the shape of an upside down cross. It moves like lava when I touch it. I get lost in Athena's world for what seems like forever as she resets time a thousand times. No matter how many times she travels back, we are never able to prevent the destruction of a knowledge so ancient even the star gods have forgotten. I wish I could describe Ixchel, a jaguar goddess whose children founded the Earth. Maybe at the end of all this, if I live, I will draw the fantastical creatures who inhabited the forests and gardens of Artemis, goddess of the hunt, and breathing things. I will need to use art, because I don't have the words to describe how it felt to be in her body and know the battle she fought for Earth and the creatures who have no voice was one she would ultimately lose.

I steal her golden bow, and a quiver of arrows with flaming tails that neither wind nor water can extinguish. The very same one I just used in my fight against Xola and her crew. Each time, it gets harder to recite the words. I am nearly mindless by the third go. Daniel strokes my fevered brow, wipes away the sweat that pours into my eyes. The rest for the most part is a blessed blur. I don't know how many hours I travel, but time itself is a jumble of confusion when I return to my own.

Eventually, I become aware of the fact that I'm lying on my side, and a sleeping Daniel rests in my arms. I notice two things instantly. One, how shallow his breathing is. Two, how it feels like I've been trampled by a two-ton Rade. My tongue is a ball of cotton clinging to the roof of my mouth. My ears are ringing, and I'm seeing double, triple maybe. I swallow hard, choking on my lack of saliva as I slip in and out of consciousness. Somewhere behind me, I hear Dayle and Rashid whispering. I understand the words, but they make absolutely no sense to my overworked mind.

Dayle's gruff voice is clearly distinguishable. "Can't stay here, girl's been glowing for hours. No boat...may have to take the old train tunnel."

"I know," says Rashid in a thick voice. I try to breathe through the searing agony in my head. The one yellow light glowing on the dash adds a false sense of heat and calm, so I focus on it and try to ignore the rest.

"Can't move her. She's too weak. I can't believe what I just saw. I don't think I'll ever get the sounds of her screams out of my head." Dayle again.

Rashid makes a sound of agreement then says, "They're coming."

Dayle makes a muffled sound. "You think they're trying to kill her because she might save a world they want?"

"Makes sense. It's what I would do."

Dayle's response comes to me in confusing segments. "Wish Valance was here...might have a fighting chance...brother is gonna kill you."

"Yeah, he is. I know it's only a matter of time before he finds us. There was no reason we should have crashed the *Gravity* where we did. She pulled him to her, I've always thought so," Rashid says this, I think, but the words fade to a loud ringing. It feels like my mind is breaking. Being stretched beyond its ability to bear. I want to sit up and ask them why the hell they're talking about me like I'm not right here. I want to tell them I'm strong enough to run and fight. That I can make it, that I can save them. Save us all. I keep quiet though because I am too spent to do as much as move my lips, also because my mother told me to never tell a lie.

CHAPTER THIRTY-SEVEN

Attack

DIVINICA

The Channel Tunnel is thirty-eight kilometers long. It actually consists of three tunnels. Two for the trains that stopped running when the waves started coming, and one for service and security. We're in the service tunnel. Slimy, layered concrete walls make me feel like I'm lost in the body of some giant worm. Bunches of old, busted wires climb the brick. The wires spark at odd intervals, raining hot showers on our unsuspecting heads and shoulders. Daniel sticks to walking down the center track, carefully avoiding the divots and gaps in the fishplates. We've been down here almost six hours, according to Dayle and his watch. Rashid hasn't said much for the entirety of this miserable trek. Head down and occasionally talking to himself, he looks like a demented pixy. I want to take his hand and tell him he did the right thing by forcing me to do what I just freaking did, but I'm still reeling from it all. I fight to keep my mind off dark things and instead focus on the ticking of Dayle's watch. If it weren't for that steady *tick-tock, tick-tock*, I think I would have a challenging time distinguishing fact from feeling.

Fact: This is all actually happening. Feeling: It feels like we've been down here forever. It's the light that confuses and tickles the mind. It moves differently, like muddy water, or liquid, opaque glass. Disturbed only by our passage and the steam emerging out of broken pipes, or the aforementioned sparks from the occasional live wire that light up our tunnel like tiny sun spots.

It's creepy as hell, gross too. The smell of rotting flesh has been our constant, unwelcome companion. Every sound makes us all hold our breath; every shadow makes us jump. I keep my eyes on Daniel's face and remember all the reasons I'm doing this. I'm less afraid than I should be, but maybe that's because I'm carrying Artemis's bow slung over my shoulder. The flaming arrows in the quiver on my back help to cast a slight light on the path, and the eye of the Fates is in my duffle bag, along with Medusa's head and all the other artifacts I collected. There's a jaguar who's been following us at a distance, ever since he came back with me through the stars. Angry, but alive, my fire bird keeps pace with our bedraggled little party. He's formed an odd friendship with Daniel, the little dude's been feeding the bird from his rations when he's sure I'm not looking. The bird stays near Daniel. Fire wings folded, he's shrieking less than normal, but I know he hates it down here as much as the rest of us. It's so morose, damp, and dingy. The worst part is it's damn cold. So freaking cold that it's hard not to get into my feelings. Such as how shitty I feel for leaving Valance the way I did. I believed it was the right thing to do, but now, half a mile underground in a tunnel stuffed with dead people, I'm not so sure. On top of everything, I have the most awful sensation that we're being followed.

I'm glad when Dayle stops to shift bodies from our path, it gives me a chance to catch my breath. Dayle pauses beside a jumble of cracking concrete dividers and twisted metal pipe to lift the body of a young woman. Despite the sores decomposing her skin, and her twisted, mangled limbs, he's gentle with her and lays her carefully on a pile of people with no faces. They're all dead, stacked on top of each other as if they had known a secret path to freedom but failed to reach it. Water all around us, I wonder where they were trying to go.

Dayle's lips thin into a pale line. "Fit little bird, isn't it? She was pretty once," he says. "I wonder if she was kind. I hate how they all die screaming."

I blink and turn away from all the things I can't fix or change. *This is how it ends*, I think, *not with a bang, but with an unvoiced scream.*

Dayle puts a hand on my shoulder, leaving it there until I meet the question in his eyes. "You good?"

A tense moment passes before I nod. I'm of course lying. I'll never be *good* again. He gives me a weak smile, but his eyes say he knows how I really feel. Time passes. We walk, we hope, we fear. Water drips from the wet walls, steady as the ticking seconds. When the dark gets thick like ink-soaked cotton, I take the light of Aether from my duffle and let it illuminate our way. It creates a soft bubble of aqua-silver brightness that extends about three feet. We move together under its aura, a united front against the tenacious dark. A viper bites me every time I stick my hand in the bag, but it's okay, the venom doesn't seem to bother me. The razor fangs hurt like hell though, so I focus on the pain, which helps distract.

Three thousand and six hundred seconds pass, then another two thousand and two hundred. Now I know we're being followed. The knot in the pit of my stomach tells me so. Five hundred and fifty seconds ago, I saw what once appeared to be a stationary shadow just up ahead, twisting and moving along the wet wall. Three hundred seconds ago, I heard a scratching sound, harsh as nails on a chalkboard. Could've been a rat. Could've been something more. I clutch Daniel's hand tightly in mine. It's so cold we can see our breath, but our palms are sweating. He keeps casting furtive glances over his shoulder.

"I know," I whisper and meet his eyes. "Don't keep looking, just be ready."

"I'm always ready," he says in a voice so small I barely hear it. He cocks his head to the side and the light of Aether glances off his smooth cheek. "I'm scared," he says.

I swallow hard. "Me too, but don't worry. I won't let anything happen to you."

Daniel rolls his eyes. "I'm not scared for me; I'm scared for you. Dummy."

"Just keep walking," Dayle says, checking the chamber of his gun with a nearly imperceptible click. Shadows on the wall behind us deepen, then shiver. Rashid meets my eyes. I see my own terror reflected in his chestnut gaze. "They're right behind you," he mouths. I nod. I know. Why wouldn't they be? We're the idiots who went deep underground into what I assume has always been their territory. I can feel them breathing down my neck, sending ice shuddering along my spine.

I squeeze Daniel's hand. He looks up at me, a question in his scared eyes. "They're here for me. Take this and go on ahead with Rashid," I say and put the light of Aether in his hand. "Dayle and I are gonna hang back a bit. You'll be fine. I promise."

"I already told you, I'm not worried about me," Daniel snaps.

"What? No way!" Rashid says simultaneously.

I look between both of them, worn down and broken by my destiny. I can't let anything else happen to them.

"Please. I need you to trust me. You swore you would. Go on now," I say, trying to put a Valance level of command in my voice. Daniel looks on the verge of rebellion. "Just do what I say, for once in your life," I plead in a shrieking whisper. Daniel hesitates. In his eyes, I see his mind debating my edict. I turn to Rashid for help. "Take him, keep him safe."

"I'm supposed to keep you safe," Daniel says. It sounds like he wants to cry.

"I can't fight if I'm worried about hurting you. I have no idea what my powers can do...what I'll do...please—"

"Oh, alright," he interrupts fiercely, his gaze zeroing in on something behind me. His look makes my skin crawl. "But, sis, if I see you need me, I'm coming. I don't care what you say."

"Fine," I mutter, but meet Rashid's eyes, and narrow my own. *"Not under any circumstance,"* my look says. Rashid nods. A sudden burst of bright green lights up the tunnel like a fired flare. I shove Daniel back. "I love you! Go! Run!" I scream, dragging a flaming arrow from the quiver and unslinging my bow. Rocking back on my heels, I draw in a deep breath and spin around. I forget to exhale. A dozen pairs of yellow eyes stare back at me from the dark.

In my peripheral, I see Rashid take Daniel's hand. A harsh stream of curses follows their retreat. As they leave, the light cast by Aether recedes until all that remains is the firelight of my arrows. Jumping, shifting flames that send shafts of gold to highlight the stern, alien features of my enemies. Ten of them at least. I see twenty feet, and twenty pairs of eyes that fold down the center like origami. Well, I've always dubbed myself a bad ass. It looks like now is my time to prove it.

I internally debate my options as I let the duffle's strap slide from my shoulder. The bag hits the ground near my feet with a thud that sounds loud as a bomb in the hung silence. We all just stand there for a moment staring googly-eyed at each other like a group of besotted fools. Xola stands at the head of the pack. Her beautiful lips are twisted in a terrifying snarl. She swipes a lock of red hair from her face, moving with an elegant grace I can only dream of. I know I'm petty, but it makes me hate her even more. I can see that she got her hands on another sword. This one appears even larger, the crackling Hades' colored flame ever brighter. Classic.

Beside me, Dayle lifts his shotgun to eye level, then takes a menacing step forward. "Well, let's crack on then. We don't have all day." His voice is loud and carries a clear taunt. Xola extends both her hands, links her fingers and leisurely cracks her knuckles, then unsheathes her sword. Something about the move is so threatening that whatever air is left in my lungs escapes in an uneven rush. I still don't know the extent of my powers, or even what they all are. *This could go all kinds of wrong,* I think, but familiar adrenaline surges through me. I have to bite the inside of my cheek to hold in the wicked cackle trying to claw its way out of my mouth. My tattoos start to glow. I close my eyes as lightning crackles in the centers of my splayed palms. It burns hot pink at the edges. I feel suddenly invincible, like my body is a brand-new Maserati, and my mind is ready to take it for a test drive. Curiosity is my dominating emotion as my feet clear the ground, and I rise into the air like a fucking angel, or goddess actually. I'm going with a goddess. I open my eyes and meet Xola's hate-soaked gaze. "I'll give you one chance to turn around," I say loudly, meaning every word. "We don't have to do this. Leave now and I'll let you live."

Xola has the audacity to throw back her head and laugh. The rest of them don't move a single muscle. They look like stone statues under the uneven light of my flaming arrows. More power surges through me, and I am unafraid. Statues can shatter.

I'm losing myself as all the other goddesses fight for the dominance of my hands and mind. "Let's fucking go, then," I say, and my voice echoes like thunder. Pink lightning shoots from my palms toward the lot of them. Sentient whips of sizzling electricity that know my targets. I smile as a bolt strikes Xola in the dead center of her chest. She screams in rage, and her tumble backward is so extreme it's almost cartoonish. Shockingly, she finds her equilibrium in the air and lands on her feet like a cat, then arches a deep red brow. Her smile is deadly as she looks into my eyes and says, "I've heard many stories about you since I was a child. They say the spirits in you are ancient and unkillable. I always thought it was my fate to test the legends." She pulls herself to her full, impressive height and flexes her fingers.

A smile lifts my lips. I think in that moment, the power thrashing through me could lay waste to a city. My words are slow and glacier cold, as I say them through clenched teeth. "Bring it, bitch!"

A single beat, then we fly at each other, screaming like thirsty banshees or sirens wanting revenge. Our bodies collide mid-air with a smack that shakes the tunnel. Her hand goes for my throat as my fingers lock around her own willowy neck. She's strong. Insanely so. With a single tug, she brings us both crashing to the ground. She lands atop me as my back slams into a wide, concrete slab, and the bow and arrow fly from my hands. Breath leaves my lungs in a roar. "Uh? Heavy much?" I gasp, working my knee between our straining bodies. I heave and shove her off me. To my right, I hear the snap of a bow string followed by the hiss of a soaring arrow. I spin and catch the shaft in a single, fluid move. The serrated metal arrow head stops less than an inch from piercing straight through my eye.

I don't have time to wonder who fired the arrow, because as soon as I manage to find my feet, Xola is on me again. She swings her blade, bathed in light green fire, directly at my throat. My body folds into a deep back bend. Xola shouts her rage when the blade sails harmlessly over me. I come up swinging. Black vines comprised of lightning and smoke shoot from the tips of my fingers, break through the ground, and split asphalt and concrete like they both have the consistency of tofu. I clench my fists and call for more lightning. It crackles and strikes the vines, scorching them. I smile again as they begin to burn. Smoke and flame drench the air.

Xola hisses and lifts her sword. Sharp thorns cut the bare skin of her upper arms as more twisting vines, hard and thorny as the ones that cover Styx, fly from my hands and surge past her. She curses at me. I open my mouth to say something hurtful and witty, but instead of words, black smoke billows past my lips. I exhale and breathe out pure darkness. Thick as ink and moving like storm clouds over an empty prairie. Xola stops slashing at the vines, the green flames coating her sword are no match for my blazing golden power. She turns to face me, then draws back her neck and surprises me by spitting a thick substance that looks too much like blood directly at me. It strikes my chest, splashes my arms with a perceptible splat, hissing and burning like raw acid. When it hits my shirt, it makes big holes in the pretty pink silk until it looks like someone used me as a cigar ashtray. This unwarranted destruction of the prettiest thing I own pisses me off more than the scorching pain. "Asshole! This is my favorite shirt!" I scream, and she laughs. I hear a foot fall behind me and spin on my heels to see an eight-foot creature looming, spear raised for the killing blow. I reach up and rip the weapon from his grasp. It's as easy as taking candy from a baby. The expression of shock that takes over his face makes me laugh.

I extend my free hand and fire a bolt of lightning into his chest. Like Xola, he too goes flying. His hard landing takes out three of his companions. I don't know what I'm doing. My body is moving on its own. I fall to my knees and press both hands to the ground, and the earth itself begins to quake, sending deep cracks racing across the ground and climbing up the walls. Something above our heads starts to rumble and it's a dangerous sound, like there's an angry creature above us made of weight and water struggling to break through. A giant fissure appears between me and Dayle who is currently involved in hand-to-hand combat with two creatures who look like they came directly from one of Stephen King's nightmares. Dayle fights like a brute, it's a beautiful thing to watch him break bones and blacken eyes. When I face Xola again, her arms are bloodied by my thorns.

I point to a particularly bad cut on her right shoulder. "First blood," I say succinctly.

Her smile is as poisonous as her spit. "No matter. This fight is to the death."

"Good," I say, then lift my hands. My lightning responds. I don't stop channeling until I start to rise off my feet again, propelled by my own power. I'm jerked back to reality when I feel a clawed hand sink into my hair, then yank my head back with enough force to snap my neck. I blink and stare up into another pair of yellow eyes that clearly hate me as much as Xola. Maybe more. What the fuck is everyone's problem?

I grab at the restraining hand, trying to disengage the strong fingers by twisting one back, then clawing at another. Xola rushes in, sword raised, green flames bouncing off her flawless skin. The blade is aimed at my throat. I lash out with my right foot, wanting to kick her in the gut, but she dodges easily. Her laugh grates on my nerves. It's a joyful, vomit-worthy sound. It makes me so angry I could spit bullets aimed at her heart. Despite the clawed hand holding me in place, I manage to twist my body at the last second. The blade misses its chance to carve out my heart but cuts deep into my stomach. The pain is bad, monstrous actually, but I don't make a sound. I'd rather die than give her the satisfaction of my scream.

I relish Xola's frustrated groan as she raises her sword for another try. I press both palms tightly to the scaly skin of the hand dug in my hair, then release the strongest electric bolt I've ever summoned. The creature shrieks and drops me. I fall to my knees, duck, and roll. Hot blood pours down my stomach, I feel it collecting in the waistband of my pants. Sticky and real. This time, Xola's scream of rage is animalistic as her sword misses me my inches. It slams into the concrete divider instead, splitting the fifty-pound cinder block cleanly down the middle. I move onto my back, then turn to face the two coming at me from my left. I half scramble, half crawl to my duffle, then reach my hand inside and grab Medusa's hissing, thrashing head. Cobras sink their fangs into my wrist. Blood pours down my arm as I lift it from the bag and point it at the two approaching figures who mean only harm. Medusa catches their gaze. Xola screams, for real this time, as her companions turn to stone.

"Hold!" Someone yells from the darkness. I can't see their face, but their voice carries a strange command, triggering something that makes me want to kneel and bow my head. I fight the compulsion and stare through my black mists at Rashid who lies face down, unmoving. Daniel is on his knees. A creature stands behind him, this one doesn't look like he carries an ounce of human blood. His sharp teeth are bared in a snarl, and he's pressing a knife to Daniel's throat.

CHAPTER THIRTY-EIGHT

Brutal capture with a side of jealousy

"Call off your powers," the old one says, as if these abilities changing my very alchemy were only some angry dogs I'd let off leash.

As I stare into his creepy eyes, my rage knows no bounds. My hands curl into useless fists as I fall to my knees. "Hurt him, and I'll kill you. Slowly. I swear it," I vow. Fear shudders through me. I want to look at Daniel, run and snatch him away from present danger. I don't because my gaze is fixed on the old one's eyes—probably the only guy here who could give me a decent fight—wise eyes that look like they've seen far too much sorrow. The lightning still crackling in my palms dies with a hiss. Black vines retract from the tips of my fingers and turn to dust, the Earth stops quaking. From the corner of my eye, I see Xola move. She comes up behind me and presses the sharp point of her flaming sword into the center of my back.

"There will be no death in this place today," the old one says, breaking my gaze to look at Xola. "She must be bathed and sacrificed in the ancient way."

"Uh, hard pass," I say. Dayle and Daniel snicker. No one else moves. All eyes are trained on the walking, talking, lizard person who apparently holds some kinda sway over my assailants. Maybe he's their fucking king. Good. I've always thought monarchies were made to be toppled. "Look," I say, proud of how I'm keeping the scream in my throat from infesting my voice, "if I fight right now, you all might eventually overpower and kill me and my baby brother, but I can guarantee I'll fuck shit up, and probably take a few of you dickheads with me.

But if you let my brother free, I'll go quietly to your morbid afterparty. Hell, I'll even let you sacrifice me if that's what you really feel you gotta do."

The old one has no hair on his scaled flat face, and his nose looks like it belongs to Voldemort, but still, I see his nostrils flare. I know if he had eyebrows, they would be raised. "Really?" he asks in a slow way, dragging out the *R* until it rolls.

The tip of Xola's blade digs a little deeper into my spine. I flinch. "Yes, fucking really! But if you or your little minions put a single mark on my brother, or my friends, all bets are off."

The old one smiles. The armor he wears seems almost Roman in design, though I can't identify the material. It moves like liquid glass, like transparent steel. Feathers adorn his headdress, blue as Aphrodite's eyes. The braces on his arms and the straps of his flat sandals are fashioned from distressed leather that shimmers like snake skin when he moves, the design of them looks like it was born in the head of Alexander McQueen. He reminds me of some rockstar at a costume party. No one moves or speaks for so long, I'm about to fucking lose it, when the old one finally lowers his knife. There's a smear of Daniel's blood on the blade. Red washes my vision, and I almost forget everything I just said about going quietly. Then, Daniel grabs his throat as he starts to crawl toward me, and all my focus is for him. I move, meaning to rush forward and pull him into a smothering hug, but Xola grabs my right arm and twists it up behind my back. My body arches as every nerve running down my spine starts to scream.

"Where do you think you're going?" Xola asks tauntingly.

"Hopefully anywhere that's not right beside you," I spit, voice dripping so much fake sweetener I almost choke on it.

"Take her, leave the others," the old one commands, tone stern, but I think I see laughter in the wrinkles at the corners of his yellow eyes.

Rashid chooses that moment to groan loudly. As one we look at him. "What the hell did you do to my friend?" I demand, struggling against Xola's fierce hold.

"Hit him on the head," the old one says. "He'll come to right at moonrise."

"Moonrise? When the fuck is that?" I shout.

Dayle kneels down beside Rashid, and glances at his watch. "About an hour," he says, his big hand pushing waves of deep green hair off Rashid's bloodless face. Dayle's eyes are a heated shade of amber as our gazes crash. "Don't let anything happen to them," I say, putting my soul in the plea.

"Screw that twice," Daniel shouts emphatically. "I'm going with you."

Denial jerks my muscles. Xola knees me hard in the back, then twists my arm higher until I feel sure my bum shoulder is seconds from popping its socket. Her blade cuts me a little, but I don't bow under the pressure.

"No way!" I gasp through locked teeth, trying to disassociate myself from the pain.

Daniel kneels in front of me. His upper lip curls and anger snaps in his wide eyes. "Well, you don't really have a say, do you?" he asks, tone tight and edged in bitterness. "I survived without you for two years. Shocking actually, that I managed to soldier through sans your bossy supervision. I know it wasn't your fault, but you left me alone to make my own choices, and that's what I'll keep doing, no matter what you say. Besides, if you leave with that crown, you're taking my memories with you—and fuck that where the sun don't shine."

Guilt twists my gut. He's right. I left my only baby brother to fend for himself while I was busy time jumping and lost in white silence. "Daniel, listen to me, I don't think there's anything I'm going to be able to do to change how this story ends. Do you understand?"

He presses his lips together for a second, and sucks at his teeth, then his eyes meet mine. Unflinching. "Yes, and I don't care. I'm not leaving you," he says. I'm shook by the look on his face. Daniel's always been a mouthy, mischievous, wonderful boy, but never a determined one. I can see in his eyes that there's no way in hell he's changing his mind. I want to tell him he'll only be a liability; I want to say something hurtful enough to make him leave. I can't though. It's just not in me. My shoulders sink as I cave with a drawn-out sigh. Daniel doesn't let loose the expected whoop of glee. His face is solemn, his big eyes are full of shadows and his mouth set in that firm line. He's tagging along to watch me die. We both know it.

They take us deep underground in a pair of strange conveyances that appear to be a twisted mashup of wooden mining cart and some interstellar craft. Green headlights and fire-soaked torches dug into the cave walls light our way. My hands and feet are bound with slender yards of glittering ropes that look like metal snakes.

The strange wooden/electrical carts take us to a world unknown. We travel down tunnels I believe few humans ever knew existed. Dank, small tunnels that were first covered in thick moving dirt, then brown mud. Soon the dirt is peppered with stringy, upside-down roots, then threads of green shoots and fluffy patches of emerald moss. An hour of travel, maybe two, and the tunnels begin to widen. The moss and green shoots turn to bushes and trees, long branches laden with multi-colored leaves, painted the colors of autumn and dawn. Down here, everything is incandescently alive with a kind of tech that seems to be airborne. It's all around us, blue and moving like slow lightning or electrically charged wind. As if we had all gone underground and into some Xbox game. The NPCs surrounding me, the ground, every breath I take seems to be fed by it, touched by its crackling mystery.

I see giant, luminous orbs like the ornaments that hung from my gran's Christmas tree every year. She used to yell at me, then slap my hand when I dared to touch them. I don't dare touch them now, but it's hard. The orbs are everywhere, like misplaced alien eggs. Resting in tree branches, nestled between rocks, or hanging suspended above our heads. No strings or wires needed; they float like unpoppable soap bubbles. They drink the aquatically embossed tech— emanating from literally everywhere—and shine like hundreds of tiny alien suns.

I move past groups of creatures who watch me through wide, judgmental eyes. I'm dragged into a series of tunnels outfitted like some ancient Egyptian spa. The tunnels are honeycombs filled with soft light and the smell of jasmine. We stop in front of a cave dripping with stalagmites. In the center of this fragrant cave is a wide, metal tub sitting on four clawed feet and filled with steaming water clearly being heated by the shimmering ball hovering over our heads.

Daniel and Dayle, holding a partially unconscious Rashid between them, tell me they'll remain outside to make nice with the locals, but maybe it's just to give me a moment of privacy while I get all dolled up to die. Xola shoves me toward the tub, I stumble, barely managing to catch myself with my bound hands. I find my balance, spin on my heels, and shove her back. Her mouth drops in round O as she falls on her ass. I let some power—just a little—surge past the barriers I constructed to contain it. Our eyes lock as I twist my wrists in opposing directions and snap my bonds like they were made of paper mâché.

"You swore," Xola yells, recovering her feet and unsheathing her sword.

"Oh, chill out bitch. I'm not going to fight you. Not right now anyway. It's been over two years since I've seen a tub. You can worry about a brutal maiming after I take a bath." I shrug out of my jacket and pull my ruined shirt over my head. Xola stares at me like I've suddenly sprouted another arm out of my ear as I kick off my shoes and unhook my black bra. I pause in the act of peeling the straps down my shoulder. "You going to stay and watch?" I ask, brow raised.

She looks away nervously. I shrug and purse my lips. "Suit yourself," I say flippantly, before divesting myself of the rest of my clothes, and practically leaping into the hot water without further ado. It feels like heaven. Like flying through clouds of liquid wonder. I moan and run my fingers through my hair, careful not to dislodge the crown as I dig my fingers beneath the twining metal and scratch my nails over my scalp, an action that sends shivers over my whole body. My moan turns into a throaty purr. Xola doesn't say anything, but she hands me a glass jar of lavender liquid that moves like shampoo. I use it to wash my hair three times, then scrub every inch of my skin until it's bright red and stinging.

Xola watches me mutely, arms crossed over her perfect breasts.

"You know, in my world, staring is rude," I inform her.

Xola snorts. "For years, Valance swore you were strong, graceful, and beautiful, even used grand words like worthy. It doesn't matter that he's right. I still hate you."

"What a lovely thing to hear."

"You are evil. You carry the soul of another alongside your own."

I make a sharp noise somewhere between a laugh and a groan. "I carry the souls of a lot of somebodies. You'll have to be more specific."

Her eyes darken menacingly. "Valance loves you. Do you love him? I can still smell him all over you."

"You sound kinda jealous. I didn't know you knew him."

"I do," she says, and there's something wistful, possessive, and almost intimate in her eyes, and suddenly the sickening jealousy is mine. I sit up straighter in the tub. She laughs, and I have an urge to wrap my hands around her dainty throat and squeeze until the urge is gone. I grit my teeth so I don't give into the irrational impulse.

"But 'know,' is a strong word," she continues. "The Liguara and the Anunnaki people have been waiting for you. We knew the moment you were created. The enchantment protecting your upside dwelling kept you safe for a time. He, Valance Lord, kept you safe when Hecate's wicked spells could not. He's killed all who've come for you."

"All? Not you, apparently. Aren't I lucky?"

Xola smiles. A slow, thirsty smile, then she licks her full lips and flicks her hair. I know it makes me petty, but I hate that she looks like some exotic cover model getting ready to shoot the centerfold. "No, not me. We fought only once. He's a great warrior, and beautiful as an arctic dawn. I let him live."

I close my eyes and turn away from her. The illogical jealousy is everywhere now, tearing my eyes and clawing at my throat. My mind races with a single, looping thought. Maybe *he* let *her* live, a far more concerning option. I dunk my head under water and scrub my hair for what feels like the hundredth time. There's moisture on my cheeks, but I don't think it's from the bath. I stay in the water until my skin is white and wrinkled.

Xola finally leaves, that taunting smile still plastered to her lips. I'm alone, and now I'm craving the sight of Valance so badly it's making me shake. "I miss you," I whisper aloud, and in my life of loss, my words have weight. Three more women with soft hands and reptilian eyes come to drag me from the bath, and I let them. They dry my hair with a fuzzy towel, then brush it until it shines brighter than it has in years. They leave the crown though, muttering and trying not to jostle it as they plait my hair in a single braid that runs down the center of my back, then stuff me into a white nightgown that appears to be made for a smaller girl. My squished cleavage challenges the strength of the delicate seams. They confiscate most of my artifacts—not the firebird, who took off when all the trouble began—or Medusa's head. It sits in the duffle, untouched and hissing. I understand the snakes and the ancient language they speak from the shadows of the half-zipped bag. They tell me I'm going to die. I believe them. I'm still not really afraid though, which is kinda weird, given the circumstances. In fact, when they haul me from the bathroom to their tribunal, the only thing in my mind is Valance. If this really is my last night on this strange earth, I wish with all my tortured soul that I was spending it in his arms.

CHAPTER THIRTY-NINE

A Celtic cross, a touch of salvation

I'm bodily pushed and jostled to the center of a torchlit circle. They give me a hard shove, I stumble, but I'm pretty proud of myself when I don't fall. I do spin though, round and round, like an unstoppable top. There's so many of them. Five hundred, maybe more. All eyes are on me. A thousand yellow lights shining from the darkness. I feel their silent sentencing like a weight on my soul. The room we all stand in is wide and high. Stone walls. Stone floor. Stone world. The rocky bronze terrain is broken up by slender trees strung with twisting vines lushly infused by forgotten colors, peppered with little insects that glow with the air's energy while they chirp and croak. The numerous torches stuck into the cervices of the rock have dancing flames that cast menacing shadows. And above it all like some Druid god is a tall, upside-down, and white as exposed bone cross dominating all the space around it. It's the oldest thing I've ever seen, from a forgotten time, back when the word 'Bible' had never been uttered. Ancient as the one standing beside it.

Behind the cross, I search the crowd for familiar faces, Daniel, Dayle, Rashid, even my damn bird or the freaking monster jaguar who abandoned me suddenly—much like my courage. I glance over my shoulder and see no friends hiding among the yellow eyes, find nothing but narrow glares of hostility that look to be fueled by a millennium of hate. I turn back to face the cross and the old one lifts his hands. The whispering crowd falls silent.

Yep. He's definitely their fucking king, I think, seconds before his leathery voice booms out. I know he's not speaking English, but I understand every word. I listen. Jaw dropped.

"Divinica Starr, Child of Prophecy. Dark blood of the ancient three who play with living strings. Daughter of Gaia," the old one calls, steady gaze trained on my face. His eyes see me, see through me. I hardly breathe as he lowers his hands and continues, "Stories of you fill our lore. You have many names. Mythmarked, Starsigned. Savior of the human race. A weapon built in a mad man's lab. A spliced soul. The treasure and curse of our people. We were once a great and powerful race. The dominant species of this planet. Children of the Anunnaki. We are ruled by the power of the stars. We utilized sciences no human mind can comprehend. We were the hunters who became the hunted. For the last three thousand years, we have been murdered by the millions. Humans have driven us underground and destroyed our world above. Even the vast seas are not safe from their filth. Now humans are finally being exterminated by a spell that should have been activated centuries ago." His eyes narrow on my face. "You, star child, you are the only one who can save them. That is why tonight, you must die. The pieces of the goddesses in you will be silenced. This world was ours first, we deserve to dwell above."

His voice rises at the last, and the surrounding crowd roars their agreement. I roll my eyes. "Fuck me, that was long winded. Keep talking, we might be able to forgo the traumatizing cross if I simply die of boredom," I say, then almost immediately hear an unmistakable snicker emerge from the belly of the crowd. Relief makes me weak. Daniel is alive and laughing at my lame jokes. The crowd parts then, as if on cue, and sure enough, there's Daniel again on his knees with another knife to his throat. He's wearing a huge shit-eating grin, and as his eyes meet mine, he gives me a double thumbs up.

The hairs on my neck rise as the old one steps off his dais to move stealthily toward me. His breath touches the shell of my ear, his voice sends shivers down my spine. "You die. He lives. I give you my word."

I turn and face him. I know he sees the bitter laugh in my eyes. "You give me your word? Oh, good. Here I was thinking you were going to give me something completely useless," I say, voice sweet as fresh honey.

The old one's glower is thunderous. Daniel starts laughing again. "That really was a good one, sis."

"Shut up, kid," someone hollers. I hear a smack, followed by a grunt of pain from Daniel.

My lightning comes suddenly, filling my palms. Sparking like I'm holding the wrong end of a live taser. The blaze in the old one's eyes could incinerate the rainforest. "Attack and your brother will die—"

"He says ominously," I sneer. I'm so pissed, I think I might be powerful enough to take them all and save my brother. I spin again to look at Daniel. He must see my intent because he narrows his eyes and shakes his head. There's something in his gaze that brings me a small semblance of calm, a tiny and dangerous thought. A shred of hope that this cave might not be where my story ends.

The feeling stays for a second until Xola grabs a handful of my freshly washed hair, and twists until it hurts. "Come bitch, time to thwart fate," she says in a nasty, hissing voice. Hope, like the hot pink lightning in my palms, dies. I don't fight. I let her drag me toward the cross. I don't move as they tie me to the cross, stretching my arms high above my head.

"Don't you think this is a bit archaic?" I inquire in a voice that trembles like my limbs as they spread my legs, then secure my ankles with ivory ropes. Xola's response to my inane question is to tug on the ropes until they twist my skin. I keep my eyes on Daniel as Reptilian soldiers pile bundles of dry sticks under my feet. I don't look away from his baby face, noting all the ways it's irreparably changed. I remember the day Mom brought him home from the hospital, the way his little hand grabbed my finger and just held on, like he knew I was his sister. I think about the way he used to scream the house down in the middle of the night. I remember the song Mom would sing to make him hush. I remember sunny days and family trips to the beach as the soldiers use torches to set the piles of kindling ablaze. The fire touches the tips of my toes. The smoke starts to rise. Still, I see nothing but trust in Daniel's eyes, and I start to believe he thinks I'm somehow going to find a way out of this. Hope dies a little more. Doesn't he know the knife to his throat holds me in place more securely than the weak ropes they used to restrain me?

The flames wrap my ankles like manacles. Aphrodite turns my toes to ice and water. I feel her symbol glowing white hot, indomitable as the power surging inside of me. The old one nods his head and the creature holding the knife to Daniel's throat twists the blade. Daniel flinches. Still, his eyes are brave and full of trust. I resist Aphrodite's magic, battle it until I feel the fire again. It burns the soft skin on the bottoms of my feet, and it fucking hurts. I press my lips together so the scream in my throat remains unvoiced. The fire starts licking up my legs.

Oh god! Oh god, oh my fucking god. This fucking hurts! I'm not going to be able to keep the scream in much longer. I gasp when the hem of the white gown ignites. Concern floods Daniel's eyes. Then I see fear. I feel that same fear as the flames climb up my body. The crowd of Liguara moves closer as my body starts to burn in earnest. I'm going to scream. It's only a matter of when. It can't be helped. The pain is like the red wave. Everywhere. Life changing. Eternal. The power writhing in my chest wants to stop it, wants to heal, and save me. I don't let it. Instead, I feel the pain. Try to understand and merge with it because it's all I can do. I won't watch Daniel die. I'll take this a thousand times if he keeps breathing. I know that my death on this pyre means I'm saving one and killing thousands, essentially damming what's left of the human race. It probably makes me a horrible person, but it's not a hard choice to make. I won't watch my brother die. *I won't. I won't. I won't.* I'd rather burn. I couldn't stop the death of our parents. I couldn't keep the wave from torturing him. I couldn't help him through two years of loneliness and pain, because those things were out of my control. This isn't.

The fire starts to eat its way through the flesh of my calves and char my bones. My nerves are screaming, my brain is short-circuiting. Around me, the Liguara begin to chant. Their song is sad, mournful even. The smell of my cooking flesh burns my throat. I start panting, then bite the inside of my cheek so hard my mouth fills with blood. I swallow a big gulp of it and shudder. Smoke, pain, burning, melting. My wracking coughs turn to husky wheezes.

Sweat pouring down my forehead blinds me. I know the pain is driving me insane because I hear a voice in my ear. Deep, husky, familiar, and so altogether wonderful I imagine I might already be dead. "Put out the fire, Divinica," the voice says, but I shake my head. I won't obey a hallucination.

"Divinica," the voice says again. "Do it right now."

I shake my head once more. I can't speak. I'm burning. I can't breathe. I can't even say his name, but my mind is alive with the word. *Valance. Valance. Valance.*

"Now, Divinica. Right now, before it's too late."

The fire reaches the underside of my breasts. My skin is bubbling like lava. My eyes open, I search for Daniel's face in the crowd. I find him quickly. There is sweat, maybe tears running down his cheeks. He isn't smiling anymore, but when he catches my gaze, he gives me a nod, and a single thumbs up. Then I flinch as I realize I might not be hallucinating after all.

I take a deep breath, then another. The power in me is easily accessed. I simply let go, the goddesses do the rest. Water pours from my skin, a great deluge of it that douses the flames. The instant surcease of agony makes me dizzy. I slump against my bonds. Then, a pair of strong arms wrap my waist and hold me up. The owner of the arms is behind me, close, so close, almost crowding me. I can feel the heat of his ragged breaths on my skin and the blue in his eyes is mercurial as they drop to my lips, then travel slowly down my body, when his gaze reaches my feet, his face goes ashen. "Divinica." His breath brushes the shell of my ear making me shake. "Divinica, Divinica." He touches my cheek. "Heal yourself, baby, or you're going to die, those burns are—" His voice breaks as he shakes his head. "Your legs look like Bolognese."

"Gross, and th…thanks…" I manage to gasp. Past Valance's shoulder, I watch as the old one drops his arms and turns toward me, seeming to finally register the absence of crackling flames. Valance nods his chin in Daniel's direction. Instantly, Dayle materializes behind the creature holding a knife to Daniel's throat and hits the lizard warrior on the head with the butt of his Glock. The Reptilian drops like hammered lead. Daniel jumps to his feet and barrels toward me. I snap my ropes with ease and hold my arms out to him. The water enveloping me turns to soft white light that heals. Daniel brushes past the old one and crashes into me. My arms close around him. My power envelopes us both. A white halo. A shimmering shield.

"I knew he was here," Daniel pants. "I knew it was going to be okay." Daniel glances up at Valance. "You sure took your fucking time. I hope you have a plan, because you're about to get jumped by a butt load of angry lizards."

Valance ignores my brother; he moves in front of me and reaches out to cup my cheek. He's a thief who steals my air and mind. "I've missed you," he whispers. The admission sounds like it was wrenched from him.

Daniel plugs his nose and makes gagging noises. I turn to admonish him, or simply stick out my tongue, but I freeze mid-motion as Valance vanishes. Right in front of my eyes he just dis-a-fucking-pears.

Daniel makes a face equal parts fascination and awe. "He keeps doing that. It's weird. Maybe he's magic too," Daniel says. I don't have time to comment. The old one moves, and he's on us in a flash. I spin and shove Daniel behind me, then face the towering monster. Fists clenched. "Come at me then," I snarl. "I was a good sport the first time, but I have my brother now, and there's no fucking way you're tying me to that cross again."

"You're actually not far off, Daniel," Valance says, reappearing in the center of the torch lit circle looking like he's always been there. His stance is casual, sexy. Dark jacket, darker jeans, wicked smile. The AK strapped to his back is as menacing as the glare he levels at the old one. Valance lifts his hand, fingers splayed to show us a diamond shaped object winking in the center of his palm. "It's Hecate's tech. Not as cool as getting hit by a particle accelerator, but not bad. I'm like a superhero."

"Your mind's the superhero, I thought I smashed that thing," I mutter.

"No way! I want superpowers," Daniel whines at the same time.

"You did smash it, you're good at smashing things, Divinica, but I fixed it," Valance says. "It wasn't hard. Fundamental when you really look at it."

The old one lifts his arms and roars, "Enough! Take him!" The command mobilizes the troops. Reptilian soldiers rush forward, their extended spears aimed in Valance's direction.

Valance smiles, then throws me a devastating wink. His moves are confident, almost jaunty. He hooks his thumbs in his pockets, the very soul of casual charm. "Divinica has royal blood, as such, according to Liguara law, she is entitled to the rights of Holmgang. Trial by combat," Valance says.

"She does not—" the old one starts. Valance cuts him off with a wave of his hand. "Athena, Kali, even your own goddess, Hecate. Nokomis, Isis...do I need to go on? All of them had royal blood, and they gave that blood to her. So, I demand the right to your own tradition. You will respect the Holmgang. Your champion against Divinica's—who is me by the way if you didn't already get that."

The old one raises himself to his full, impressive height. "I am the champion of the Liguara. You will fight me. When I rip you to shreds, I will kill her in a way that makes the pyre seem kind."

Against my chest, I feel Daniel's shoulders shaking and realize he's laughing. "You think it's funny? Valance is about to get killed by a mythical creature in a place that shouldn't exist."

"Yeah, but..." Daniel gestures at the two towering men circling each other. "I mean come on, boss battle."

I start to stand. Daniel grabs my arm. "Hey, where the hell are you going?"

"To stop this shit!"

"No, Div. He's got this."

There's such trust in his eyes I don't have the heart to tell him that I don't need a damn white knight, but I suspect he's right. Valance does look like he's got this. I can see his aura, hot and pulsing. His sparking adrenaline heats the air. He looks like a guy spoiling for a fight.

"To the death," the old one says.

Valance's laugh is wicked. "Winner gets the girl."

The old one draws his sword. Green fire bathes the blade. I jump harder than necessary, then scoot back. Daniel moves his body to shield mine. "Don't worry, sis. I won't let them burn you again. That was the worst for me."

"Really? Well, it was great for me," I say sarcastically.

Daniel smacks my arm. "Shut up! I'm serious. I'll have nightmares for years. You must really love me."

"Of course, I do."

Daniel looks over at Valance. "You love him too, don't you?"

I don't say anything, but I'm afraid my answer is shining brightly in my eyes because Daniel rolls his. "No one can deny the guy has presence."

"Oh my god. No. I don't love him. I can't, so I don't."

Daniel pulls one of his faces that says he knows I'm full of it. "I don't see how you couldn't. Shit, I think I love him."

I scowl. "Traitor." A flash of movement in the corner of my eye quickly diverts my attention to Xola who's stepping toward the circling pair of masculine time bombs. Her own sword is drawn and blazing.

Valance turns his head to look at her. My heart flips over, then halts completely. Xola stops when she's close to him. Too close. "This doesn't have to happen," she says loud enough for all to hear.

Valance draws his brows together; his gaze is knifelike. "I warned you exactly what I would do if you ever tried to take her from me."

Xola frowns. "As I recall, she's the one who left you and got herself in this mess."

Valance bares his teeth. "You tied her to a fucking cross and set her on fire."

Xola lifts a defiant chin. "It isn't a cross. It's an Iona. A symbolic representation of the four elements. An ancient symbol of the gods who built the first stone circle. The first star portal."

"Please spare me the history lesson of the lost Druids and your nearly exterminated race. You were going to stand here and watch the girl I love fry. That's cold, babe. I thought we were friends."

Xola stomps her foot. "I'm not going to stand here and watch you fight my father."

Valance's smile is toxic as poison. "So bring me someone else. I don't much care who I kill right now."

Valance and Xola are standing so close now, their lips are almost touching. I want to rip them apart. Rip her apart. Just before I do something stupid, the old one steps between them. "The challenge has been extended and accepted. The rites of Holmgang will be observed. You, daughter, have no power to stop this. Go now. Find your place with the others."

Xola spins to glare at me for a long second before she directs her rage back to Valance. "Don't do this. She's not worth it."

Valance glances over Xola's shoulder. His eyes crash into mine. The world just stops. "You're wrong. Divinica is worth everything."

My heart hammers in my ears. As usual, Valance locks me to him with simple, powerful words. I can't find it in me to break his stare, even after Xola turns, then storms off.

"Ugh!" Daniel moans, looking away from my lovesick face before he throws up a hand to cover his eyes. "You two are totally rated R."

Xola steps closer to her father, eyes for Valance alone. "The magnitude of what you're about to do cannot be undersold. Humans have proven themselves to be diabolical stewards of this planet. Obviously, there are the good, brave, and pure, but the evil ones do such irreparable damage. They would destroy the cosmos if they could," Xola says.

Her words grate on my ears until I literally can't take it anymore. "Oh my god, will you please shut up. You're lethally dull. Humans are bad, blah, blah, blah. Same old off-key song. Do you know how many humans were fighting for this Earth before the damn savior device was activated? Thousands, maybe millions. I'm sure the goddesses had a freaking reason for what they did—or are still doing. But they were shortsighted, and so are you!" I stand up and realize I'm yelling. Shaking all over, but my voice is strong and clear. "I think I might be the most powerful person alive, or should I say awake? If you weren't so busy trying to turn me into charcoal, you might be able to see that. See that we could work together, help each other."

Xola makes a sound somewhere between a laugh and a yawn. "Talk about long winded."

I'm so wound up by my little speech that my breathing is jagged. I know it makes me childish, but I flip her the bird, slowly…by cranking it up.

Valance clears his throat loud enough to demand our attention. "So…is it like a ready, set, go thing, or…?"

"Valance, there's another way," I say.

He shakes his head. "No. Your way has a high body count. This way, it's just one. If he kills me and tries to burn you again, you have my full approval to give your way a whirl."

"If you think I'm going to stand here and watch him kill you, you're out of your damn genius mind."

Valance puts a hand to his heart and makes a face of mock hurt. "Wow. Love the faith. Come on, this guy's old. Easy money."

The old one straightens his shoulders. "Human scum. I was champion of Holmgang when this Earth was young."

Valance gives me a befuddled look. "What's he saying? I've barely understood a word since I got here."

"He said he's killed tons of cocky guys like you before," I offer.

Valance blows me a kiss. "Ah, darling, we both know that's a lie. I'm clearly one of a kind."

"If you step from the circle, you forfeit your life. If your weapon touches the ground, it is forfeit," says a nameless voice from the crowd in flawless English.

Valance leans down to pull a knife from his boot. "Don't drop, don't fall, don't die. Got it."

"Just like your game of human chess," the old one says in broken English.

Valance snorts. "Don't know what kind of fucked up chess you've been playing," he says, then some idiot hits a gong, the sound making me jump about a mile in the air, and the fight is on.

The old one swings his sword in a wide arc, the movement is so fast it's hard for the eye to follow. Valance smiles, a big cheesy grin and vanishes again, but the clear imprint of his feet in the wet, mossy ground proves that he never once breaks the rules. He reappears mere seconds later. The cold muzzle of his AK pressed tight to the back of the old one's scaly head.

Valance leans close to speak near the creature's ear. His voice is violent. "Checkmate motherfucker."

CHAPTER FORTY

Trauma leaves a thick scar

Valance paces. Sits. Tinkers with the cloaking device. Paces. Sits. No one says anything. Finally, after a time that seems perpetual, he rounds on me, shoulders hunched, eyes staring past my face. Not seeing me. He looks like he wants to yell, and he's breathing like a winded stallion. He opens his mouth, but I can see the words won't come. Don't know if I'm sad or mad about that. I don't know how to feel. Guilty, angry, tired, hungry enough to eat anything, living or dead.

"Oh hell, spit it out," Daniel demands. He's sitting beside me. Since the moment he crashed into my arms, he hasn't let go of my hand.

Valance runs both hands through his wild hair. "DNA is a storage medium. One gram of DNA can store over seven hundred terabytes of data. Repeating zeros and ones, endless streams of information."

Rashid lifts a theatrical brow. "Yeah? Your point?"

Valance doesn't look at me, but he throws a thumb in my direction. "She's basically a walking USB drive. The human body can store thirteen point five billion years of data. Coincidently, that's roughly the age of our universe. Humans have all the information of the universe stored in our brains from the beginning of time to this moment. Her DNA? That's something extraordinary. Like I've said a thousand times, there's code buried in those tattoos. We can extract the code, along with her blood, then give it to the damn stone circle instead of her."

Valance pauses to take a breath. Rashid holds up his hand before Valance can keep spouting more confusing, amazing things. "You know what? That actually might work. It will be painful for her, but I just saw that girl get burnt alive without making a sound. I think she can take it."

"You know, you both have an annoying habit of speaking around me," I snap, tone more vitriolic than I intended. Claustrophobia smothers me even though the room we occupy is cavernous. The arched rocky roof hangs low. Stone surfaces shine wetly under the torch light as if they had all been rubbed in some glitter drenched body oil.

Dayle shoves himself off the boulder he's been leaning against and rolls up his sleeves. Sweat soaks his tight T-shirt, the moisture has turned the cotton into a dark burgundy. He looks drawn and pale. Like a guy who just woke from a bad nightmare. "I don't know how much longer we can bunk here. They're going to think we're plotting."

Rashid shakes his bandaged head. There's a patch of blood on whatever cloth the Liguara women had used to wrap the wound. "No. He," Rashid tosses his chin in Valance's direction, "spared their king's life. To the Liguara, he's like a god now. If he'd killed their king, the overlordship would've been his."

"So, you're a god again. Shocker!" I say, trying to catch Valance's attention with my voice and eyes. He doesn't take the bait. Daniel keeps me from doing something rash by making an alarming sound. The mutant child of a guffaw and a snort that clears his throat. "A god of invisibility with superhero powers — damn, kinda want to be you, dude."

"You and me both," Dayle says. He and Daniel share an exhausted smile.

"What?" Valance snaps, making me jump again.

Rashid lifts both hands in surrender. "I ain't got nothing to say."

Valance raises a tell-tale brow. "You think I should've killed the old guy? Sorry, I didn't have it in me. Felt like I'd be destroying a piece of history, like bombing the Sphinx."

Rashid bites his lower lip. "No, but you didn't have to promise to give him half the world if he swore to let your girlfriend live."

"Like that asshole could kill me if I fought back," I say. No one says anything for a few deafening seconds. We all shuffle and fidget. It couldn't be more awkward. Finally, Valance clears his throat and says, "It's done now. The king leaves her alone, and we go save the planet."

"Then give half of it to them," Rashid mutters.

Valance returns his gaze to the glittering cloaking device. It looks like a thousand diamonds stuffed haphazardly into a glass prism. Even from where I sit, about ten feet away from him, I feel the power of the apparatus. Its essence is like the pure light of Aether mixed with a touch of Hecate's cunning, topped with the barest hint of Athena's terrifying calm. It narrows my existence, gives me a focal point, and draws me in. Pulls me to its owner. Him. Always him.

I give up trying to catch Valance's attention and drop my eyes. He hasn't looked at me since we left the room where I almost died. I wasn't sure at first, but now I'm positive he's intentionally ignoring me. Varied feelings roll over me like breakers on a beach. I don't blame him for hating me, but I just want a moment alone with him to explain why I did what I did. I want to tell him everything, but I don't think he'd care to listen. *He'll forgive me,* I think, casting hidden glances at his granite features. I note the hard set of his mouth, the hooded condition of his eyes and fear my heart is lying to my mind. Valance has more qualities than I care to count, but I don't think unbridled forgiveness is one of them. I betrayed him, plain and simple.

It's too much. He's too much. I close my eyes, finally letting his previous words filter into my churning brain. I can't make sense of them. "Valance, explain it all to me again. In English please."

"I need blood and tech from your tattoos. Hecate took blood from each of your goddesses and infused it with the ink of their corresponding tattoo."

"They're not *my* goddesses," I mutter.

Valance ignores me and continues talking. "I've actually been planning this for a while, ever since you took those photos for me. If you look closely at the high-res images, you can see silver threads running through the black ink of your tattoos. I would've told you all about it the other night, but I was busy getting stabbed with two tranquilizers by a hand I thought belonged to a friend."

I rest my chin on my drawn-up knees and laugh. It's a horrible sound. "Friends? Really? Is that what we are?"

"Yes, Divinica, we were friends."

Heat prickles me. "Were?"

Valance sighs. "Yes, Divinica, were. Now you're just a girl who tranquilized me."

"Let's not forget about all the stabbings," I snap bitterly, blithely digging my own grave.

I open my eyes in time to see the corner of Valance's mouth kick up. "Right. God forbid we forget about those."

I sink further into myself, my hands squeezing the tops of my thighs until my knuckles whiten. Guilt churns. I wait for a moment, and then, "You really think I might not have to die?"

Valance shrugs and starts placing the diamond/glass prism thingy back into the little pocket he stitched in the center of his Kevlar glove. "Well, I was thinking we could try a few things before instantly resorting to a sudden and abrupt execution. Unless you want to die. In that case—"

I draw back, stung. "Of course, I don't want to die! Why would you even say that?" I glance around the room looking for support, then sigh. Not sure when they all left us to our bickering, but Valance and I are alone. "I don't want to die!" I say again.

Valance tsks. "Touchy. Me thinks she doth protest too much."

"Really? Shakespeare?" I squeal, and still, he doesn't so much as bat an eye in my direction.

"What do you expect me to think, Divinica? I saw you on that pyre. You fought your powers!"

I leap to my feet as my breathing turns erratic. "I was trying to save my brother."

Silence for a second, then Valance slams his fist down on the stone table, and everything in the room seems to tremble. "You were giving up!" he roars. Finally, finally, finally, his eyes lift to meet mine. "Fucking selfish, Divinica. Did you even stop to consider what your death would do to me? To Daniel? To the damn world?"

"I actually did," I mutter.

Valance is so incensed; he's past hearing me. He moves from behind the table and strides in my direction and doesn't stop until he's towering over me. I stumble back. He advances. "I begged you to trust me. Swore I'd find a way, but you—" His voice snaps. "You don't even want to bother trying other options. For you it's just, 'where's the nearest sword, let me fall on it!'" His hands flash out. I can feel the steady tremble in his fingers as they wrap tightly around my upper arms. My own fingers tangle together across my stomach, twisting around each other until I hear the knuckles crack.

Valance's head moves dangerously close to mine. His voice when it touches my ears is grainy as dry bark, mesmerizing as strawberry wine. "Can you even comprehend what the thought of losing you does to me? The idea hits my brain, the images of your corpse come, and I can't think—can't breathe!" He yanks me closer. "Just the mere thought tears my insides, it guts me. You gut me, Divinica."

I shove away from him, but Valance as always is an immovable object. His stance remains sure. His grip on my arms only tightens. His smell is all around me, playing havoc with my senses, warping my mind. Smoke, gunpowder, and rain. His aura screams masculine power, deep hurt, and endless rage. I want to soothe his madness, erase it, but I can't because it has infected me.

Enough. I pull power from my crown, from my core, feel it in the fingers I press against his chest. I shove again. This time it's enough to bowl him over. He doesn't lose his grip on me though, so we both go down. The landing is jarring. We roll. The stone is hard and ice cold. Valance is hot as the damn sun. He pins me beneath him, then grabs both my wrists and locks them above my head. His eyes find mine. Pierce me, pin me down. "Why, Divinica? Why?"

"Because you overbearing bully, I could lose everything in a second. Lose my brother. Lose you. I can't. Do you understand? I won't go through that again. I'd rather save you than forget you."

We stare at each other. It's a silent war of wills. A battle of broken hearts. Finally, he shoves off me and stands, running both hands through his hair, yelping when a few golden strands tangle with the cloaking device in his glove. "Ugh! Fuck me! I can't do this anymore! I can't keep caring—" he howls. Each word strikes my skin like a poisoned dart.

"Interesting," I say sarcastically. "I didn't know that caring about each other was a switch we could flip off and on." I stand slowly, brushing my hands down my ruined dress—burnt beyond repair.

Valance shrugs, then snarls, "I don't know, I think I could do it. I've always hated cowards."

"You know what, Valance?" I ask, storming past him, preparing to make my grand exit from this particular miserable cave.

"What?"

"Fuck you! That's what."

Valance's arm lashes out and wraps my waist. He spins and pulls me to him, his mouth descends on mine in the same shattered breath. I fight him, but the first touch of his lips melts my icy rage. The taste of him invades my senses. My hands fall to his chest, my fingers curl, grabbing fistfuls of his shirt. The kiss is harsh. Fierce. Punishing. I crave all of it. We tremble in each other's arms. Then, with a muffled curse, he tears his mouth from mine and steps back from me. I stumble. His face is haggard, his eyes haunted. "I can't do this anymore. I just can't, Divinica. You leave me in shambles," he whispers. The devastating pain in his eyes makes hot moisture gather in mine, my lashes flutter closed. When next they open, he's gone.

CHAPTER FORTY-ONE

For better or worse, 'till death do us part.

VALANCE

I storm away from her without looking back. I don't know where I'm going. I'm too angry to think. I stop at the mouth of the cave and lean against the wet wall, just out of Divinica's line of sight, then try to catch my breath and attempt to bring my body under control. Hand clutching the unreasonable pain in my heart, I keep walking, if I don't, I'll go back in there and tell her I forgive her. Would probably forgive her for anything if she would just stay with me.

In the adjoining cave, I find Xola waiting. One hand wrapped around a luminous torch, the other she's holding out to me. I don't take the outstretched hand, but I do fall in step beside her. I've known this princess for two years. I met her three days after I first saw Divinica. I think it was on the day Hecate scripted Divinica's final tattoo that the Liguara knew the creature they had waited millennia to kill had finally been created. The first time Xola and I met, we fought on the grounds of Styx. The old place was invisible at the time, the cloaking device in perfect working order, protecting the girl inside.

It was on that day Xola told me Divinica would bring about the end of their race. I was still trying to get over the fact that her race existed to make much sense of the rest. The wave doesn't affect the Liguara, so she and I formed an odd friendship over the years. She was there to kill Divinica, I was going to stop her, but apart from *that* conflicting dynamic, she was someone to talk to. Just her knowledge staggered me. The two of us talked for endless hours, about the stars, ancient civilizations, and the steady, unstoppable passage of time. I poured my soul out to her about my feelings for Divinica on numerous occasions. Xola was understanding, if not sympathetic, and I almost started to care about her. Now it's back to enemies. I'll never forgive her for the way she just stood there and watched Divinica burn.

Xola glances up at me now, a clear question in her big, dazzling eyes. "Trouble in paradise?"

I don't answer her because fuck—what is there to say? I do tell her my plan, though. I told Divinica I can't keep doing this, but apparently that was a lie. It looks like I have one more try left in me. Xola takes me to the Liguara healing caves, or life dens, as she calls them.

"Tell me what you need," she says when we're standing in a central cave with stone shelves cluttered by tiny glass jars, test tubes, and the bright blue orbs which serve as the Liguara's interconnected power grid.

"Ever since I saw the mercury running through her tattoos, I've wanted to take a needle and suck it out. It's what saves and kills her."

"She'll need a human hospital," Xola says, lifting a syringe that looks like it was meant for bulls and stallions. "This needle will interact well with the star tech, but your bodies are weaker than ours. If the incisions get infected, our medicines will not save her. Bacteria don't bother Liguara cells. So, we are not stocked with human antibiotics, and she'll need them." She shrugs casually, as if we were discussing an obnoxious change in the weather. "If you do it down here, she'll probably die."

I grunt. "Don't get too choked up about it."

Xola shrugs again. "I would shed no tears. My race would control the earth, and you would be mine if it weren't for her. We're friends. Maybe even good friends, and I know you find me beautiful."

I can't lie. "Very."

Xola runs her fingers across my chest, scraping me lightly with her nails. She purrs her question against my neck. "But…you don't want me?"

With Divinica's face in my mind, her question has an easy answer. I barely miss a beat. "No."

She chuckles, it's a low, rich sound. "I think I could get your body to disagree," she says, glancing down to what she wants.

I don't actually think she could. I don't tell her that though. I don't want her to know the extent of Divinica's power over me. Instead, I cross my arms and try to sound casual. "Girl, that's not a boast. I haven't been properly naked with a woman in two years, my body currently thinks it belongs to a fifteen-year-old boy."

Xola's face flexes into a sad, fake little pout. "You don't lie with her?"

"You know I don't."

Xola throws up her hands. "Must you snipe at me? I thought maybe…since the crown and her memories—"

I cut her off. "No."

"Maybe you should. Take the girl, get it out of your system, then forget her."

Her words make me imagine it. Divinica, twisting, arching, gasping my name. I bite down on the inside of my cheek to keep from groaning. "If only *she*, or *it* were that simple."

Xola's eyes find mine. Doe eyes, wide and honest. "Then use me to get her out of your heart and mind. You spared her life today, but that girl is destined to die. She wears her doom like an aura." Xola tentatively runs her fingers down my arm. "It would not be so strange. Our kind frequently mates with humans. Even my own mother is a half breed."

I don't need to hear her pedigree. The girl's a stunner, but she's not Divinica. Divinica, the girl I covet, the girl who will never be mine. The girl I can't bring myself to leave but refuse to betray. Some part of me craves the notion of pulling Xola under me, ripping off her skimpy clothes with my teeth and forgetting. Even if it's just for a few scattered moments. Why am I doggedly staying faithful to someone who consistently does everything in their power to leave me? I'm an idiot. That's why. A glutton for torture. A masochist clinging to the path of a disintegrating heart. Xola presses herself to me again, this time I lock my teeth, and don't move away. If I do this right now, I fear it will break something irreparable between Divinica and I. Maybe, deep down, that's what I want. Maybe that's the way it must be. A goddess supreme like her was never made for mortal men like me. The three days I tracked her were torment, the long nights so much worse. I fantasized about killing Dayle and Rashid. I was their captain—which makes what they did a damn mutiny. I suppose the pledge we made on Mars—blood brothers until the end—was shortsighted.

In the light of day, I don't blame either of them. It isn't their fault. They are caught in this orbit same as me. None of us could have anticipated her. Her. Her. Her. Her. Her.

When Xola grips the back of my neck to tug my mouth down to hers, all I see are Divinica's eyes. *Let me forget*, I think. *It's better this way. Just let me fucking forget*, yells my mind, but the entirety of my physical form rebels at the thought. *No. Just, no.* I grip Xola's upper arms and step back.

"I can't. I probably should because Divinica seems to thrive on breaking me, and in the end, it will probably be her who kills me. Still, I can't. I love her," I say, acknowledging the full truth of the matter and accepting the three simple words that have the power to seal fate.

Divinica
Swords kill. Jealousy is sudden death.

The party is Bacchanal. Drums, torches, scantily clad writhing bodies swaying to the savage beat. Thick, golden liquor flows like water. Someone hands me a cup. I drink it down in one gulp, then gasp. Fire liquid stings my nose as it burns a path to my stomach. I braved this madness about fifteen minutes ago for the sole purpose of finding Valance. I stood frozen for a while after he left me. Staring at nothing, wondering why I didn't just run after him, throw myself in his arms and tell him that I love him. Whether alive or dead, I'll always love him. I want to tell him that I no longer wish to yield to fate or trust destiny. I want to tell him that I'll try it his way. Happily. I don't wish to be a martyr, regardless of the cause. On the floor of the bathroom, I found the duffle bag, stuffed with all my artifacts and the dress I filched from the mall. My solitary relic of a lost civilization. I put it on and thought about all the things I'd say when I found him.

That was then, this is now. Now I'm lost, turned around in this catacomb of caves. This underground forest of myth and majesty. The steady, pounding drums are hypnotic, my stomach churns like an old washing machine, my palms are sweaty, and the crown on my head is suddenly far too heavy. Liguara pause to stare as I pass. Some reach out and brush their scaled fingers down the soft cloth of the dress. They touch my arms and hands; say things I don't believe.

"Grateful you're still breathing," says one.

"Never wished to see you burn," proclaims another.

"Goddess," some say. "Goddess, goddess, goddess."

"Bless you, Freya," another cries.

In turn I ask them, "Have you seen Valance? Tall guy, likes to vanish on a whim?"

"No," they all repeat. "No, no, no, no."

Eventually, I see Daniel and Rashid's faces in the crowd. I rush to them. The guys are drinking and laughing. Spirits are high regardless of current circumstance, or maybe, because of it. Daniel's cheeks are bright red. He's making moon eyes at a pretty little girl. I ask them the same question. "Have you seen Valance?"

"Nope, haven't seen him," Rashid says.

"Not for a while," Daniel tells me.

A dark feeling begins to snake through my gut. "What about Xola? Have you seen her?" I ask, shouting over the beat of the drums. The obnoxious chorus of 'no's' starts up again.

When I finally battle my way to the fringes of the dancing crush, my head is spinning, and my lungs struggle with the smoky air. *He's with her,* my mind tells me. *He's with her,* my heart agrees. I start moving faster, feeling like I've swallowed a tornado of serrated knives. The sound of the drums trails my hasty retreat, banging with every step I take. To me, the drums sound like warning bells. My mind and heart are at war. *He has every right! No, he doesn't. Let it be. I'll kill her if she touches him, kill them both,* the darkness in me replies.

I run through tunnel after tunnel feeling like something is chasing me all the while. I pass rows of blue orbs dug deep into the rock walls. I encounter odd sounds and a few curious faces. Then, from a cave to my left, I hear a laugh that stops me dead in my tracks. I fight down the power that's trying to claw its way out of me and round the corner. The scene that meets my eyes makes me see red, deep, bloody red. Valance and Xola, he's holding the top of her arms the way he holds mine before he kisses me. Xola is gazing at his face with fucking cartoon hearts in her eyes. Her full lips are pursed and tilted toward him. Her invitation clear in every line of her sensual frame. I know it's irrational, maybe a little crazy, but all I can think is, *No, he's mine. Mine. Mine.* Fury is a bright red blindfold, and I can't see through the dense cloth, can't feel in the sudden darkness. I am frozen. Forever ice. Then, Xola takes a deep, intentional breath that drags the tips of her breast up his chest. Something inside me snaps with a resounding twang, and I can only react.

A feral, inhuman sound rips from my throat as I fly across the room, clawed hands reaching. Xola's jugular is my flashing target. I slam into their bodies. It feels so good to wrap my fingers around her throat. She squeals, I squeeze. She tries to dislodge my grip and shove me away, but I'm stronger. I hold on. Together we crash to the ground. She kicks and scratches, draws back her lips, lets her twin fangs extend, then spits her poisonous, venom infused blood. But burning and healing only made me stronger, her nails and teeth can't penetrate my skin, and the poison hisses and dies in the air before it ever touches me. She breaks free of my grip to punch me in the face. The hit feels like the lightest brush of a butterfly wing. We tussle for a few seconds before I tumble her under me, then straddle her waist. I draw back my fist ready to deliver a hit that's certain to pulverize bone. A muscled arm snakes around my waist before my fist can make contact and hauls me off her.

"Divinica, today's not a good day for killing princesses," Valance says as he drags me backward.

"Take your hands off of me," I say, my voice is cold, dead, my teeth clenched so tight I fear they are in real danger of chipping. Valance steps back and folds his arms across his chest looking like sin and bad decisions. He cocks a brow while Xola struggles to pick herself off the floor.

Valance stares at me for a long moment before he says soberly. "Nothing happened."

"Yet," I spit.

"Ever," he vows.

Xola moves behind Valance as she tries to slip silently from the room. I track her passage, my eyes marking her for death. *Strike three, bitch.*

When she's gone, my eyes travel back to Valance's face. We stand there in suspended animation. Time and silence stretch until both begin to buzz. Threads of lightning start to sizzle in my palms, and thick black vines made of smoke and mercury slowly extend from the tips of my quivering fingers. It's not fear that moves me, it's unbridled rage. The harsh glow falling from my tattoos touches everything, paints the lines of his face in a thousand shades of gold. In the center of my crown's base platform, a storm is brewing thunder and more lightning.

Valance's gaze drops to my hands, then flicks back to my face. The bitter look in his eyes dares me to do my worst.

"Don't glare at me like that. You have no right to judge. What if our positions were reversed? What if you walked in and saw me wrapped around another man?"

"She wasn't wrapped around me," he says obstinately.

"Fine, if you came in and saw me and a man, standing like that?" I ask, motioning lamely to the spot of air that still holds imprints of their previously twined energies.

"I would kill him," he says simply.

"So you can, but I can't, is that it?"

Valance takes a deep breath. "Yes."

I throw up my hands. "Oh my god the patriarchy called; they want their outdated bullshit back," I say, stepping up until I'm in his face. "So, tell me? If I wouldn't have walked in just now—"

"Nothing would've fucking happened. She wanted me, and I told her no. The end," he says harshly.

I hug my arms across my chest and ask the question I know I don't want the answer to. "Did you think about it?"

Valance inhales a long, deep breath, like he's bracing himself for a dunk in liquid ice. "Yes," he finally says, the word blending with his exhale.

Yep, you didn't want to hear that, laughs my snarky mind. Tears stab my eyes. "Why?"

Valance shrugs casually, but there's a depth of sincerity in his voice that staggers me. "Because I'm yours. Irrevocably, painfully, unconditionally yours, and I don't want to be. Because, as thrilling as it is in my head, in reality, I think I'd find the romance with a dead girl to be one-sided. Because these last two years have driven me permanently mad. Pick whatever reason suits you but leave the blame with me. I wanted to forget, but there was no point, I knew it wouldn't work. All I see is you."

The lump in my throat is made of poison, and I'm unable to suppress the shudders wracking my fame. "Maybe it's better if you do end up with a girl like her. I'm walking death. You're safer with someone uncursed."

Valance closes the remaining distance between us. I see him clench both fists until the knuckles turn bone white. I think he's doing it to keep from touching me. "No, Divinica. It was just a thought, quickly discarded. I know in my soul there's no forgetting you. Not in anyone else's arms," he says with such authenticity that I want to fall to my knees, fling my arms around him, and beg him never to leave me. I want to pour out my soul to him, tell all the emotions inside me, the ones I have no adequate words to express.

Instead, I fold my arms across my chest to keep myself from doing something emotional and stupid. "Don't say things like that to me anymore. I clearly ended whatever this is with us the day I tranquilized you. You shouldn't have followed me."

"And you should've trusted me," Valance bites out each word.

I can feel his rage like a brand. It makes my bones quake feverishly. I square my shoulders and lift my chin. "Why? Because you're going to be the one who saves the day? All you've been trying to do is stop me. You're insufferable," I say quickly, trying to get the words out before I scramble to take them all back.

Valance's smile is dagger sharp. His left hand flashes out and catches the back of my neck before I can turn away. He runs his other hand up my torso, fingers skating along my throat and over my lips, then he touches his forefinger to the tip of my nose. "Maybe I am insufferable, but you my dear, are a coward."

I knock his hand away as my spine goes ramrod straight. "I told you I'm not trying to die, I'm just trying to save my brother, and maybe if I can—the world."

"Fuck the world!" he says flatly. "All I care about is you."

"Don't you see? That's what's going to get you killed," I cry.

Valance takes my chin between his thumb and forefinger and tilts my face, so our eyes meet. "Then allow me the opportunity to die for you. Let us help you. Stop throwing yourself into danger. Tell me, love, how were you planning to help Daniel by letting the lizards burn you? You would've been dead, which means the waves will remain unconquered, so the radiation will still kill him."

"They had a knife to my brother's throat, I would've done anything," I shout.

Valance matches my tone. "But you didn't do anything, did you? You just stood there and let them burn you."

"So what? To punish me, you went off alone with the girl who's been actively trying to cut me to pieces?"

"Yeah, consider it a trauma response."

"Trauma? You son of a bitch! You told me you loved me."

Valance swallows hard. His hands clamp down on my hips, then he leans forward and almost snarls, "I do love you! That doesn't mean I want to or have to!"

His cruel words make me want to drop through the floor. They make my hackles rise. Literally. My hair flies off my neck, lightning sparks and bites at my fingers, threading through the vines decorating my crown. I can feel the heat of it buzzing against my scalp. My toes curl, my body starts to rise off the floor. Valance's grip on my hips intensifies, and he drags me back down.

He opens his mouth to say something, but I shout over him. "Want to? Have to?!" I can feel my dress whipping around my legs, his hair starts to blow across his face obscuring his rage-filled eyes, the very air is spinning. "That's the stupidest thing I've ever heard! I could be thrown through centuries, ripped from my own body, separated from memory and sanity. It would only take one look at your face for my heart to tell my mind that it's in love with you and will always be in love with you. Always." I whisper that last word, wrenching away from him. He doesn't reach for me again. I turn on my heels, wanting nothing but to escape him and all the stupid pain. Run from it. Run from him.

"Where the hell are you going?"

I don't turn around. "I don't know, Valance. Maybe somewhere I won't be tempted to kill you."

CHAPTER FORTY-TWO

Dear Divinica

This world is an illusion. The illusion is based on what you know. The rules are decided by your soul. Right and wrong is a matter of choice.

You don't know why you're writing this. You don't have to read it because you're probably already dead. However, on the off chance you make it out of this still breathing, and you forget everything, the above passage is all you really need to know. Maybe even the secret of life.

As to the rest: You live wherever you open your eyes. Germany and Styx feel far behind you. You crossed the British Channel using Liguara tunnels. The world beneath was a revelation. As green below as it was above. The tunnels let out onto some ancient Celtic burial ground, a rolling stretch of the Salisbury plains where sits a marvel of engineering. Upright stones towering over twenty feet and weighing upward of forty-five tons. Stonehenge. Horizontal slabs—Valance calls them lintels—crown the huge pillars. These giants are made of sarsen. A local sandstone that is harder than granite. Nestled among the sarsen stones is a circle of smaller stones, blue stone, transported from Wales, perhaps even more remarkable than the sandstone giants.

If you are the weapon, they are the battery that powers it.

Freya remembers these grounds. She has walked them before. She tells you about it incessantly. Overall, the voices in your head are getting louder. You suspect it's the crown but refuse to take it off. Daniel loves it here. He says the ground is soaked in old magic, says anything can, and has happened here. The goddesses in you know he's right. You see them, and hear them, all the time. Ghostly shadows at twilight. You feel your own soul fading away.

Your friends are about to torture you to save your life. You're going to let them even though you're 99% sure it won't work. Imminent death is an unshakeable sense. A taste in your mouth that won't quit. You feel the grim reaper lurking. You fear he means to harvest your soul, here in this place of magic and legends.

Then, there's Valance and damn if it isn't still complicated with him. For a genius, he's a total dumbass. From the looks of it, he doesn't plan to change anytime soon. Time. What a strange, tiny, all-encompassing illusion. An illusion you won't have to worry about for much longer. The aforementioned states it plainly. You feel it in your soul. All the Hail Mary's in the world won't save you. Your time is nearly up.

And if that's how it all shapes up in the end, well then, that's all right. Good, bad, wicked, or just, the goddesses who fucked with you really did save the world. And isn't that what it's all about? Saving this beautiful planet. Third rock from the sun in a solar system of a jillion stars. If by chance you are meant to burn again, look down at your tattoos, watch them glow and remember the end probably justifies the means. The end is salvation. Salvation for your brother, your friends, and the cowboy you love more than life.

Don't close your eyes. Don't dream. Don't wish on any stars. From stardust you are, Divinica, to stardust you will most certainly return.

Tomorrow is the shortest day of the year. The world is a thousand shades of winter ice. Cold that crawls under your skin to infect your bones. Daniel is your warmth. He's been more affectionate than normal. You want to hug and kiss him every second. You don't. You try not to get too close in the hopes that maybe it will be easier for him when you're gone. Valance has been giving you the cold shoulder, but you're not overly bothered, you've been giving it right back. He's being a world-class ass because he's scared. You all are.

You don't know why you're rambling on right now. Maybe, in a way, this is your suicide note. On the bright side, if you do go out, it will be with a bang. Not everyone is so lucky. If by some chance you live, the power of the solstice sun is real. If you become something more, well then, I guess, look out world 'cause here you come.

CHAPTER FORTY-THREE

I'm sorry.

I rest my chin on my knees and watch the boys lay out a transparent plastic sheet—which they got from fuck knows where—a coil of rope, and a syringe with a needle the size of my forearm. They work. I stare and hope for the best. Rashid catches my eye. Whistling, he strides over, then takes a seat beside me. He's having a pink moment today. Hair, brows, lashes, and buffed, immaculate nails. His curled lashes flutter when he notices me looking with what I'm sure is pure incredulity on my face. To call my hair a bird's nest would be an insult to the organizational skills of birds the world over. Earlier, I took a dunk in Lake Avon, dress and all. I left the crown on, scrubbed my hair with air and water, then used my fingers as a brush. The effect? I look like a wild woman. Give me a Celtic cross and some black lipstick, and I would be Freya reborn. At least I got the dirt stains out of my killer dress.

Rashid sees my mind's path, and flips his shiny hair, to twist the knife, I guess. I roll my eyes as he flashes me a smile fit for angels.

I shake my head. "Rashid, you look—" Words fail.

"I know right. Don't let anyone tell you fashion dies at the end of the world."

"Makeup? Hair dye? You probably have a bottle of shampoo stashed somewhere."

"I do. I'll give you some if you forgive me."

I drop my eyes. "There's nothing to forgive."

Rashid laughs. "You have dirt on your cheek, Divinica. Did you know that?"

"Of course not," I say, scrubbing my right cheek vigorously.

"It's on the left side, love." Rashid wipes the pad of his thumb over the offending spot, then he smiles wryly and drops his hand. "Valance is right behind me, isn't he?"

I discreetly peer over his shoulder. "Yep, glaring daggers," I whisper.

Rashid makes a non-committal sound. "I can feel them stabbing into my back."

I snort. "He's a world-class dick."

"Still mad at him about Xola huh?"

"Humph." I cross my arms.

"You know nothing happened."

"I don't really care," I lie. "But having a chauvinistic lord and master wasn't really on my vision board." I finish acerbically, then sigh. "Okay maybe I care, but that last part was true."

Rashid lets out a crack of laughter. There's a sparkle in his eyes, and I want to laugh with him, instead, I stare at the ancient landscape of Stonehenge. The tree stumps we are sitting on used to be a mighty circle of cedar trees so tall their branches seemed to pierce the rumbling belly of the sky, or so I've gleaned from Hecate's consistent diatribe that's been going on in my head since I stepped foot on this place.

Rashid looks at me from the corner of his eye. "Still hearing voices?"

"Yes. They're really loud here. I keep thinking Hecate has found a way to communicate with me telepathically. She's the chattiest, but they all chime in. Some of them think Valance's idea might work, others are skeptical. Actually, I think a few of the goddesses might even be rooting for me to live."

Rashid moves suddenly, then takes my cold hands between both of his, eyebrows scrunched, face earnest. "I'm sorry, Divinica. So sorry for my part in all of this. I do want the world back. I want the waves and the death to stop, and I don't want to lose you. If I believed there was any other way—if we had some time—"

I sigh, reclaiming my hands. "It's not your fault. You're thinking about the greater good. At least one of us should."

"If I could take your place in that circle I would," he says, leaning in to give me a quick kiss on the cheek, then he pulls back and nods his head in Valance's general direction. "He would, too, in a heartbeat. I know you need to be mad at him right now, but don't judge him too harshly. It's hard loving someone you know is going to die, the heart and brain automatically try to protect themselves. He's doing surprisingly well, given the circumstances. Before all this started, I would've bet good money that boy couldn't keep it in his pants for two days, much less two years. He tends to gravitate toward random pussy when he's hurting. He's playing it cool right now, but I don't think he will ever recover from watching you burn. The way you held yourself in those flames, dying on purpose. I know I won't."

While I listen, my eyes go to Daniel, Valance, Dayle, then back to Daniel again. "Rashid, if this all goes to shit, promise me you'll take care of them."

"You know I will," he says, and I don't feel great, but I feel a little better. We don't say any more as Dayle walks over to us and lifts me into his arms without preamble.

I link my arms around his neck. "Is it time?"

"Yes," he says, deep voice sad.

"I can walk you know," I say, gripping his neck even tighter.

"I know, Div, but I'm about to help torture you, carrying you is the least I can do. Besides, Valance is staring hard, and from the looks of it, he's going to try and kill me or bust an artery. Either option would really lift my mood."

"Give her to me," Valance demands when Dayle gets close.

Dayle shoulder chucks him out of the way. "I've got her, dude," he says, and places me in the center of the old cedar circle on the plastic sheets they laid out to catch my blood.

"This is so freaking weird," I whisper as my head touches the ground.

Dayle's voice is gentle as his retreating hands. "What is, doll?"

"The goddesses, Freya, Hecate, Athena, Kali, and the others have all visited this circle at different times in history."

Dayle makes a confused face. "Yeah, so?"

"So, I randomly can see all its unique stages of evolution. Simultaneously."

Dayle shudders. "Freaky. This place is—" He lets the sentence hang for a few seconds, then shudders again. "Let's just say I'm very aware of my skin."

Daniel pipes in. "Makes my teeth hurt."

I crane my neck to stare at my brother, loving the way the wind tosses his hair. "You shouldn't be here, Daniel. You don't need to watch me scream my head off."

Daniel laughs and steps around Valance, then hunkers down and takes my hand. "You, scream? That would be the day."

"I mean it, Daniel. I don't want you to see this."

"I told you, you can't tell me what to do," Daniel says, voice a little shaky. He has my hand in a death grip between both of his.

I roll my eyes at him. "You know, they're probably going to have to strip me."

"Ugh! Seriously?" Daniel groans as he lets go of my hand and jumps to his feet. "Fine, but I won't go far."

I smile at him. It feels strained, but it's all I've got. Daniel blows me a kiss, then turns to look at Valance. "If you hurt her, I mean more than you have to—" he starts.

Valance shakes his head. "Not a chance, kid."

Daniel nods. "Good, because I'd probably have to try and find a way to kill you."

"Sounds fair," Valance says seriously.

Daniel saunters off, hands in his pockets. I try to watch him leave, but a shadow falls over me blocking out everything, even the haunting, bloody light of the setting sun. Valance just stares at me hard, like all my secrets are right there on my face. I close my eyes, so I don't have to look into his. Still, I jerk when his hand falls to the row of buttons and laces running up the front of my dress. His fingers brush my skin, and I feel him. Not just his touch, but him. His energy is chaotic, angry, and scared.

"Divinica, closing your eyes isn't going to make this any easier," Valance says, voice low and right next to my ear.

In defiance, I squeeze my lids tighter. "Oh yeah, smart guy? What will?"

"Look at me, take my strength if you can," he says simply, as if people said stuff like that every day.

"No," I say churlishly.

"Why not?" he asks, then I sense his body going still as he waits for my answer.

I can feel a pout forming in my bottom lip, so I bite down on it. "Because I'm mad at you."

"And looking at me will ruin that?" he asks, deep voice gone all soft.

I open my eyes and stare up at his face. Then, I tell him the truth, because I want to, because he looks like he needs it. "It always has, in the past." I say, and fold my hands across my stomach, inhaling a breath. My tongue is dry, and I gulp at nothing.

Valance groans. "I'm sorry, Divinica. I'm so fucking sorry for going anywhere with her. I must have been out of my damn mind. You have every right to hate me, and when all this is over, I'll give you a knife, then stand still while you do your worst, but right now, I need you to take my strength, because I can't stand the thought of hurting you."

I level him a lethal look.

"Fine," he says, "hurting you more than I already have."

"I can't take your strength, Valance. One, I don't want to. Two, I don't know how."

"Legends say Athena does, I think Athena wants to. Let her."

"No,"

"Divinica," Valance hisses, "if you aren't the most stubborn creature—"

"Valance—" I start, but lose the thought, his hands are on the buttons of my dress again and my brain is suddenly mush. This is honestly pathetic. I'm pathetic. The fight goes out of me, I'm too scared right now to keep yelling at him, instead I say, "I'm sorry for tranquilizing you." My voice is a threadbare whisper. He's silent for so long, I think he didn't hear me. He's blocking my world view. All I see is his face framed by a multi-colored sky, the world is darkening, but he is bright and golden, like he swallowed the sun.

"Damn it Divinica, I'm afraid to think about what I'll become if I lose you," he says crisply, almost to himself. I hear it though, and it shatters me. He always shatters me.

Mist rises from the ground as if summoned, enveloping us, making the air coasting over our skin dewy and warm. His forehead drops to mine, and his lips touch my sweat-dappled brow. "I don't want to hurt you, shit! I don't even know if I can."

"I know, Valance. It's okay. I want to try. I want you to be right. I want this to work. I want to live…with you. I want to go back to California one day and swim in the ocean. I want to drive to the top of Big Bear and make a snow angel. I want to fall to sleep in your arms and wake up to the sound of your voice. Most of all, I want to remember you…us. Remember us for as long as we both shall live. If there's a chance that going through this gets me even half of that, then it's totally worth it."

"Take some of my strength, Divinica."

"No, you need it. It's not going to be easy holding me down."

"You're impossible," he says.

"Look who's talking. You're impossible. I honestly hate you."

Valance touches his lips to the tip of my nose. "Little liar. You love me. Let's face it, I'm probably the love of your life." His eyes are serious as they lock with mine. "I love you, Divinica. I'm going to save you."

I shake my head. "Your hope is a dangerous thing, Valance."

"Why?"

"Because it's really contagious."

"Good," Valance says softly, then louder, "Dayle, you better get over here."

CHAPTER FORTY-FOUR

Umm...ouch.

Dayle holds me immobile with a solid grip on both my shoulders. I take a bracing breath, Valance whispers my name, once, then pierces the thick needle between my eyes. There's a distinct *pop, pop* as he stabs the ink forming Aphrodite's symbol. The second Valance starts to draw blood, I hear a sharp scream that nearly shatters my eardrums. I jerk hard, Dayle's hands press me further into the earth, but he doesn't know that I'm not fighting the pain, only the horrible scream. The pain is there, of course it is, but the real agony is from the goddess who is reluctant to be parted from her host body. Again, I'm overcome by that sense of terrible purpose. The shine in the thread of destiny that tethers me to my fate.

Time starts to whirl as Valance reaches Magu's tattoo. When he digs the needle in the center of the mark, then starts to draw my blood, I'm alert, present, rushing on a heightened sense of clarity. I see time for the silly construct it really is. A matrix designed to be shattered. The eternal sunshine of a spotless mind, a lake of souls for the damned. My newfound prescience limits as much as it reveals because my soul is still stuck in this human avatar with no ability to respawn. I'm just a player in a game.

Valance reaches the Isis tattoo between my breasts. Some part of my cognitive self understands that my body is shaking and sweating, but my mind is far away, drifting with planets and stars that twinkle to the rhythm of a heartbeat.

"God damn it, Dayle," I hear Valance shout. "Hold her!"

"Shit man, I'm trying, she's strong. Rashid, get her legs!"

"What do you think I'm doing?!"

Their voices come at me from far away. I'm running through that endless tunnel in my mind, it's all covered in shiny white tiles, my tunnel doesn't understand pain. I've come to think that this mind tunnel is actually another dimension where wings exist, and mosquitoes don't bite, they sing.

"Divinica, baby, I'm so sorry. God! I'm so fucking sorry. Rashid. Do something." Valance again. His voice sounds odd, maybe broken.

"What the hell do you want me to do?" Rashid wails. "I've never heard her scream like this. Damn it! I've never heard anyone scream like this."

Was I screaming? How strange. I wonder why.

"It's going to be alright, Divinica," Valance lies. Then he pierces the needle into the center of Isis's mark, and I start to feel it. Hecate's tech, fighting, clawing to stay inside my body. I open my eyes and stare at the distant rolling hills, bright green and wrinkled like a velvet bedspread the morning after. The green hills make the moment feel illusionary. *And why not?* I think it's the first green I've seen in years. I close my eyes again as more pain comes. It feels like ragged little glass shards are slicing their way through my skin. Valance growls through his teeth. It's a low, agonized sound, deep and wretched as if he's just taken a bullet to the gut, and I realize I must have screamed again.

I want to say something, I want to tell him that somehow, everything is going to be alright, but I can't. My brain is stumbling, tripping sideways in time to a place in my mind reserved especially for him. I remember the first time I saw him, the first time I stabbed him, the first time he made me laugh, the first time we touched. When he untied me for the first time, he was sitting across from me and my bean bag, his finger brushed my wrist and the spark between us was visible and almost holy. He had dropped my hands, but a second later, he reached out and tucked a lock of hair behind my ear. He told me he thought I might be magic.

I remember how Valance pulled me onto his lap just seconds before our first kiss. I remember the way I couldn't stop staring at him, how my skin tingled when I thought he might kiss me.

"Kissing you is a crime," he had breathed against my lips. I recall the way I thought I might faint right there on the spot and miss it all.

"There are no more crimes at the end of the world," I had told him. For better or worse, I suppose that's probably true.

Valance

I can feel the split second when Divinica passes out. I live in the moment when her agony finally eases. Relief makes me weak. I set the syringe next to the silver bowl that holds less than a teaspoon of mercury and half a pint of Divinica's blood. Rashid kneels next to me and scrubs a hand across his face. He's white as a sheet. "What now?"

"I don't know. The wave will hit in less than twelve hours," I tell him as my eyes drop to the bowl of blood. "I'll bring her blood to the altar and hope Stonehenge takes the offering instead of my girl."

Rashid sits back on his heels to bury his head in his hands. "And...and if it doesn't?"

"Don't think about that," Dayle says. "But if it comes down to it, I'm pretty sure Divinica's going to give her life, she's noble and cool like that." He shrugs when I turn my glower at him. "You know I'm right, dude. I watched her burn. She let those flames toast her, took all that pain on the off chance that it would save her brother."

"Dayle's right," Rashid says, head still in hands, voice muffled. "If your bowl of blood doesn't work, I don't think heaven, hell, or even you can stop that girl from sacrificing herself."

"Don't sound so glum about it! Isn't that what you wanted?" I ask, then feel like absolute shit when I see Rashid flinch.

"Val, how can you even ask that? You know I love that girl. I helped her because it was what she wanted, and because it was the right thing to do. The only thing to do. You've been my best friend for years. We survived the academy together, hell, we left the planet together. I know you, and I know you love her. I love you, Val. Even if I hated her, I wouldn't want her to die, for your sake."

"There's always a chance that even if the blood bowl doesn't do the trick, Divinica might survive," Dayle says, coming over to drop a consolatory hand on Rashid's shoulder. "I mean, we both saw her in action, she was—"

"Spectacular," Rashid says, then shrugs. "Anything's possible," he finishes blandly. "I guess we'll know when we know."

My fist meets my palm, and I'm standing before I think about doing so. I'm angry all over again. I understand it's because I just figured something out about my best friend. He does love Divinica, maybe a lot, but he would kill her himself if he knew for sure it would stop the waves. Right now, he's pale and strained. His eyes are huge, his lips thin and tight as tripwire. He wouldn't like it at all, but he would do it.

"You'd do the same if you weren't so in love with her," Rashid says, reading my eyes, then my mind in that annoyingly accurate way of his. I look away from Rashid to Dayle. When Dayle catches my gaze, he lays a blood smeared hand on the top of Divinica's head. "She might not die," he says again, and all at once the sheer scale of what we are trying to do crashes down on me.

"What if it doesn't work? What if I put her through all this pain for nothing?" I yell. Goddamn it. I really sound like I'm on the verge of tears.

"No, even if there's the slightest chance this works, that's enough to have warranted a proper try," Dayle says.

"Divinica knew what she was doing when she asked me to bring her here," Rashid says, casually adding insult to injury. "She never wanted to hurt you, Val."

It takes real effort not to pull a Divinica and violently roll my eyes at him. "Rashid, please. Hurting me has been the one consistent thought in Divinica's mind these past two years," I say wryly.

Rashid gives me a smile that looks real. "Yeah, well, what woman hasn't thought of doing bodily harm to the man she loves, at least once or twice. When that man is you—" Rashid shrugs, and lets the sentence hang, which clearly implies I should have the self-awareness to finish it for him. I hesitate, then offer him my hand.

Rashid gives the extended limb a weird look before he takes it with a grimace. "Don't expect a thanks," he says, jumping to his feet. "You should be nice to me; you nearly broke my jaw."

"Payback for my nose, which you did break."

Rashid pulls a face. "We were eighteen, man."

"Still counts," I tell him.

CHAPTER FORTY-FIVE

All those dreams of grandeur

DIVINICA

I'm awake, I think. I'm standing in my white dress, my bare feet resting on a cobbled path that winds off into the distance like the stone body of some prehistoric snake. My hair is shockingly brushed, clean, and falling in soft waves past my hips. I'm not wearing Freya's crown, but I know exactly who I am. I'm Divinica. This time, I'm Divinica.

I open and close my hands, noticing how buffed and perfect my nails look. Gone is the blood, travel sweat and ashes, I smell like jasmine and a fresh bouquet of hot-house roses.

I drop my hands to my sides and dare to glance at the sky. It's twilight, and my world is a spinning ball of mists. Only…if I squint, I think I can see the trace of embers flashing in the fog. I decide to follow the path and the phantom firelight. A dense army of trees flank me on either side, their gnarled branches tightly linked above my head.

Halfway down the path, I'm convinced I'm dreaming. For one thing, I'm not in pain anymore—an anomaly in and of itself—quite the opposite actually. I feel perfect, light on my feet, strong as if I could run for miles, maybe even fly. I feel invincible.

I keep walking. The mists are practically blinding now, but I'm not afraid. I hear voices in the distance, singing, laughing. I smell fire, and something else, something sweet like melting sugar or candied popcorn. My mouth waters as I start walking faster. It seems the mists begin to clear. Maybe I can just see through them now. I feel like running, so I do. I'm allowed only a few seconds of unbridled freedom—mists in my eyes and wind in my hair—before I falter. The cobblestone path comes to an abrupt, messy end. I teeter, swinging my arms as my toes hover on the edge of the broken stones.

I find my balance and my sight, and as the fog lifts completely I realize where I am. Stonehenge dominates the distance, nearly illusionary in its solitary, ancient splendor. The first thing I notice are the flowers, thousands of them. On the ground, draping the stones, hanging from the very sky. Blankets and bushels of them. Acacias, orchids, pansies, African daisies, amaryllis, bergamots, fuchsia, and roses, always roses. The flowers are dancing, throwing their colors at the night stars, the goddesses are dancing with them. Somehow, I know they are waiting for me, that they have been waiting a long, long time. They turn as one to look at me. All of them are smiling.

I've passed the test. Trial by actual fire—I guess. Whatever the case, for better or worse, I think I'm one of them now. Am I already dead? Did the mercury extraction kill me? Is Valance still somewhere in the mortal realm holding my breathless body in his arms?

Who knows? Not me. I lift the hem of my dress and run toward the flowers, toward my sisters of life, blood, and death. The fire in the circle's center blazes high, casting more embers that flitter like fireflies.

Athena is the first to reach me. Her chestnut hair is loose, her cloak long and golden, on her head she's wearing a crown of planets and stars. Altogether beautiful and trippy as my tattoos. I reach for her without intending to at the same time she takes my hand in both of hers and pulls me close, then throws her arms around my neck. "You courageous, strong girl," she says. "You are more than worthy to bear the title of goddess. Tomorrow you will ascend, and Gaia will have another powerful protector."

I open my mouth to say something, anything, but Athena places her fingers over my lips. "You are one of us now, Divinica." She takes my hand again and tugs it. "Come, tonight we drink, dance, and celebrate the continued survival of this earth."

"It is the most precious in our cosmos," says Nokomis as she presses a glass flute in my hand. The liquid swirling inside is as bright purple as the feather in her hair. I take a deep breath, then sip the drink. The instant the violet wine slides down my throat, it's like someone pulls a sparkle filter over my eyes. Everything suddenly seems soaked in layers of glitter, even the now full, risen moon.

Ixchel falls to her knees in the grass, then tugs on my free hand until I sit down beside her. "We did it. We have saved the earth, now your life will rescue humanity," she says, voice like an earthquake. No whites or pupils mar her eyes, only galaxies and milky ways. Her captivating honey skin is decorated in brilliant markings and gold symbols that glow as bright as my tattoos. When she shakes her head, flowers fall from her hair. They bloom the second they touch the grass. Gardenias, orchids, and roses. Ixchel places a fingertip on my cheek. Her touch is soothing as moonlight and clear water. "You've restored a hope in me that was nearly lost, especially these last thousand years."

"My oceans," moans Aphrodite, knocking back her drink before pulling another straight from thin air. "They were dying. Because of you, Divinica, my creatures can breathe."

Artemis sighs. "My forests. I will always weep for my monster trees. Because of you they can grow again—"

"What about all the people?" I ask sharply, unable to keep the questions in a second longer.

"Some will live, and those who live will remember," Ixchel says. "They will tell stories of this time. They will realize this Earth is not theirs alone. Gaia is the true cradle of life in this distant solar system. They will learn that she must be respected and treated as such."

"Perhaps in time they will forget as they have in the past," says Hecate's left head. "And we will be here to remind them of all that stands to be lost," says the right.

"Our hex protected this Earth and conserved the foundation of life, as we have always done, but now it is time for you to break our spell, and let the rest live," Athena tells me.

Magu sits beside me, then rests her head on my shoulder. "It's time to die. You will be one of us. Blessed, cursed, eternal."

I know they all believe what they are saying, I know they think they are in the right, but each word further infuriates me. I stare at the leaping flames, now blazing so high I fear they will singe the moon.

"What about all those dead girls, and those people the red wave killed?" I ask in a whisper.

"Life always demands death," says Atropos the inflexible, the youngest sister in the fate trio. As she speaks, her baby-soft white cheeks start to wrinkle, deep lines slash the creases by her eyes, her full, red lips shrivel, then turn black as chunks of hair start plummeting from her scalp, her eyes fall from their sockets, and blood pours. "Humans die every day with no purpose. Those girls had nothing, no one in the world who cared at all. They were nothing. Now they are heroes who will live forever among the stars."

I can't look anymore at the horror Atropos's face has become. My eyes lock on Hecate. "You killed my father."

Hecate's lips turn down. "I did it to save you and your brother. I see the future, remember? I knew what leaving him alive would mean for both of you."

"He had to die," Isis says.

"This is the path of all women who desire to be goddesses," Hecate adds stoically.

I stand in a rush, fists clenched. "I never desired—" I start hotly, then pause on a choked breath as I remember the young girl in the mirror. She had dreams of grandeur that somehow turned into wishes with gravitas.

"For every girl we killed, a million other humans met their inglorious end. War, famine, genocide. Even Gaia did her part. Earthquakes, tsunamis, volcanoes. The lives we took were a sacrifice for a worthy cause."

My fists clench even tighter, I've never wanted to hit something as bad as I do right now. "Still, it wasn't the way."

Athena touches my hand. "It was the only way. The only choice."

"I have seen all possible futures," says Hecate, and I find myself wondering if her voice will still sound like honey when my hands are wrapped around her various throats. "Divinica, every destiny I traversed led to the same thing, the extermination of this planet. The future only changed when you were in it. Yet you were one in billions. A mere grain of sand on the beaches of eternity. I had to find you."

"By murdering thousands? You're monsters, all of you! There was another choice, something, somewhere. You just chose not to make it."

"Chose not to make it," Hecate repeats.

"Chose not to make it," Athena confirms.

"Chose not to make it, not to make it, not to make it," the other goddesses chant, eerie, hollow voices pitched low. The flames rise higher. The goddesses close in on me, smiles widening, teeth sharpening. Their eyes are black all the way through, their skin lit by swallowed stars. Some start to laugh. Others begin to scream. All move closer. Their clawed hands reach for me. The violet liquid in my glass turns to blood. I drop it. The delicate crystal shatters in slow motion as my body starts to rise. My head is thrown back violently, neck twisted until my wide eyes see only the burning, rushing sky. My arms fly out and my spine bows until I hear it creak. A beam of brilliant light spears the dark body of the sky and pierces me through the heart. Lightning strikes and shivers through my seizing limbs. I hear the world tremble and planets spin off course. I don't scream. I know it's a dream. I simply tell my mind to wake up, and I do.

CHAPTER FORTY-SIX

Bad liar

DIVINICA

I'm in Valance's arms, and he is gazing down at me like he managed to capture the essence of primordial magic in his hands. I blink and watch the way his face hardens when he sees me wake, then we just stare at each other in that timeless way of ours. It is a stare that holds a thousand thoughts and a million tones of silence. His fingertips coast slowly over my cheek, the bridge of my nose, lightly touch the corners of my mouth. When he leans his forehead to rest it against mine, the moment is so tender, tears prick my throat and flood my eyes.

"How are you?" he asks, and I can see in his face that his sanity hinges on my answer.

"I...I..." My voice cracks, then I cough so hard I taste blood. "Actually, my throat is a little sore," I manage to tell him.

Valance grunts, then props me up and starts to rub my back. "I'd be shocked if it weren't raw. You screamed. A lot."

"Did I? Really? I don't remember much—just—" I press my hands to his chest and struggle to rise into even more of a sitting position, but his locked arms keep me immobile.

"Don't move. Not yet," he rasps against my neck. "Just let me hold you for a few seconds."

He's already holding me so tight I can hardly breathe, but it's all right. I settle my head into the crook of his shoulder and close my eyes. I feel that the sand in the glass timer of my life is draining fast. I want to spend each grain that remains with him. I open my eyes, tilt my head, and take a breath. After that dream I had, I don't think his bowl of blood is going to work, which means it's almost time to part. I shouldn't let him get too close. I swallow hard, preparing to tell him to let me go.

Valance shakes his head. His hands grab my waist, and he pulls me tighter against him, stares into my eyes and reads the words straight out of my mind. "No. Don't say it. I'm not going to lose you. Do you understand? I'm never going to let you go."

"Valance, the goddesses, fate, the stars themselves are standing between us."

"Then I will burn them all down! Do you hear me, Divinica?"

I shove at him again. "No! You're crazy! It doesn't matter how many lives we find each other in, one of us is always destined to die. It's the nature of a blood spell to take lives. I should know since I cast the damn spell."

"So what? You're saying there's no hope?" he asks, and his voice sounds like tearing metal.

"No. That's not what I'm saying. There is hope for everyone, just not for us," I say, finally disentangling myself from his hold and scrambling a safe distance away. Valance's fists clench, but he lets me go.

I wrap my arms around myself, missing my cloak. It's terribly cold without him. The wind is sharp, and the night sky is hanging so low, it seems possessed by that kind of monstrous dark that devours starlight, while closing its foggy teeth over the moon. "I read somewhere that it's a two-mile walk from this cedar circle to Stonehenge. I've always wanted to sleep between the blue stones and watch the sunrise. Will you walk with me?"

Valance stands quickly, then places his right hand to his heart like a salute and drops into a curt bow. There is something noble, rather than mocking about the gesture. "Walk with you, die with you, as always, I am at the disposal of my goddess."

I stand too and shake the grass from my dress as the thread of tension between us dissolves. "Oh please, be serious," I giggle.

"I've never been more serious in my life," Valance says, and holds out his hand to me. "Shall we?"

I take his hand. His fingers are warm and close around mine like an unbreakable seal. We stroll in absolute silence for a time, each risking occasional glances at each other, and quickly looking away when our gazes collide. The air between us seems thicker than the air around us, and I can almost taste the magic in it.

"I had a weird dream," I tell him.

Valance glances down at me, the slight hint of a smile cracks his stone face. "Don't you always?"

I kick a lonely rock. "Yeah, I guess."

After a few beats of silence, Valance nudges my shoulder. "What was your dream, Divinica?"

"I was in Stonehenge with the goddesses."

"Which ones?" he asks.

"All of them I think, at least anyone my soul has colluded with sometime in the last however many thousand years. I was yelling at them about their methods, but really, who am I to talk? I've killed people too and not for any grand purpose, except to save my own life. I guess you can say I've been choking on my own hypocrisy since I woke up."

Valance stops walking so abruptly I almost crash into him. He crosses his arms and stares up at the sky. "I'm not judging. I'd kill anyone to save you."

"I know. It's one of the primary reasons I'm mad at you. It's why I left you the way I did."

I turn away from him to keep walking, but Valance grabs my arm and holds me firmly in place. "Divinica, wait—"

I twist my arm and shake off his hand. "No. Don't say anything else."

Valance reaches for me again. "Divinica—" His voice cracks on my name.

Mine is breaking too. "No! I have to do this, for Daniel, for our friends, for your people. For everyone. And if you keep saying—keep telling me—that you... want...love—" My words die as I throw up my hands then bury my face in them. "You have to stop. I don't want you anymore. Please, just stop!"

Valance reaches me in a single stride and yanks me into his arms. His words fall hot against my throat. "I can't stop! I won't ever stop! I've protected you, loved nothing in this world but you for two long years. You can't ask me to give up now. I won't!"

"I don't want you anymore!" I yell again, trying only to hurt him. "Now that I have my memories, I want nothing to do with you. Why can't you just leave? I don't need you! I don't love you!"

Valance touches my chin, and our gazes crash. I see the intent in his eyes as he dips his head. I slam my hands against his chest. "Valance, wait!" I gasp, but he means to wait for nothing. His head lowers the rest of the way and our lips lock. My vision blurs. I struggle against him, kicking his shins and pummeling his chest. Valance is unfazed. He drags me down to the soft grass, then rolls me beneath him.

Forcefully, he grabs my wrists and locks my hands on either side of my head. I arch my body and bite down hard on his lower lip. Valance flinches back, hissing. We stare at each other, panting. A drop of blood forms where my teeth cut a groove. His tongue flicks out to lick it away. "Divinica, bite me, fight me, stab me, but if you want me to let you go tonight, you're gonna have to kill me," he says darkly, then he kisses me again, and steals that last, tiny piece of my soul that didn't yet belong to him. The kiss is like a vow, made with only the muted stars and the moonless sky as our witnesses. Valance is all around me, he smells like thunder and rain, like lust and desperation, like whisky and man. He smells like something that belongs to me.

Breathless minutes tick by. Somewhere in the haze, I feel him let go of my hands to sink his fingers in my hair. My mind tells me to push him away, to harden my soul, embrace cruelty and break his heart, but I don't. I wrap my arms around him and pull him closer. I allow myself a single moment to just hold him while my mind screams how much I love him, love him, love him, love him.

Valance breaks the kiss to whisper more scalding words against my neck. "Can't believe you actually think I could stop, especially tonight." His fingers drop to the buttons running down the bodice of my dress. He kisses my lips between words. His hands are shaking. His body, hard as diamond, grinds into mine. I've wanted this, wanted him for so long. The gods are truly cruel to tear this away from me in the ninth hour, but if I take what I want, what we both want, if being with him becomes reality rather than dream, I know there is no way in the world I will be able to leave him. No way will he let me. I feel my dress sliding down my shoulders and my mind starts screaming. *Hurt him. Make him hate you. Push him away. Save him. Save them all.*

Valance's head dips again. His lips disintegrate the words writing across my mind. I wrench my head away. "No! Stop! I don't want this! I don't want you!"

"You're a bad liar, Divinica. Really bad."

He's right. I'm the worst. I buck and twist my body, thinking of more words to stab him with. "Seriously? Valance, stop! Are you actually going to force me?" That last catches Valance off guard. His whole body instantly goes deathly still, then the world starts to move in slow motion as he climbs off me.

Valance sits back on his heels and crosses his arms; his crooked brow is at an all-time high. Teeth clenched; I stare up at his face. My heart is pounding a mile a minute, my stomach is churning and everything is different shades of blur, but I straighten my spine and return his devil stare. He smiles at me. All teeth and ice. "No, Divinica. I'm not going to force you, but I've heard what you really want a dozen times, one lie isn't going to sway me."

"I was wrong! Confused! You were right. Thirteen days isn't enough to really know anyone. You're just another stranger to me. How many times do I have to say it? I don't want anything to do with you. I hate you! You're a villain. A monster who took advantage of a confused girl."

After I spit that last lie, Valance's expression turns thunderous. He goes from man to avenging angel in a flash. His eyes narrow, and he looks like he wants to throttle me. He puts a hand to his chest and rubs a spot just above his heart while glowering.

"Ouch, nice try. You forget that I know you better than my own heartbeat. I know how noble and ridiculous you are at your core. You're only saying this crap because you're scared. You think cutting my heart into miserable little shreds will somehow save my sanity, or my life. I can't figure out for which you're shooting. It won't work. I'm tethered to you. Even you don't have the power to cut that cord." He says the last sentence with so much feeling it is impossible not to believe him. I don't move as he grasps my icy fingers. "Stop fighting, baby. Tonight, I'm stronger than you."

"Why?" I ask in a defeated whisper.

Valance takes my face between his hands. "Because right now, you're fighting yourself too."

"Valance. Please. I'm going to die tomorrow. There is nothing anyone in the world can do to stop it."

Valance nods. "So be it. I'm tired of this fucking world anyway."

I shove at him again, and my desperate words come pouring out one on top of the other. "No! Don't you understand? In this life, you actually get to live."

Valance chuckles. "Who the hell wants that? Please at least allow me the dignity of my own choice."

"I need you to swear to me that you'll live no matter what happens," I beg. "You can have anything you want with me tonight, if you just swear—" My head falls, and I fight the tears in my eyes that are burning their way down my throat. "Valance, please. That's all I want."

"No deal baby," he whispers. "This place is the worst. Don't ask me to live here without you."

I lose the battle with my tears and shove him again. "You're such an idiot! Why won't you listen?!"

Valance uses his thumbs to wipe the tears from beneath my eyes. "Because you're not saying anything I want to hear," he says, and something inside me breaks.

I stop pushing him, instead I grab his biceps and dig my nails in. "You stubborn bastard, have it your way!" I practically sob. Then my fingers find the back of his neck and this time I'm the one kissing him. My sudden attack takes him by surprise. His arms go around me and together we tumble, then roll across the damp grass, lips and limbs intertwined. Somehow, he gets the buttons of my dress undone, then sweeps the flimsy piece of cloth over my head without breaking our kiss. I tear off his shirt with my teeth and nails. His bronze skin is brushed with starlight. Memories come then, fast and blinding as a rain of bullets. Memories that fortify each time his skin touches mine, and he touches me everywhere. The memories become my reality.

I stare up at him. Framed by Stonehenge and the moonless sky, I can see all my different lives with this man and how much I loved him in each of them. I remember all of our first kisses. I recall each of his deaths, but I also remember how vividly we lived. Childhood sweethearts, best friends, fated lovers. Regardless of how hard I fought, no matter what I tried, there was never a life where I got to keep him. Ancient god of light, Celtic prince, demon warrior, Egyptian god, but always just Valance, smart, strong, loyal, true. He is my only wish, forever unfulfilled.

With him, right now, everything is new and achingly familiar. The cool blades of grass against my naked back, the night wind in my hair, the drying tears on my cheeks. His mouth, an open flame on the tip of my breast, his tongue tracing a line of beautiful agony down the center of my body, brushing each of my tattoos in turn. His low whisper against my inner thigh, his lips moving higher, higher. I tug on his shoulders. I need him. I must say something that mirrors my thoughts, because Valance laughs, then kisses his way quickly back up my body. He drags his teeth down my neck. "You sure?"

"Yes. I've never wanted to die a virgin."

Valance brushes his fingers down my ribs. "You think that's funny, Divinica? You're not going to die. Take it back!" he commands.

I narrow my eyes and start to shake my head when his fingers skate up and down my ribs, and my whole body breaks out in goosebumps.

"I won't," I wail. Valance moves his fingers again, and my scream turns to a giggle. "Oh, my gods. Stop it," I holler. It's pure torture. I twist and squeal, but Valance lies fully atop me, locking my legs between his knees and holding both my hands firmly in one of his. "Valance, stop, I can't breathe," I demand, but he's not listening, he's laughing. The sound is everywhere, reverberating off earth and sky and it's beautiful.

"Bet you wish you had your knife right now, don't you?" Valance asks, voice husky as he flexes his hips and licks the column of my throat.

"Yes!" I gasp, shivering as his teeth nip at my earlobe. I buck and kick my legs free of his hold, wrap them around his waist, and roll him onto his back, then sit up straight with my knees pressed into the grass on either side of his narrow hips. His hands drop to my thighs as his eyes ignite. Suddenly, neither of us is laughing anymore.

"God damn," Valance hisses, "look at you glow." He stretches out his arms, then rests both hands behind his head, and looks up at me through lashes so long they have no business belonging to a man. "Well, darlin,' you've managed to subdue the dragon. What do you plan to do with him now?"

I smile. I can't say the words out loud, but I think he knows.

Valance

If I am human, and the ground I lie on is earth, then Divinica is the stars. She leans forward to put both her hands against my chest, her tumbling hair makes a curtain around us. Smoke infused violet lightning shoots from her fingertips, sending bolts of electricity racing through my limbs. The feeling is indescribable, it feels like her, and she is magic. Her hair is swirling everywhere, alive with more lightning. The glow falling from her tattoos has become a moving sphere of light encircling us in symbols and star-studded galaxies. As I stare up into Divinica's eyes, she starts to change. Quick as a flickering bulb, she morphs into different versions of herself. Greek goddess, Egyptian ruler, lady of the moon, Gorgon queen. I remember the way she looked in all our other lives, and it's like a thousand locked doors open in my mind. Suddenly, the tables turn and it's me who has been inflicted with amnesia all along. Me who was blind.

Divinica tugs my jeans, her hands frantic, her expression desperate. I lift my hips and let her do what she wants. She gasps as she glances down at the part of me she just bared. I watch her swallow hard. Divinica licks her lips, and I barely bite back a groan. It hisses between my clenched teeth as she wraps her fingers around my cock and all the blood in my body rushes to her touch. She dips her head, and I catch her shoulders. "No," I pant, but I need her mouth there more than I've ever needed anything.

Divinica smiles like a siren and shimmies down my body. She purrs, and I see her pink tongue flash before she licks the length of me. I almost lose the little hold I have on my control right then. My head falls back into the grass, and I can't stifle my groan as she tries to fit all of me in her mouth. I stare down my body and meet her blazing gaze. Divinica's too brave to drop her eyes, her cheeks are flushed, but she stares at me anyway as she slides her lips over me. She doesn't stop until I hit the back of her throat. I watch her eyes water, and I get harder than I've ever been in my life. She makes a hungry purring noise and my hips buck. "You're going to kill me," I hear myself rasp.

Divinica's smile is beatific, and something primal in me wants to devour her. I grip her shoulders and drag her up my body. She resists the pressure of my fingers and wraps her hand around my cock, going up on her knees, an adorable look of focused determination on her face. I don't tell her it's going to hurt—I know my Divinica better than that. We are staring directly into each other's eyes when it happens, and I swear I witness the fusion of our souls.

I'm mere seconds from coming by the time I'm fully inside of her. Sweat glistens on my skin as she moves experimentally, lifting her hips slowly, then slamming back down with enough force to make me beg. She rakes her nails down my chest, and my body is a live wire of sensation. I start to move my hips, needing to fuck her. Hard. Now. Divinica clamps her knees on my waist, keeping me still.

"You said you've imagined us like this a thousand times. Do I hold up against a dream?" she asks breathlessly.

I run my fingers down the center of her body to settle between her legs, and her breathing turns jagged. "No, baby," I murmur, voice guttural with need, caressing her, gently tracing the place our bodies are linked. "You're a goddess, mythmarked, divine. You're the rarest, hottest thing I've ever touched. You're better than any fantasy I could conjure."

Divinica's head falls back as I touch and stroke. She's so fucking perfect. I kiss her lips and tell her so. Her legs start to shake and her hold on me loosens, then I'm free to move as I wish. Behind us, above us, all around us, her lightning splits the sky, and smoking sparks spatter the ground like electric rain. Her eyelids tumble closed as she starts to rock her hips. I let her ride me for a few moments while I simply stare at her until I can't take it anymore. I sit up, grab the back of her neck, and pull her lips to mine. I taste it when she whispers my name. The motion of her hips is an intoxication that might drive me mad. I run my fingers through her hair, down the silky line of her back. Divinica undulates against me, and it's all I can do not to flip her over and lose myself in her tight heat. She locks her ankles at my lower back as I thrust up into her, and again, until the glow of her tattoos puts the light of the moon to shame.

My hands grip her shoulder blades, and I grate my teeth over the tip of her breast, then suck it into my mouth and listen as her splintering gasps turn to screams. "Valance, gods, Valance," she breathes. I'm seconds from rolling us both over when light shoots between my fingers and Divinica arches. Visible, sizzling energy explodes from her back like electric wings, or a butterfly nebula unleashed. I stare, transfixed. Her glory takes my breath away. In my eyes there is only her, there will only ever be her.

Divinica's lightning moves to the cadence of her hips. I kiss her as we rise into the air. A little human, a lot god. Together, we are the raw essence of passion. Unchained love wrapped in immortal fire. It's a long time before we land. When we do, I keep my promise. I don't let go of her all night, and I find out at least a half dozen times how many lumens make those tattoos turn to stars.

CHAPTER FORTY-SEVEN

The final countdown.

Valance and I reach the summit of the Henge before dawn. He lets go of my hand as the first streams of light touch the mist drenched air. Everything is deathly silent. Even the rising sun seems to hide its golden face from the approaching red wave. The sky itself looks terrified with the black clouds, grumbling in places and skittish in others. Daniel stands beside me holding my hand like it's the end of a rope that's swinging off the edge of a cliff.

"It's coming," he says.

I nod, just the same as the times before. "I know. Don't worry. This time, I won't let it touch you," I say, then smile. That's a promise I've never been able to make.

"Sis?"

"Yeah?"

"Do you think Dad knew he was bringing you to Germany to die?"

I swallow hard. "Valance asked me the same thing."

Daniel glances up at me. "What did you tell him?"

I shrug. "Does it really matter?"

Daniel sighs. "No, I guess not."

"Daniel, Dad loved us. I don't know how much he knew, or what all his reasons were, but I'm choosing to think about the good times we had instead of decisions made under end-of-the-world duress. There were tons of good times. Like, remember how horrible his Sunday pancakes were?"

Daniel starts to laugh, but I get the feeling he's trying not to cry. "I always got the biggest lump of flour. The edges were burnt black, and the middle was gooey." Daniel scrunches his nose. "Pure grossness. We always told him they were the worst."

"But we always ate them," I say.

"Yep, so he never stopped making them. That might've actually been our bad." Daniel sniffs, and pinches his nose, blinking rapidly. "I think practice actually made him worse."

Smiling, reminiscing, we both fall silent, eventually turning away from each other to stare up at the towering stones.

"They look like sleeping giants," Daniel says after a time.

"Earth beasts, sons of Kronos," I mutter, recalling something Aphrodite once named them.

Daniel nods again, but doesn't seem to have anything further to add, so we just continue to glare at the ancient monument. *Admit it, Divinica,* my mind demands. *As far as choice spots go, it's not a bad place to die. Pretty epic actually.* Internally, I roll my eyes. I choose not to share my thoughts with Daniel, due to their emotional nature. Instead, I watch the boys set the bowl of my blood on the stone altar situated in the dead center of Stonehenge.

Rashid fusses and fiddles with the bowl, trying to get it level with the uneven divots running across the surface of the stone slab. Dayle holds up his hands toward the still rising sun and makes odd directional and pyramidal shapes with his fingers. I can only assume he's trying to judge the sun's positioning so we can get the timing exactly right. Dayle then drops his hands and locks them behind his back. He does a walk around the circle checking the placement of each of my artifacts on the blue stones. Twelve artifacts on twelve corresponding stones. The proof positive of my star door travel. So many stories, the evidence of so many lives. Medusa's hissing head. Artemis's golden bow. Kali's curved scimitar. The Fate's gooey eye. Even my squawking bird holds his perch. Aphrodite's shell takes a tumble when Dayle leans down to adjust it. Rashid moves over to help sort it out.

Valance doesn't move a single bulging muscle. He stands behind the altar. His face is hidden in the deep shadow cast by the heel stone, queen of all the stones. His arms are encased in leather and crossed over his bare chest, his eyes are on me, blue and brilliant as wolf eyes seen by the light of midnight. Our gazes crash. Lock. Ignite. He starts to walk toward me. Time moves until it's an infinite whirl around me, and I can see the past as clearly as the present. The stones fix their ruins, the wind changes course and tugs the angry red clouds away. Suddenly, the Valance I'm looking at is not the one this body knows. The Valance I see now is a Celtic prince again, wild and unfettered as this sacred land. He's walking toward me with intent, sword and bow in hand. The vision reverts to the present as quickly as the past crept in, and it's Valance again. Just Valance. Him.

I look down at Daniel, then back to Rashid and Dayle who follow Valance like dark guardians. I love them all. I would die for them all. The three of them come to a stop in front of Daniel and me. Rashid and Dayle stand on Daniel's left, Valance stands on my right. None of us say a single word. As one, we wait for the wave to come and the sun to set. For a few hours, no one sits, no one sighs, no one moves, even my artifacts seem to be holding their collective breath. Together we watch the sun climb to the center of the black and maroon sky.

Soon the sun starts its descent toward the western horizon. The glowing orb darkens, and the wind picks up its pace, whistling softly while it moves the sparse blades of grass. I've alternated between looking at the sky and the restless grass. I'm afraid to look anywhere else. I can feel Valance's eyes on me. In all this time, I know they have scarcely left my face. Hot chills attack all the spots his eyes touch, my neck, my cheek, my lips. Finally, at long freaking last, Dayle breaks the silence by loudly clearing his throat. He then leans down to rifle through his backpack until he retrieves his canteen of water. He looks up at the sky and takes a long noisy drink until the water runs down his chin. Eyes trained on the forerunners of the approaching wave, Dayle wipes the back of his hand across his mouth then says, "You know, today reminds me of the day my daughter was born."

Valance, Daniel, Rashid, and I turn our heads as one to give him each our own version of the same befuddled expression. Dayle smiles back at us and takes another drink before he hands the canteen to Daniel.

Daniel grins. "Thanks man. And…" Daniel glances toward the sky, then back at Dayle. "How is this anything like a baby being born? This shit looks like the end of the world."

Dayle laughs. "It has a lot of similarities. A lot of waiting, a lot of tension, a lot of red. It was the best and worst day of my life. My wife screamed at me for about ten hours straight. Swore she hated me, even called me a spawn of Satan, I think. It was all a bit much, to be honest. Then, oh then the baby came, screaming its little head off, all bloody, slimy, and gross. She was the most beautiful thing I had or will ever see. She was perfect, absolutely flawless. Ten fingers, ten toes, wide open, alert brown eyes. I held her in my arms and cut the cord with a hand shaking so bad it could hardly hold the scissors." Dayle takes a deep breath, then his eyes travel to me. "If the five of us save anything at all by doing this, I hope we save moments like that."

Rashid makes an unexpected gagging noise. Now we all turn our accusatory glares on him. Rashid shrugs. "What? I watched my mom give birth to my little sister. The miracle of life was a traumatizing bloodbath. Scared me straight gay." Rashid shifts his stance, then trains his sole attention on me. His eyes are rimmed in scarlet. Scarlet as the sky. Suddenly my legs feel boneless, and I sway a little. There is an ominous sound in the distance, a sound that moves closer with each passing second, closing in on us like the crackling storm. It is the sound of a dozen gears, each larger than the moon grinding together in discordant synchronization, intertwining with the wail of one of those fabled Nephilim trumpets. The sound is huge, echoing as the ground starts to tremble. Behind Rashid's head, the threads of star-studded lightning already stitch the sky, each reaching for the bowl of blood in the center of the charging stone circle. My artifacts hum and glimmer. My fire-bird screams.

It's not going to work, I think. *No way, impossible, it can't work.*

Rashid reads my face and throws me an indulgent smile. "Give it time," he says glibly. "I have a good feeling about this." He keeps smiling, but the tremor in his voice tells me he is lying. Everyone hears the fear in his tone. Daniel is squeezing my hand so tightly all my fingers have gone numb. I steal a glance at Valance, then quickly drop my eyes. The man looks like he wants to strangle something—maybe me. Rashid shoves his hands in his pockets, then sits down on the grass, his hazy eyes staring out at nothing and everything for a few moments before they trace back to me. "My sister and I grew up in Tehran, did I ever tell you that?"

I nod. He had.

"Yeah, well when I was eleven and she was five, someone set off a couple bombs in our city's commercial district. Iman Hossen square. It was—" Rashid's voice cracks as he shudders. "It was...well it was unspeakable. Our parents had both been dead for almost two years. My sister was all I had in the world. I was holding her little hand when the first bomb detonated. The blast ripped us apart. I'll never forget the moment our fingers lost touch. I was thrown about twenty feet and broke my right leg. But that was nothing, all I could seem to care about was her. It took me two days to find her. I dug through rubble and severed body parts until my hands were a bloody wreck. When I finally found her—" Rashid drops his head into his hands briefly, then presses the heels of his hands into his eyes and inhales a deep breath that sounds like falling hail. "When I finally found her, she was hurt, weak, dehydrated, but she was alive. I hadn't shed a single tear while I was looking for her, but when she threw her arms around my neck, and I felt her little heart beating against my chest like a broken butterfly wing, I bawled like a baby. Like full on scream-cried. The feelings I experienced in that moment, love, relief, gratitude, and inexpressible joy all rolled into one—that's what I'm trying to save," he finishes, eyes and voice impassioned, begging me to understand, and of course I do.

When Rashid looks at Daniel, Daniel makes an exasperated face, then rolls his eyes. "Don't look at me. There's no way I'm joining this little circle jerk." Daniel throws a finger over his shoulder in Valance's direction. "Ask this dude, he looks like he's got sap busting his seams." Daniel swivels all the way around and wiggles his eyebrows at Valance. "Tell us big guy, what are you trying to save?"

Valance's response is the soul of monotone. "Your sister."

Daniel rolls his eyes, again. "Shocker."

Red thunder roars in the distance. Daniel's eyes flick to the sky, and his lips fit themselves into a thin white line. The wave is visible now. It looks angry, and very hungry, desperate to torture us in a tsunami of stars. My heart starts to pound so hard I think the others will hear it. I twist my fingers together in front of me, that way, no one can see how badly they tremble. The bowl on the altar appears similarly affected. The thing is having a damn seizure. Those threads of galaxy saturated lightning creep from down from the sky to the bowl and play with the bloody mercury, making it heat and sizzle until the bowl looks like it's full of electric rain.

My eyes return to Daniel's white face. His nose is bleeding again, he's wiped it on his sleeve about ten times in the last hour. *There's no way he's making it through another wave*, screams my mind. *This one will kill him for sure.* The bowl trembles again, its contents start to bubble like a cauldron. *It's not going to work. It's not going to fucking work!* My mind and heart continue to roar, and in that moment, I feel like a drop of water caught by a lusty wind.

"Seriously, dude? What are you trying to save?" chirps Daniel, still craning his neck to get a good look at Valance's face.

"Love," Valance says simply.

Daniel raises his thumb and forefinger to delicately pinch his nose, then he waves his free hand in front of his face like he just encountered targeted flatulence. "Omg. I'm gonna hurl. You're such a dork, perfect for my sister, actually."

"I mean it. Most people who find love aren't even looking for it. But I feel like I was always searching. I looked into the faces of a thousand women trying to find her. Then, just when I thought hitting the Earth in a spinning ball of fire and surviving was going to be the wildest thing that happened to me that day, I saw her eyes. If love at first sight truly exists, if other people in the world have a chance to feel the way I did in that moment, then it's worth it. I would save the world for love; I think it's the only thing strong enough to fight fate."

Daniel is on the verge of re-rolling his eyes, but he never gets the chance. A blue bolt of lightning cracks the sky less than a second before a bellow of thunder rocks the earth. The bowl starts to rise, there is no reciprocation or action from my artifacts. They remain stable, their individual glows muted. The sun slides between the stones, inching ever downward as the wave gets closer and closer, until it's almost directly over our heads, only a few seconds before it engulfs us in torture. The bowl starts to spin, as it continues to rise, and for a wonderful moment as the wave reaches toward my blood, I think that we all believe it just might work, that we hold onto hope until the metal bowl shivers, then shatters like it was made of hard candy. It rains blood and mercury onto the ground. We all hold our breath, but nothing happens. The wave keeps coming.

"It didn't work," Valance says, stating the words in my mind.

"I guess that's my cue," I say as my body jerks instinctively toward the altar, and my feet get ready to run.

Valance's arms come around me before he takes his next breath. He crushes me to his chest. "Don't you dare, don't you even think about it," he whispers into my hair.

"Valance." I tilt my head and meet his eyes. "Valance, please."

"No! God damn it no! Don't ask me to let you go."

The terror in Valance's voice and eyes make me start to cry. Slowly I let go of Daniel's hand. Daniel grabs a handful of my dress and twists it. "No, Divinica. If you die, I have no one," he says, and tears spill down my cheeks. I wrap my arms around Valance, press my palms to his heaving back, then hug him as tight as I possibly can. I lay my cheek against his chest and hear his rasping breaths and count his heartbeats. I tilt my face down so he can't see before I turn and lock eyes with Dayle, then Rashid. "Please," I whisper again, but this time my words are for them not him.

Dayle shakes his head, and mouths the word 'no,' Rashid starts to cry. His tears make mine fall faster. Valance kisses the curve of my neck, the side of my face, the corner of my lips, all the while I beg the boys with my eyes. *Help me. Help me hold him, hold him back, hold him down!* I mentally yell. *You know he'll never let me go. There's no other way.* Dayle stands and locks his teeth. I can see a strong, distinct ticking in his jaw. Rashid gives me the slightest nod as Dayle leans forward and drops his shoulder like a quarterback about to take on the defensive line. Valance notices Dayle's stance and all his muscles tense. Dayle and Rashid charge. Valance lets go of me with one hand to take a swing at

Dayle's face. Rashid catches Valance's arm with both of his hands and locks his fingers around Valance's wrist. Dayle spins and drives a knee into Valance's back. My heart breaks for what feels like the final time as I watch Valance fall. I have just enough time to tear myself free of Valance's grip, allowing myself to voice a single, miserable wail as Valance and Dayle hit the grass like toppling mountains.

Valance roars. He reaches for me with the hand that Rashid isn't using all his body weight to restrain. I look down at his face and feel all the blood drain from my mine. Valance's cheeks are flushed red as the wave. His eyes are a bloodshot wreck, and his expression is that of a man caught in the grip of his very worst nightmare. He fights with Dayle and Rashid, cussing them out with an unending stream of ear-searing profanities.

"I love you, Valance," I whisper, and blow him a kiss.

"If you loved me, you wouldn't do this!" he shouts.

I shake my head. "You're wrong. I'll love you until the last star in this galaxy dies." I turn away from him then, and it's the hardest thing I've ever done. Shaking, I lean down to kiss Daniel's cheek and tussle his hair. "I love you too, kid. Take care of him for me, yeah? Take care of each other." I'm crying so hard now it's difficult to talk. I face Dayle, careful not to look at Valance again. If I do, I won't go. "Dayle, Rashid," I call as I give them both a salute, and a teary wink, "It's been real," I whisper, then in a lower voice, "I love you all."

There's nothing left to say, the grains of sand in my timer fought until the last man, but now, all have fallen, the base of the glass is full of my dead warriors, each is a precious moment I can never retrieve. I spin on my heels, then I'm running. Running to die.

CHAPTER FORTY-EIGHT

Mythmarked

VALANCE

I stare at Divinica's receding back for a few seconds before my head is rudely shoved into the grass. She's fast. Too fast. Her legs move with such velocity, the skirts of her white dress are little more than a foggy blur. Every single fiber of my being wants to run to her, but Dayle's knee, the one he's pressing deep into the center of my spine, pins me to the ground. Motherfucker is heavy, like a Rade and a semi-truck had a giant, misshapen baby.

"Dayle, Rashid, I'm begging you," I rasp, my voice barely recognizable as human.

"Fucking hell," Dayle rumbles. "Valance, we're begging you! Don't make this any harder than it already is."

"If she dies, I'm going to kill you both," I rage.

Rashid sniffs. "Sounds fair," he says, his tone twisted by tears.

"It's her choice," Daniel says in a defeated voice. He slumps down near my head, shoulders shaking as he starts to cry in earnest. I want to comfort him, but all I can think about is how if I dig my own knee into the grass with the right amount of force, I might be able to buck Dayle off my back.

I'm just about to make my move when I hear a sound that freezes me in place. It's the distinct twang of a fired arrow, followed by the hissing whisper as it flies, and the sickening thud when it hits its mark. Divinica lets out a cry of pain that tells me the arrow struck her. I struggle to lift my head and see her.

Dayle shoves me further into the dirt, and Rashid twists my arm a little higher. "For fuck's sakes guys! She's hurt! Let me go to her!"

"It's Xola," I hear Daniel breathe. "Guess she doesn't give a shit about the treaty."

I fight harder, desperate to see. "Xola?"

"Yeah, she shot Divinica with an arrow that's about as tall as I am, and she's gonna fire another one," Daniel says almost conversationally. I see only his muddy boots and the torn legs of his jeans as he turns away from all of us. His words, and the dead tone he says them in, make adrenaline jolt through my veins, and I start to fight harder than I ever have in my life. In a shuffle of crazy movements, I manage to jam an elbow between Dayle's ribs and drag Rashid— who still has a firm hold on my arm—and me, into something of a sitting position, one where I'm nearly on his lap. Dayle re-enters the fray by reaching between Rashid and I, then locking both his arms around my chest and squeezing until I fear my spine might crack. It doesn't matter. I can finally see her clearly. Dayle can break me in half for all I care. I won't take my eyes off her again.

Divinica is still running. Xola's arrow protrudes from her right shoulder blade, the twisted bolt jolts up and down with every beat of her racing feet. A ribbon of scarlet decorates her pretty white dress and drips down the back of her leg. I watch her stumble, quickly right herself, then keep going, just as another hissing sound makes me flinch. The next arrow flies toward Divinica in slow motion. When the three-pronged tip buries itself in the base of Divinica's back, puncturing her left kidney, all I can see is red. All I hear is Divinica's scream.

Divinica's back arches as she pitches forward. Swinging her arms in an attempt to maintain balance, she falls to her knees. Shock, or regret hopefully, loosens Rashid's grip on my hand, finally giving me access to the rigged cloaking device that won me the Reptilian duel, still coded with Hecate's indecipherable tech. I was lying to Divinica when I said it was easy, I can reverse engineer with the best of them, but even the basic fundamentals of this device were far beyond the limits of my personal smarts. Honestly, I'm not really even sure how I fixed it.

Trying not to draw attention to what I'm doing, I slam my thumb down on the misshapen diamond. White strands of thready energy jolt across my fingers, but nothing else happens. I hit the device again, desperately. Again and again. Nothing. Nothing. Absolutely nothing. On my final try, there's not even a spark. Helplessly, I watch Xola draw another arrow from her quiver as Divinica struggles to her feet. Xola nocks the arrow. Divinica keeps going. Her steps are labored, each footfall seems more dramatic than the last. She reaches the outer ring of stones and stumbles again. This time when she falls, her weak cry feels like a flaming dagger is carving out my heart. Literally. I've never felt someone's agony like it was my own.

Xola draws back her arm. "Xola! No! Please!" My voice is a bellow I know she hears. Her stance falters a little, but her head doesn't even flick in my direction.

"Hey, bitch!" Daniel shouts, and I look up at him in time to watch him draw back the hammer of the .45 pistol he's holding between steady hands. "I bet my bullet flies faster than your arrow," he says, and promptly pulls the trigger. He braces for the recoil. In his clear eyes, I see nothing of the boy I've come to know. I just see a dude pushed past the limits of sanity, prepared to kill in order to save the last person he loves.

The bullet sings as it soars, and Xola screams when the hot metal tip splatters through the flesh of her upper arm. It's a well-placed shot. The arrow drops from her suddenly useless fingers as blood spurts from her shoulder. I struggle with Dayle, hoping his hold has weakened in the last few moments and find—much to my chagrin—that it has not. He restrains me with insulting ease. "Please, please, let me go to her," I beg, my voice cracking over every word.

"I'm sorry man. Fuck, you don't know how sorry, but…it's what she wants," Dayle says.

"She made us promise," Rashid says.

I want to shout out my helpless rage, but Dayle's right. It is what Divinica wants. Despite the two arrows embedded in her, Divinica is lying on her stomach crawling toward her goal. I watch her grab handfuls of grass, dig her fingers into the dirt, and desperately drag herself forward inch by painstaking inch. It's the most pitiful thing I've ever seen, it's also the bravest. Right now, in this moment, with the wave less than thirty seconds from impact, I love her so much I feel the whole Earth should be somehow changed by the sheer strength of my feelings.

Divinica makes it to the altar with mere moments to spare. She reaches up to grab the edge of the stone slab, but she doesn't need to bother. The maroon sun slides into place between the two center sarsen stones, and a beam of light spears straight through Stonehenge. The light catches Divinica and lifts her and her artifacts into the air. Divinica's body goes limp as she levitates, her arms hang lax at her sides, but her crown is alive with blue lightning, her eyes are wide and alert. She's staring directly at me when the concentrated beam of light funneling through the heel stone hits her in the chest. The same light is being fed through the charging ring of blue stones, then connecting to, and streaming from, each of her artifacts in long funnels of twisting brilliance. The light from each artifact appears to be sentient as the twelve individual beams search for, then link themselves to their corresponding tattoo on Divinica's body until she looks like some strange variant of jellyfish with twelve glowing tentacles intent on siphoning her soul.

Above our heads, the incoming wave pulses then retreats, clearly driven back by the force of Divinica's effervescence which is now initiating a chain of eruptions in the sky. The red wave implodes in places and altogether vanishes in others, like a semi-visible dome is shattering. The twelve streams of light connected to the tattoos on Divinica's body grow brighter. They resemble halogen tubes, only each one is filled with mercury and her blood, and I can't decide if the artifacts are giving her strength or sucking what remains of her life. Whatever the case, Divinica is turning into a star before my eyes, and I know I only have seconds before she goes supernova.

The sun touches the tip of its toe to the horizon and the glow of the girl hovering in the center of Stonehenge reaches a crescendo. Suddenly our world is rocked by a low boom with the treble of an underwater sonic blast, and the earth shakes hard enough to knock Daniel off his feet. Divinica's back arches further as light sprays from her mouth, her eyes, her very pores, then the air explodes in a rushing wave of rippling molecules. The light wave smacks us with blinding force and sends each of us flying at least a dozen feet through the air. The landing is hard. I blink twice as something in my ankle twists with a sickening sound and my mouth fills with blood.

I jump to my feet before Dayle and Rashid have shaken off the pain. Before either of them realizes I'm free, I'm already running, all the while hitting the useless tech in the center of my palm. "Hey, ancient earth powers, you want a blood sacrifice?" I yell as my feet pick up speed. "You want a life? You want a soul? Fine, fucking take mine!"

Divinica.

Reels of twisting light—like brilliant, transparent pipes or glowing antennae—funnel the trapped pieces of each goddess's soul into me, and I feel it all. Their pain, ecstasy, despair, rapture, life, and death. Old earth powers infuse my molecules down to the last atom and re-write the hydrogen bonds in my DNA. The same light rockets from my mouth and eyes creating beams that traverse outer space, and I feel my human shell begin to disintegrate. Under the force of my brilliance, the electric edges of the red wave start to fray, then unravel like a tossed spool of thread.

The spell cast in this stone circle, in this very spot so many millennia ago, is finally rupturing. I am the catalyst, the key, the end of the world and its beginning. I will pay the blood price because suspended in the air like this, with tentacles of light sprouting out of my body—making me look like some alien-hybrid creature—I am now a full believer. Valance is right, I am mythmarked, this is my destiny, and it has always been my fate.

The heat of the sunbeam slicing through the center of Stonehenge and crashing into me intensifies as the seconds tick. I burn for the second time in forty-eight hours, but this time, there is only ten percent pain, and ninety percent power. Power greater than the combined forces of the Earth's oceans, stronger than gravity. The arrows in my back turn to smoke and drift away, the wounds in my body heal themselves with ease, and I am instantly stronger, healthier than I ever have been before. I understand my father's writings, and I know what will happen to my soul when all this is over. The goddesses have whispered in my ears and told me in exacting detail. I can see it like fluctuating pictures in my mind, paintings of dread I can't erase.

In my changing, unlocking brain, I also understand that the merging of souls in me has created a new breed, a modern goddess, too powerful to quantify. I am now an anomaly, an unknown. Thus, I am dangerous. The goddess circle that did this to me would never allow such a wild threat to exist. I could change it all, alter their fates or straight up destroy them if only I wished it. So, it's obvious they never meant for me to survive this. Which figures because the only thing I can't do is save my own life.

A sharp burst of rebellion makes me momentarily see red. Rebellion against the ones who did this to me, rebellion against meekly submitting to their master plans and dying here on this universe pyre. Yet I don't move away from the sunbeam that is steadily killing me, instead, I straighten my body and find my line of sight through the beams of light shooting from my eyes, then I focus my gaze on Daniel's face. His left hand is gripping the handle of a still smoking gun, his right is reaching for me. Both Dayle and Rashid have their arms wrapped around his slender, trembling body. I know they will take care of him, and some of my desire to run from death escapes me. My attention drifts from my brother, and I register that I'm searching for him. Valance. Seems some way, somehow, I always am. For a terrifying second, I can't find him, he's not where I expected him to be—struggling under Dayle's bulk. Then I see him, hear a scream, and realize it's mine.

He's dashing toward me, running like a storm wind. *"Nooo!"* The shout that booms from my throat is the loudest sound I've ever heard. Seriously. It sends out a visible sonic wave that knocks Valance backward a few steps, but he braces his strong legs and keeps his footing. I yell his name, and my voice sends out another rippling wave. Seconds before it hits him, Valance disappears. I search for him with my goddess eyes, but Hecate's spell tech is as smart and stealthy as she is. Valance is invisible as a thought.

He'll be okay, he's at least a hundred meters away, and you have mere seconds left, says my mind, trying to soothe my frantic heart. *He will live, they will all live, they will! They will!* I internally chant. All around me, the blue stones are humming, fully charged, and the sunbeam is now hot enough to incinerate. The bodice of my dress starts to smoke, the lace hem catches fire. "Bastard," I mutter, still searching for him. "Fuck you Valance, you, and Hecate's vanishing magic shit! All I want is to see you one last time. Please, Valance. Please." I close my eyes and let tears fall.

Suddenly, impossibly, magically, I feel a warm, familiar hand curve around the back of my neck. It's a dream defining touch that sends hot and cold shivers running up and down my spine.

"I'm right here, baby," he whispers, then his lips are firm and warm against mine. My own lips part on a gasp and he's kissing me. The kiss is hot and deep It renders me thoughtless, senseless, breathless. His tongue brushes, then captures mine, my hands come up, my fingers twist through his hair, and then we just kind of sink into each other. It feels like the type of kiss one might give to their true love when there are no more words with which to say goodbye, and that scares me.

Distantly, somewhere in my swooning mind, I notice my dress has stopped smoking. For a second, all I register is how wonderful it is that I'm not burning anymore. When the reason *why* dawns on me like a slap in the face, my whole body goes icy with shock. I'm not burning because Valance has managed to throw his body in front of mine and his back is currently taking the full force of the blast.

He doesn't seem to care. He's still kissing me with soul-melting ferocity, tilting my head back with his lips and owning my mouth. "No! Don't you dare!" I manage to gasp. Valance answers by locking his arms around my waist and pulling me closer, kissing me deeper. I shake my head wildly, tearing my mouth from his and leaning back so I can look into his eyes. "Valance, no! It's *my* destiny to die for the world. It's *my* fate."

"Maybe, darling," he drawls, smiling his crooked, sexy smile and dragging me even closer. "But I don't believe in fate, and I like to think we make our own destiny. Besides, I'm not dying to save the fucking world. I'm dying to save you."

"Please don't do this! My dad was right. Breaking this blood spell will shatter your soul, the stones are activated. They will send the pieces through time," I tell him, crying harder now.

"Then get them, love. They all belong to you anyway," he rasps, the look in his eyes says he's memorizing my face. I can see the glowing tentacles extending from each of my artifacts and siphoning through my tattoos start to move toward Valance, like the light of Stonehenge is calling them.

"Oh god!" I shove at him again, but the light is making him strong, his arms are steel traps. "You idiot," I whimper, internally gathering my power, prepared to knock him the fuck out if I must. *It's okay, I can save him,* I think. It's the last thought I have before the color of the sunbeam changes from gold to scalding white and cuts a visible hole straight through Valance's chest, just like the bolt of lightning did to that Celtic prince Freya loved so long ago. Valance is still kissing me as his heart catches fire. The beating organ blazes between us, and I can actually feel him dying. I use all my strength to fight with him, but I know it's too late. The blood price is paid, and the spell is broken. I'm really going to lose him. Valance kisses me tenderly once more, cups my face in both his hands, then whispers my name.

"I'll get the pieces of your soul, whatever it takes, I'll find a way. I swear I'll fix this. Wait for me," I sob.

Gently, he brushes away the hair sticking to the tears on my cheek and tucks the strands behind my ear. "Don't cry, Divinica. I love you. Everything is exactly as it should be," he says. They are his last words. We are looking into each other's eyes as the light piercing him implodes with an internal detonation, and our world erupts in a mushroom cloud of phosphorescent light, setting off a series of blinding flashes so formidable they ripple our solar system. The expanding sphere of light attacks what remains of the red wave and turns the killing electric blaze into harmless, scattering bits of sparkling dust soon to be swallowed by starlight.

Tears run down my cheeks as I curse each of the goddesses by name. When I reach the name of the witch who marked me, Hecate materializes in clouds of glitter-soaked vapor and starlight. Gossamer veils drape her three heads. Transparent material that blows in the visible winds enveloping her. All her heads are smiling, teeth like sharpened fangs. A circlet strung with stars crowns the center head.

I hold Valance tighter to my chest, linking my fingers around his waist so she can't take his body from me. Drunk on the agony of loss, my words pour out sans any real sense. "You dare show yourself to me? You fucking, murdering bitch. I'll rip your throat out," I scream.

"There's no blood on my hands. I did not want this. I did not foresee this future," Hecate says, glancing down at Valance's dead body in my arms, all six of her brows draw together, and she appears confused, perplexed even.

"Impossible," the left head hisses.

"We don't understand," the right head wails.

"It was always you who was meant to die," the left head informs me. "Never him. This is not good. We did not see this."

The right head runs her tongue slowly over her fangs. "How did it happen?"

"We don't know...don't know," the left head cries.

I want to take advantage of her rare moment of shock and attack her. I don't because she looks strong, I'm weak, gutted, spent, and terrified. I drop my head and more of my tears rain on Valance. "I do. He used your magic against you. Even you, with all your stupid omniscience, can't see through the invisibility shield you created. He was smarter than you thought."

Hecate's heads lift in a haughty tilt. "I didn't think about him at all."

"That was your problem. He was the best of us."

Hecate's laugh falls cold and lifeless before it rises up and coils around me, rootless in a phantom wind, kindling my unquenchable rage. Inky power explodes from my chest and the tips of my fingers. It shoots toward Hecate's heart. She blocks the blast, but it sends her reeling backward. "So strong," she croons, like I'm a child she's training. "So angry. But all the anger in the world cannot kill fate."

"I'm willing to test that theory," I snarl.

"To what end, Divinica?" the left head asks.

The right head cackles. "Will you turn back time and let the waves destroy what remains of humanity, your brother—just to save him?"

Tendrils of black fire ripple around her as Hecate reaches for Valance.

I twist my body mid-air, moving Valance from her reach. My hands are so slippery from his blood, I almost drop him. "Don't," I scream. "Stay away. You can't have him."

Hecate's mouth quirks to the side. "I must admit, I am interested to see how this all plays out, and I haven't found interest in anything for thousands of years. It has been exquisitely captivating to watch your love story, Divinica. However, one has to wonder if the beauty of your tale would shine as bright absent the pain?"

"Shut the fuck up!" I command through a wracking sob. "Who cares? This has all just been a game to you, hasn't it? A story with a predestined end. We're just characters in your convoluted plot, distractions you eventually kill off. I swear to you on all the old gods, Hecate, my revenge will make it very real for you. If I have to walk through Hades' hellfire, I'll make you feel my pain. Feel all our pain."

"Oh Divinica. Your fight is not with me. I protect the rock you stand on, not the bugs that inhabit it."

I shake my head, watch my tears fly. "I stopped the waves. Humans will survive."

"He stopped the waves," she says, flicking all her eyes toward Valance. "But it will take a thousand years for humanity to become the beast it once was. For a time, Gaia will be safe, and she will heal. Come for me if you will, I do so long to be entertained, you cannot imagine the tedium found in eternity."

"I will kill you; I will kill you all." My words are a promise, a spoken prayer that becomes a vow.

Wind howls through the Henge sounding like a death scream. Hecate vanishes as quickly as she appeared. Her maniacal laughter lingers.

I sink to the earth with Valance's lifeless body cradled in my arms as the sun melts into the horizon and we enter the witching hour. The earth falls silent. The blue stones lose their crackling charge. I sit motionless just staring at his face. The unearthly light that took Valance from me diminishes in stages. When I regain some semblance of situational awareness, the moon is bloody, and the night is black.

—To be continued.

SNEAK PEEK OF SMOKE AND OTHER STORMS

By: J.L. Delavega

I was born with two shadows. One is thrown by the sun. The other is the Stranger.

The dried brush hugs the abandoned walls as I leave the rough grass and walk toward the fort, a thing of dust and focus. It looks dead, but there is a difference between things that are dead and those that only appear that way.

Twenty-nine—the number of steps I take before the fort shadow hits me. The Stranger counts them for me.

Few people can see her. But she's always with me. Watching my back, counting my steps. It's not enough to notice details if you can't remember them later. The Stranger remembers everything. She is a second pulse, sensing danger, sharp edges that frighten others. The one thing my mother managed to give me.

My shoulder to the bleached wall, I listen deeper. Around me, the Rim hisses behind a slow-moving wind. Behind the fort's chipped stone is silence. I drag my scarf off my face and whistle to my sister Leagan waiting downslope with the wagon.

We are alone, the Stranger confirms.

Rock cracks as the horses get moving.

I slip my hand through the gap to lift the plank from the inside slot, walking the gate open as the wagon rolls inside.

Leagan hops from the high seat, landing with a fresh cloud of dust. Her face is muffled with a blue scarf and goggles. The right eye is a red sniper's lens with distance dials, the left all-purpose amber to dull the sun.

I drop the plank back into its slot and shake the gate. There will be no surprises from behind.

The smuggler's cache is in the jail room.

"Eighty-six crates of Exodus brand ammunition..." Leagan tugs at one of her buns and stabs another pin through it. "And we get to carry all of them. Thanks a fart-load to our favorite arms dealer, Raleigh."

Leagan's hair is fire red, twisted on top of her head like two cinnamon buns, lipstick always black. The colors of her two moods. "You're my favorite arms dealer."

And she blushes.

The familiar tic rises in my chest with each step. It doubles when my gaze makes a pass over the other five doors facing the courtyard. The Stranger again.

I've picked through all those rooms before, but the Stranger won't let me leave here without doing it again. It's always been this way.

After we get the ammo dug up and loaded.

Seventeen steps.

I sweep open the door ahead of Leagan. Bottles and piss still lurk in the corners. Another gang was here not too long ago. I drag away the flabby mattress covering the recently disturbed dirt in the first cell.

"Catch." Leagan tosses the shovel.

The wooden lid peels back, and the tang of metal hits me. Loose dirt continues to trickle in around the ammo boxes. Rows of fresh, brass-capped lead. Heavy. Not something an unprepared bone picker just walks away with. But I look into the entire top layer of boxes, to be sure no one got to this before us.

Leagan breathes in the gunpowder, humming as she closes her hazel eyes. "Fresh."

An earthy whistle scours across the wind. I go still.

"Did you hear that?" Leagan eases a hand toward the rifle on her back.

It sounded like a train. But the Stranger and I know better than to turn our backs to a stray sound. "Stay with the stash."

Thirteen.

The midday sun is beginning to burn through my back despite my clothes. Pieces of my white hair stick to my neck as I reach the top of the wall.

Smoke.

A train glides southwest along the red bank of the river *Sol*, a copper snake. Against the clear sky, both smoke and steam spread dark blue, but straight out of the stack, at its most concentrated point, it looks like boiling midnight. Black means it's burning Hannah's pyrite quartz, better known as black gold.

East blood—prospectors, settlers, and fools.

The cars spool around the rock bend, out of sight. Heat ghosts twist the hillsides out of place, false pools of water appearing under them, but the sage-bristled landscape near us doesn't move.

The sun is strongest during Moon Season. Even under the wide shadow of my hat, my neck has a hot pulse. I'm definitely burning.

"Well?" Leagan says.

"Train. Headed for Vantage."

"Alkaline." Her smile slants. "Enjoy the Rim, you fools." She holds out a bottle of Sun Fire whiskey. "I think this is supposed to be our smuggler's bribe."

"Lucky for Aunt Tess." She's the only one who drinks that sludge and likes it.

"Aunt Tess isn't here hauling this. Next time they should send us something we can all enjoy. Silver pinchers."

"Such as?"

"Oh, I don't know…" Leagan grabs another crate. "Some books…or a puppy."

"Tell Raleigh. I'm sure he can find one for you."

"I'll tell him to stop working with such a cheap-ass supplier. It just makes him look bad. I think by now he owes me a dog and you a horse because we always get stuck doing the wretched heavy-lifting jobs."

"A horse doesn't fit on the train."

"A dog would. We can share it. And name it…Barley."

The bed of the wagon gets lower as we fill it.

"You know why we're here?" I ask.

"Why?"

"Because no one else can actually lift these besides us." I squeeze Leagan's flexed arm. "They just won't admit it."

"Still," she says. "It's the bribe that counts. And I'm not feeling very persuaded."

As soon as we finish loading Raleigh's ammo, I return to the jail, rake the dirt back over the smuggler's cache, and then cover the disturbance with the soiled mattress. The Stranger's pulse is clicking again, deep in my chest and in my head. Once again, I feel the rooms I haven't looked in. They pick at me like nails in my spine.

Thirty-two.

The first door breaks apart a spider's web. Relief from the sun. Army-issue cots still clutter the floor, a scorpion shell and nothing but rat droppings in the gun cabinets. We haven't done a pickup here in eight moon cycles. But I still have to look. With each opened cupboard, the Stranger's clockwork pressure winds down until it's no longer a weight I have to breathe past.

Leagan sits up in the wagon, reading.

"Ready."

My horse looks me in the eye as I untether him from the wagon and run my hand down the wide white stripe marking his face. I've only known him since this morning, but he's proud to be strong, taking people where they need to go. I can see it. And I want him. But we don't stay in one place long enough for a creature like him to be satisfied. Horses are like us. They need the wild air. They need to run.

Someday I'll have a horse I don't have to give back at the end of the day. But for now, the rails are my freedom.

Two miles outside the town of Vantage, something dark moves beyond the creek crossing. I put up my hand, and Leagan stops. The water is low and sharp on the red-brown rocks. We haven't had rain since the red Season moon rose, won't until the Season is over and there's only one moon again.

A group of four men huddle on the opposite bank where the trail is steep. Their cart bed is cracked, no tack, no horses, a yellow flag to signal help clinging to a brittle limb.

"This looks like a bum uncle," I say.

"Yeah, it does." Leagan lets go of the reins and brings her boar rifle around. *Verdict,* she calls it. "I'm ready when you are."

My horse obeys my nudge into the creek. The water doesn't even touch his ankles. Leagan stays where she is, partially obscured by the brush.

Eyes up.

"Hello there, missies." The man wearing an oversize felted hat lifts a dirty hand. "Think you can spare a minute?"

When I don't speak, he and another move in.

"Thank the good Lord Providence you came along. Thought we might be stranded out here."

"You're only two miles from town," Leagan calls. She tilts her head in Vantage's direction. "I can walk that far, can't you?"

"I dunno. Got a bad leg. Token of the war."

He's not old enough to have been in the war.

"Think you can give us a hand?" He hums to steady my horse as he reaches to gather my reins. "We'd be ever grateful."

He clamps his hand tight. I slip my feet from the stirrups. From the other side, the second man grabs my arm and belt, ripping me from the saddle. He locks an arm around my waist, the other pinning my elbows to my sides. Fool's gold, he smells. They always smell.

I wait.

The roadman digs into my scarf, greasy nose to my neck, breathing deep. "Ah...ignore the color, boys. This one smells clean."

A revolver sets on my temple. "Don't move, don't scream."

They're not from here. Gangs that have been on the Rim very long know there's no advantage in threatening victims into submission. There's usually no one around to hear a scream, and even if there is, no one is going to risk their life for a stranger. It might be different in the cities back east. But out here, you're on your own. You use violence to get what you want. You wield it to survive.

The roadman holding the gun chuckles, ripping down the yellow flag.

The arms squeeze me. "Never trust a stranger, little girl."

I don't. Only mine.

"What do you have for me, huh?" He moves his hand across my stomach. "You're too pretty to be a fox. Too pretty to be out here alone."

My scarf comes up past my nose and the brim of my hat down to meet my goggles. He has no idea what I look like. But I know they'd still try me even if I had one red eye and pointed teeth.

Leagan won't make a mistake or strike too soon. She never has.

He slides the hand between my legs, and she fires. It's the roadman holding the gun to my head who drops, an echo and spray of blood coating my cheek and ear.

Leagan's already lined up her next shot. "She's not alone."

"Sweet Jezebel—" The fourth still crouching by the busted cart leaps up. He's dead next.

"Stay back," the roadman still holding on to me yells at Leagan, using my body as a shield against her. "If you ever want to see your friend alive."

The back of my heel snaps up into his groin. The arms crushing mine break away as he doubles over. My elbow catches his head first. Then as he folds, I shove my heel deep into his stomach. He lands in the creek, red spooling in the water from his mouth.

I draw my pistol. "Never trust a Stranger."

"Get back!" He tries to spit blood on me as I crouch over him. I make sure he feels my hand in his pocket, stealing from him.

"Shady bitch!" He grabs for my throat.

I shoot.

One more. The Stranger turns her attention right. The one in the felted hat. He lets go of my horse.

"Fuck." He backs away, palms up.

Two.

My horse tries to shy away when I catch the reins, but I don't let him. The man slips on the clay bank as he tries to avoid me, but he keeps his hands up.

"We're the Reveres." Leagan stands up in the wagon seat. "Heard of us? You should've. Now pay the toll."

"Sure, miss." Both gold and silver standards fumble between his fingers. "How much?"

"Your friend insulted my sister, so everything you've got." Leagan gives the coins he presents an unimpressed nod. "Is that all?"

"That's all, I swear."

"Bone picker," she sneers.

I step to him. "Holster off. Set it all on that rock."

His hands skid off the buckle, slip again. "Fuck."

"Now that's how a real robbery is done," Leagan says as he obeys me. "Without that gold, you'll be able to run faster. Maybe you'll make it to town."

I push my hat back, just enough. Sun hits my skin and hair, white enough to blind. I'm not disappointed as his breath staggers.

"Please don't eat me," he whispers.

My jaw hardens. *Shady* doesn't bother me anymore, but there's still something about being called cannibal that does. "If anyone asks what happened to you, tell them you met a Stranger and a Raptor on the road and made the mistake of robbing them. You paid the Reveres and were saved."

"No, ma'am. I mean, yes, ma'am—"

Leagan takes hard aim again. "Now run, fool."

He bolts like a rabbit.

The angry breath goes to my head as I let go. "Amateurs."

We check the bodies one at a time, thoroughly scavenging each pocket, removing each bullet. Leagan takes a handful of silver standards off one and adds them to her own belt. There is a decent knife with a fat grip, perfect for hollowing to add a hidden vial of poison or flash fire, so I shove that into my belt.

The blood splatter is already crust on my face.

Leagan stalks around our wagon, checking the axels weren't caught on any snags going across the creek. She kicks one of the spokes. "This is a piece of shit. Did you hear it groaning? I think Abel gave us his worst one."

The water is skin warm and sulfur tainted, but I scrub my cheek anyway.

Leagan dumps the bullets from one of the revolvers and throws the gun downstream. "Garbage."

"One of the fools on that Jezebel train would have bought that. They don't know the difference."

"I have my principles. I do not sell anything with Matthan-Atlas parts."

At least she took the bullets like I taught her. It's a sin to leave free ammo behind.

Don't stop now. Keep reading with your copy of SMOKE AND OTHER STORMS today!

And don't miss more from JP Roth. Stay up to date on all of her release information, cover reveals, sales, and giveaways by visiting her at www.rothic.com

**Don't miss more from JP Roth coming soon, and find out more at
www.rothic.com**

**Until then, discover SMOKE AND OTHER STORMS
by City Owl Author, J.L. Delavega!**

**Welcome to the Rim. Come seek your fortune in a paradise of endless sun.
Land is cheap and the possibilities endless, where the edge of the map meets
the end.**

The mining campaigns always forget a few details. Moon Season makes storms
volatile. You're more likely to be killed by your neighbor than strike a crystal
vein, and there's only one name you should bother knowing around here:
Revere.

Moira and her granddaughter Adelaide are professionals. Smugglers, thieves,
and arms dealers, the Revere women have lifted their family business from the
dust, and with their train they've become the most notorious gang in the
territory.

After an accident damages her sister's eyes, Adelaide finds an opportunity that
will not only pay for a sight-saving operation but pull the family from the
shadows of the back market for good. Accompanied by her sisters, Adelaide
guides a survey crew into the uncharted West Rim—a poisonous desert
concealing untapped riches—with the full intent to claim the fortune for
themselves.

But when Moira learns a bounty has been placed on the family, she discovers a
deeper plan already in motion that will change the Rim forever.

Please sign up for the City Owl Press newsletter for chances to win special subscriber-only contests and giveaways as well as receiving information on upcoming releases and special excerpts.

All reviews are **welcome** and **appreciated**. Please consider leaving one on your favorite social media and book buying sites.

Escape Your World. Get Lost in Ours! www.cityowlpress.com

ACKNOWLEDGMENTS

To the best girlfriend in the world, Dawn McTeigue, who listened to each word of this story about a hundred times on the hundredth time. From character design to endless moral support, none of this would be possible without you.

Special Acknowledgements to Stephanie Hanson for believing in my characters and helping me bring them to life. To Dan Schwartz for always coming up with the coolest names in the world. To the fans who have been with our Divinica every step of the way, you guys are the reason she breathes.

ABOUT THE AUTHOR

Author, dreamer and wild child extraordinaire: JP Roth is an American Novelist, and owner of Rothic comics, founded in 2012, through which she has produced and published five of her original series. JP Roth lives in California with her beautiful family, and their adorable Bichon Frise. Her days are spent writing fanciful stories, walking on the beach, and attending comic conventions across the globe. While JP Roth enjoys travelling to exotic locations, she admittedly prefers to stay home, wrapped in a soft fluffy blanket, drinking tea and penning her next novel.

www.rothic.com

X x.com/IamJPRoth
♪ tiktok.com/@jprothic
⌾ instagram.com/jprothic
f facebook.com/JPRothic

ABOUT THE PUBLISHER

City Owl Press is a cutting edge indie publishing company, bringing the world of romance and speculative fiction to discerning readers.

Escape Your World. Get Lost in Ours!

www.cityowlpress.com

facebook.com/YourCityOwlPress
x.com/cityowlpress
instagram.com/cityowlbooks
pinterest.com/cityowlpress